BREATHING WITHOUT YOU

The Courtlynd Series Book 2

CHRISTINA MARIA

To all my naughty smut loving sluts out there...
Be my good girl and turn the page...

That's it... you listen so well my dirty little slut
Now go on... read those pages like the good girl or good boy you are
♡♡♡

CONTENT WARNING

Please note, this book contains sensitive subject matter.
To view the trigger warnings, please see the end of the book.

1
EMERALD

"Mind if I dance with you?" I hear someone whisper into my ear, as their warm, somewhat muscular arms come around my waist as I get lost in the music. I'm sweating from all this dancing and enjoying girls' night with my best friends.

Mystery man's body starts grinding against my ass making me smirk, hoping he's a hot guy around my age. Winter, Chastity, and I are dancing at Black Velvet, waiting for country night to start. We're doing our normal dancing like hoochies having a blast, grinding up on each other and shaking our asses. I look over at Chastity because she's diagonally across from me, her eyes going wide as she stares at the man behind me. She starts trying to shake her head no without making it too obvious and shit I don't want to turn around but if she's giving me that look then that means I'll have to tell him to get lost. Why does this always happen to me? I take a deep breath in and turn. Fuck...of course it has to be a man who's old enough to be my dad and creepy enough to drug me and leave my dead body in an alley way. I watch way too many crime shows, but it's true, he has 'run now' written all over him. He's a tall, somewhat heavy-set man, somewhat muscular with barely any hair left on top, at one point he could've been attractive but with the look he has on his face tonight he has creep written all over him. He's drunk too as his glossy eyes look me up and down, drinking me in with this disgusting smirk on his face. He licks his lips slowly as his eyes stay focused on my shirt that's way too low, staring at my cleavage. But hey I'm allowed to dress like this for a night out with my girls.

"Sorry, I'm just trying to dance with my friends while our boyfriends get us drinks." I lie a little, but he doesn't need to know that. That's something we always do if we don't want to dance with a guy, we back each other up on our imaginary boyfriends when we come here alone. Usually, it works but sometimes we get the assholes who just don't want to listen, kind of like tonight.

Except I'm the only single one here tonight. My best friend Winter's fiancé, Carsten, is part owner of Black Velvet so he's working tonight, and Chastity, I'm not sure where her boyfriend is tonight. I'm surprised she's allowed out alone, he's usually up her ass, the controlling dick head that he is. I hate the guy but I'm a supportive friend and I'm there when she needs me.

"C'mon baby." He grabs me a little tighter around the waist, pulling me closer to him. "I watched you walk in; I didn't see you with a man. Dance with me." He starts grabbing my ass pulling me closer to him and his junk. Ew, I think I can feel his boner on my stomach. That's fucking gross. I turn my head back to the girls and mouth "Help" to them and right as I'm about to turn back to him to try and push him off since he's not taking the hint, someone comes up to me placing their hand on my lower back.

"Hey babe, sorry I took so long to get back over here to you." I look over confused at the familiar voice. I see Creedence standing there looking at me with a big smile on his handsome face and boy does he look fucking hot tonight. His dark washed ripped jeans are tight in all the right places, hugging his junk and his ass perfectly. Fuck, he's always been so attractive to me. It's been hard living next door to him and not throwing myself at him every chance I could. He's wearing a tight fitted white T-shirt that looks like it could be painted over his skin, that's how tight the thing is on him. But that's because he's pure muscle. You can see the lines of his abs as his shirt forms to the definition, trailing down to that defined 'V' that goes right down to that large bulge in his pants. Fuck I would love to see what his cock looks like. What is wrong with me?

"Hey man, I was dancing with her first," the creep says to Creedence, trying to pull me away from him, pushing Creedence's hand away and replacing it with his on my lower back. The guy has a nasty look on his face like he's pissed off at him for stealing "his" girl, but I already know who is going to win this fight.

"The fuck you are, you're not dancing with my girlfriend, back the fuck off before I make you back the fuck off myself." He pushes his hand between me and the creepy man while gently pulling me back towards him to get me away from him.

"I already told you I'm dancing with the girl; you back the fuck off." The creep pulls me closer, his lips curling up at the corners, with an angry look on his face. I place my hands between us trying to push myself away so I'm not so close to him but it's no use, the guy's grip on me is too tight and I can't push myself away.

"Excuse me, I'm right here, stop fighting. Sir, I'm not interested in dancing, and I told you I was waiting for my boyfriend to come back, now get off me." I push him again and this time he loosens his grip on me, but still keeps his hand on me, like he still has a chance to win this little fight he created.

Creedence pulls me away from the creep and my body slams into his. At the same time, he places his hand at the nape of my neck, his hand tangling through my hair, he leans down, his mouth crashes into mine, his tongue swipes across my lips and I part them without hesitation. Holy. Shit. Goosebumps break out across my body, and chills shoot through me, my stomachs doing somersaults... What the fuck, I've never felt this way over a simple kiss but there's something about this kiss that's different than just your normal kiss, I just can't put my finger on it.

He finally pulls away from me, his breathing a little heavier from how intense that kiss just was. Then he looks over at the guy who's standing there with a pissy look on his face but also a look of defeat like he can't believe he just lost me, when I was never his, or something.

"Back the fuck off and leave my girl alone," he says in a husky voice, he sounds out of breath from the kiss we just shared, like it affected him as much as it did me. I can't help but stare at him and how handsome he truly is, his beautiful brown eyes and his light-brown beard that's trimmed close to his face, that I'd love to run my fingers through. The tattoos that run up his hands and both arms and around his whole neck that make my thighs tighten together, making my pussy wet from how much they turn me on. Fuck, he's so sexy.

The creepy guy finally gets the hint and walks away, shaking his head. I don't care if we pissed him off, I'm not trying to get murdered tonight, and like I said before–he definitely looked like the type of guy who would leave my dead body in an alley after having his way with me.

Creedence looks down at me as butterflies form in my stomach from the way he's smiling at me, he's still holding his hand at the nape of my neck, and the other one on my lower back.

"Sorry." He pauses, the corner of his mouth turning up. "Well, honestly I'm not sorry for sharing that kiss with you, but sorry for kissing you without a warning." He looks down into my eyes with a somewhat apologetic look on his face while shrugging his shoulders a little.

"Umm...it...it's okay." I brush some of the loose strands of hair out of my face, then look back up at him. "Thank you, for uhhh, helping me out there. I appreciate it. That guy was a creep," I say shivering, not sure if it's still from the way Creedence is touching me or if it's from that guy creeping me out.

"No need to thank me, I'm glad I was walking by and saw you." We're standing there in the middle of the dance floor, shouting to have this conversation. We probably look crazy to everyone around us for just standing here and not dancing. But I don't care, I don't want him to stop touching me or stop talking to me, and I'd love to feel his lips against mine again.

I glance over and see both Winter and Chastity dancing together giving me an excited look. Chastity nods her head and gives me a thumbs up and Winter shoos me with her hand as if to tell me I'm fine and to keep talking to him. They both know I've had a thing for him since seeing him in my driveway, that being the second time I've actually met him. But the day he and Carsten came over helping me unpack Winter's things after her dad had beat the shit out of her, he introduced himself again. Then kissed my hand instead of shaking it and butterflies instantly swarmed my stomach. I didn't know if it was because I'd never had a man do that or if it was due to being attracted to him. I'm leaning more towards because I've had a thing for him since I moved into the house a few years ago. They moved in a couple months after me and holy shit when I saw I was living next to four hot guys I felt like the luckiest girl ever, but Creedence was the only one who truly kept my attention. Only thing is I've never seen him with girls at his house before, so it makes me wonder why he doesn't date. Or why it seems like he doesn't date. Maybe I just don't pay enough attention to it. Ha. Who am I kidding? I pay way too much attention without it being noticeable to Creedence's house and what he's doing and who comes and goes with him. Maybe I'm a little obsessed but I can't help it. I'm too much of a chicken to come out and say anything to him about how I feel. I don't even know him enough to even be feeling this way. But fuck, the man is so dreamy it's hard not to be obsessed with someone as sexy as he is.

"Why were you walking by on the dance floor instead of around the dance floor by the tables?" I look at him confused because that would seem to make more sense to walk around the dance floor, not through the dance floor. The way the dance floor is set up it's in the middle of the bar, and there's tables with chairs set up around it and then the booths and pool tables border the rest of the bar. So, it would've made more sense to me to go around the dance floor to get to the bar.

"Well shit, fine do you want the honest truth?" He gives me that half fucking smirk again making butterflies form in my stomach, yet again. What is this man doing to me? God I just want to lick him when he smirks at me like that. He even has a small dimple that forms on his right cheek when he gives me that smirk of his. Fuck is he sexy.

"Sure, as long as you don't tell me you were planning on killing me or something like that last guy probably was. Actually, scratch that, don't tell me if you were going to kill me because then that'll ruin this moment. I'll take my chances." I start laughing, I'd rather hear what he has to say anyway, hoping it's something exciting. Besides if I'm gonna die I'd rather it be from someone as sexy as him than that creep that was old enough to be my dad.

He starts shaking his head while laughing. "No, definitely not. You're way too beautiful." Damn, I feel my face heat up from him making me blush. "I'd never do anything to hurt you. Well, hold on, that's not the only reason why I wouldn't hurt you, but you get what I'm saying." He looks at me with a nervous look while licking his lips, and I'd give anything to run my tongue across his lips the same way he's running his tongue across his lips.

"Yes, I totally understand what you mean, but I am very curious about what you were going to say." I smile up at him, he's a lot taller than me, well over six feet and I love it. The DJ changes the music, and a slow song comes on, perfect, maybe he'll want to dance now so we don't stand here awkwardly on the dance floor anymore.

"You want to dance?" He asks me as he removes his right hand from my lower back and holds it out to me. He has the sexiest smile on his face, I'm beginning to think everything about this man is sexy though.

"I'd love to. Now stop stalling, I need to know, it's driving me crazy." I look up at him, taking his hand while he places his other hand on my lower back now and I place my other hand on his shoulder and move my body to where it's right up against his.

"Oooh feisty, I like that," he chuckles. "Okay, so I'm probably gonna come off creepy, but hopefully not as creepy as that last guy. I saw you come in; I was sitting at the bar talking to Carsten, he had to go make some shots real quick so he walked away and I just so happened to look at the entrance as you walked in. Truthfully there's just something about you. I see this beautiful girl, with green and black hair, covered in tattoos walk in and I'm drawn to her instantly. Holy shit, she takes my fucking breath away, right? Then when you finally looked up. My heart stopped for a minute when I realized who you were. The smile you had on your face; goddamn baby you are absolutely gorgeous. But then I just couldn't take my eyes off you." He's staring straight into my eyes telling me this, he didn't look away once, I don't even know if he blinked. But my heart feels like it's about to pound out of my chest and it feels like it's up in my throat and those butterflies are back. Holy. Shit. Damn, talk about making someone weak in the knees. If he wasn't holding onto me, I think I would've fallen.

"Wow," I practically whisper. Suddenly I can't talk and I'm at a loss for words. I slowly lick my lips, hoping that wetting my dry mouth will help me find words somehow. But that's not the case because I feel like my mouth is even more dry than it was before. So dry that my tongue almost sticks to the roof of my mouth as I try to open it again to form words.

"It's a good thing I was watching you, because if I wasn't I wouldn't have been here to stop that creep," he says, leaning in closer to me and I'm hoping he's going to kiss me, I would love to feel his warm, soft lips brush against mine again.

"Th...tha...that's not cr...creepy at all." I gulp, still having a hard time forming words. What the hell is this man doing to me? I've never had a man affect me the way Creedence has each time I've been around him and I would be lying if I said I didn't like it, because honestly? I love the electric feeling that shoots through my body whenever he's around.

"Was that sarcasm?" He raises an eyebrow at me. He has kind of a sad look on his face too and it makes me want to kiss it right off of him.

"No actually," I say quickly because I don't want him thinking that I think he's a creep, because that's definitely not the case. "I don't think it's creepy at all. You're not a creep like that guy was. Plus, I'm glad you were watching me, you protected me from him when you didn't have to. So, thank you, again." I look away for a second to see if Chastity and Winter are still around us, but I think they went to the bar for more drinks, or possibly outside for fresh air.

He leans down next to my ear. "I want to kiss you so bad right now," he whispers, slowly pulling his head away, as it's tilted to the side, half his mouth curled up into a smirk.

"I wouldn't tell you no." And before I can say anything else his hand that was on my lower back comes up to my cheek, his thumb in front of my ear and his fingers underneath my ear, his palm resting gently on my cheek.

His lips slowly meet mine. Giving me soft, slow kisses I never want to end; I think I might be in love. Can you fall in love from a kiss? Listen to me, I sound like an idiot. Then he pulls away, going towards my ear again to whisper. "You smell like vanilla and sugar, good enough to eat. It makes me want to taste you." He lightly licks my ear, making me shiver. "What do you think, Sugar?" He stands up straight winking at me. Shit. That nickname, goddamn, it makes my pussy throb, and I instantly tighten my thighs together.

"I love the nickname." I smile up at him, his golden-brown eyes staring down into my eyes.

He gives me the sexiest smile ever. I don't think this man is capable of giving me a smile that isn't sexy.

"Well Sugar, are you tasty enough to eat? Do you taste sweet like sugar baby?" Just as I'm about to answer, we're interrupted by Winter and Chastity.

"Hey Creedence, you know I enjoy having you around but I gotta kick you out of our girl's night," Winter says to him, laughing as his jaw drops, with a playful look on his face like he's joking around about being offended that he has to leave.

"Yeah, bitch it's girls' night. Sorry Creedence, go back to your lover boy at the bar," Chastity says, patting him on the back.

"Sorry Mister, looks like the ladies spoke and you gotta go." I smirk at him, biting my lower lip. I was excited to see where this was headed and what he was going to say next, looks like I'll have to find another way to hear how this conversation was going to end.

"Mmm, Mister I kinda like that." His voice is deep and rough. "You ladies interrupted me asking Emerald if she tastes as good as she smells." Their jaws drop and my face instantly heats up as I blush. I'd love for him to taste me. Fuck, he even licked my ear and that turned me on like crazy, especially the way he was whispering to me too.

"Damn, down boy." Chastity's smiling but with a look of shock still on her face like she can't believe he just said that out loud.

"Guess you'll have to take a raincheck and find out another night. Now go keep my man company, he looks sad over there." Winter playfully pushes him away from us.

"I'll see you tomorrow then, Emerald," he says with his drop-dead gorgeous smile. He is so sexy. He recently shaved his beard down so it's not as long as it used to be but it's still noticeable, especially for being a light-brown color. His white T-shirt clings to his muscular tattooed arms to the point it looks like it could rip if he moves wrong; his tattoos, fuck, they are like the icing on the cake. His full sleeves from his hands up to his neck; I'd love to lick every single inch of them. And I mean every. Single. Inch.

"See you sometime tomorrow, Creedence." I blow him a kiss and wink at him. It's something Winter and I have always done with guys, without even realizing the other did it until one day we did it at the same time.

He stops and catches my kiss and holds it to his heart, then looks to Winter and Chastity. "I don't know how you ladies expect me to just walk away after that." He starts slowly walking towards me, the look on his face, like he's undressing me with his eyes. He comes up to me placing his fingers on my chin lifting my head up to look at him, then leans down giving me a gentle kiss. It's like he's trying to remember the feel of my lips against his, until he gets to kiss me again. "I'll definitely take you up on that raincheck," he whispers, leaving me speechless as he turns to start to walk away.

This has probably been the craziest night of my life. I'm not even dating him. I've talked to him more now due to Winter dating Carsten, but he's never shown much interest, and now he's kissing me like we've been dating, and I didn't know about it. He walks away leaving me breathless and wanting more. I stand there probably looking like an idiot with my mouth open like I can't believe that just happened. Then for him to just walk away like nothing even happened and not say a single word. Guess tomorrow when I see him, I'll be playing a little hard to get if that's the game he's trying to play here. At least I might play hard to get, I might turn to mush the second I see him and give in.

"Holy shit, I can't believe he just did that to you," Chastity says with her hand on her chest like even she's in shock from the kiss we just shared. "I feel like I just fell in love with him, and I didn't even get to feel that kiss." She laughs a little looking at him with a dreamy like look in her eyes, even though she has a boyfriend.

"Right, I can't believe he just kissed you and walked away without saying anything ...like at all. Mr. Mystery man there. That was really fucking sexy," Winter says, pushing my arm lightly with a smile on her face. We all just stand there like idiots as we watch this sexy man walk away from me.

I finally snap out of it. Long enough to say something to them finally. "Well shit, that was an intense kiss. I need to go get some air." It's all I say as we head outside. I'm still in a daze replaying everything that happened tonight in my head, from the minute he walked up to me to the minute he walked away. Was I dreaming? Or did that actually happen? Every time I think about the feel of his warm, soft lips against mine I get butterflies in my stomach.

2

CREEDENCE

Courtlynd is your typical town where the cops are assholes and harass you if you ever do anything wrong. Everyone in this town knows everyone and everyone knows your business even when you don't want them to. That's why I don't sleep around, and I try to date girls that aren't from around here, that way if we break up people won't be in my business; they won't know shit I don't want them to know.

I look like your normal polite gentleman, but covered in tattoos, from my neck to my hands, along with my stomach and my back. I'm pretty quiet and enjoy keeping to myself but you know what they say about the quiet ones...

It's the quiet ones you gotta watch out for, they're usually the freaks with unexpected behaviors and I definitely am a freak, but not how you'd think and the way I behave in private is something that always catches most girls off guard.

"Fucking great," I mumble to myself as I pull off to the side of the road from the flashing lights and police sirens behind me. This is all I needed was to get pulled over. This is also a perfect example of what I was just talking about as well. I've been pulled over plenty of times, arrested for stupid shit a couple times too. I'm not an asshole who gets in trouble all the time. It's just dumb shit I did when I was younger with my friends that you can pretty much say I was in the wrong place at the wrong time.

"Good evening officer," I say politely, hoping it'll get me out of this situation quickly if I cooperate. Killing them with kindness usually works with people, so hopefully it'll work in my favor this time and I won't get a ticket.

"Good evening, is there a reason why you were speeding?" The cops in this town suck. They don't do their jobs right because they don't think they have to. They just think because they're cops, they're in control, and that's why they can run things however they want to.

But what am I supposed to say to him, sorry officer I was rushing out of this girl's house that I just fucked, because she was starting to become clingy and on the verge of tears because I didn't want to sleep over? That my friends are convinced I only sleep with girls when I'm in a relationship because I don't share my sex life. Why not? Because I don't need them knowing what kind of shit I'm into, I like to keep that private and that's why I'm careful about who I sleep with. I'm just hoping that Daisy keeps her fucking mouth shut, I wasn't as intense with her as I usually am because I know she likes to talk, but she definitely enjoyed what I did with her. I knew I shouldn't have slept with her, but I couldn't resist, she's got some-thing about her that I just couldn't walk away from. I should've just stayed away from her though, especially after what her best friend Brynn did to my best friend Carsten. But like he said about Brynn in the past, I feel the same way about Daisy right now, the pussy is just too good to let go, that's why I keep hooking up with her.

"Sorry sir, I umm didn't realize I was going that fast," I say, trying to keep it cool and not get pissy; I just want to get home. I'm tired and have to work in the morning, and it's not that easy tattooing when you're half asleep, especially when your eyes are heavy. You gotta stay focused so you don't fuck up the lines, or any of it really.

"Can I have your license and registration please?" He has a cocky look on his face, of course he does, I feel like he's the only one who ever pulls me over in this town. Like he's the only cop who ever works. I'm just convinced that since he arrested me that one time, he just has it out for me, so when he sees me he pulls me over.

"Um yeah, give me one second to grab it from my wallet and glove box." I'm getting annoyed, I feel like he's dragging this out, which I know he's not. I'm just impatient and don't want to be here. I'd rather be in my comfy warm bed right now. I actually could've been pulling into my driveway right now if he wouldn't have pulled me over.

"Creedence Knoxx?" he asks, looking at my license, he looks at me then back to my license, what a tool. He acts like we haven't gone over this before, like he's never pulled me over. At this rate he should just walk up to me and say, "Good evening, Creedence." That's how often we go through this.

"Yes sir, that's my name." I try not to roll my eyes, still not sure why he's acting like he's never done this before, or we've never been around each other before, like I said he's the only cop that ever fucking wastes my time and pulls me over.

"I'll be right back," he says, taking my information with him. Great, another thing to waste my time. Usually I'm not disrespectful, but like I said before, I'm tired and annoyed already, so I'm just grumpy. Plus, fucking Daisy didn't do anything to get Emerald off my mind, not after tonight at Black Velvet and how fucking sexy Emerald looked, and the way her soft, plump lips felt against mine, damn I need to kiss her again it's like I can't stop craving her, I've never felt lips so soft, so perfect. They fit against mine like they were always meant to be there.

But instead, Daisy and I had already had plans to fuck. It was boring sex because I wasn't really into it, my mind was on Emerald the whole time, I think at one point I had to pretend that Daisy was Emerald just to get myself off. Then after we fucked, I got dressed and left. That's why she was being so dramatic because I didn't want to stay, which I usually don't, so I don't know what was different about it this time. I think it's best I cut things off with her anyway. I think the psycho is starting to catch feelings and I'm not about to have another crazy bitch on my ass about where I'm at and who I'm with when I can be a free man to do as I please. I wouldn't say I'm a whore, I sleep around, but I stick to the same girl for a bit or the same few girls for quite some time, not quite relationships but I guess you could say fuck buddies.

God I can't wait to see Emerald tomorrow, it'll probably only be in passing as we both head to work but still, her beautiful fucking face, it's stuck in my mind all damn day anyway, and that ass of hers, mmm looks so fucking delicious I just want to sink my teeth into it. She's got curves for days. But then I'm interrupted from my thoughts by Officer whatever his name is–I didn't quite catch it. But I don't care to remember it either.

"Here you are Creedence." He hands me back my stuff. "I'm feeling nice today and it's been a while since you've been pulled over for speeding. Have a nice night." And he just walks away leaving me in shock, he doesn't even give me the chance to respond. Which I'm fine with. I'm just surprised he didn't want to give me a ticket for speeding, oh well I'm not complaining.

I drive off lost in my thoughts about Emerald still, I can't get her out of my mind. I think it's safe to say I'm on the verge of being obsessed with her, that is if I'm not already obsessed. Yeah, now that I think about it, I'm fucking obsessed and I won't be happy until she's mine. I can't wait to taste her sweet fucking lips again, mmm vanilla and sugar.

I get home and walk in through the garage walking past my blacked-out Harley Davidson Chopper, stopping for a minute to stare at it; I fucking hate the thing. It's a good memory and a fucking nightmare all in one. I should've just gone to therapy, maybe it would've helped me cope with the nightmares and the horrible flash-backs, but for some reason thinking about talking to someone makes the guilt worse.

FOUR YEARS AGO

"You ready jackass?" my younger brother, Xander, asks, shoving my shoulder like he always does when he calls me a jackass. He may be younger than me, but he and I are best friends, we've been close our whole lives and I love it.

"Yeah, fuck face. Just remember to be careful please. It's slippery out since it rained, don't ride like an ass," I tell him. We pulled off at a restaurant to eat while it rained, figuring we'd play it safe instead of riding through the rain, since it was pouring. But now that it's drizzling, we gotta get back home before it's too late. He just got his motorcycle license a couple months ago so it worries me that he thinks he's untouchable and sometimes rides like a jackass. I just hope he'll use his head now.

"Yeah, yeah. Stop trying to be my dad and go back to being my big brother, how about that," he says jokingly, but I hate when he tries to act cocky, like he knows it all. Which I get, I've been eighteen before, not that I'm that much older, I just turned nineteen last week, but I know how to use my head when it comes to doing stupid shit on a motorcycle, especially in the rain.

"I'm not trying to be your dad, you know that. Now let's go before it starts storming again." I give him a serious look, I hate that he doesn't take me seriously sometimes, the jackass always thinks I'm trying to be his dad, when really, I'm just worried about his safety.

"Be careful big bro," he says, now all serious, something telling me he's not feeling confident at the moment, his cockiness seems to be wearing off.

"You too, little bro." They're stupid nicknames but it's something we've always called each other. Something I didn't know I would never be able to call him again.

We get onto the highway to head home, it's the only way home from where we're at, so we don't have a choice. There's a lot of traffic so I'm making sure he's driving ok, especially since the jackass and I didn't wear helmets. Looking back and forth between the both of us, I end up switching lanes cause we're getting closer to our exit, which I don't think he notices cause he looks over at me to see where I went and right as he does his bike hits a puddle, which makes him lose control causing his bike to spin out from underneath him as his bodies thrown off of it, the impact from the way his body lands, smacking his head into the ground, killed him instantly.

I snap out of my flashback, shaking my head to wake myself up from it. That whole day changed my life. If I wouldn't have switched lanes that would've been me, it should've been me. We didn't wear helmets that day either, so I know what happened to him. It could've been different if we did wear our helmets, but every day I think to myself...it should've been me. I relive that nightmare every night in my sleep. Or lack of sleep, since I barely sleep anymore–the night-mares keep me up. Losing my brother keeps me up, the fact that it could've and should've been me is another reason I lose sleep every night. But I haven't been the same since. There's a heaviness in my chest that I carry around with me daily that will never go away, the constant reminder that I lost my baby brother, it kills me.

I wake up the next morning to get ready for work, hoping I'm timing everything right to see Emerald in the driveway, even if it's long enough to just say hi, I'd love to walk over and kiss her again, but that all depends on the timing. I rush to do my normal morning routine and get out the door. I see her car is in the driveway, so I set my stuff in my truck and wait. I fold the bed door down and sit there, like the obsessed creep I'm becoming. What is wrong with me? I'm turning into Carsten, when he stalked Emerald to talk to her about Winter, except this time I'm just stalking Emerald because I need her, and I won't stop until I have her.

I finally hear her door shut about ten minutes later and look down at my phone seeing we both have at least five minutes until we have to leave. We don't work together but we work close to each other, so I know her work schedule pretty well. That's not even the obsessive part either, we've been working the same work schedule for years now, except I work two hours later than she does, so she usually gets home first.

I hop down off my truck bed and walk over to her driveway meeting her by her car before she gets there.

"Well good morning...stalker." She laughs, blushing a little as she looks down. I love how much she blushes around me. I don't even know what I do that makes her blush, but I love it. I don't think there's anything I dislike about this girl. Everything about her is perfect, absolutely fucking perfect.

"Good morning, beautiful. I just wanted to come over and tell you to have a good day at work," I say, waiting for her to look up so I can make my next move.

"Really?" She finally looks up at me with a confused look on her face. "Why's that?" She's biting her bottom lip and it's the sexiest thing ever; it's making my dick semi hard just looking at it.

"Well Sugar, because I want you." I don't even care how blunt I'm being, I'm telling her how I feel because I don't want to waste either of our time. I know what I want, and I'm not going to stop until I convince her to give me a chance. I don't just want her sexually either, I mean I definitely do, don't get me wrong. But I want more than that. I want to call her mine, and she's going to be mine.

"You...you want...me?" she asks slowly and quietly, almost at a whisper towards the end of her sentence. It's cute how she almost becomes shy around me, and I know she's not shy.

"Yes, beautiful. I want you in more ways than one." I stop, stepping closer, tucking her hair behind her ear, she looks down again. "And I won't stop until you're mine." I place my finger on her chin, raising her head to look up at me. She's nervous, her breathing has picked up a little and I can tell by the way she's swallowing her mouth is suddenly dry, and if it's not it's on the verge of being dry.

These are all the things I've paid attention to about her when I'm around her. Call me crazy... but I want to learn everything about her. Maybe I'm a psycho, I don't care. I'm going to make her forget about any man she's ever been with, and I will ruin her for any man she plans to be with in the future that isn't me.

"B...b...but why? What makes me so special?" She swallows hard again, you can hear in the way her tongue sounds, that it's sticking to the roof of her mouth as she talks from how dry her mouth is.

"Everything...everything about you is special to me and I want to show you every time I'm with you why you're special." Then I lean down cupping her face and I kiss her passionately, showing her just how much I want her. I swipe my tongue against her lips, and she instantly opens, allowing me to deepen the kiss as our tongues dance together. My cock is painfully hard now and it's taking everything in me to not convince her to fuck me right here. But instead, I take her hand and place it on my hard cock.

"See what you do to me, Sugar. How hard you make my cock," I whisper down into her ear as she gasps. "I'd love to show you more, but only when you're ready to take it all." Then I kiss her forehead and start walking away. Wanting to tease her. To leave her wanting more. "I'll text you later, free up your schedule. We're going to Black Velvet tonight and getting drunk, Sugar. We're about to have some fun," I tell her as I get into my truck and shut the door, leaving her standing there, jaw hanging open, cheeks rosy from blushing. Her chest rising and falling from how quickly she's breathing. It takes everything in me not to get out of my truck and go back over to her, push her up against her car kiss her, then fuck her, but I need to be patient.

I'm bored during my break at work so I decide to text Emerald, to keep myself busy, and because I can't keep my fucking mind off her. She's literally consumed all my thoughts today. I can't wait to see her again, and to press my lips against hers.

Credence
Don't forget to be available tonight 10:30

Emerald
you're awfully bossy

Creedence
nah, I just know what I want

Emerald
ehh, I'd say bossy ;)

Credence
no... I just want you. Sugar ;)

Emerald
I like a man who knows what he wants. But I still
think you're bossy lol

Creedence
do you like to argue?

Emerald
sometimes...

Credence
I'd like to punish you for that

Emerald
yeah? How so

Creedence
spank that delicious ass of yours

Emerald
shhh you're making me blush

Creedence
good, I love it when you blush, want me to
continue?

Emerald
nope, maybe you can show me sometime.

Creedence
I'd be more than happy too...

Emerald
good, I'll meet you in the driveway tonight at
10:30

Creedence
are you leaving me?

Emerald
yep. Gotta get back to work

Creedence
no fair

Emerald
bye mister

Shit, her and that mister shit. Makes my dick hard. Who would've thought that a simple word coming from those plump lips of hers could make my dick so hard.

I spend the rest of my workday trying to keep myself busy and my mind off Emerald as much as possible, but of course I fail miserably, but that's ok it helped the time pass by quickly.

I head home so I can shower after my long, drawn-out day at work of tattooing people. I recently started working at Carsten's uncles shop Crazy's. I love it. I started tattooing a couple years ago and it's something I've enjoyed doing since, just some days the people can be annoying is all. Like today, girls who whine the whole time because it hurts... Well, no shit, it's supposed to hurt. I shake my head to myself thinking about it, but what's a tattoo without a little pain. After my shower I head downstairs to make something to eat and end up running into Carsten while I'm down there

"Hey man, how's it going?" I ask him as I open the refrigerator looking in the drawers to pull out the lunch meat. Sandwich it is. I plan on convincing Emerald to grab something to eat at the diner Winter works at, either before or after the bar, so I won't need a ton of food.

"Hey Creed. Just got done working out before I have to head into Black Velvet for my late shift tonight. How was Crazy's today?" He takes a bite of his sandwich that he must've made before I came down here.

"It wasn't terrible. I love doing it, but man, some of the people whine a lot. The last girl I tattooed took forever because she kept crying that it hurt." He shakes his head laughing.

"I mean yeah some of them hurt like a bitch, but don't you go into it knowing that?" he asks in a confused tone. You would think people would go into this knowing that a tattoo hurts like a bitch, but I think some underestimate just how painful some areas can be.

"My thoughts exactly. But I'm pretty sure she thought the exact opposite or something because she was very surprised with how bad it hurt." I shake my head as I put a piece of Salami in my mouth while I make my sandwich.

"Some girls are strange man. Speaking of..." he asks, giving me a look, but I'm not giving in yet.

"Speaking of what?" I ask like I have no idea what he's talking about. I know damn well he's talking about that gorgeous fucking woman who lives next door, but I'm gonna pretend I don't know what he's talking about, just for the fuck of it. Because I'm an asshole like that.

"Nope, don't you play dumb with me. I've known you since we were kids, you know damn well what I'm talking about." He crosses his arms over his chest. "You and Emerald bro, I saw you dancing together, kissing her. So, what's going on?" He raises one eyebrow at me. There's no fooling him. We can basically read each other's minds; I just have to look at him and he just looks back and we're instantly on the same page. I guess you can say that's a part of our bromance that we get made fun of for sharing. I guess that's what happens when you grow up together, and spend every school break, and weekends together, summer vacations too. It was rare when we weren't together.

"Nothing yet. I just haven't been able to stop thinking about her man. The more I see her the more, I don't know, obsessed, I feel like I'm becoming. I feel like a fucking psycho bro." I laugh after saying that because I really do feel like a psycho. "That's how into her I am, it's so weird. I've never been this into a girl like this, where I just can't stop thinking about her and then I get this feeling inside me that's even more fucked up. What's wrong with me... we haven't even slept together. We're not even dating." I sigh after getting all of that out, I can't seem too crazy. I've known Emerald for a few years, but just started talking to her more these past few months so it's not like this is completely random that I'm showing interest, I've just never been this way before with women.

"Sounds like you got it bad man, that's how I felt with Winter, like I couldn't, well still can't even fucking breathe without her. That's how I knew I was in love with her," he says, grabbing a bottle of water from the fridge and opening it.

"Well damn, that's what I was thinking but then I thought I was being like a chick and overthinking it." Laughing, I take a quick bite of my sandwich. "We're going out tonight. I told her we're going to the bar to get drunk and have fun, so we'll see what happens." I take another bite feeling like I'm running out of time as it's already almost nine at night.

"Well let me know how it goes when I see you tomorrow. I'm sure I'll see things while you guys are there, but I'm gonna be like a chick now, I want full details tomorrow dick," he says running up the stairs.

"Will do man, glad we can act like chicks together," I yell up to him and hear him laugh in the process. I finish up my sandwich and go head upstairs to shower and get ready for the night texting Emerald again in the process.

Credence
don't be late, or I might punish you

Emerald
I'm a girl, I'm always late. What kind of
punishment lol

Creedence
If I told you that would ruin all the fun now
wouldn't it?

Emerald
yes, but I hate surprises, now I'm pouting

Creedence
I'd love to bite that pouty lip of yours and suck it
into my mouth

Emerald
holy shit, if you talk like that I'm curious what
your punishments look like

Creedence
well if you show up late you might find out, or
you might just find out either way

Emerald
Damn, now I'm getting excited over here. Promise
I can find out either way?

Credence
pinky promise, sugar

3

EMERALD

Pinky promise... What the fuck is this man doing to my damn heart here. I can't believe he just said pinky promise. I wonder if he's heard me say it before because that's something I've stuck with since I was a kid because I just always loved pinky promises. Is he making fun of me? No, he can't be. But now he goes and says it and it's making me like him even more. He made my fucking panties wet in the process. Now I'm debating if I should change them or not since I just got out of the shower not too long ago.

I decide to keep them on, that way I can tease him and tell him how wet they are later, that's if I can work up the courage and just be straight up blunt instead of shy. For some reason he makes me shy, and I blush around him more than I've ever blushed around a man before. He makes me feel like a little kid. But not in a bad way.

I get dressed in my black fishnet tights, my black leather skirt that is on the verge of being dangerously too short, but I don't care I'm dressing to tease him tonight and then a hot pink fitted halter top. I'm also wearing my black high-top converse, which happens to look really cute with my outfit. Hopefully he likes how I look tonight.

I grab my small purse, my gum, and my phone and I head downstairs. Thankfully I'm home alone so I won't be late from getting distracted talking to Winter. I have five minutes to spare before he considers me late, so I don't waste any time. I grab a jacket in case it gets cold and head for the driveway.

As I walk towards my driveway, I see Creedence standing by his truck and holy shit, he looks so fucking good, my stomach does somersaults. He's wearing a plain fitted black T-shirt, that's so tight on his muscular arms, with dark wash jeans, making my mouth practically water just looking at him.

"Holy. Fuck. You look fucking gorgeous, Sugar. Good enough to take a bite out of." He starts slowly walking towards me and grabs my hand.

"Thank you, Mister, you look really fucking good as well, I'm practically drooling over here." I laugh walking towards him, closing the distance between us.

"Thanks Sugar." The side of his mouth curls up in a smirk. "Every time I see you, I just want to kiss you, is that okay?" He cups my face with his thumb in front of my ear and long fingers through my hair.

"You don't have to ask anymore. If you want to kiss me, please do." And before I can say anything else his lips crash down on mine, he swipes his tongue out and I open for him immediately. I swipe my tongue against his and pull his lower lip into my mouth sucking on it, he lets out a growl.

"Fuck, Sugar, what are you doing to me?" he asks, pulling away from the kiss "You're driving me absolutely crazy," he says taking my hand and placing it on his rock-hard cock, again, and my god if it feels like this through his jeans, I'm kind of afraid to see him with nothing on.

"I'm not doing anything at all handsome, just being my normal self," I say, pulling him down towards me by his shirt to kiss me. He grabs me by my hips, picking me up and I instantly wrap my legs around his waist. He pushes my skirt up a little and grips my ass tightly with both hands making me moan into his mouth as he lets out a groan.

"Fucking shit. If we don't stop, we're never going to leave," he says, pulling away again.

"And trust me you won't want me fucking you out here, you'll want me to take my time with you," he says, whispering into my ear and nipping at my earlobe.

"Let's go Sugar, I promise we'll have a fun night tonight, but let's go out together and have some fun. It'll be a good time." He kisses my neck slowly; his lips feel heavenly against my skin, so soft and warm. I never want to stop feeling his lips against my skin working their magic like they were made to be a part of me, sending chills through my body, sending a throbbing sensation straight to my pussy. I never thought I'd want someone as much as I want him right now and all we've done is kiss.

"Well, if you'd stop trying to seduce me then I'd be able to get down so we can leave." I start giggling, trying to pull my neck away, as he gently sucks on the skin right below my ear, making my body heat up with even more excitement. Shit, I'd give anything to feel his lips against me all day long. They're the softest lips I think I've ever kissed. They're the perfect thickness, and form to my lips perfectly, I'm convinced they must've been made just for me.

"Fine I'll stop, but this isn't over with." He puts me down slowly, like he's already regretting this decision to stop kissing me and walks around to open his truck door for me. I instantly regret my outfit choice, not sure how I'm going to get up in this thing without showing my ass and vagina off to the world with my skirt sliding up around my waist. That should make Creedence happy.

"Oh my, such a gentleman." I smile at him. "Thank you, I appreciate you opening my door for me," I say, grabbing his hand to step up into his truck since I'm having a hard time with my skirt keeping it down like I thought I would.

"Damn, I just saw your ass and it took everything in me not to bite it." He laughs while wiggling his eyebrows at me. That fucking smirk on his face that comes so naturally. It takes everything in me not to pull him towards me and say fuck it for going out tonight.

"Well how about I let you bite it later. When I show you how wet my panties are from you." I say winking at him, his jaw drops as he shuts the passenger door and quickly walks around to the front.

"Is that a promise?" he says as he opens the door climbing into the driver's side, with the sexiest look on his face. This man and his many panty dropping smiles and facial expressions.

"Pinky promise." I hold my pinky out to him as he interlocks his with mine.

"I love pinky promises." He smiles down at our hands.

"Really? Are you fucking with me? I always say pinky promise and everyone always makes fun of me for it." I'm kinda shocked hoping that he's not messing with me. I don't think I'd be embarrassed but I'd feel stupid for just admitting something like that the first time we're going out together.

"Hell no, I'm not fucking with you, I've been saying and doing pinky promises since I was a kid, they've always been my favorite. I will always be one to pinky promise people, no matter how old I am. That's one thing I will never break either is a pinky promise." He leans down and kisses my hand. The kiss is so light and gentle it's almost hard to feel his lips press against my skin. But I can feel the warmth from his kiss, and I miss it the second it's gone.

"Same here, wow... I've never met someone who loved doing those like I do." I look down at our hands and I feel giddy almost like a child.

We walk into Black Velvet and it's not that crowded yet, which I'm thankful for. I hate crowded bars, but I'm sure it'll pick up since it's a Friday.

"What do you want to drink, Sugar?" he asks looking down at me, I love how tall he is compared to me. For some reason it just makes me feel safe with how big he is.

"How tall are you? I know that's random, but I keep meaning to ask." I look up at him feeling so short in my five-foot five height.

He smiles, giving a slight laugh "I'm six foot five. Why shorty?"

"Rude." I laugh. "I was just curious; I love how tall you are is all." I smirk a little, I love tall men, it's so sexy to me.

"I'm just kidding, I love how short you are," he says, wrapping his arm around my waist as we wait at the bar for Chase or Carsten to get our drink order.

"I can't get over how sexy you look," he whispers down into my ear sending chills through my body.

"God, I love it when you do that." I shiver again, suddenly feeling cold now that the warmth of his body isn't as close as it was.

"Do what Sugar?" he whispers again, and I feel like if he whispers in my ear again, I might jump his bones right here in front of everyone. I don't fucking care at this point; his deep rough voice is so fucking sexy and hearing the hoarseness in his voice as he whispers makes my pussy throb and my panties even more wet than they already were.

"Whisper in my ear, god it's so sexy." I turn my head up to look at him hoping to God he kisses me again soon. I've never had someone turn me on so much from just a kiss, but honestly, I feel like his kiss alone is enough to get me off. Or maybe I'm just that horny, it's been a bit since I've slept with anyone. So, I think at this point he could blow on me and get me off. That's how badly I need to be with this man.

"I love how honest you are with me and how you're not afraid to tell me what you like, you're going to be fun later." He pulls me even closer to him, I can feel his erection against my lower back and it's so hard not to turn around and wrap my hand around it as much as his jeans will allow me to.

"I couldn't imagine not being honest with you, I feel no need to lie to you or not tell you what I'm into or not into. Even just in general I always try to say how I feel about something," I say back to him. Loving the fact that it feels like we've always been this way. Like he's never been a stranger.

"Well please, keep being honest with me. Don't hold back," he says, leaving light kisses on my neck, right below my ear and slowly kissing his way down my neck. I'm usually not one to be this way in public, but right now I don't care. I want everyone in this bar to know he's off limits.

"What can I get you guys?" Chase asks. "Oh hey, I didn't realize it was you guys, do you want your usual?" he says, looking back at us with a confused look on his face.

"Yes please, cherry vodka and Sprite," I remind him in case he forgot.

"Ohh cherry vodka, another thing to make you taste sweet later," Creedence says, letting go of my waist and sitting on the stool next to me, pulling me into him. My stomach pressed up against his hard cock, from where I stand.

"You sure sound positive that something will be happening later." I look up at him, he's still taller than me sitting down so I have to look up to look into his eyes.

"Well, I won't force you to do anything you don't want to but I promise you you'll love it," he says with that sexy side smirk of his. That smirk is going to get me pregnant one day. I can't believe I just thought about having a baby with Creedence, what is going on with me? Not that having a baby with him is a bad thing, but because it's so soon and we aren't even a couple yet is why the thought shocked me.

"Maybe I'll make you wait and just tease you all night." I smile at him, maybe I'll stick to that idea. I'm not sure if I want to sleep with him yet. I don't know if he's a man whore and sleeps around, so I'm afraid if I do that'll be the end of this and I'm not ready for this to end yet.

"Here you go guys, do you want me to start you both up a tab?" Chase asks us while setting our drinks down in front of us. I grab my purse to get my card out, but Creedence beats me to it and gives Chase his card.

"Yeah, that's fine, I'll be paying for Emerald's drinks as well," he says, shooing me away with my card, he's holding my arms in one of his hands, that's how huge his hands are, that way I can't give my card to Chase, or fight him. I'm not gonna lie the thought of him holding my wrists' during sex is turning me on. What is wrong with me? First, I talk about him getting me pregnant now I'm talking about us having sex. I need to get laid soon.

"Alright gotcha man," he says, taking his card from him and walking away. I lost my fight in trying to pay for anything tonight because being here where Chase and Carsten both own the bar, they're going to take Creedence's payment over mine.

"Thank you, you didn't have to do that. I can pay for my drinks; I would feel bad making you pay for them." I turn to look at him so I can see his face better now. Every time I look at him, I feel like I find something new I like about him, whether it's a facial expression, a different smile on his face. His facial features, I don't know. I could study this man over and over and never get tired of looking at him.

"I know I don't have to, but I want to and besides I'm the one who said you were coming out with me, so I'm going to be paying for your drinks." He pauses for a second. "Remember I said we were going out getting drunk and having a good time." He leans in and kisses me slowly. I open my mouth instantly inviting his tongue before he even swipes his against my mouth, then I suck his bottom lip into my mouth and bite it. He lets out a soft growl before pulling away and placing his forehead against mine.

"You're driving me crazy; you know that?" he asks. "Damn Sugar, I don't think I'll ever get enough of you," he says pulling me in by my waist, loving the way his strong arms feel around me.

"What do you mean?" I'm curious now, I think I know what he means, but I want to be sure, and I want to hear him say it.

"I have a feeling that no matter how much I'm around you or how much I get of you, I'm going to keep wanting more…from you and only you." He wraps his arms around me, hugging me before standing up. "Let's go dance, Sugar." He starts pulling me with him to the dance floor.

It's a slow song so he wraps one of his strong arms around my waist pulling me in close. I could get used to this; I love the way my body feels close to his. I feel safe with him. I put my right hand in his and my left hand on his shoulder. I lay my head onto his chest and can hear his heart racing; it feels exactly how mine is racing right now. He makes me feel different than any other man has ever made me feel before, which is so strange for someone I really don't even know.

I've dated men for years or months and haven't even experienced these feelings before.

4

EMERALD

WHEN THE SONGS ARE OVER, HE PLACES HIS FINGERS ON MY chin gently lifting my face as he leans down and kisses me, his tongue swipes across my bottom lip. I open my mouth trying not to moan out, his tongue swirls with mine, his other hand slides down my back to my ass, and he grips it tightly, possibly tight enough to leave a mark on it. I can't control myself as a moan slips out of my mouth and I pull away before I get too carried away.

"God damn babe, that was sexy," he groans into my ear. "I can't wait to hear you moan my name," he says, licking my ear lobe slowly. He gives me goosebumps, something else I've never experienced before with other men. I love it though.

"Oh Creedence." He cuts me off before I can finish what I was going to say.

"Do you like it rough, Sugar?" he whispers gruffly, pulling away from my ear, the intense look of hunger in his eyes. That is if hunger had a look. Mr. Creedence fucking Knoxx, this sexy man standing right in front of me is now the definition of the look of hunger. He is the owner of this sexy look. He stands there staring at me with a look like he wants to eat me alive but in the best way possible, and I'm all for it. This man can do as he pleases to me, and I don't think I'd stop him. I don't think I'd have it in me to tell him no because whatever he has planned for me and my body I need it, I crave it and I don't even know what it is yet, but I won't complain because as long as it involves his body and mine, I'm ready.

"I...umm, I don't know honestly. I've never been with someone who was into rough sex or anything like that." I look up into his brown eyes that look like pools of whisky. His mouth curls up into a delicious grin showing off his sexy dimple.

"Mmm damn, well I can't wait to see what you like." He winks at me, his grin growing into a full smile. God his smile does something to my heart that makes it feel like it's racing but beating slowly at the same time.

"Come on, let's go take a shot." He laces his fingers through mine and walks towards the counter with me. Everything about this man next to me just makes me feel safe, and the way he holds my hand and pulls me closer to him makes me feel wanted, needed in more than just a sexual way.

"Okay, wanna do a lemon drop? Those are my favorite," I yell to him so he can hear me since I'm slightly behind but pulling me close to him while holding onto his hand tightly, so I don't get lost in the crowd that slowly grew while we were dancing.

"Anything for you, Sugar," he yells back down to me. I bite my lip trying to hide my nerdy, cheesy grin that's trying to creep up on my face because of what he had just said to me. It wasn't even anything super romantic or sexual or whatever but something about the meaning behind it

Anything for you Sugar. I think he truly means that he'd do anything for me. Unless I'm overthinking it. You know like most girls tend to do. What's next, I'll be planning my wedding with Creedence? Calm down Emerald, you're reading too much into this.

We both grab a stool, and I spin sitting to where I'm facing towards him, so he pulls me closer to him and spreads his legs around each side of me to where my legs are between his then he places his hands on my hips, scooting me a little closer. I love how he's always finding a way to touch me and have his hands on me. It makes me feel wanted, like he needs me near him to feel complete.

"So, tell me about yourself," he says to me while we wait for Carsten or Chase to come over this way.

"Well, what do you want to know?" I ask because I'm not good at talking about myself, I'm my least favorite subject to talk about. I know it's sad but it's true I hate talking about my life.

"Well for starters, how old are you? I'm only asking cause I wasn't sure if you were twenty-four like me and Carsten or if you were twenty-three like Winter is now." He looks right into my eyes as he speaks, and I love that he always looks into my eyes. Eye contact always makes me nervous and twitchy, but for some reason with Creedence it's easy. It happens without me even thinking about it and I just feel comfortable being in the comfort of his eyes.

"I'm twenty-three, I just turned twenty-three last month." Not sure why I mentioned my birthday, it's not like I celebrate it anyways. The only reason I celebrated my birthday was because Winter made me go out, if it wasn't for her, I probably would have stayed home.

"What's your favorite color?" I ask him. I like that he cares about getting to know me, all the men I've been with I've always had to ask the questions which have always annoyed them, and they didn't care too much to know about me, it was mainly about sex even when I was in a relationship.

"Uhh, I'd say blue, Cerulean blue." His lips twitch a little like he's hiding back a smile, and it makes me laugh a little because that's my favorite blue crayon. It's always my go to whenever I have to use the color blue.

"That's my favorite blue crayon to use. If I ever use crayons, that's the shade I go with." I smile looking away, blushing a little. I can't believe I just said that to him. Admitting I color sometimes, another thing to scare the man away. But it's true I'd rather stay home and color or read or snuggle up to a good movie than go out. I've always been that way even when I was in high school. Home is just the best place to be. Forget the drama of the outside world, I'd rather be home.

"Why are you blushing, what's wrong?" He turns my face gently with his fingers. A serious look on his face.

"I just embarrassed myself telling you I still like to color, is all." Might as well be honest, no point in trying to make something up, especially if something comes of this, then he'll be around me enough to see that I color.

"Nothing wrong with that, why are you embarrassed though? Listen, you don't ever have to be embarrassed around me ever, I will never judge you or make fun of you for liking something." He leans in, leaving gentle kisses along my lips.

"Thank you." I pause for a minute. "I mean that, that means a lot to me." I lean in kissing him again. Then pull away. "Most people around my age are all about partying and getting fucked up constantly. Which is fine I get it, but it's not my thing. I'd rather be home and comfortable, doing whatever the hell I want than out at some bar, or a frat party." I give a half smile. Unsure of how he's going to react. "I mean I do enjoy going out, but I don't need to go out," I add in nervously.

"I'm the same exact way. I'd rather stay home and do my own thing than worry about getting fucked up at some party or the bar." He kisses me again, a little more intensely this time. Right as I'm about to open my mouth to swipe my tongue against his, we're interrupted.

"What can I get for you two lovebirds?" This time it's Carsten who comes over to us. A cheesy ass grin on his face and a look that says he's happy for his best friend.

"Two lemon drops please." Creedence pulls away to look over at him, laughing and shaking his head. They have a relationship just like mine and Winter's, they've known each other their whole lives practically just like the two of us.

"Lovebirds, huh is that what we look like to everyone around us?" he asks me then stops for a second. "What's your favorite color?" I'm actually surprised he remembered he didn't ask me my favorite color, or that he still cared to carry on with our other conversation.

"Pink, but not just any shade, it has to be hot pink," I say glancing over at Carsten who is setting our shots down on the counter for us.

"Thanks man, appreciate you," Creedence tells him as he sets them down then slides them towards us.

"Yes, thank you very much," I tell him. "I can pay for these ones though." I go to reach for my purse and they both tell me no at the same time. The smiles on their faces are pretty much the same, these two are too much alike.

"Gosh calm down." I laugh. "Can't a woman pay for drinks for herself and her man?" I ask them as Carsten shakes his head walking away. Like he's not about to get involved.

"Ohh, so I'm your man now?" He smirks at me, god just that smirk in itself makes me wet. It makes me want to lean forward and kiss or lick him. Maybe both. Mmm the things I'd love to do to this sexy man.

"Well, no, but like I don't know, you knew what I meant." I blush, putting my hands over my face trying to hide behind them. I can't believe I just said that when I don't even know one hundred percent if he's that into me.

"Hey," he says, trying to pull my hands away but I don't let him. I feel stupid that I said that when this is the first time we've hung out without our friends with us.

"Hey, Sugar. It's okay." He pulls my hands down this time. "I honestly liked that you said that, it was cute. And it made me feel, I don't know special that you called me your man when this is our first date." He looks down like he's nervous, which makes my face redden a little more with embarrassment for some reason.

"Well, I like you, I honestly have liked you for quite some time. I was just afraid to act on it," I say putting my hands on his knees, might as well get it out in the open now. That way if he doesn't see things going any further, he can tell me. What is my deal? Why am I being so negative?

"Same here, when I kissed your hand that day in your driveway, I haven't been able to get you off my mind since then." He smiles. "And I'm being serious, I've been wanting to take you out, but just didn't think you were interested." He looks into my eyes now, but he still wears the nervous look on his face.

"How could you not tell?" I question, thinking it was so obvious... "I blushed when you kissed my hand and every time we hang out as a group, I flirt with you." It's so easy to be open with him, he makes me feel comfortable like I don't need to shy away from what I want to say.

"I honestly just thought that was just how your personality was. It took me a minute to realize that you were flirting with me." He smiles at me. And we just sit there staring at each other, neither of us bothering to speak. It's not weird or awkward because I enjoy his presence.

"Let's take our shots, Sugar. I want you warmed up for tonight." He winks at me. The smile on his face is to die for, the way his lips curl up in the corner and the dimple forms on his cheek, it makes me want to stick my tongue out and start teasing him.

"Man, you are just so sure that were gonna fuck aren't you," I whisper-shout to him so no one around us can hear, and for some reason it comes out breathy, probably from him turning me on.

"Well, I'm not forcing you, but don't tell me you're not wanting to yourself, am I right?" He gives a sexy side smirk. "You even told me about how wet your panties were, correct me if I'm wrong but that usually means you're in the mood to fuck someone huh?" He winks again, and I officially think I could watch this man wink all day, something about the way he does it and the smile on his face is enough to make my heart feel like it's going to explode.

God everything this man does is so sexy, it's like he stepped out of my fantasies with how I always pictured my dream man to look and has all the perfect qualities that I always look for in a man.

"Ready?" he asks, handing me my shot, his cheeks moving as he smiles at me again.

"Of course." I take it from him, and I nod my head letting him know I'm ready to drink it and we take them both at the same time.

I make a grossed-out face, because no matter how many shots I take they'll always be somewhat gross to me, even my favorite ones. Alcohol in general is just nasty, I don't even know why I drink honestly. I truly just don't like the taste of it.

He sets his shot glass down and looks at me. "That was cute," he says. "The way your nose scrunches up when you make a certain face, I love it." He stands up, closing the space between us.

My body heats up and I don't know if it's from the alcohol or from how close he is and how much he turns me on. He cups my face and leans down to kiss me, groaning in the process. "You have no idea how much I want you right now, Sugar." His husky voice sends a wave of chills through my body making me shiver.

"Same here." Is all I can manage to get out before he comes back down for a kiss. I open my mouth letting him in instantly, I love the feel of his tongue against mine. The way it moves perfectly with mine, like we were made to share these kisses together. I just hope that he's falling as hard for me as I am for him and that I'm not just some obsessed freak who is making this stuff up in her head.

"What do you say we close this tab and go back to my place?" He stops, resting his forehead against mine.

"Sounds good to me," I say breathlessly. I'm so turned on right now and he's barely even touched me.

As we walk to the car, he walks me to the passenger side and stops. He places his arm on the left side of me and then his other arm on the right side of me, caging me in, then slowly closes the space between us.

"I don't usually just sleep around, usually if I sleep with a girl, it's because I'm interested in things going further with her," Creedence says to me quietly, but seriously.

"That's good to know, I usually don't sleep around either. I usually only sleep with a man once I'm in a relationship with them, that's why I've been so unsure about whether or not I wanted to tonight, but my gut is telling me to just say fuck it and go for it," I tell him, looking down at my shoes while he looks down at me. I feel so small between his arms even when he's not physically touching me. But when he is touching me, it feels like electricity is shooting through my body. He makes me feel alive. "There's something about you that just keeps drawing me in, I don't know what it is, but it makes me not want to follow my rules that I have for myself and just go with the flow," I say, finally looking up at him, the butterflies in my stomach swirling faster.

He's staring down at me with hunger in his eyes, like he could devour me at any second and he wouldn't give a fuck about being in public, the look is intoxicating, and I love it.

"I'm giving you a warning, that I'm not into your typical normal sex. What we plan on doing I don't want you to repeat at all, do you understand?" he says in a firmer voice than he was talking in before, and it instantly makes my panties even more wet than they already were.

"What do you mean?" I ask a little nervously, but excitedly hoping he's talking about the type of stuff I've been wanting to try but haven't found a man willing to do it; they just look at me like I'm some crazy freak.

"How about I show you instead of tell you, because sometimes saying it sounds scarier than actually doing it," he says, leaning down and kissing me deeply. He moves his hands cupping my face and kisses me with need like no matter how much he kisses me he can't get enough. He pulls away looking into my eyes.

"God you're like a drug Sugar, maybe that's why you taste so sweet, sweets can be addicting, and you babe are so fucking addicting. I need more of everything I get from you. I haven't even had the rest of you yet that's the crazy thing. I know once I do, I'm going to be in big trouble." His tone is husky as he steps back and picks me up at the waist opening his car door, then sets me inside.

"I figure I'd save you the trouble of climbing up into my truck since your skirt is tight and short, don't want you teasing me anymore or we'll never get back to my house." He laughs a little.

"Well thank you, maybe I wanted to tease you more. I already teased you earlier with my ass, and my wet panties, you should feel how wet they are now." I give him a wicked grin giggling a little.

"Woman you're killing me, you're lucky we're in public or I'd rip those tights off of you, lift up that skirt and fuck that wet little cunt of yours." He leans in whispering to me and holy shit I didn't think I could get any wetter than I already am but I'm sure my panties are soaked all the way through, and my tights are wet. I can feel it between my thighs. The things this man does to me and the control he has over my body, and he doesn't even know it.

He walks around and gets into the driver side of the truck, shutting the door behind him. He puts his key in the ignition and starts the truck, before reaching over and placing his hand on my thigh, dangerously close to my throbbing pussy and he squeezes hard. I let out a soft whimper, so turned on I can't wait to get to his house.

5

CREEDENCE

We pull into my driveway, and I quickly shut off my truck, eager to get inside and get started. I'm horny and can't wait to feel her pussy on my cock for the first time. I jump out of my truck and walk over to the passenger side opening the door for her, as she's about to climb out I stop her and wrap my arm around her waist.

"Nope, I don't think so, Sugar. I'm carrying you." I throw her over my shoulder. Making her squeal.

"Excuse me, Mister." She lets out a cute laugh. "I can walk, just so you know." She starts pounding her small fists on my back like it'll make me put her down. And man is it sexy, to have this gorgeous girl thrown over my shoulder, ass by my face, close enough to bite if I really wanted to, but I'll just keep her guessing, making her wonder what my next move will be.

"No Sugar, I'll be carrying you." I smack her ass hard, hoping to leave a red mark. I'm ready to start leaving my marks on her. To show people who she belongs to. Because after tonight she won't belong to anyone else. She'll never be able to be with another man. I'll ruin her for anyone else. She'll be mine and only mine.

"Fuck, Creed." She lets out a quiet moan, and it is so fucking sexy the sound goes straight to my already hard cock making it even more painfully hard.

"Mmm, did you like that babe?" Fuck did her moan turn me on. And I need to know if I'm turning her on the same fucking way.

"Yes...yes I did." She's panting in between her words, her sexy cracked tone making my cock twitch. I feel like she's already about to come just from me spanking her. We walk through my front door and thankfully no one is home, or they'd get a full view of her almost bare ass, with whatever her barely-there thong and fishnet tights are covering.

As I start walking past the kitchen towards the hallway that my room is down, I spank her again.

"Ahh shit. Creedence, please." Fuck, she practically moans those words and it's probably the sexiest sound ever. Something about the way her voice sounds as she's moaning really gets me going. I could listen to the sound of her voice all day it's the prettiest sound I've ever heard especially when she moans and her voice cracks, fuck. Man, she is going to be a lot of fun to be with.

"Mmm you're going to be so fun to play with Sugar, already begging me to fuck that pretty pussy huh?" I smile at her because I can't wait to play with her. I can't wait to feel her pussy around my hard cock. I'm getting myself going even more with just these thoughts alone. At this rate I'm not going to last long at all if I don't calm my ass down.

"Damn, I guess I am." She laughs, and I'm sure if I could see her face she'd probably be blushing too. Because for some reason she blushes around me a lot and it's really fucking adorable.

We get into my room, and I walk over to the bed gently throwing her down. Her cheeks are still rosy from blushing, just like I thought she would be. I climb onto the bed next to her, leaning on my right elbow.

"Why are you embarrassed, Sugar?" I ask even though I already know the answer. I want to hear her say it. Her saying it will be such a fucking turn on.

"Cause I can't believe how desperate I sound, practically begging you to fuck me before you even touch me. I don't know what my problem is. But you drive my body crazy and make me react in ways I never thought I'd react to a man, and you've barely even done anything to me." She's turning her head away almost like she's ashamed or something.

"Listen Emerald, you need to stop being embarrassed, I already told you before I'm never going to judge you." I turn her head to look at me, then I smirk at her. "Besides, I'm going to have you begging me to do a lot to you. It really fucking turns me on, and I promise it'll turn you on too." I lean in to kiss her. I swipe my tongue letting her know I want her to open up for me and she doesn't hesitate, she opens her lips for me right away. Swiping her tongue against mine in the process before she sucks on my tongue making me groan, because if it feels that good with her just sucking on my tongue, fuck it's going to feel so good with her mouth around my cock.

"Fuck, if you suck my tongue like that, I'd love to know what it feels like with you sucking my cock like that," I whisper into her ear, making her shiver.

"I can't wait to suck your cock," she whispers back to me, giving me a devilish grin. And holy shit, if I wasn't rock fucking hard already, I would be now after she said that.

I lay back and pull her on top of me, then I scoot back to where my back rests against the headboard and she's straddling me.

"Fuck." I let out a growl. She feels so goddamn good, and this is just my cock being pressed up to her pussy. "Do you feel how hard my cock is for you, Sugar?" I ask as her pussy rests against me, closer than it was before. God. She. Feels. So. Warm.

I sit there staring at her. I'm so fucking horny. I'm not even sure how I want to go about doing this tonight, which is rare since I usually have ideas in mind. I need to remind her again though, just in case she forgot and that way she knows I was being serious about what I said.

"I gave you a warning and told you I was into dark shit." I pause, placing my fingers on my chin thinking about whether or not I can really trust her to not repeat anything that happens tonight to her friends. Especially Winter, I don't need her telling Carsten about the shit I'm into. He'd probably never let me live it down, or he'd tell the other two and then that's all I'd hear, and I don't feel like listening to a million questions.

"I know." She swallows hard, seeing her throat move up and down.

It turns me on thinking about my dick being in her mouth when she does that. But I'll have to be patient. Good things come to those who wait... and this woman right here is going to be the one who makes me come undone. She's going to be my weakness.

"Whatever I plan on doing to you tonight stays between you and I, do you understand?" I ask her again, placing my fingers on her chin, gently lifting her head to make sure she's looking up at me. Since I'm still taller than her when sitting down, I want to make sure she's paying attention to what I'm asking of her so eye contact is very important to me right now.

Her breathing gets heavier, her chest rising and falling, I think she's excited about what I have in store for her tonight. "Ye...yes Creedence. I understand." She practically moans out her answer.

I make her take her tights off because I'm not ready for her to be fully naked yet, I still want to tease her.

I pull her back over me where she's straddling me but kneeling; I don't want her fully sitting. I lift her skirt slowly by her thighs, pushing it up her waist. Then I bring my fingers close to her pussy.

"Understand that sometimes it will hurt, but I promise baby, you're going to love it. Do you understand?" I slowly move my fingers closer to her panties. I can't wait to feel how wet she is for me, how soft she is and my favorite part, how warm she is. The need to be inside her somehow is very strong and I don't think I'll be able to stop until I get to taste her and then once I taste that sweet pussy of hers, I'm going to fuck her until it takes all my cum from me. I'll spill my seed into her as she grips my cock, squeezing it, while pulsing around it grabbing it tighter into her already tight cunt milking every last drop of cum from my cock.

"Yes, I understand," she whimpers. Fucking shit, her delicious pussy is going to feel amazing wrapped around my cock, I can't fucking wait.

"Good girl, I bet your pussy is soaked for me, am I right?" I lean in to kiss her pouty lips, then I pull away to allow her to answer. Fuck, I can't get enough of her fucking lips I would love to kiss her lips all day, suck them into my mouth, feel them wrapped around my thick fucking cock. Mmm. I can't fucking wait.

"Yes, so wet." She's out of breath from how heavy she's breathing from how turned on she is.

"My sweet, sweet Sugar, such a good girl getting my pussy wet for me." Her chest rises and falls quickly. Her breasts, fuck they look so perfect through her shirt, I can't wait to see them, and put my fucking mouth all over them, hickies, bite marks. Mmm, she's going to be so much fun.

I touch my fingers to her panties, and they're soaked all the way through, shit I let out a wicked groan. I can't control myself; she drives me absolutely crazy.

"Fuck, I haven't even touched you yet and you're so wet for me, Sugar." I smile at her as I move her panties to the side. I can see how wet she is just from looking at her perfectly smooth pussy.

I swipe my fingers across her slit. "Goddamn babe." I practically growl as she lets out a moan. "Your pussy is so wet, I bet it tastes amazing, doesn't it?" I watch her, waiting for a reaction but there isn't one, I assumed she tasted herself before.

"I..." She bites her lower lip nervously. "I don't know, I've never done that." Is all she says as she shies away.

"You've never done what?" I ask because I want to hear her say it, I know it'll turn me on, and if I'm not turned on enough already, why not add to my torture and work myself up even more.

"Tasted myself," she whispers as her cheeks turn a light shade of pink, like she's embarrassed or ashamed.

"Now, now Sugar, don't be embarrassed, you have nothing to be ashamed of, but you know what I'm going to have you do?" The corner of my mouth tilts up as I smirk at her waiting for her response. She swallows nervously. Fuck, this is going to sound so amazing hearing this come out of her mouth.

"Taste...my...myself." She looks away, like she's shy all of a sudden. Which I get, I'm only putting her on the spot telling her to tell me if she's tasted her pussy or not. Damn, I can't wait to taste her wetness.

"Good girl, Sugar." I swipe my finger through her pussy again and she lets out a soft moan, her eyes slightly rolling as she does it. I watch as goosebumps spread across her body, shit, she is so perfect.

"Tell me if you taste good; open up for me." She slowly opens her mouth, slightly sticking her tongue out. I bring my fingers up and place them against her tongue. She catches me by surprise, closing her mouth around my fingers, swirling her tongue and sucking them into the back of her throat. I groan, even more turned on than I already was, my cock even more painfully hard now.

"That's a good girl," I whisper to her. "How'd you taste?" I smile again, she is going to be so much fun to play with. I can't wait to fuck this tight pussy and see what she wants to do for me, and how far she's willing to go.

"Umm..." She bites her bottom lip, still nervous, not sure why after she just teased the shit out of me with sucking on my fucking finger like she was sucking on my fucking cock, with those delicious lips of hers.

"Don't be shy now, beautiful, not after you did that. Tell me, how'd you taste?" I look down at her waiting for her response as I tower over her small body. Everything about her is perfect and I haven't even seen her naked yet, but I already know she's going to be the most perfect thing I've ever laid eyes on.

"I tasted...umm...sweet," she says, blushing again as she looks down. Like she can't believe she just did that and how could she be okay with tasting herself. I thought it was fucking hot as hell.

"Mmm, I knew you would." I stop, looking at her. Her beautiful cheeks that are red from blushing, and the beautiful shade of brown that her eyes are.

"God you're so fucking gorgeous." I practically whisper because I think I might be in love with her, and it just hit me like a ton of bricks. Or maybe it's the alcohol intensifying my feelings, at least that would make me feel a little less crazy than already being in love, but who am I kidding. I think I already know the truth.

"Thank you." She looks down as she says it. She gets so shy every time I compliment her. I'm hoping to eventually change that, she doesn't need to be shy around me. She's too gorgeous to shy away from me.

"Why are you looking away?" I'd like to get the truth out if she'll tell me.

"I just... I've never had a man compliment me as much as you have, and I'm not quite used to it. I almost don't know how to react when you do it. I don't mean to be rude and shy away, because I do appreciate them. Plus, I'm very self-conscious, it's hard to feel confident when you lack confidence." She finally looks into my eyes. I can stare into her eyes all fucking day; man, I think I've got it bad.

6
CREEDENCE

I PULL HER DOWN TO KISS HER, SLOWLY AT FIRST memorizing the way her mouth moves with mine. The way her tongue feels against mine. The way she moans into my mouth as I deepen the kiss. I grip her ass with both hands, hard. I want to leave bruises, I want to leave my mark every time I touch her, so when she looks at herself when she's naked she remembers she belongs to me. Not in an abusive way either but more of an obsessive I need to mark her way. Like she's mine, to make sure she remembers every time she feels how sore her body is from the rough sex or when she looks at my marks, I leave on her. Fuck, the thought alone makes my cock jump in excitement.

I push her pussy down onto my hard cock making her moan out, still swallowing her moans I refuse to stop kissing her. I can't get enough of her lips against mine. She slowly starts grinding against my cock through my jeans and I know she's going to leave a wet mark on me, that's how wet she is, and I don't even care.

I pull away and start unbuckling my jeans to pull them down a little, I don't want the roughness of them to irritate her through her panties and I wanna feel as close to her warm pussy as I possibly can. It's going to be a while before I'm fully inside her. I lift my ass and remove my belt from my pants wanting to use it on her so she can't move her hands.

"I'm going to tie your hands behind your back with my belt, okay?" I'm not sure if she's ever done anything like this before so for the first time, I want to make sure she's okay with everything I'm doing before I do it. "I don't want you to freak out since this is the first time I'm doing this to you, usually I just do it without asking but I don't want to scare you. Do you understand?" I ask to make sure she's still on the same page before we get too far, and she backs out.

"O...okay." She bites her bottom lip like she's nervous or not sure what else to say.

I take her hands and push them behind her, bending them at the elbows and take my belt, looping it tightly around her wrist, tight enough to leave a mark. I smile as she hisses in a breath.

"Does that hurt?" I give her my sexiest smirk, hoping she says yes so I don't have to redo it.

"Ye...yes." Is all she says as she arches her back trying to see if she can straighten her arms.

"Good, it's supposed to hurt. I want to leave my marks on you, Sugar. I need people to understand that you're mine and only mine. Do you understand?" I ask her to make sure again that we're on the same page. I don't want her to be too surprised for her first time. She nods as she understands what's about to happen.

I reach up and pull her halter top over her head letting it fall to the front, exposing her breasts.

"Fuck babe, your tits are perfect." I breathe out as I reach up and start rubbing them, and lightly pinching her pebbled nipples. I look at her heavy eyes, slowly closing as I rub her nipples with my finger-tips, pinching them a little a little harder this time. You can tell she's turned on by the look in her eyes, the heaviness, the look of fire dancing through her honey-brown eyes. They practically roll to the back of her head as I intensify my grip on her nipples. She arches her back a little, enjoying the mixture of pain and pleasure that her body is starting to feel. I grab one full breast with my left hand squeezing it, feeling my dick getting harder as I do. I feel like my dicks about to snap in half from how hard it is, and I know she can feel it because she looks at me with a slight side smirk as it happens and slowly grinds herself down into me a little.

"Tsk. Tsk. Emerald, I didn't tell you that you could move yet did I baby?" I smile, fuck she's going to be so much fun. My cock is so excited to be inside her warm wet pussy.

Her head falls back as she slowly starts grinding on me again. Completely ignoring what I had just said to her.

"Emerald." I groan, because fuck does it feel good and I'm not even inside her. I still have my boxers on and she's still wearing her panties and I'm reacting like she's completely naked rubbing her wetness all over my hard cock.

"Yes?" It comes out in a breathless tone. Her wicked grin telling me she knows exactly what she's doing and she's enjoying this.

"You're a bad, bad girl, aren't you?" I grab her hips, holding her still for a minute, afraid I might get off with her just rubbing against me.

"Why are you going to punish me?" She slowly slides her tongue across her bottom lip, making me wish it was brushing the tip of my cock instead of that plump lip of hers. Who knew you could be jealous of someone's body part, but I sure am jealous of her lips getting to feel that warm tongue against them.

"Oh Sugar, you're going to love everything I'll do to you and not just today. Always baby." It's true she's never going to be unsatisfied when she fucks me.

I don't know how much more I'm going to be able to take with her beautiful body on me like this. I might not be able to do what I have in mind.

To get my mind off things I slap her breast lightly and her head snaps down to look at me as she moans.

"Shit Creedence," she moans out. "Do that again." She practically begs, and I smile. I knew she was going to be fun to play with.

So I slap her breast a little harder this time and pinch her other nipple, then lift her body to smack her ass, hard. She lets out a tortured moan. The kind where it feels so good it's almost like torture, because you need the release.

I grip both of her ass cheeks, I'm not nice about it, because she winces when I do it. I lift her body up and slap both of her ass cheeks, then push her down and grind her onto my hard cock. She starts grinding herself onto me as I reach up and pinch her nipples again.

"God, Creedence," she moans. I love the way my name sounds on her lips. I slide my hands down her body and stop when I reach the top of her shirt, grabbing the fabric I rip it straight down the middle exposing the rest of her body to me.

"Shit, that was my favorite shirt." She's not angry though, she smiles at me with a look in her eyes like it excited her more. "God, that was so hot though," she groans, her eyes full of lust. She is just so beautiful.

"Sorry babe, I'll buy you another one," is all I say. The only thing you hear is her heavy breathing. Well, both of our breathing really because I'm getting even more worked up too. The sound of her breathing, mixed with all the different sounds of her moans, is an even bigger turn on.

I slowly push her off me where she's sitting on her knees and get to my knees as well. Then I pull my T-shirt off, throwing it on the floor and then I pull my jeans off all the way. Leaving me in just my wife-beater and boxers. You can see how hard I am from my erection straining against the fabric of my boxers. Emeralds eyes go wide as she looks down, I'm not exactly your average size and you can clearly see that from just my boxers alone. It's hard not to smirk a little at her reaction. Or the red color that's creeping up her cheeks as she blushes from me catching her reaction.

I push her body back onto the bed, smirking a little when she winces from the pain of her tied up arms. Trust me I'm not just some asshole, I just like to make sure the girls I fuck are sore, with marks left on them to remember me by. Everyone I've fucked has always enjoyed what I do. If they don't, we stop, I don't force anything on anyone. That's why I like to double check as we do things to make sure we're on the same page.

"Fuck, my arms Creed, they hurt." She wiggles her body to try and find a comfortable position.

"Good, they're supposed to," I look over at this beautiful masterpiece lying on my bed waiting for me to use her for my pleasure. The only thing that's left are her panties. I pull them ripping the fabric making her whimper as the torn fabric bites her skin.

"Shit, please Creedence," she moans out, I bring them up to my nose sniffing them, making her blush. Fuck. If she tastes as good as she smells I'm about to die and go to heaven just from eating her pussy alone.

"Fuck, Sugar. Your pussy looks so good, I can't wait to see how you taste." I push her thighs open.

"Look how wet you are for me, baby." I swipe my finger through her slit, a moan escaping past her lips.

"Please Creedence, I need you!" She cries out breathlessly. I think this is enough torture for the both of us, I guess I'll have to save the rest of it for next time.

I scoot her to the edge of the bed getting down onto the floor, kneeling down my face right in front of her pussy. Fuck I can't wait I know she's going to taste so good. I throw her legs over my shoulders, placing my hands on her thighs to hold her in place, I don't want her moving on me. Then I swipe my tongue across her pussy. Lingering on her clit before sliding my tongue back down and pushing it inside her. Fuck, this mouthwatering sweetness is something I'd love to eat daily, my favorite fucking meal of the day.

"Ohhh Goddd!" Her voice cracks as she moans turning me the fuck on. I'm rock fuckin hard, it's almost painful. I slide my tongue back down, sticking it inside her entrance again and I let out a groan myself. Fuck is her pussy amazing.

"Goddamn baby, you do taste sweet. Just like fucking sugar." And

I slide my tongue back up to her clit, swirling it around before wrapping my lips around the sensitive nub and sucking on it.

"Ahhh god, please Creedence, please," she pants, and I can tell she's already getting close.

I pull away and take my finger, swiping it up and down her pussy to get it wet before sticking it inside her, she cries out as I pump it in and out of her slowly, torturing her with pleasure.

"Don't you dare come yet, Sugar," I tell her because I won't let her come until I'm ready for her to come.

"Wh...what? Please Creedence I'm so close," she whimpers, breathing heavier.

"Ah. Ah. Ah Sugar. Not yet," I say before I start licking her clit again, in just the right spot that I know will get her where I want her, even if I won't let her come just yet.

Her body starts trembling, her legs shaking on my shoulders, and I know she's there, she's about to come. Shit does my cock hurt, I can't wait to thrust inside her fucking pussy.

"Creed, please... I'm about–" And then I stop and pull my finger out of her. "Fuck, please, I was about to come," she says, pouting a little.

"I know you were, but not yet Sugar. Don't worry I promise it'll be worth it." I smile at her and then stick my finger into my mouth sucking off the rest of her wetness. Mmm I could taste her every day and never get sick of her.

"God, you taste so fucking good, I could lick your pussy all day baby," I tell her as I help her sit up.

She moves her arms trying to relieve some of the pain, making a pained face in the process.

"My arms are going numb," she says quietly. Like she's upset about it, and that's the last thing I want is for her to be upset when I'm just trying to please her.

"Are you okay? Do you want me to stop?" I double check, making sure I'm not going too far with her.

"No, not yet. I'll let you know if I do." She gives me a wicked grin, showing me she's ready for more, making my cock twitch in excitement with what I'm about to do next.

"Good, now get on your knees." She's about to be surprised. I smile to myself as I watch her get down onto her knees, I hold my hands out just in case to help steady her since she can't use her arms. I can't wait to feel my cock in her mouth.

I step back and remove my boxers, and her eyes go wide. I smile again. This always brings a smile to my face when I watch someone's reaction to my piercings.

7

EMERALD

I SIT THERE AND STARE AT HIS THICK, LONG COCK, TERRIFIED by the size to begin with, but then I see piercings lining the whole top side of his shaft. I've never seen anything like it, and I've definitely never had sex with someone with piercings on their cock before. Holy shit, my pussy throbs, making me tighten my thighs together, to relieve the ache since he stopped before my orgasm. He slowly pulls his wife beater over his head, smirking as my eyes go wide. His tattoos cover his chest, and his arms down to over his hands and over his fingers. Fuck they're so sexy the way they form to his muscular body perfectly like they were made just for him, molded perfectly to every single dip and crease. My eyes travel down to that drool worthy 'V' that makes his body look delicious in so many ways. God he is so sexy

"It's called a Jacob's ladder." He gives that smirk of his that instantly makes my pussy wet. I should say more wet than it already was because my thighs are officially wet. "This is why I didn't want you to come yet because it's going to feel amazing when you do baby." His smirk grows into a full-blown smile as I nod my head. I have no idea what to even say to him, so I just nod my head and stay quiet. I'm too scared to ask questions, I'm too busy trying to figure out how I'm going to fit this thing inside me with his piercings and all. Will it fit inside me?

"Now I want you to be my good girl and open that pretty mouth of yours then stick your tongue out." I decide to say fuck it, push my thoughts aside and have fun. I am so turned on right now I don't want to wait any longer.

I stick my tongue out slowly, swirling it around the head of his cock. Mmm he already tastes so good that the precum dripping from his cock makes me moan from how good it is. I suck the tip in making sure to get it all as I look up at him from my knees staring into his eyes. His hooded gaze as he stares into my eyes with hunger, like he wants to tear me apart and eat me alive that's how badly he craves me.

He throws his head back practically growling. "Fuckkk." His Adam's apple bobs up and down as he swallows hard. It is so hot. He hisses in a breath and looks back down into my eyes again. "Goddamn baby, your mouth." He breathes in quickly like he's struggling to remember how. "I knew it was going to feel amazing." He hasn't even had my full mouth around him yet and I'm just getting started on how good I'm about to make him feel. He wants to tease me though? I can play that game too.

I remove the head of his cock from my mouth and tilt my head to the side, sticking my tongue back out. I slowly lick the underside of his shaft, swirling it as I lick him, loving the way he tastes. He throws his head back again as I swirl my tongue to the top of his shaft, licking my way back down to his head before going back to the underside taking my time over his piercings. I never knew something like a piercing could turn me on so much. I make my way back to the tip and wrap my lips around him and suck him back in, swirling my tongue around his thick length as I slowly work him into my mouth, pushing him to the back of my throat and I swallow.

"Fucking shit, do that again please Emerald." He hisses out as he moans, then he finally looks down at me, I smile up at him the best I can with his cock in my throat and he growls down at me.

"You look so sexy right now." He breathes out slowly, between clenched teeth. "Fuck you sure know how to use that mouth of yours baby." His smile is to die for, I'd suck his dick all day long if it meant I'd get to see that look every time. Because I'm the reason he's hard. I'm the one pleasing him right now. That look is made just for me.

He grips his hands into the back of my hair and starts slowly moving my head. I nod my head giving him the okay and I start sucking back down to the tip. He takes his hands pushing my head forward pushing his cock back into my throat, and I gag on his cock because I wasn't ready. Tears start forming in my eyes because I'm not getting the chance to fully breath as he does it.

"Mmm, I love listening to you choke on my cock, Sugar." He turns me on, making my thighs automatically tighten together.

"Look at those pretty tears baby." He takes his right hand and wipes the tears away with his thumb. Then he takes his thumb to his mouth and licks my tears off his finger.

"Mmm, even your fucking tears taste sweet," he says shoving my head back down to where his cocks back in my throat. I gag again, drool now spilling from my mouth, dripping down my chin.

"Mmm," I moan out onto his cock. I'm so turned on; I can't wait for him to fuck me. If the piercings feel this good in my mouth, I can't wait to feel what they feel like in my pussy.

"You like that baby?" he asks me and to tease him more, instead of nodding my head I moan out.

"Mmhmm," I drag out the sound, the vibrations making him moan more.

"Fuck Sugar, I'm getting close," he groans, goddamn he sounds so sexy. I nod my head to let him know I heard him.

"Look how good you're doing for me Sugar. You're taking my cock so well in that warm mouth of yours." Fuck, if he keeps talking to me like that, I'm going to come from his words alone.

I can't wait to taste him, I tighten my lips and suction my mouth, sucking and swirling my tongue as he picks up the pace of how quickly he's moving my head. Tears stream down from my eyes, spit flies from my mouth and I can barely breathe, but I am soaking fucking wet. I'm so turned on I feel like I can come just from this alone. My pussy throbs with need, and I'm so glad he made me wait to come because this orgasm is about to be fucking amazing.

"Here it comes. Get ready baby." He grunts out, making me moan. "I want your eyes on me as you swallow my cum, Sugar." I nod my head again as the warmth squirts into my throat. Holy shit, he sure has a way with his words, turning me the fuck on with everything he's saying. He pushes his cock all the way into my mouth, as he spills down my throat. I swallow it all, moaning as I do because I am so turned on from him getting off in my mouth. I'm even more turned on by how good he tastes. He lets go of my head and I slowly slide my mouth back to the tip, sucking as I go making sure to get every last drop from his thick, hard cock. I look up at his heavy eyes, his muscular chest rising and falling quickly, he's still panting, trying to catch his breath. Spit still dripping from my mouth, I'm sure along with his cum. I suck on his cock one last time to swallow the rest before pulling it out of my mouth, making sure to make a popping sound as I do it.

He looks down at me, a sexy side smirk on his face as he rubs the spit on my chin with his thumb, his other hand wiping the tears from my left cheek.

"Fuck, look at those tears, Emerald. You look so beautiful with wet eyes, your tear-streaked cheeks, and my cum dripping down your mouth all over your chin."

"You taste so good, Creedence," I moan breathlessly, I'm still out of breath from him taking control while sucking him off. He gives me the sexiest smile after I tell him that.

"God that was fucking sexy." He cocks his head to the side a little, looking into my eyes as his hand strokes my cheek.

8

EMERALD

I CAN FEEL MY WETNESS DRIPPING DOWN MY THIGHS FROM how turned on I am. I've never been this wet before, I've never even been this turned on before and holy shit am I turned on.

"Stand up Sugar, I want to feel how wet you are for me." I don't think I could tell Creedence no even if I wanted to. The way he talks and demands things is so attractive. I slowly move my legs, they're sore from being on my knees. He reaches out and places his hands on my arms, helping me up as I slowly stretch my shaky legs. I turn my head to wipe my chin on my shoulder, but he stops me before I can.

"Give me one second baby, let me take care of you." He walks away into the bathroom for a second and comes back out with a washcloth in his hand. Walking up to me he gently wipes the rest of the spit and I'm assuming cum off my mouth and chin.

"Thank you." I smile at him because it was sweet of him to do it for me when I could have done it myself.

"Anything for you, Emerald." He gently kisses my forehead before walking away again to put the washcloth back into the bathroom.

He keeps walking towards me until he's right in front of me, stopping until his chest touches my nipples. The warmth sends goosebumps across my skin, making my nipples harden more.

"I need to feel you inside me," I whisper to him. Then he leans down, his mouth crashing against mine.

"You sound so sexy saying that, Emerald." His lips find mine again before swiping his tongue against my lips and I instantly open them for him. He swirls his tongue against mine, sucking it into his mouth making me moan, before he bites my lip.

"Please Creedence, I need you to fuck me." My body is wound up so tight, if I don't get some release now I feel like I might explode.

"Is that what you want, Sugar?" His hoarse voice causes the butterflies in my stomach to stir a little. It almost sounds like a growl. "You want my cock in that tight pussy of yours?" He's out of breath as he speaks, you can tell he's turning himself on even more in the process of saying it.

"Yes..." I breathe out. "Please Creedence, please fuck me. I... I–" I don't get anything else out before he pushes me back onto the bed, landing on my sore, tired arms.

He slowly crawls over me pinning me in with his arms on each side of my head. His cock sitting at the entrance of my pussy, I thrust my hips up, the tip sliding in a little. Holy shit he's huge, god he's going to feel so fucking good.

"Fuck Sugar," he breathes out again. "Your pussy is going to feel so amazing." And without warning he thrusts himself inside of me, making me wince from the pain of him not allowing me the time to get used to his thickness or piercings. It makes me feel so good and so full.

"Shit," I moan out. It hurt, but fuck did it feel so god damn good. "Please don't stop... I need to come," I groan out as he thrusts back in deep, filling me all the way and I cry out from the pleasure. It feels too good to keep my moans in.

His piercings sliding against me inside, sending chills every time he thrusts in and out of me. He wasn't lying when he said it would feel amazing, because I've never had sex feel this good before. This is the first time we've had sex, and I think he's just ruined sex with anyone else.

"Tell me who your pussy belongs to Emerald." He gives a slight smirk, it's almost like he read my mind and knows what I just thought about, because that's exactly what just happened. My pussy just became his and he knows this., I will no longer be able to have sex with anyone else now. His cock is too good. It's like it was made just for me.

I moan out because it turns me on hearing him say that. "You Creedence, my pussy is yours. Oh god, it's yours," I moan. "Please, make me come." My body is wound up and my muscles are tight and sore. My pussy won't stop throbbing in the best way, I need this release, and I can't even touch myself to fix that.

He pulls out of me and I instantly pout. "Don't stop, please I was so close. I need to come Creedence," I groan out.

"Don't worry baby, I'm not done with you yet," he whispers into my ear and shit it is so sexy the way his voice sounds deep and husky. Another thing to add to the list of things Creedence does that turns me on. He sits up and flips me over onto my stomach, bringing my ass up into the air, and thrusts right back into me. I turn my head to the side so I can breathe and watch him bring his hand up and smack it down hard onto my right ass cheek. Sending a sharp burning pain through me that makes me moan. I never thought I'd like being spanked but holy shit.

"Ohh goddd," I moan because it feels even better this way with his piercings, and him smacking my ass intensified the pleasure. He rubs his hand against the sensitive skin and slaps again, making it sting more. "Shit, don't stop Creedence."

"Fuck, I couldn't even if I had to. Your pussy is amazing, Sugar," he practically growls, and he smacks down again onto the same spot, the stinging even more intense than it was before, but it's getting me closer.

He's pounding into me. Gripping my hips hard now, hard enough to where I know I'll have bruises, and I don't even care. Let him leave bruises. He lets go of my hips and grabs me by the back of my hair pulling me back towards him, my back to his sweaty chest, he pulls my head to the side and bites down onto my neck hard.

"Oh god Creedence please." Is all I can keep saying because it's like my body just keeps getting wound up tighter and tighter. Like a bomb waiting to explode.

He sucks on my neck hard. I'm sure it's hard enough to leave a hickey and I don't even care, let him claim me, let him leave his marks on me, I'm his canvas to use however he pleases.

"You like when I suck and bite your neck baby?" He licks my neck where he was just biting before sucking on the same spot again. God his tongue, the way it moves across my body feels magical.

"Fuck yes," I moan out, my body starts shaking, I can feel the intensity of my orgasm building in my core. Whatever is about to explode inside me is going to kill me, I just know it. He brings his hand forward, reaching between my legs. Putting his fingers against my clit massaging it and fuck does it feel so good. Sooo fucking good. I could cry from how good the pleasure feels. That's how intense everything is right now.

"I'm getting close Sugar, are you ready to cum with me?" he asks, panting into my ear, he groans out a deep groan. I don't think there's anything this man does that isn't a turn on because fuck was that sexy.

"Yes, yes I'm about to please...don't... Shittt Creed." And then my body explodes, my orgasm shooting through me, my pussy clamping down around his large cock, the piercings intensifying everything. I scream out my moans, I can't even control it, the pleasure is so intense the moans come out into screams naturally. Yep, I'll never be able to sleep with anyone else ever again.

"Fuck, that was amazing." I barely get the words out because I'm so out of breath.

"Goddamn that was." He collapses onto the bed next to me, we lay there panting, staring at each other. "Shit, let me untie your arms babe." He gets up undoing the belt as my arms fall slowly to my sides, I lay there letting the feeling come back to them.

"Your pussy and your mouth are like fucking drugs I swear," he laughs, shaking his head. "You're going to become a very addictive problem for me, Sugar. I don't know what you did to me while we were fucking with your pussy, or while you were sucking my cock, but damn." He lets out a long sigh and I giggle a little. He makes me feel so good, not even because of the sex. He makes me feel alive, happy, and other feelings I'm not sure how to put into words yet.

"I mean, really you did all the work; I couldn't do much with my arms tied." I let out a breath before I continue talking, because I'm still a little out of breath from the sex, and right when I go to open my mouth to talk, he cuts me off.

"Oh no, don't you give me all the credit. That mouth of yours. Mmm fuck. And your pussy, fucking sucked me in like it wasn't going to let go, shit you're so fucking tight it's amazing." He starts laughing and then he looks over at me and slowly moves me onto my side, pulling me into him. He wraps his warm, strong arms around my waist, and I lay my head down next to his.

"I wanna go get some fresh air after that, it's stuffy in here and I'm fucking sweating. But I don't want to move yet." He's still trying to catch his breath. I watch as his tattoo's rise and fall across his muscular chest and my thoughts go back to how I still want to lick across his muscles, maybe leave a few hickies on him, leave my marks too.

"I gotta stop at my house and grab something to change into, unless you need me to leave." And he cuts me off again with a kiss, his lips gently brushing against mine a couple times before he pulls away.

"Shut up." My jaw falls open and I have a confused look on my face, while I try not to laugh because I'm so confused as to why he just told me to shut up. "You're not going home; I'd love for you to stay the night if you can," he says, pulling me in closer to him, and this is why he told me to shut up. I guess this passes as a good enough reason to cut me off for the second time, especially if sleeping over involves his cock inside me again.

"I was gonna say, excuse me, why did you tell me to shut up, but now it makes sense." I laugh now, because I can't hold it in anymore. "I'll still need to run home really quickly to grab some clothes though." I roll over sitting up, wrapping my arms around myself since I'm cold now that his warm body isn't next to me. I could get used to being around his warmth all the time, especially since I'm always cold.

"Who said you'll be wearing clothes?" He laughs, wiggling his eyebrows. All he has to do is flash that smile and I can't say no, it is humanly impossible to say no to a smile that sexy.

"This is true, but I'll need you to keep me warm or I'll freeze all night." He gets up and walks over to his closet grabbing a hoodie for me to wear and throws it onto the bed next to me.

"Ooo yes! I hope this wasn't a favorite because you're not getting it back now." I stick my tongue out at him playfully. He doesn't say anything. Just walks towards me slowly. His sexy, muscular body, slightly shiny still from sweat.

He grabs my hands, pulling me up, lifting my chin with his fingers to make me look up at him. His lips come crashing down onto mine, I open my mouth up letting his tongue swipe mine. He continues to kiss me as he reaches down, lifting me up below my ass cheeks, bringing me up to his waist as I wrap my legs around him. I can feel his cock growing hard the longer we kiss and I'm already ready for round two. He walks me over to his bedroom door and pushes my body up against it, positioning his cock at my soaking wet entrance and roughly thrusts inside me.

"Fuckkk baby, your pussy was made for me," he groans out as he's pumping in and out of me.

"Mhmm, your cock feels so good Creed," I moan wrapping my arms tighter around his neck to help hold myself up better.

He pounds my body hard into the door, adjusting his grip on my waist with one arm, as he reaches up and places his free hand onto my throat, choking me, not completely stopping my airflow but making it hard to breathe.

"Ohhh g...goddd," I struggle to moan out, his thrusts and my body hitting the door making it harder to get even breaths in, which makes it harder to moan.

"You like that, Sugar?" he asks, giving me a deliciously sexy smile. Everything about this man is perfect.

I nod my head the best I can, as he tightens his grip a little on my throat, I'm starting to feel dizzy and lightheaded from the lack of air but all it's doing is intensifying the pleasure and I don't want him to stop. The way his pierced cock feels rubbing against the inside of my pussy is amazing, it sends chills through my body as goosebumps break out across my now sweaty skin.

"Fffuckkk," I struggle to breath out; it feels too good. My body doesn't know how to react to what is happening to it.

"Let go baby, just relax and feel the pleasure intensify, don't worry I won't let anything happen to you," he moans into my ear as he rests his head on my shoulder for a second, before he starts, moving a little faster again. I relax my body against the door as he holds me up, my arms still wrapped around his neck, I'll probably have scrapes and bruises from the way my body slams into the door each time he thrusts into me.

My body's starting to shake as I feel the tension building in my pussy, my orgasm getting ready to soar through me. I don't know if my body can handle another orgasm after how intense the last one was. I feel so lightheaded and right now as I try to gasp for one last breath, my vision goes blurry, and I think I might pass out. But it feels too good to make him stop. He thrusts into me harder, my back now scraping the door even more.

Everything feels like a high, every nerve feels alive. My body wound up tight from how intense the pleasure is.

"Come with me Sugar, let me feel your pussy swallow my cock as I come baby." And just like that my body comes to life. I gasp for one last breath, my head feeling heavy, and then he lets go of my neck, and my body feels like it bursts apart as my orgasm takes over, my whole-body trembling as I cry out from the pleasure. His cock pulsing inside me as my pussy grips it pulling it in as he thrusts in deeper, I've never had an orgasm feel so intense before, I think it actually beats how intense my first one was.

"Holy. Fucking. Shit." I cough, my throat dry from struggling to breathe. My body goes limp, and I feel like I could fall asleep as he carries me over to his bed. He lays me down onto his black comforter, covering me with a warm fuzzy blanket before I fall asleep.

9

CREEDENCE

After she falls asleep, I walk away to go run a bath for her. I know her whole body is going to be sore and tired, especially after the last orgasm she just had. Breath play really takes a lot out of you, but I could tell she really enjoyed it. I just want to make sure I take care of her body correctly afterwards, I might like to cause pain, a good pain. But I do my best afterwards to make sure I can comfort and help them with whatever they need. Especially Emerald, she's different.

I go into my cabinet and grab some bath salts and soaps to make it bubbly, you know stuff girls are into that I keep on hand just in case. I just bought this one yesterday for Emerald. The scent is warm vanilla sugar, what she smells like and what she tastes like, so I can smell it on her as we sleep.

When the bath is ready, I walk into the room and slowly uncover her naked body. I pick her up and carry her into the bathroom and step into the tub. I slowly sit down and position her between my legs to where her back and head rest against my chest. She slowly starts to wake up as her body adjusts to the hot water. I made it hot enough to soothe her sore muscles but not too hot because I'm not trying to burn her.

"Creedence?" She looks around for me still groggy from putting her body through so much.

"It's okay Emerald, I'm right here with you. I told you I'd wash you after, so I figured I'd get you into a nice hot bath to warm you up and help your sore body," I tell her leaning to the side so she can see me as I look down at her.

She slowly turns her head up to look at me, her neck probably sore from my hand. I hope I didn't leave too big of a bruise. I want people to know she belongs to someone, not to think she's abused.

"Sss...sorry for falling asleep." She shivers, giving me the cutest half sleepy smile.

"It's okay Sugar, your body needs it after everything. It's normal to be sleepy after breath play," I tell her because it does take a lot out of your body. Everything we did takes a lot out of your body, I'm sure she'll still feel out of it tomorrow as well.

"Breath play?" She looks confused.

"Yes, when I put my hand around your throat, blocking your air, that's considered breath play," I answer her because I want her to be aware of what I was doing. I wasn't trying to hurt her; I just like to have a darker kind of fun.

"Just so you know, when I do that to you it's not to harm you." She cuts me off before I finish, smiling at me.

"I know, I enjoyed it. I wouldn't be mad if you do it again." She leans in kissing me. God I could never get tired of her kissing me, she's like a drug, no matter how much I get of her it's never enough, she's the high that I always want to keep chasing.

She pulls away and rests her head against my chest moving her hands through the warm water, then she sits up slowly looking down. "Wait, what did you put my hair up with?" she asks, confused.

"Well, I figured you wouldn't want to get it wet. Yesterday I went to the store and bought some warm vanilla sugar body wash and bath salts for you, since you know you smell like vanilla and taste like sugar." I stop, winking at her. "And I was walking away and saw they had a hot pink scrunchy it reminded me of you, so I grabbed it for you." I can't help but smile at her, she brings out my happiness, a happiness I haven't felt in such a long time.

"Wow." She stops for a second, it looks like she has tears in her eyes, or maybe it's from the water. It's hard to tell since she's looking down. "I can't believe you bought all this stuff, or even thought of me like that." She sniffles getting the bubbles off her hands to wipe her eyes.

"Wait, wait." I stop cupping her face with one hand to look at me. "What's wrong, Sugar? Why are you crying...did I hurt you?" I start panicking, hoping that whatever I did to her the pain isn't kicking in and causing her discomfort, because I don't want to hurt her at all, that's the last thing I want.

"No, no it's nothing you did. It's just stupid is all." She bites her quivering bottom lip. "I'm okay though." I don't want to pry, but I'm gonna ask anyway. She'll tell me if she doesn't want to talk about anything.

"What's wrong? Please tell me." I still want to make sure she's not hiding it if I am the reason she's upset. I don't want to make this beautiful woman in front of me cry or cause her any discomfort. Fuck I'm such an asshole.

"It's just that, my last boyfriend. The guy I dated for about a year. I broke up with him about a year ago and I've been single since. He treated me like shit he never cared to remember anything I like or my favorite color, anything. He just cared about using me." She sniffles again, wiping away her falling tears. She's breaking my fucking heart.

"Well Sugar, I can promise you right now, I will always listen when you talk, and I will never treat you like shit. I couldn't imagine being an asshole like that and treating you wrong. I...I..." And for some reason I want to tell her I love her, but I stop, not wanting to scare her away. I know it's too soon even if it's how I feel.

"I'm sorry he put you through that, but I promise to always treat you right, Emerald. Always." I lean down and bring my lips to hers, leaving slow, gentle kisses on her trembling lips, showing her I also know how to be gentle and caring.

"Thank you. For everything, for the bath stuff and the scrunchie, I love it all and thank you for showing me that not all men are assholes." She gives me a sad smile. Which crushes my heart even more to think that any man could even think about treating her like shit. But in a way I'm glad they did because she wouldn't be here right now if they didn't. And I'm a selfish asshole, she's mine. I don't want to share her with anyone, ever.

"Turn around and straddle me, Sugar," I tell her, readjusting my constant hard cock. I think it's broken because it's always hard around her. My mind doesn't know how to stay away from perverted thoughts, but it also doesn't help that she has the body of my fucking dreams, literally everything about her is everything I love and look for in a woman. Even if I'm not thinking them, my cock still knows those thoughts don't just go away. She turns around straddling me and my cock instantly moves towards her entrance, and she lets out a quiet moan. Fuck, she's so sexy.

"Sorry, I was just thinking myself how I'm broken, I can't calm my constant hard dick down around you." She laughs, making me laugh. I'm glad she can find some kind of humor in this situation, instead of thinking I'm just a typical man who only thinks with his cock.

"It's okay, I'm not complaining, just finding it hard not to put it inside me right now." She gives me a seductive look, her lips curling up to one side as she starts to smile a little. She looks right into my eyes with a confidence I don't think I've ever seen in a woman before and it's the biggest fucking turn on ever.

"What if I ask you to ride my cock, would you?" I practically whisper, afraid I might be asking for too much. But my cock doesn't care, as soon as I say the words my cock jumps in excitement. I'm sure she felt it move against her pussy, because I felt it touch her more and fuck, I just want to be back inside her.

"Go ahead, ask me," she says, readjusting her body to where the tip is slightly inside her entrance ready to slide in her still wet pussy. Shit, it takes everything in me not to just shove myself inside her and feel her warmth again. I let out a low growl so fucking turned on right now from how sexy she looks with that seductive look in her eyes, and the way her voice sounds quiet and breathless like it's torture just sitting there.

"Will you ride my cock, Sugar?" I ask her with a smirk on my face. That's all she needed before she pushes her body down, hard on my cock making me groan. Her pussy is so tight it feels like it's trying to push me out as she sinks down. "Fuck, baby." I breathe out slowly trying to calm myself down, so I don't get off too soon.

"Mhmm, fuck you feel so good," she moans as she throws her head back. I put my hand behind her head, gripping her hair at the nape. Pulling her in for a kiss, needing to taste her lips while I'm inside her. I swipe my tongue quickly against her mouth, silently begging her to open. She immediately opens her lips, so I take the opportunity to deepen the kiss, as my tongue dances with hers. Her body slowly grinds into mine, torturing me with every movement. Having her tight pussy around my cock right now is my form of heaven. She feels so good, too good. She rides my cock like she was made to ride me and only me. Fast and going in as deep as her pussy allows her too. I can't get enough of how amazing she feels. I pull away from the kiss as a groan escapes my lips at the feel of her pussy tightly wrapped around me and practically swallowing my cock like it's getting lost inside her every time she sinks down. God, she feels fucking amazing, I don't think I'll ever be able to fuck another girl after her.

"Your body was fucking made for me, Emerald. You're being such a good girl taking my cock the way you are." I thrust my cock up into her, hard. Her cries making it so hard not to explode. Fuck. It's the sexiest sound I think I've ever heard. To listen to this woman who is straddling my lap, losing herself in pleasure, the pleasure that I'm responsible for that's making her feel so good she's able to let go and let the pleasure take over is everything in this moment. I don't think I've ever seen a woman ride me like this before, the heavy look of lust in her eyes as her fingers dig into my shoulders. Her eyes roll back every time she sinks back down onto me. Her head falls back every time she grinds herself into me and I thrust myself up. She keeps her eyes on me except in those moments. She's not afraid to show me how much she's enjoying the pleasure my cock is giving her. I lean in, pressing my lips to hers, it's sloppy but I don't care I need her mouth against mine. She slides her tongue against my lips, and I meet her with mine. Our tongues are going to war with each other as I taste every inch of her as I rub my hands along her body memorizing her curves with them.

I pull away from the kiss. "Fuck Sugar, I'm going to come soon." I want to spank her so bad, but I can't because of being in the water, so I grip her ass tightly, hard, helping her body move up and down while she rotates her hips. It'll probably leave another mark. I can't wait to see how beautiful she looks with all these marks I've left on her. I lean down sucking her nipple into my mouth making her moan before moving up, sucking on her breast to leave another hickey. I love my girl beautifully painted in my art of pleasurable pain and love.

10
CREEDENCE

I'm not abusive at all. I love to be rough and leave marks and cause pain of pleasure. I like to make sure they know the difference, but I don't think she is questioning any of it, she's enjoying it all too much.

"Come with me Creedence, please come in my pussy," she groans out, and that's all it takes for me to lose control completely. I lean in to kiss her, wanting to feel her lips against mine as I come. Her pussy tightens around me, and I feel her trying to pull away from my lips. Deciding to let go of her so I can watch the look of pleasure on her face as she comes undone, her heavy eyes fluttering, her breathing is heavy and uneven as her orgasm shoots through her.

"Oh goddd baby your pussy is going to be the death of me." My voice hoarse. I'm barely even able to get the sentence out, because the pleasure takes over my body, this orgasm more intense than the last two, as I cum inside her again.

"I can't have sex anymore tonight. I think you're on the verge of breaking my pussy." She laughs sliding into the tub in front of me, her legs still around my waist.

"I'll give you a break for the rest of the night, I can't wait to see all the marks on your body," I say to her hoping she won't freak out, making sure she is aware that there will be marks left on her. My love marks, I've never actually called them that before. I never had a name for them until now, until Emerald made me feel things I wasn't expecting to feel.

"I have a feeling seeing them will just turn me on again." She shakes her head. "I don't know what it is about you but damn I've never had sex with someone this soon before or this much in one day." She covers her face in embarrassment, so I reach up pulling her hands down and lift her chin to look at me.

"Look at me, Sugar," I tell her, making sure her full attention is on me. "I'm glad you trusted me enough to do all of this tonight, but I'm really happy you enjoyed it all," I tell her, pulling her in for another kiss. Everything about this girl is addicting. I always want to be addicted to her; I never want to become sober from her as my addiction if it means losing her.

After we finish up in the tub we get out and dry off. I give her clothes to change into, so she doesn't have to go to her house. Then we head outside to get some fresh air, we walk out of the house through the garage so we can get to the back patio. But before we can get out back Emerald spots my motorcycle.

"Oh shit, is this your motorcycle?" Emerald asks right away; I mean it's the first thing you see when you walk out the garage door so it's not really a surprise that she asks. It just sucks, I hate the feelings that come rushing in along with the flashbacks that suck me in. Sometimes it feels paralyzing like no matter how much I try to escape or get away from these memories I can't, I couldn't run away from them even if I tried, I'm stuck with them for the rest of my life.

"Yeah, she's mine." My brother and I used to call them our girls so whenever I talk about my motorcycle, I call her a she, another horrible memory that haunts me, the guilt of being alive and still getting to call my Chopper a she.

"Can we go for a ride? I've never been on one before and I've always wanted to go on one." She asks with a big smile on her face looking down at it. The look of excitement on her face is fucking adorable and I hate the fact and hate myself for the fact that I'm about to crush her excitement.

"Well not tonight since I've been drinking." She cuts me off, the excitement still on her face.

"Shit, I forgot we were drinking but another day I meant." She finally looks up at me, a concerned look on her face. "Are you okay? Did I do something wrong?" She moves closer to me as she talks, making me feel nervous.

"No, you didn't do anything wrong, I just, I don't ride anymore is all." A lump forms in my throat, I look away to blink back the tears that threaten to form. Something that still happens every time I think about him.

FOUR YEARS AGO

What the fuck just happened? I think to myself as I pull over onto the side of the highway. Where the fuck did Xander just go, did I really just see that? My mind is freaking out, my body shaking, I walk to the side of the road dry heaving, and then I start vomiting up everything we just ate. I can't control it. I need to go see where my brother is and what just happened, but I can't stop the puke from coming up. I hear cars slamming on their brakes, sirens in the distance.

Someone is behind me talking but I can't hear what they're saying. My head is in a fog, I feel like I'm in some kind of tunnel, everything sounds muffled and far away. I feel like I might pass out, but I need to get to my brother. The tears start coming as I finally stop myself from puking. I slowly turn around and there's a puddle of blood surrounding a contorted body.

"Xander? Xander?" I scream to nobody but myself as I run to his body, he's lying there, blood coming from his head and other parts of his body, I just can't see from where. I'm afraid to touch him because I know what I'm going to find once I do and I'm not ready to see it.

"Xander please." Spit and snot flying as I scream and cry next to him.

"Sir...sir, we're going to need you to step away from the body. Sir, my name's Officer Jacobs, I need you to please move so the paramedics can move the body.

I've been in my own world. I didn't even notice the paramedics around him. I didn't notice the other people standing around freaking out or crying as I screamed and cried for my brother.

"Creedence?" Emerald says in a panic. "Creed?" she says a little louder this time. "Are you okay?" She shakes me back from being lost in the past. The memory I always find myself getting stuck in, the memory that still haunts me every, fucking day.

Lost in a nightmare, that I will forever keep living. It should've been me that day, but I was the asshole who switched lanes and let my little brother, my best friend, die.

"Hey, hey it's okay. Where'd you go Creed? I'm right here, it's okay." She grabs me, hugging me tightly while looking up at me. She reaches for the back of my neck, pulling me down by my nape to look at her.

That's when I realized I've been crying. I reach up with my hand and wipe away my tears. Turning my head from her, embarrassed. I usually don't cry in front of people over this, I usually leave the room or blink the tears away. So, I'm surprised that my mind or my body, something trusts her to be comfortable around her, at least enough to just let go.

"Sorry." My voice, gravelly. I clear my throat a couple times to get my voice back fully. "Sorry," is all I can manage to get out. It's a hard topic for me to talk and to think about.

"Creed, why are you apologizing? I should be the one saying sorry, I obviously triggered something, and I feel like an asshole now." She shakes her head as she says it.

"Don't, it's not your fault it's mine. Let's go umm." I pause, taking in a deep breath trying to calm my nerves. Damn I feel like a bitch, the only woman I've ever allowed myself to cry in front of is my mother. "Let's go sit on the front porch instead," I say and clear my throat again to get rid of the hoarse sound.

"Okay." She says quietly letting go of me, looking down. I needed to get away from that garage and my motorcycle, so I changed my mind about going on the back patio. You can tell she feels bad though, so before we walk outside, I lean down and give her a soft quick kiss, to hopefully let her know I'm not mad or it's not her fault.

I grab her hand and lead her out the garage door to the front porch and sit on the stairs, it's too nice of a night to sit on the porch swing. She sits down next to me and it's quiet, too quiet. So, I figured I should probably explain where I went mentally and why I was crying.

"I'm apologizing in advance in case I cry again." I place my hands together and look over at her.

"Never apologize for feeling, for expressing yourself. Never apologize for crying around me. I'd never judge someone for showing their emotions." She scoots a little closer to me as she talks.

"My brother Xander and I were in a motorcycle accident. Well, he was. I just missed it," I start off, clearing my already scratchy throat from the tears that are threatening to start filling up my eyes.

She doesn't say anything, she sits there with a worried look on her face, listening as I start from the beginning, how we pulled over from the rain, ate some food while waiting for the storm to pass. How I could just tell he felt nervous about riding after the rain. How we were stupid and didn't wear helmets that day.

"We were riding on the highway; we didn't have a choice as that was the only way we had to get home. We probably should've waited longer before getting back on the road, but it was getting late, and I didn't want him out in the dark. He had just gotten his license a few months before that, so he wasn't used to riding at night, or after the rain." I stop, looking in the other direction, trying to calm my nerves and blink back the tears that just keep falling without me allowing them too.

I continue on with more details, the condition of the roads. How we probably shouldn't have been driving as fast as we were.

"I sped up to get ahead of him so I could switch lanes because our exit was coming up. I just assumed he'd switch lanes right after me. But instead, he sped up, his bike hit a puddle causing his bike to spin out, he hit another car causing him to fly off his bike. Which caused his head to hit the concrete first." I pause again, wiping away my tears, this is the first time I've ever really spoken about this to anyone, besides Carsten, Chase, Axton, or my parents since it's happened. But it feels kind of good getting it out after all this time.

"It all happened so fast I didn't want to believe it, I thought maybe I was seeing things or imagining it. And after all this time it's still my fault that he's dead," I choke out. "It should've been me, if I wouldn't have switched lanes before him, I would've been the one not him." I shake my head as I stop talking just letting my tears continue to fall.

"Fuck, Creed." Emerald sniffles, wiping her own tears. "I'm so sorry you had to go through that." She says putting her hand on my lap over one of my hands.

She stops, removing her hand from mine. I look up at her confused. She moves my arms and steps up, then sits down on my lap, straddling me, it's not meant to be sexual. It's comforting.

"Don't say that. I don't know your brother, but I know he wouldn't want you blaming yourself and I think deep down you know that." Her voice sounds sad. "You can't live your life blaming yourself babe or you won't enjoy it." She finally looks at me and I see she has tears in her eyes that are ready to spill over.

"I know I just can't be happy knowing it should've been me, and I try to tell myself that he wouldn't want me feeling this way, but I just... I just feel guilty. Like if I go on living a happy life it's not fair to him." I pause, taking a deep breath.

"Creed, please don't blame yourself. I promise you it's not your fault and I'm not going to stop telling you that until I can convince you that it's true."

She looks into my eyes, as she cups my face, wiping my tears with her thumbs in the process and leans in giving me a soft, slow kiss. I wrap my arms around her middle, hugging her tight while I deepen the kiss more, kissing her passionately. The fact that she took the time to show me how much she cares with just those sweet words and simple gestures means more to me than she'll ever know.

I pull away from the kiss. "Thank you, Emerald." My voice is husky from the way she's sitting, how it's starting to affect me. It's hard not to get worked up when this beautiful woman straddles your lap. Now I'm emotional and horny, what a terrible combination to feel at once. But I push the sexual desires away and focus on her showing me that she cares. Even if she's not saying it with words anymore, she's showing it. She lays her head down on my shoulder, wrapping her arms around my neck and we just sit there in silence. There's something about the comfort of her presence that makes me feel at home, at peace. She helped take a weight off my shoulders tonight that I hadn't realized I'd been carrying. Just by listening and allowing me to feel something. I turn my head and open my eyes, her green and black hair in my face and I smile. She still has the pink scrunchy in her hair that I put in, I thought she'd take it out after the bath. I've only ever seen her with her hair down, even in passing before work, her hair's always down.

"I like that you're still wearing the scrunchie." My voice comes out a mix of a rasp from crying and a husky tone from being turned on, again. My voice is not wanting to cooperate since crying.

"It's my new favorite." She lifts her head, turning to look at me as she smiles. I lean forward and gently kiss her cheek, her skin as soft as velvet, I could touch her all day, kiss her all day. Yep, I think it's safe to say, I'm obsessed, and I might be in love with this woman right here.

I look over as Emerald starts to yawn, making me yawn myself, realizing how tired I am. It's been a long day.

"You wanna go in and eat something then go to bed?" I'd love nothing more than to sleep with her next to me.

"I'd love nothing more than that." She kisses my neck, then bites it lightly, instantly making my dick grow hard.

"Down boy." She giggles as she slowly grinds herself into me. "God, I can't resist you, Creedence," she groans out. "I can't have sex anymore, but I need to feel you again tonight," she tells me between breaths.

"You have no idea how badly I want to be inside you right now, Sugar. I'm just going to have to get used to the fact that my dick is constantly going to be hard around you." I laugh, shaking my head at her.

I lift her up under her ass and she tightly wraps her legs around my waist.

"Mmm," I growl out from the heat of her pussy pressing against my hard cock. "I might not be able to control myself. I know you said I'll break you if we have sex again, but Emerald...my cock is throbbing for you," I whisper into her ear in a hoarse voice.

"Oh god that was fucking sexy." She practically moans out, her body moving like she just shivered.

"Maybe I can go one more round. But food first, please. I'm starving." She laughs as I carry her through the garage back into the house into the kitchen.

We settle on making bacon grilled cheese together, it's one of her favorite meals, even though it's simple. She said it's something that makes her happy, and it sounds fucking delicious to me, anything with bacon makes me happy.

We head to my room and eat in my bed while watching a movie together. Then we both end up falling asleep instead of another round of sex, which is fine with me because having her snuggled in my arms next to me with her head on my chest is the best feeling in the world. I could get used to this. Falling asleep next to her every night would be the best.

11
EMERALD

The next morning, I wake up with a warm body snuggled up behind me, along with Creedence's arm wrapped around my middle, holding my hand and I smile. I don't remember the last time I actually enjoyed waking up next to someone. I start stretching a little before I feel soft kisses against my shoulder blade. I ended up taking my shirt off in the middle of the night due to being too hot and I usually sleep best naked, plus I figured he wouldn't mind waking up with me lying next to him naked.

"Mmm, already ready for me?" His voice is sleepy as he talks, the raspiness to it is so sexy. He tightens his hold around my waist pulling me closer to him as he pushes his erection into me.

"Keep doing that and it'll take everything in me to not get on top and ride you." I giggle hoping to get him going more. Because now I'm horny, how could I not be waking up to a sexy ass man like him.

"Well, if you keep talking like that it'll take everything in me to not pin you down and fuck that delicious wet pussy of yours," he whispers gruffly in my ear.

"Mmm, please Mister. Don't punish me." I practically moan, I'm so turned on over something so simple. This man is a dangerous, dangerous man. The things I'd let him do to me just to be fucked by him is crazy.

"I'll fuck that tight ass of yours as a punishment." The way his voice sounds as he talks sends chills through my body. I never thought I'd be into anal, but him just talking about it makes me ready for it, and willing to give it a try. Although I'm sure with his piercings it would hurt. But all the pain he was inflicting earlier only felt good. It barely hurt before the pain turned into tortured pleasure.

I turn over facing him and look up into his eyes. "You sexy, sexy man. The things I'd do for you." My voice comes out in a whisper because I don't think I can find my voice right now.

"I'd do anything for you, Emerald," he says, but not in a sexual way this time. So, I question it.

"Anything?" I say, curious as to what he means.

"I'd do anything for you, anything to protect you, anything to keep you safe no matter what," he says in a hoarse voice and it's so sexy.

So, I challenge him with what he's saying. "What would you do if I were in danger, how would you protect me?" I am curious as to how far he'd go for me.

"Sugar, I'd set the world on fire and not let a single flame touch you, I'd cover you with my body if it meant I could keep you safe and protect you from anything that could ever harm you, anything that could ever take you from me." His husky voice is filled with emotion.

Holy shit, did I just fall in love? I mean I knew I was falling before but fuck, the butterflies, the chills and goosebumps that spread across my skin and I actually shivered after he said that.

"Wow." I pause thinking of what to say but he doesn't give me the chance. He cuts me off with a slow, sensual kiss. I open for him, allowing his tongue to swirl against mine, he leans over me, the way his strong body covers mine, making me feel so small yet safe under his big muscular frame.

He gets on top of me, holding himself up by his knees and fore-arms then he leans in letting his erection settle between my legs. I let my head fall back when he begins kissing my neck, moaning out from the intensity of the pleasure from something so simple. His delicate kisses as his tongue dances and sucks across my skin, he bites into the sensitive flesh as I cry out, so turned on I feel like I can come just from this little bit of contact.

He shifts his weight to his right forearm and yanks my head back with his left hand to give himself better access, biting and sucking harder, probably leaving his delicious marks that make my pussy wet just looking at them. I noticed some of them last night as I was drying off from the bath we took and they instantly made me wet and start throbbing, picturing him pleasing me like that. He makes his way down to my breasts sucking my hard nipple into his mouth and licking it as he sucks. Then biting it hard, making me cry out while sending chills up my spine, he moves from my nipple sucking on my lower breast as he makes his way down my chest to my stomach licking and sucking along the way.

By the time he reaches my pussy I'm so turned on I'll probably come instantly. My pussy throbbing as he pushes my legs apart.

"Mmm so wet for me, Sugar," he growls out before he swipes his tongue across my slit.

"Fuck. Oh God." His tongue focuses on my clit, hitting the spot that makes my toes curl. That feels like torture and pleasure mixed into one because it feels so good that you never want it to end but it tortures you because you're so close to orgasm but not close enough. I grip his hair, needing something to hold onto as he eats up my pussy like it's his last meal. He licks my pussy at a torturously slow pace. Driving me absolutely wild. His tongue swirling and sucking my clit, his finger working my G-spot inside me as he works a second finger into me, fingering me slowly, torturing me by not giving me my release. Right when I didn't think the pleasure couldn't get any more intense, he turns his fingers and slowly sticks his thumb into my ass, not all the way but enough to make the pleasure and pain soar through me. I've never had anything in there before and I'm not upset by it, in fact the pleasure is so intense I need more.

"Please Creedence, more," I moan. He moves his mouth away for a second. "No, don't stop," I pout and he gives me the sexiest grin.

His lips glisten from my wetness and it only turns me on more knowing the grin on his face is for me, and the wetness on his lips is from me.

"Don't worry, Sugar I'm not done licking this pussy of yours. You want more, you said?" He's making sure we're on the same page.

"Yes please, I need more." He starts circling his thumb around inside me a little more, pushing it further in my ass as he does. The pain and pleasure mixing together. Fuck, I never thought something like this would feel so good. He thrusts his thumb roughly, all the way in making me cry out, the sting from the pain shooting through me a little because his finger wasn't wet. But it feels so good, too good.

"Oh god it's too much I need to come, please Creed," I practically shout because my body is about to explode and then he comes back down sucking my clit hard and pumping his fingers in and out of me faster, and harder. Before reaching up with his free hand and pinching my nipple, pulling and twisting it and that's all I need, my pussy clamps down on his fingers as the most intense orgasm shoots through me. My body exploding with waves of pleasure.

He comes up to his knees licking his two fingers that were just inside me, growling in the sexiest way. "Fuck Sugar, I could lick your sweetness all day baby. I think your pussy is becoming my new favorite flavor." His low, husky tone mixed with what he just said is so fucking sexy. Making my already throbbing pussy pulse and throb some more.

He lowers his body down positioning his hard cock at my wet entrance before thrusting in fully, without warning. God, it hurts as he stretches me, but it feels so fucking good.

"Ohhh goddd," I moan, panting from the pleasure and still trying to catch my breath from my first orgasm. Still riding the high from the intensity of it, I'm so sensitive, his piercings intensifying it all. I feel like I could cum again already but I try to hold out so I can orgasm with him.

"God damn, Sugar," he groans, it's the sexiest sound ever. He takes my legs, pinning them to where my knees are bent to my shoulders, pushing my pussy and ass in the air overstretching my sore muscles. He looks down at me with heavy hooded eyes and a wicked grin on his face. His eyes fluttering with each thrust. He looks me in the eyes one last time thrusting in before looking down and watching his cock slowly slide in and out of me. Grunting with hunger in his eyes.

Being able to watch his large cock sliding in and out of me and come out even more wet each time is such a turn on. He reaches down, his smile growing as his hand starts rubbing and gently massaging my ass cheek. Then smacks my already sore ass twice in a row, hard, before rubbing it to soothe the burn from it. He then moves to my ass massaging it with a finger. He drops his head down, spitting right into his hand then rubs it on my ass lubing my butt for whatever he has planned for me.

"God baby girl, your ass is perfect. I'd give anything to be able to shove my cock into it right. Fucking. Now," he says between thrusts as he rubs one of his fingers on my tight entrance.

"Creedence," I whimper as he starts pushing one of his fingers in my ass before shoving it in roughly making me cry out from the pain and the pleasure. He quickly pumps his finger in and out of my ass, he's done so much to my body that it's on a pleasure overload and I love it. Everything feels good, my whole body is sore from being stretched in all the best ways. I don't think any of the sex I've had has ever come close to how amazing sex with Creedence has been.

"Fuck Creed I'm so close but I want you to come with me babe." I'm out of breath from everything happening to my body right now.

"Don't you worry, Sugar." Then he comes down onto my body, his chest on the back of my thighs slightly smushing me but not enough to hurt. He takes his left hand and wraps it around my throat and my eyes roll to the back of my head from how much that one movement turns me on. The intensity from his large, pierced cock thrusting into me, his finger pumping in and out of my ass and his hand constricting my breathing. I feel like I'm high, it's such an amazing feeling, the pleasure so intense I feel like I could cry from how good it all feels. He tightens his grips on my neck, and I can barely get air in or out now but I don't care. I trust him. He spits again and I feel it dripping down on me as he slowly pulls his finger out and rubs his spit around. He spits again.

"Sorry baby. I'm just making sure you're ready." He rubs two fingers against my tight entrance now and I can't help but tighten my body up afraid of what two will feel like.

"Relax Emerald, I pinky promise it's going to hurt, but the pleasure in the end will outweigh the pain. You'll love it." His voice comes out rough and deep. It's so fucking sexy. And for some reason him spitting on me really turns me on. To think I'm turned on by a man using his spit as lube on my body. And that fucking pinky promise, god my heart.

"I'm trying babe, I'm just nervous it's going to hurt bad." I'm honest with him because I don't want to ever hide anything from him. That's not how I like things to be with anyone so I'm always up front and honest.

"Shhh, it's okay, Sugar." He starts gently massaging me there with his fingers and it feels too good to not relax a little. "Good girl, open up for me, Sugar. Show my fingers what it's going to feel like when this tight little hole is being filled with my thick cock." He slowly starts thrusting two fingers into me as more spit drips down onto me.

"Fuck Creed, I need." He thrusts into me a little more, making me hiss out in pain. "Shit."

"It's okay baby just relax, open up for me and let me in," he groans as I relax a little more trying not to tighten my ass around his fingers.

"My sweet Sugar, you're doing such a good job baby. Relax just a little more for me." It comes out in a deep rasp. I never thought I'd be this turned on by a voice before, but I could listen to him say dirty things to me and probably get off from that alone.

"Fuck you're going to feel amazing when you finally let me fuck you here." He practically growls through clenched teeth. He starts pumping in and out of my pussy a little faster before he finally

shoves his two fingers fully into my ass, sending me over the edge from the pleasure and pain. My pussy clamps down around his cock the same time he lets go of my throat intensifying my orgasm.

"Fuck babe, I'm coming," he says holding himself up with both hands as he thrusts into me, spilling himself inside me.

12

EMERALD

I STRETCH MY SORE LEGS OUT AS HE COLLAPSES ONTO MY body, my eyes heavy from the intensity of the orgasms. I still feel like I'm on a high riding a wave of pleasure. We both lay there breathing heavily, his head on my chest as my hands come up and start rubbing his sweaty back. The wetness from the sweat turning me on, knowing everything he just did to get that sweaty. But I'm too tired to act on it. This man is going to break me, he's constantly turning me on and all I want to do is fuck him whenever I'm around him.

"Shit, I could get used to this," Creedence says, rolling off me and laying his head onto the pillow next to me.

"Get used to what?" I hope he's thinking what I was thinking earlier.

"Waking up next to you every day. Amazing sex every morning with you." He brushes loose hair out of my face with his hand.

"Going to sleep with you every night, sex before bed as well." I roll over, moving closer to him. Then I lean in to kiss him, soft, slow kisses placing my hand on his face in the process. "Sometimes you scare me." I pull away whispering.

The look of panic forms in his eyes. I think he's worried about some of the stuff he's done to me, thinking he's hurt me or like I said, that he's scared me.

"What do you mean?" His voice is slightly rushed and panicked. "I'm not trying to hurt or scare you ever and if I have you need to let me know so I know what to avoid the next time, Emerald." He looks at me with worry in his eyes.

"No, no sorry it's nothing to do with sex. I just can't believe how quickly things are moving and it scares me, but I love it." I smile. "I feel like I've known you forever." I look away hoping I don't scare him, but he lifts his hand gently turning my face with my chin.

"Please don't look away from me. I could get lost in your eyes, Sugar. I could stare at you all day and never get tired of the view. I love looking at how beautiful you are. You're my favorite thing to look at before bed and you'll be my favorite thing to open my eyes to in the morning." He leans in and kisses my forehead. Before pulling away and looking into my eyes, again.

"You've never felt like a stranger to me. When I first met you everything about you was so familiar, like I've known you for a lifetime, you've felt like everything I've been searching for, everything I've always needed and that right there scares me," he says in a hoarse whisper. "Because I've never felt this way about anyone before." Then his lips crash down against mine, his tongue inviting itself into my mouth as I open for him. I pull away looking at him, I never thought love at first sight or falling in love this quickly was something that was possible but since meeting him I definitely feel like it's possible. I feel crazy for feeling this way this soon, but it seems like he might be on the same page as me and that makes me feel a little less crazy.

"Holy shit, I'm glad you said all of that, because I feel the same way." I kiss him, then pull away. "I thought I was a psycho feeling like this." I kiss him again and pull away. "Like I was going crazy or something." Tears fill my eyes. What the fuck is wrong with me? Why am I about to cry?

"Emerald, it's okay baby," he says but I cut him off.

"That's why I said you scare me, because I was afraid how I was feeling was going to make me sound like I was a stalker or something." It comes out quiet because I'm embarrassed by what I'm saying.

"Emerald," he says but I cut him off again.

"Now I'm crying, and I have no idea why I'm crying." He probably thinks I'm crazy now for crying.

"Emerald…" he says a little louder this time, trying to get my attention.

"God, what is wrong with me?" He cuts me off again, and I'm about to say something until I hear what he says.

"Emerald, I think I'm in love with you." His tone is serious along with the look on his face. He looks into my eyes, but it doesn't register as he says it.

"Why did that make me so emotional, I can't believe I'm about to scare you away by saying this." I pause and it finally hits me what he said.

"Wait, what did you say to me?" I look at him confused, raising one eyebrow.

"If you'd shut up long enough." He laughs. "And stop rambling long enough to let me talk." He shakes his head laughing still. "I said I think I'm in love with you, Emerald. Sure, I've loved people before, but I've never felt this way for anyone before and that scares me too." He lets out the breath he's been holding, a look of relief and nervousness flashes across his face.

"No, I don't have to think about it because I know what this is. I was just afraid of saying it too soon. But now I don't want to keep it in, especially if you're feeling the same way." He gives me his sexy smirk, my favorite smirk that makes me feel weak in the knees.

"What did you just say?" I'm shocked, I must be hearing things, there's no way he just said what I think he just did.

"I said I think I'm in love with you, actually no I don't think. I know I'm in love with you, Emerald."

"Fuck, thank god that's what you said." The tears fall faster now. I can't believe I'm crying over this but now I can't stop them from falling. Fuck I'm such a baby.

"I love you, you handsome, handsome man. Fuck." I laugh. "I'm glad I'm not the only crazy one for loving someone this soon, because babe I think we're both crazy right?" I'm laughing and crying; I feel like such a crazy person, but he isn't even paying attention to it. He's smiling and laughing right along with me. Maybe we're both crazy and we bring it out of each other.

"I love you baby, so fucking much it's crazy. I feel crazy too, so I guess we can feel crazy together." He leans in and presses his lips against mine. The kiss is slow, passionate. His tongue swirls along mine in a slow torturous dance.

"I love you, Creedence. God this is crazy right? We're crazy but I don't care, I don't want anyone else, and I don't want to be crazy with anyone else but you." I kiss him, pulling away smiling.

"Good because I don't want to be crazy with anyone else either baby. Throw me all your crazy baby girl, nothing will scare me away. I'll still love you, show me your worst baby, go ahead, don't be shy. I'll still fucking love you, Sugar. Give me all the crazy you've got and guess what? You're still going to make my cock painfully rock fucking hard, and I'm still going to fucking love you, because you're my kind of crazy." He pauses for a minute then looks away before looking back at me with a different look in his eyes.

"I'll always be there to catch all your crazy. It won't scare me. I fucking love crazy, you my crazy, fucking gorgeous, Emerald you're my crazy girl no one else can have you." He leans in and presses his warm lips to mine, he slips his tongue between my lips the same time I open my mouth, his tongue explores my mouth, it invades me, like he's tasting me, and a moan slips out, the kiss so intense I can't control the pleasure it brings to my body. It's like he knows how to please me in every way my body didn't know could find pleasure without even trying. It's like he was made with the answer key to all my buttons that lead to pleasure that I'm not even aware of. This is why he's perfect for me, he knows me better than I know myself, yet we're still sorta strangers, getting to know each other.

We lay there together in his bed, my head on his chest, I keep thinking about his brother and their accident, well his brother's accident. I can't imagine how Creedence feels witnessing something like that. It makes my heart ache for him.

"Can I ask you something?" I rub my fingers up and down his chest, nervous about how he'll respond when I ask him.

"Of course, beautiful, you can ask me anything." He rubs his hand up and down my back after he responds. His warm hand spreading chills down my cold arms.

"I don't want to upset you when I ask this, so please if you don't want to talk about it I completely understand." I feel his body tense up a little at what I say to him like he knows what I'm about to talk about which I'm sure he does with how I went about it.

"When is the last time you rode your motorcycle?" I slowly ask the question, shutting my eyes tightly, unsure of how he's going to react.

He clears his throat. "A week after he passed everyone we knew who had a motorcycle rode it at his funeral, sort of like in his memory kind of thing. I knew he would have loved to see all the motorcycles and his friends riding together, and I haven't been on it since. I can't bring myself to do it." He lets out a breath like he was holding it this whole time.

"Wow, that's so sweet. I'm sure that would have been something amazing to see. I don't know your brother but I'm sure he would have loved that." I pause again afraid to ask my next question. "Will you ever ride again?" I ask quietly wondering if he even heard what I said.

He waits a few seconds before he slowly starts responding. "I... I just... I'm honestly afraid to. I feel like how is it fair that he died because of a motorcycle, something he had loved since we were kids, something he couldn't wait until he was old enough to get. How is it fair if I go on enjoying something that killed my little brother, I don't think I'd ever be able to find joy in it ever again." He sighs, a sad look on his face.

My next question really makes me nervous, but I figured as he's answering them, I'm just going to ask. "Do you think he'd still want you to ride and not stop because of him? Like he'd want you to find joy in it and ride for him?" My body tenses and I shut my eyes tight again waiting for him to be mad.

"I think about that all the time and the guilt I feel from it eats at me, but I'm also afraid what if I ride and get into an accident. I couldn't imagine doing that to my parents." Shit I didn't even think about his parents in the situation. I feel like an ass. Then I think about his friends who were mutual friends of him and his brothers and how they'd have to go through that heartache all over again. First losing Xander, and then something happening to Creedence. Then the thought of me losing him if something were to ever happen if he rides again. The thought makes me sick.

"I think maybe one day you should try it again. I'm not trying to push you or anything, but I feel like if it's something you think will make him happy too you should maybe try it again one day, I can... I can help you and be there for you when you do it if you want." I hope I don't sound as nervous as I feel, so I bite my bottom lip again to distract myself from waiting while tightening my eyes shut. Not sure why I keep waiting for anger, when he's not like my ex.

"Maybe one day. I would like to in the future, just not sure when. I guess I'll know when I'm ready though, I just don't want to push it ya know?" The sad look on his face breaks my heart. Makes me want to take his pain away, to see such a wonderful person experience such a loss, hurts me in ways I've never experienced before.

"I hope you don't think I was pushing you; I was..." He cuts me off before I can finish what I was saying, and I hope I didn't push too far.

"Hey beautiful, don't you worry. I promise I don't feel like you're pushing me to do anything. I was just saying I don't want to push myself into it is all. It's something that runs through my mind all the time and sometimes I think to myself just fucking do it and stop being a baby about it but I'm afraid if I do push myself then what if

I'm not ready and I do get into an accident." He pauses for a second. "I miss riding I really do, but fuck I miss my brother so much and I wake up every day thinking it'll get a little easier, then I see my motorcycle in the garage when I'm leaving, and it hits me like a ton of fucking bricks and it just fucking sucks." He sniffles and I look up at him to see tears falling freely down the side of his cheek from the way he's lying and it breaks my fucking heart to see him like this.

I reach up and wipe his tears for him with my one hand and he smirks a little as I do it as he looks down at me.

"I'm sorry," I tell him, because if I wouldn't have brought this up then he wouldn't be crying right now.

"Don't be sorry. For some reason whenever I talk about it to you it helps me feel a little better. Like I'm not carrying so much weight on me, my chest doesn't feel so heavy." He squeezes me a little, hugging me.

"I'm always here for you, Creedence. I'm happy I was able to help you." I squeeze him back looking up at him.

"I love you, Sugar." He fully turns onto his side so he can lean down and kiss me. I stretch my body up to meet him and kiss him back before I pull away.

"I love you, you handsome, handsome man." And then I lean back in to continue kissing him, opening my mouth for him as he takes his time to deepen the kiss.

13

CREEDENCE

After Emerald leaves, I head to the bathroom to shower and get ready for my day. I need to run to Crazy's Tattoos to get some sketches done for the upcoming week and I'd rather do them there with less distractions. Whenever I try to do them at home, I just say fuck it and never get them done. Before I head to the car, I check the mailbox and smile because my packages are here. This will be so much fun using these on Emerald.

I head to my truck tossing the package into the passenger seat and head on into Crazy's. As I walk in, Kane is standing behind the counter.

"Hey man, how's it going?" he says to me when he looks up and see's that it's just me walking through the door.

"Sup Kane, it's going, just another lovely fucking morning." I laugh. "How about you?" I haven't seen him in a few days. The last few times I worked it was either by myself or with Carsten.

"I feel that. It's going, just another busy week coming up for me, I have a lot of my regulars coming in to either finish up a piece or start something new." He crosses his arms leaning against the counter next to the register.

"Damn that's awesome, I'm about to draw up some sketches here myself for some of my regulars comin' in this week too, I think

Carsten has a busy schedule as well. I know he was drawing shit up at home yesterday while Winter was working," I tell him, it's always good when we all have busy weeks. I love my job and love giving people new pieces of art. I wonder if Emerald will ever let me tattoo her. I'll have to ask.

"Awesome, if we get any walk-ins and we're not busy you can either take it if it won't cut into your time with any of your regulars or schedule it for a future time with yourself that way we stay busy. Or schedule it with one of us if you're going to be busy." He says as he starts walking towards the back room.

"Alright cool, I appreciate you doin' that man." I follow behind him to walk into the room I always work in, my office. I don't share it with anyone else, actually none of us share, our office is ours to set up how we please with our supplies.

I set up everything for my sketches and hear my phone ding. Looking down I smile, seeing it's a text from Emerald.

Emerald
I miss you, you handsome, handsome man

I love how she does that, the way she says it twice, for some reason it makes it more unique to me.

Creed
I miss you too Sugar. Wanna get dinner later?

Emerald
what do you have in mind?

Creed
well, I already know that I want your pussy for dessert

Emerald
mmm promise?

Creed
Pinky promise

Emerald
Can't wait ;)

Emerald
now what about actual food lol

> **Creed**
> I have something in mind, just be ready by 7 is
> that okay?

Emerald
perfect how should I dress

> **Creed**
> wear something sexy for me Sugar, please?

Emerald
got it you sexy, sexy man you

> **Creed**
> we can go get drinks after, I got a surprise for you
> so the alcohol may help when we get home ;)

Emerald
ooo I love surprises

> **Creed**
> good, this one will be different than normal, I'll
> text you in a bit someone just walked in the shop.
> Love you Emerald.

Emerald
Love you babe

I walk out the front to see someone standing there that I definitely wasn't expecting or wanting to interact with at all, especially now that I'm with Emerald. "Fucking shit," I mumble to myself, but it must've been loud enough to hear.

"Well hello to you too, Creedence." She rolls her eyes.

"What do you want Daisy? I thought I told you we were done seeing each other." I cross my arms already annoyed by her presence and she just got here too. I don't know why I ever gave her the time of day, she's annoying and needy.

"I wanted to see you; I miss you," she pouts, an ugly ass pout at that, it's not even cute at all. Usually when a girl pouts it's a weakness of mine but when she does it, I want to smack it off her face. I obviously would never touch a girl like that, but you get what I'm saying.

"Well, that sucks, I just said we aren't seeing each other anymore. I told you that. I also have a girlfriend, I'm dating Emerald. So, you can leave now," I say, turning around to walk back to my office, but she stops me.

"Wh...what? You're dating someone?" Her whiney voice gets even whinier than it is naturally, and I roll my eyes before I turn around to look at the ugly pout that's still on her face. I don't know what I saw in her, I know it's not all about looks but now that I'm with Emerald I see that she is just an ugly person because of her personality, she's very selfish and always has been. But I know when we fucked it was just for that and that only. We weren't a couple ever, I only called her to fuck her and that was it.

"No wait, remember I have an appointment today with you?" She panics, trying to stop me before I walk away.

"What?" I turn around to go look at the book on the desk that we keep our appointments in so that way when we have walk-ins, we can schedule things easier. "Fuck," I whisper shout, already wanting her appointment to be over.

"Gee thanks, sound a little more excited why don't ya." She rolls her eyes this time, while blowing out an annoyed breath.

"Sorry I just forgot I had an appointment today, I'm not mad at you," I say trying to change my attitude. I don't want to be annoyed for the next hour tattooing her left side, plus I don't want to come off as rude and make her feel uncomfortable while tattooing her, I gotta be professional still, just in case.

"It's fine, I can wait out here until you're ready." Her mood changing back to her annoying whiny voice.

"Nahh, you can follow me back. I already have your stencil drawn up, I can put it on you and we can let it dry while I set the rest of the stuff up for it," I tell her as I walk back towards my office, looking back to make sure she's following me.

"Cool thanks." She follows me down the hallways and makes a left into my office with me.

This is the last thing I wanted to do today; I can't believe I forgot about the fact that I scheduled this over a month ago. I was that booked up that I had to schedule over a month out. Which is good that I'm busy but fuck I don't want to deal with her bullshit today. Or ever really. I wish I would have just listened to Carsten or thought about the bullshit he went through with Brynn before I got involved with Daisy. Hopefully she's just not as psycho as Brynn is who faked a pregnancy with my best friend, more like a brother to me, to try and trap him into staying with her and loving her.

An hour and a half later I'm finally done with her side tattoo, she had me tattoo flowers connected with vines going down her side. Covering her whole left side.

"I'll meet you up front for you to pay, I just have to throw all this stuff away real quick," I tell her as I dispose of the needles in the hazard bin and throw the used paper towels and stuff away.

I walk up front to see her standing by the window waiting with a smirk on her face. I don't even want to question it. So, I charge her for the tattoo and of course she pays for it with *daddy's money*, like everything else she gets to buy, daddy pays for. After she's done, I walk out from behind the counter at the same time the door opens, making the door ding and Daisy rushes into my arms hugging me, too tight wrapping her arms around my neck and kisses me right on the lips. I push her away as fast as she kisses me, curious as to why she fucking kissed me, or even touched me.

"What the fuck Daisy?" I say the same time Emerald says. Shit this isn't going to be good. What the fuck.

"What the fuck is going on?" Tears form in her eyes as I look at a smiling Daisy and a crying Emerald.

"See you later babe," she says, winking at me. The amount of anger that builds up in me, she's lucky she's not a guy because I'd love to fucking punch her right about now.

"No, you fucking won't. What the fuck was that about?" I yell at her as she walks out the door the same time Emerald sets the bag and coffees on the counter and runs out.

"No Emerald, stop," I shout after her.

"I'll be right back Kane," I yell down the hall as I rush out the front door down the sidewalk to catch up to Emerald.

"Emerald... Emerald please stop." She's opening her car door and now it all makes sense. She parked in front of the coffee shop across the street and walked over. Daisy probably saw her and that's why she was smiling the way she was, because she knew she was coming here next. What a fucking psycho bitch, I can't believe she would even do this.

"Fuck." She speeds off in her car before I can get to her and I run back inside to get my keys and phone so I can go after her, I am not letting her leave here thinking I just cheated on her. Or that I was planning on cheating or have been cheating because I'm not that kind of guy, if I was going to cheat, I wouldn't be in a relationship to begin with, I'd just sleep around and stay single. I run through the front door of Crazy's and practically run into Kane.

"Fuck dude, sorry I gotta go, I can explain later." I rush out running back into my office to grab my truck keys and my phone, rushing out the front door not even hearing his answer. I run to my truck, unlock it and get in. I feel like a dick for leaving without explaining more to him about what happened, but I can't stay any longer, the further Emerald gets from me before I can get to her the more fucked I am.

I start the ignition and speed off, checking for cops in the town center where the speed limit is ten mph less than the main roads, but I don't care. I need to get to Emerald to clear things up. I can't believe Daisy did that, or how she even saw Emerald, but it must've been perfect timing when she walked up to the window. It all makes sense now as to why she was smiling that way she was when I walked out of my office, that fucking bitch. What is it with her and her friends wanting to ruin other people's relationships?

I finally pull into my driveway eight minutes later, my heart racing like crazy. I'm scared she won't believe me when I tell her what Daisy did. Now I sort of know how Carsten felt when he went through everything with Winter. I can't lose her. I won't fucking lose her; she means too much to me already to lose her without a fight.

I practically jump out of my truck after taking the key out and rush over to her front door. I knock a couple times before Winter comes to the door with a confused look on her face.

"I need to see Emerald. Daisy fucked things up and I need to talk to her. Please," I rush out so quickly, I'm surprised she even understood what I was saying.

"Of course, fucking Daisy and Brynn, messing up shit for everyone. Stupid bitches," she says, talking to herself like she forgets I'm here.

"Umm Winter, I need to get to Emerald please," I rush out again.

"Oh, shit sorry, she's through the kitchen, down the hall, first door on the left is her room," she says pointing as I realize her room is like mine through the kitchen and down the hall. I run through their kitchen down the hall and knock a couple times not saying anything because I don't want her to ignore me anymore.

"Come in Winter, gosh you're so impatient." I hear her laugh through her sniffles, and she freezes when she sees it's me instead of who she originally thought it was.

"Get out." She might be tiny but she's scary when she's angry. "I don't want to see or talk to you, Creedence. I can't fucking believe you." She sniffles as fresh tears form in her eyes. Her tiny fists balled up at her sides. She looks so sad it's fucking crushing my heart.

"Please. I promise you Emerald, she planned that, and I can explain the whole thing, please?" I pause, out of breath a little from sprinting from my truck and through their house, plus rushing my sentences out without breathing. It's kinda catching up to me now.

"No, I don't want to hear it, Creed. I saw what I saw and there's no excuse for her kissing you. Her lips touched yours, what don't you see?" she shouts. Her chest rises and falls quickly while she tries to control her anger. Her cute little fists now in front of her like she's about to punch me or something. I try not to smile at her anger, Emerald is tiny so to see this adorably angry, yet scary woman look like she's about to pounce on me, fuck. Is a turn on. But she's too tiny, she couldn't hurt me even if she tried. I'm willing to stand here though and let her take her anger out on me if that's what she needs right now. I'd do anything for this gorgeous girl right in front of me. So yes, even if she wanted to fight me right now, I'd stand here and take it if that's what she needed to feel better about this situation. Then I'll punish her for it later. I'll be rough with her pussy and make sure she's sore enough to remember everything I did to my pretty pink pussy and make sure she enjoys every minute of it.

"Listen to me, please. I pinky promise. Are you listening? You know I take my pinky promises seriously, Emerald." And her head snaps up as she wipes her eyes, still sniffling.

"Fine, I'll give you five minutes to explain." Her voice is so sad. It breaks my fucking heart, but the look on her face is fucking soul crushing. I never want to be the reason she has this look on her face again.

I come over and kneel on the ground in front of her, as she sits on her bed. I want her to see the sincere look on my face as I talk to her.

"Daisy had scheduled an appointment with me a month ago before you and I started dating and she had already put a down payment on it to keep her appointment. When she came in today, I completely forgot she was getting tattooed. I was originally going in to draw up sketches for my future appointments. But then she came in, reminding me that she had the appointment." I pause taking a couple breaths since I got all of that out without breathing.

"I told her I had a girlfriend. That I was dating you and that I had ended things weeks ago with her. We weren't even a thing, we just hooked up a couple times, the worst mistake ever," I state because it's true she was nothing but drama, I should have ended it after the first night. Or listened to Carsten when he tried to warn me. But sometimes good pussy makes you blind and stupid and it's too good to pass up when they're practically throwing it at you. I'm probably an asshole for even saying that. But do I care? Ehhh not really. Especially when it comes to girls like Daisy and Brynn who are so desperate for attention, they'd do anything for you even if that means to use them.

"Then when I was getting ready to charge her for the rest of the tattoo she was staring out the window with a strange smirk on her face, so I think what happened was she saw you, then as she was paying she kept staring out the window until you finally walked in and she rushed over to hug me and she kissed me." I rush out the rest of it taking a deep breath. I need to stop doing that to myself where I hold my breath while talking.

"So, she did it on purpose?" She looks so small and fragile right now. Like if I say the wrong thing I'll break her and that's the last thing I want to do right now. You can tell she's not sure if she wants to believe me, and I don't blame her. I haven't really given her much to go off of besides what truly happened and even that can come off as iffy.

"Emerald, look at me." I reach out tilting her chin with my fingers. "I wouldn't lie to you; I have no reason to go into a relationship and lie to you. I wouldn't be in a relationship to begin with if I wasn't serious about that person. I was never serious about Daisy, we slept together a few times, and I broke it off because I was interested in you." I smile at her thinking back.

"Remember when Carsten and I went to your house looking for Winter and I kissed your hand." I smile at the memory because I was so fucking nervous about seeing and talking to her that day. I just tried to play it cool in front of Carsten before we left because I didn't want him to see how much of a pussy I was being crushing over a chick the way I was. But to her I wanted her to see how much of a gentleman I could be before I introduced her to my darker side.

"Yes, that was the second time we met, and I couldn't believe you kissed my hand, it was something so sweet and so simple, yet it made me feel so special." She blushes and it's so adorable. I love the fact that she's being this honest with me even if it involves watching her cheeks turn a couple shades of pink. Although I wish it were her ass I was watching turn those shades of pink, because the things I'd love to do to that perfectly plump ass of hers. Mmm, shit. I need to get my mind out of the gutter and my thoughts back on the right track.

"I did it because the first time I met you, I was with someone, so I didn't really pay much attention. I was pretty buzzed and just being stupid. But damn, Sugar I kept seeing you in the driveway every morning when we would both leave for work. I wasn't sure if it was on purpose or coincidence, and I couldn't get over how beautiful you are. I wanted to just go over there and say hey, but I didn't know if you had a boyfriend, so I didn't." I pause just staring at her for a minute. At her natural beauty that her body just naturally carries. The way her tattoos hug her skin just right, the way her curves are in all my favorite places. I slowly move my way up her body with my eyes, trying not to think dirty thoughts as I come back to her beautiful face, and I just can't get over how beautiful she is.

"Then that day Carsten was looking for Winter. I took it as a sign that we were meant to talk to each other that day. Then when I saw you up close and really paid attention to you, god you are just so beautiful, but I knew right then and there that I had to have you because I knew I was going to love you." I laugh for a second. "Call me crazy but I do believe in love at first sight, and I swear that's what I experienced with you. I love you Sugar, I'd never do anything to hurt you." I lean in and kiss her, not even waiting for a response or an argument. I need to feel her lips against mine. To show her that I can love her in more ways than one. I open my mouth swiping my tongue against her lips, she opens for me, she never hesitates, allowing me to slip my tongue into her mouth, swirling my tongue with hers. She lets out a whimper as I wrap my arm around her waist and pull her closer to me, her arms come around my neck fisting my black T-shirt in the process. I let out a low growl because everything she does turns me on, including gripping my shirt. I stand slowly, not breaking our kiss and push her down onto her bed as she wraps her legs tightly around my waist. She starts thrusting herself into me making it hard to resist her, but I have plans for her tonight and I want to make her wait, make her beg for me to fuck her pussy. I pull away from the kiss leaving her breathless while I stand up.

"Get ready, I'll be back to get you for dinner in an hour," I tell her before walking out of her room leaving her there in shock. I know we just made up from our first argument, but I have things I need to get ready before we go to dinner.

14
CREEDENCE

After dinner we head back to my place. I didn't feel like going to the bar. I want to have fun with her tonight and boy do I have some fun in store for us.

"I hope you enjoyed your dinner," I say to her as I open her door in my driveway and take her hand. She's wearing a tight black skirt that comes just below her ass, with a pink crop top. I think my favorite part of her outfit is the pink scrunchie I got her that she wears on her wrist.

"God yes, it was so good, thank you again." She smiles up at me as we walk towards my front door.

"How was your food?" she asks me, looking over and up at me, even in her heels I'm still a lot taller than her and I love it. "It was very good, except now I'm too full from eating too much." I laugh. "But don't worry I always have room for dessert." I wink at her as she blushes. I love that I can make her blush over something so simple. I shut the front door behind her, and I turn to look over at her just looking at how beautiful she is before I lean down to kiss her, I want to get her worked up, so she's so turned on she begs for me to fuck her.

She opens her mouth for me right away, I love that she doesn't hesitate to open for me ever. I lift her up by her ass and her skirt lifts in the process, my hands rub against her lace thong making my fucking cock twitch in excitement. I was almost hoping she wasn't wearing anything underneath but then that would ruin the fun of me ripping them off her later. She pulls away for a minute.

"Is anyone home? I don't want them to see my ass, Creedence," she whispers, just in case.

"Don't worry, Sugar, I wouldn't be showing off your ass if anyone was. This is mine." Then I let go and smack her ass hard making her moan into my mouth as she kisses me again. I carry her down the hall into my bedroom and drop her gently onto my bed. Before I step away and take off my shirt.

"Mmm, you sexy, sexy man. I'd love to lick every inch of your body, especially your tattoos." She bites that fucking pouty bottom lip of hers. Goddamn it's so sexy when she does that. I smile at her; I don't think any woman has openly admitted to wanting to lick my body before or even my tattoos. "Don't worry, Sugar, I'll let you do that one day. But today is about a surprise I have for you," I tell her as I walk over to my bedroom door to shut it and lock it just in case anyone comes home. I don't want anyone barging in especially with what I'm about to do to her.

I slowly walk over to the bed where she's sitting. Her legs dangling over the edge. She looks lost in my California king-sized bed. The bed frame I made to be higher up off the ground, so her feet don't come anywhere near the floor.

I tip her chin up with my fingers as she places her hands on my stomach, feeling my abs, tracing my tattoos that cover my whole stomach. She leans forward and kisses my stomach right above my jeans before she sticks her tongue out and slowly licks up. I throw my head back getting lost in the thoughts of her choking on my cock, but that'll have to wait for later. I slowly step back before I give in and ruin my plans, and she pouts.

"I was having fun." She crosses her arms. "That's not fair." She scrunches her face looking at me with the cutest look I've ever seen her give me before and it takes everything in me to not say fuck it.

"Don't worry, Sugar, you'll get a turn soon enough," I tell her, stroking the side of her face rubbing my hand from her temple down to her chin. I lean in and kiss her again before leaning away and whispering to her.

"Take your shoes off and lay in the middle of my bed," I tell her, but she sits there confused.

"Excuse me, Sugar. I said take your shoes off and lay down in the middle of my bed. Or I'll spank that sexy little ass of yours." My tone is a little firmer this time. She smirks at me while she starts sliding backwards onto the bed more and pushing her heels off with her toes.

She finally gets to the middle of the bed, her arms down at her sides, her legs slightly bent, and one leg crossed over the other. God, she looks so sexy and innocent laying here. I can't wait to do the dirty things I have planned to this gorgeous fucking girl right here.

I get on top of the bed and undo the button of my jeans so it's easier to take off later when I need to. Then I climb on the bed, resting my body over hers. I hold myself up by my knees which rest on each side of her body, and I hold the top half of my body up with my hands.

I lean down and give her soft slow kisses before pulling away leaving her breathing a little heavier than she just was. I lean up a little balancing on my knees as I push her hands above her head and slowly rub my hands down her arms and stop right before her armpits. Then I lean back down pulling her shirt over her head. I was going to rip it, but I don't want to keep ruining her clothes, I'll be nice about that this time. Then I move down to her skirt pulling it quickly down her body before getting to her thong that I pull on until it rips off her making her cry out from the pain. Good, I hope it leaves a mark, I want her pussy wet every time she looks at a mark I left on her body.

I lean down and suck one of her nipples into my mouth, licking and swirling my tongue over her while her body starts slightly jerking underneath me.

"Fuck, Creedence," she moans, her head tilting back, damn this is going to be so much fun with all the toys I bought her. I suck her other nipple into my mouth hard, making sure it hurts but feels good and she moans again. I knew she'd be fun. I stop sucking on her nipple and lick my way up, stopping right before I get to her neck.

"Have you ever been tied up before?" I whisper in her ear. Fuck, my cock is so painfully hard, I can't wait to be inside her pussy again.

"N...no...nope," she pants. Her tits jiggle with each rise and fall of her chest. Turning me on even more. "Just when you used your belt but never by anything else." Her breathing picks up and I reach down and gently slap her right tit a little, making it bounce. Fuck that was so hot. I've always been into boobs. That's one thing I can look at and get hard instantly and I'm not picky. I love all size tits. Well, I shouldn't say all of them because if they're too big I'm not into them. I at least like them to fit into my hands even if they're smaller than my hands. That's perfectly fine too.

"Well today's your lucky day, Sugar." I bite down on her neck, sucking her skin...making sure to leave a mark. To let people know she's my property. "Cause I'm about to tie you up and make you forget the name of every man who's ever fucked you." I smile down at the nervous look on her face. "It's ok beautiful, I'm only gonna please you. You don't have anything to worry about."

"Okay," she says in a moan. I reach down and swipe my fingers against her pussy, shit she's so fucking wet for me, it makes my dick grow even harder.

"Damn baby, your fucking pussy is so wet for me. I can't wait to taste you on my fingers. I bet it tastes like sugar just like you always do." I lick my fingers and groan out; fuck she tastes amazing. "Fuck...you taste so fucking good. You wanna know what else I can't wait for?" I hope she doesn't guess because I love watching her cheeks turn different shades of pink as I make her beautiful face blush.

"What's that?" she whispers as her tongue comes out and swipes her bottom lip and I wish I was feeling her tongue against mine right now. But that'll have to wait.

I lean down by her ear, turning my head to face her too so I can watch her reaction. "I can't wait to get my face between those legs and lick every bit of you. I crave you, Sugar. I'm fucking starving and I'm ready to feast on your delicious fucking pussy." I grin at her as she's biting her lower lip. I take her right leg and slide the fabric underneath it, bending it at the knee, tying it tightly to her right wrist, she hisses in a breath from the pain, making me smile because I'm making sure it'll leave a mark. Now her leg is spread wide open, then I tie her right wrist to the right side of the headboard post and repeat the same with the left leg and wrist. So now her hands are spread wide above her head and her legs are bent but spread wide open. Her breasts moving up and down from her heavy breathing. Her nipples are nice and hard which will be perfect for the nipple clamps I'll be using on her.

If I need to punish her, I can still smack her ass. That's why I tied her up this way. To keep her ass on display for me to do what I need to as I please. Seeing her spread open and this fucking wet for me is such a turn on. When I get to eat her juicy fucking pussy and make her come multiple times, she won't be able to close her legs. She'll have to beg me to stop. I'm going to make sure she's so sore by the time I'm done with her she'll never forget what I did to her. She will probably blush just thinking about the memories of it all. I know one thing; it'll make her pussy wet every time she thinks about it and I can't wait to be the one to take care of her every time she needs to get off.

I reach above her grabbing a blindfold and place it over her eyes and her body tenses, I can see the fear set in.

"Don't worry, Emerald. I'm not here to hurt you, Sugar, trust me you're going to love this." I make sure the blindfold is tight around her eyes so she can't see.

"Do you trust me?" I ask, smiling even though she can't see me. I can't help it, she's absolutely breathtaking so it's hard not to practically drool over her. Looking at her with this blindfold knowing she's trusting me enough to leave her body for me to do whatever I want with.

"Yes, I... I trust you." She sounds nervous, she doesn't sound confident in her trust. I reach down and pinch her nipples. The whimpering sound she makes turns me on even more. Fuck, I can't wait for her to make those noises while my cock is inside her.

"That doesn't sound too convincing, now let's try this again. Do you trust me, Sugar?" This time I lean down close, whispering it in her ear.

"Yes, Creedence, I trust you with everything." She groans out like I'm teasing her but I'm not even touching her yet.

"Good girl, now I don't want you asking me any questions, I just want you to relax and feel the pleasure, do you understand me?" My voice comes out hoarse, I'm barely able to control how horny I am.

She lets out a whimper, not answering right away. I grab her by the throat this time, not enough to hurt her but enough to leave my marks. I cut off her air, maybe this time she'll answer me.

"I said don't ask me any questions, Sugar do you understand me?" I lick her ear lobe, down to her jaw and slowly down her neck biting it. She lets out a strangled moan, she moves her mouth trying to talk so I let go of her throat, she gasps for air.

"Y...yes Creedence, I won't ask any questions." She breathlessly gives me the answer I craved. To have full control. To make sure she enjoys everything I do to her. I want her begging for more, I want her to need more every time she's not with me. I want her to be obsessed with what I do to her; I want her to crave the things I do to her body whenever I'm not around. I want her to need me always, to be the only one to fulfill her sexual desires. To be the only one who understands my good girl's needs. Fuck. She's dangerous, the things this woman can do to my heart. She could destroy me. But that's the chance I'm willing to take, because that's how much I need her to survive. I'm fucking obsessed and without her I'm just not complete.

I look at her sexy body, the way her pink nipples harden at my touch showing me just how much she wants me. Her chest rising and falling quickly making her breasts slightly jiggle some more, making my cock throb painfully against the fabric of my jeans that are still holding my cock hostage. I unzipped them to give my dick some room, but that still does nothing. The annoying jean fabric still restrains me from getting what it needs. From getting closer to her wet entrance. But I guess it's a good thing so I can't just slide it in there and say fuck it and ruin my plans. I don't want to ruin my plans with her, I want to enjoy my time with her and make sure she enjoys her time with me. I want her to love everything I do to her beautiful body. I want her wanting more before it's even over with.

Fuck, as I stare down at her I can't get over how fucking perfect she is. This woman is the definition of perfection, literally everything is perfect. The natural heart shape of her face, the way her winged eyeliner makes her eyes look seductive without her even trying. The way her freckles scatter across her nose and cheeks lightly, they're almost not noticeable until you're this close. My eyes slowly travel over her plump lips that fit perfectly with mine and feel too good against my own. Down to her perfect tits that are rising and falling as she pants still catching her breath from being worked up. Down to her small stretch marks on her stomach that practically make my mouth water with how delicious they look, right along with her curves. I love a woman with curves, a little loose skin in the belly area and meat on the love handles. Those stretch marks though, there was nothing sexier than a woman with stretch marks; those were lines of a woman, her body's natural art.

Her tattoos going down her sides the way they form to her curves just right. I love that she's covered in tattoos, by the time I'm done with her she'll be covered in the sexual art I leave on her, marking her as mine, painting her with beautiful bruises and marks of pleasure.

I reach over and open the drawer to my nightstand, grabbing everything I need. The nipple clamps, butt plug, lube and the vibrator that I just bought for this occasion. I grab the vibrator, not needing the lube like I thought I would. I take it and swipe it at her entrance letting her wet pussy lube it for me. After I make sure it's wet enough, I slowly work it inside her, gliding it in and out. "What...what is that?" she stutters a moan; I take out the vibrator.

I slap her ass hard, leaving a red handprint on her, just the way I like it, mmm she looks so sexy with the mark of my hand on her ass.

"What did I say, Emerald?" I ask, leaning down, sucking her hard nipple into my mouth.

"Fuck, Creedence, please," she moans out, her beautiful cries sounding like tortured pleasure. I'm sure it feels so good to her yet it's just not enough to get her where she needs to be. That's my favorite part. To build up her pleasure to the point where she's begging. God I can't wait to hear my name on her lips as she's begging. She's going to love it though, especially when I finally give her the orgasm her body desperately needs. It's going to be so intense her cries of pleasure are going to be burned into my brain on repeat whenever I'm not around her. That's how much I think about her, that's how much I need her, how fucking obsessed I've become.

"Tsk, tsk Sugar, what did I tell you before?" I sucked the other nipple into my mouth making her cry out, her body shivering.

"Don't...ask...questions," she moans out her response.

"You're enjoying this, aren't you beautiful?" I ask her, while swiping the vibrator at her entrance again.

"Yes, please, Creedence, I need you," she practically begs. My good girl already doing as she's told; I knew she was going to be so much fun to play with.

Once I put the vibrator inside her I turn it on a low setting enough for her to feel but not enough to get her off yet, just enough to tease her.

"Ohhh goddd," she groans out, trying to twist her body and close her legs but the way she's tied she can't close her legs at all, and I smile to myself, fuck she looks so beautiful laying like this. So exposed for me and my eyes only. All this beauty on display and willing, just waiting for me to do as I please.

I reach over grabbing the nipple clamps. "Now this might pinch but I promise it'll feel good." I want her to be aware of what she's going to be feeling but I don't want to give away what I'm doing, I want it to be a surprise. I place the clamps on each of her nipples tightening them just enough to hurt a little but mainly just to hear her moan because it's fucking sexy as hell listening to her moan.

"Fuckkk, Creedence wha..." But I don't let her finish what she is going to say.

"Ah...ah...ahhhh. What did I tell you?" I shake my head even though she can't see me with her blindfold on as it is.

"Don't. Ask. Questions," she moans her response and it's the sexiest thing ever. God I'm addicted to everything this woman does. Literally everything.

"Good girl, Sugar." She blushes, I've noticed every time I call her good girl she blushes, and I love it.

I grab the lube and butt plug because I might want to cause her pain, but I'm not an asshole. I would never do anything to cause her discomfort or too much pain at first. That's why I'm starting off small, I want her body to be ready for me for when I'm ready to fuck this tight little hole of hers, to feel it swallow my cock.

"Now this is probably going to hurt, and be uncomfortable, but again, I promise you'll love it, Sugar," I tell her so she's aware pain is coming.

"What are you going to do?" Her voice comes out in a quick panic.

"Oh, my sweet Sugar," I chuckle. Here she goes again, not listening to my rules.

SMACK.

I slap her ass hard right in the same spot I did before then I gently rub it while I slowly pull on the nipple clamps.

"Oww shittt," she hisses out. "God that feels so good." And it quickly turns into pleasure. I knew she would enjoy this. Smiling, I go back to putting lube on the butt plug and then I take my fingers and lube up her ass. I put a decent amount on there before using my finger to circle her tight hole before gently pushing my index finger inside, I feel her muscles tense and she tightens around my finger making my cock twitch. Shit she would feel so good with her tight ass wrapped around my cock.

"Relax beautiful; I promise it'll hurt." My shoulders shake with a slight chuckle at my sick joke. It's all fun. I don't want to cause any real pain. Only the pain that's followed by pleasure, which I know she will enjoy.

"But I pinky promise you're going to love it too." I pause. "And you know I don't break my pinky promises," I tell her.

"Okay," she says quietly. I'm not sure if she's nervous, I hope she's not scared.

She's breathing heavy, the vibrator still doing just enough to tease her. I slowly remove my finger and apply more lube to her entrance before I slowly place the tip of the butt plug against it. I start gently pushing it in and she hisses out again.

"Fuck, Creedence." She winces a little, her body stiffening, and I stop what I'm doing waiting for her to tell me to stop but she doesn't.

"Sorry babe, I told you this would hurt." And I don't waste any time as I shove the rest of it in her ass. I was already halfway in, but how would it have been fun if I didn't cause any pain.

"Fuck, shit Creed," she whimpers, I slowly twist it, and she lets out a groan.

"See babe, I told you you'd like it. I'm sure you feel so full don't you, my little slut?" I ask her as I turn up the speed a little on the vibrator.

"Ohh goddd please, Creedence I need to cum," she cries out moaning the sexiest sound ever. This time it is from a mix of me torturing and pleasing her, but still not enough to get her off just yet. I want it to build up, she's about to have the best orgasm ever.

I straddle her stomach the best I can with the way her legs are positioned, not putting any weight on her before I lean down and start kissing her. Slowly at first until I need more. Her kisses are addicting, she opens her mouth for me and her tongue dances against mine, scraping the roof of my mouth as it twirls around. I moan into her mouth, swallowing her moans with my own.

Her tongue is amazing, I can't wait to feel its softness running along my cock. I push back the dirty thoughts that are about to start. I'm so worked up and ready to fuck her but I can't just yet I haven't teased her enough. Then I smile, getting an idea.

"Fuck, Emerald, I want to fuck your mouth so bad right now." I groan, my voice raspy, I'm out of fucking breath from how fucking sexy this woman is, she literally takes my breath away.

"I'm not stopping you," she practically moans out, arching her back, trying to find some release.

"Tell me to fuck your mouth, Sugar." My heart rate picking up, my cock pulsing, it's so fucking painful how hard it is right now.

"Please." Is all she says. Her breathing is still heavy, her tits jiggle a little with each rise and fall of her breathing. Her eyes flutter and sit heavy from how aroused she is.

"Tsk tsk." I reach, pulling the nipple clamps making her cry out and I smile. I love how quickly her yelps turn into moans.

"What did I ask you to do, Sugar?" I say patiently waiting to shove my cock into that beautiful mouth of hers.

"Please. Do I'll fucking beg if I have to, is that what you want baby?" she groans. "Please fuck my mouth, I wanna feel your cock on my tongue, I wanna feel your cock slide in and out of my mouth, down my throat. Fuck, Creedence let me swallow all of you baby," she says, giving me this sexy devilish grin. You can tell she's worked up, everything my little slut is saying is probably soaking that delicious fucking pussy of hers.

"Good girl, now open up for me and stick that tongue out beautiful," I practically growl from excitement. I've had plenty of blow jobs in my life, but none have felt as amazing as the way her mouth feels on my cock. And her tongue the way it feels like it was made for me. Fuck I love it.

She opens her mouth, sticking her tongue out and I smile at how well she listens to me.

"Good fucking girl, baby." And I'll make sure in the end that she knows how well her listening works for her.

I place the tip of my cock on her tongue and she instantly pulls it in with her tongue closing her soft pouty lips around the tip and starts sucking on it like it's a god damn lollipop., She swirls her tongue on the underside of my shaft and circles it around to the top, gently playing with my piercings and fuck...my little slut knows what she's doing and I can't help but smile. God her velvety warm tongue, swirling around my cock. Fuck, her mouth is heaven.

"Goddamn, baby your mouth is fucking amazing." She moans around my thick cock the vibrations intensifying the pleasure. "Mmm don't stop," I growl. "Don't stop until I'm coming down your throat, Sugar." She lifts her head at a certain angle, opening up for me like my good fucking girl.

"Look how well you're taking me into your throat, Emerald." I throw my head back, it's so hard not to lose control but she's doing so good it's so hard not to.

"Mmm, you taste so good." She groans around my cock intensifying all the pleasure I'm feeling.

I rebalance my body, holding myself up better. Placing my hands on each side of her head and my knees on each side of her ribs, my cock lines up with her mouth perfectly. She leans up taking me back into her throat again while swirling and sucking before she swallows, my cock like she needs it to fucking survive. Fuck. I start thrusting my hips before she relaxes her head back onto the blanket behind her. And I start fucking her mouth not wasting any time with making her gag. I look down as I see tears fall from behind the blindfold as they stream down her cheeks. I wish I could see her beautiful honey brown eyes as those tears fell so I removed the blindfold and sure enough her eyes filled with tears. She blinks a couple times as fresh tears fill her eyes from each time I thrust too far into her throat making her gag. She usually doesn't gag but the way I'm fucking her mouth I'm making her gag on purpose because fuck, it turns me the fuck on, and why wouldn't I want my little slut choking on my cock and cum?

"Shit, Sugar, this mouth was made for my cock huh?" I ask her and she moans almost like she was saying "Uh huh." And the vibrations take me closer to the edge. "My cock was made for you, huh baby?" I ask her between thrusts. "Fuck I'm getting closer, Emerald. Get ready, baby. I'm about to fuck that pretty little mouth of yours really fucking hard, baby."

But I stop for a second and turn the setting on the vibrator up a little more before grabbing the remote for the butt plug and I turn the vibrations on for that as well.

"Mmm," she moans onto my cock, so I pull out for her to speak. "You okay, Sugar?" I ask making sure everything is good.

"God, Creedence, it's too much, I feel so full, fuck," she breathes out, spit flying from her mouth a little. "I need to come please," she begs and it's so fucking sexy the tone of her sultry voice as she begs.

"Fuck, Sugar, don't you worry I want you to come with me." So, I turn the vibrator up a little more.

"Fuckk yes," she moans and then I shove my cock back into her mouth and she sucks me at the same time I make her gag, spit drips down her cheeks as her eyes water from how fast I'm going, not letting her get much air in, but it's okay it'll only intensify her orgasm. I can feel my Jacob's ladder scraping her teeth a little and then sliding against her tongue and it feels so good, each time I hit the back of her throat she sucks and swallows. And I'm about to lose it but I don't want it to end, I don't want this pleasure to be over yet.

"Fuck, Sugar, get ready for my cum baby, I want you to suck me dry." She nods her head the best she can underneath me, while moaning. And that moan is all I needed. It sends me over the edge the same time her body tenses, her legs begin to shake, and she moans out onto my cock her orgasm taking over her body as I spill my warmth into her throat. She sucks everything out of me, I go to pull out and she sucks me back in swirling her tongue one last time making sure she gets every last drop. Damn that was so fucking hot, I've never been with a girl who swallows as willingly as she does.

"My dirty little slut," I say to her as I look into her tear-filled eyes. "Is that what you are, baby? My good little slut, milking my cock and taking every last drop huh?"

"Yes, Creed, I'm your dirty little slut," she groans and holy shit my cock went from half hard to full attention just from that. "Now please fuck me, Creed, I wanna feel your cock inside me you sexy, sexy man." If I wasn't already in love with the girl this would've definitely added to my feelings for her. I knew she was going to be fun doing all of this with. She's more like me than I realized she was. My dirty good girl and I are going to have a lot of fun as long as we'll be staying together.

"Not yet babe, I'm not done making you come," I tell her as her body writhes back and forth from the intensity of the orgasm and the vibrations filling both her holes.

Then my mouth crashes down on hers, I don't even care that she just swallowed my cum, her lips are addicting. I think it's safe to say that not only do I love this girl, but I'm obsessed with this beautiful woman.

My tongue pushes into her mouth without permission, scraping across her teeth and the roof of her mouth before swirling around hers, her tongue instantly meeting mine, swirling and sliding with mine. I pull away slowly kissing down her jaw till I get to her neck. Then I start sucking and biting, making sure I leave bite marks and hickeys along the way.

"Oh god, Creed." She's panting, her breathing picking up, her chest rising and falling. I remove one of the nipple clamps, because I need her breast in my mouth. I can't get enough of her body. I want her to remember my mouth all over her, as I suck her nipple into my mouth and her body starts to shake. Yep, she's about to cum again.

"Please, Creedence, I'm so close." I keep sucking and licking her nipple while turning up the speed for both the butt plug and vibrator, they're still on pretty low setting I don't want to go crazy too quickly with it and ruin all the fun, I still want to tease her while making her come over and over.

I suck harder while pulling on the other nipple clamp and that's all she needed to send her over the edge again, that's orgasm number two. She's going to be exhausted and sore by the time I'm done with her.

I place the nipple clamp back onto her nipple and start kissing, sucking and biting my way down her stomach making sure to leave more bite marks and hickeys along the way. Like I said before I want her covered in my art. She wiggles and moans underneath me, thrusting her hips to try and get some relief. But I don't allow her that contact she needs, not yet. I continue licking my way down and stop right above her throbbing, wet pussy. Biting my way down her thighs and sucking on them. God she is so fucking beautiful, but she's going to look even more beautiful by the time I'm done with her. I smack her ass hard this time on the opposite cheek, leaving a red mark, I look over to her right side and there's still a red hand-print from before.

I finally make my way to her pussy and don't waste any more time. I stick my tongue out and gently swirl it around her clit, massaging her swollen nub with my tongue.

"Fuck yesss," she cries out. "Don't stop, please god don't stop." I love the way she tells me what she wants, she's not afraid to speak her mind.

"Don't you worry, Sugar, I'm just getting started on this delicious pussy of yours." I pull the vibrator out of her pussy, and it's dripping wet. God I can't wait to get my tongue in there and taste her. I swirl her clit, sucking and licking on just the right spot that makes her toes curl and her back arch, she tries bucking her hips, but with the ways she's tied it's impossible for her to do it.

"Fuck, Creed your tongue feels so good," she moans out. "Please, please don't stop." She's so out of breath I'm surprised she's not gonna pass out from lack of oxygen.

"No way, I could feast on your pussy the rest of the night. Shit I could eat you every day for every fucking meal," I tell her and then get right back to sucking and licking her clit before licking my way down her slit and sticking my tongue inside her soaking entrance.

"Mmm," I moan out because she tastes fucking amazing. I reach down and tug on the butt plug a little and spin it around making her cry out from the pain and pleasure.

"Mmm fuck," she groans as her body starts shaking. I had a feeling once I started to play with it, it would get her closer to another orgasm. I lick my way back up to her clit swirling and sucking slowly with a little pressure and I continue to do that until her body loses control as her orgasm soars through her body and I feel her pussy throbbing and her juices all over my mouth. Fuck I can't wait to fuck her pussy.

"Shit, Creed, that was amazing." She's still out of breath. Fuck, she sure is gorgeous. She sure is something to look at, as of lately my favorite thing to look at.

"I'm still not done with you, baby girl," I tell her, getting up on my knees, as I pull the nipple clamps hard and smack her ass even harder with my other hand.

"Ahh fuck, you're going to kill me," she shrieks, moaning out.

"Death by orgasm doesn't seem like a bad thing," I practically whisper because I'm so turned on by this beautiful woman in my bed, allowing me to do whatever I want to her. Loving everything I've done to her so far. God I love this woman. "But don't worry, Sugar, I won't let you die. I love you too much." I smile down at her beautiful face, lost in her beautiful eyes.

"I love you, you handsome, handsome man," she whispers back, still out of breath.

I waste no time taking my hard cock to her wet pussy, swiping it up and down to get it wet before I thrust in hard, I don't ease it in, I can't wait any longer the need to be inside her. To feel her warmth wrapped around me, is too intense.

"Fuccck, Sugar," I groan. Her pussy feels so tight around my thick pierced cock, and I love it. I could never get sick of the way her pussy feels.

"Mhmm you feel so good, Creed," she says in a broken-up moan from me pounding her pussy hard.

"You like that my little slut?" I ask smacking her ass, watching it jiggle making my cock twitch inside her, fuck everything about her is perfect.

"Ohh goddd." Is all she says, so I smack her ass again and then pull on the nipple clamps.

"I asked you a question, Emerald." She'll know I'm being serious using her real name since I've been calling her Sugar more. "Do you like that, my little slut?" I ask this time as I reach between my body and hers playing with the plug, tugging it in and out of her tight ass.

"Yes," she moans. "Yes, I do. Fuck, your cock feels so amazing," she practically screams.

I look down watching my cock slide in and out of her tight pussy, still playing with the plug in her ass, pulling it in and out while twisting it.

I let go of the plug and increased the vibrations on it making her groan as her eyes roll back. Then I turn the vibrator on to the lowest setting and place it on her clit, she moans out breathlessly. I reach forward and grip her throat, this time gripping tight enough to cut off the air flow and she panics, shaking her head no the best she can. But I don't let go, I know she's going to love this.

"Do you trust me, Sugar?" I ask her in a husky tone, it's taking everything in me not to come yet. She nods the best she can with my hand around her throat.

"I pinky promise you're going to love this now just relax," I tell her, I hold my hand around her throat and the other one with the vibrator on her clit, while pumping in and out of her hard and fast. Her eyes are starting to get heavy, and I know she's going to need air soon, so I pick up the pace slamming into her hard and her eyes roll into the back of her head.

"Are you okay, Sugar?" I ask making sure she's not in any pain, because this is supposed to feel good and intensify everything, not hurt. She nods her head the best she can, and I continue to fuck her tight pussy getting closer to the edge. I let go of the vibrator and grab the remote, turning it up one more before placing it back on her clit. And her mouth opens like she's trying to let out a moan, but nothing comes out. Her body starts to shake and that's when I know she's about to come and just then I feel her pussy tighten around my hard cock and I lose control myself. I let go of her throat and she gasps and moans, her orgasm super intense from all the pleasure coming from all different angles of her body, her body goes limp as her orgasm dies down and I finish spilling inside her.

"Shit, Creedence, no more I can't come anymore...please," she whimpers. "I'm sore, my body needs to stretch please." She looks at me with a tired, yet satisfied look on her face.

"I wasn't done playing yet, but I'll give you a break, for now." I wink at her and smirk.

"God you're gonna kill me aren't you," she asks as I start untying her from the headboard, and then remove the ropes from her wrists. She starts slowly moving her arms as I start untying her legs and I help her slowly stretch them while massaging them a little.

"Don't move them too quickly, you don't want to hurt yourself, Sugar," I tell her, because it'll probably hurt moving them too quickly, and although I like to cause pain sexually, I don't want her to be in pain that's caused by something else.

"My legs are numb." She laughs a little, trying to wiggle her legs.

"Don't worry I'm gonna run you a nice hot bath," I tell her, and she pouts. "What's wrong, Emerald?" I ask confused, not sure what I did to make her sad.

"Are you gonna take a bath with me?" She smiles now.

"Of course, baby, who's gonna wash you if I don't." I stand up now that she's fully untied.

"You lay there and stretch your body; I'll go get the bath ready." I turn around and start walking towards the bathroom.

"Um Creed?" she says as I start walking away.

"Yes, Sugar?" I stop and turn around slowly.

"Umm can I remove this plug?" she asks blushing, I love how easy it is for me to make her blush. It's the cutest thing, she gets a certain look on her face as she blushes and it makes my heart go crazy, she makes me go crazy.

"Oh shit, I can't believe I forgot about it." I put my hand over my head. "I'm such an ass."

"No, you're not, it's just getting a little uncomfortable now is all." She blushes more and I smirk a little, she seems like such an innocent girl when she blushes, but my sweet dirty girl is no angel.

"Sugar, don't be embarrassed, it's okay," I tell her, walking back over to the bed, grabbing the remote to shut the vibrations off.

"Bend your knees a little for me," I tell her as I gently tug the plug from her ass and place it on the nightstand next to me. I'll clean everything off later. "Now give your body a good stretch while I go and get the bath ready for us." I turn back around and walk towards my bathroom.

15

EMERALD

I LAY THERE STRETCHING, MY MUSCLES SORE IN THE BEST way. I don't think I've ever been this sore from being fucked before, and I've never had any of that stuff done to me…ever, and I loved all of it. I'd definitely let him fuck me like that every time we have sex, even anal. I never thought I'd be into butt play or anything physically being in my ass. And again, call me fucking weird, I loved everything about it and can't wait to explore more with him. But damn am I going to be even more sore tomorrow than I am right now and it's going to suck standing and walking around at work all day. I've been working at Lisa's Diner with Winter for a few months now, the hours are a little different than my other job but she's way more flexible and understanding so I love it there, minus working with that bitch Stacy who tried to steal Carsten from Winter when they hit a rough patch and broke up for a little bit there. Anyways, at least I'll smile thinking back to where all this soreness came from.

I hear Creedence walking back out of his bathroom and turn to look over at him, giving him a sleepy smile, I've never had that many orgasms in a row before and I'm fucking tired. I don't think I'll make it in the tub. He walks over to me smiling. Watching my body, his gaze lands on my boobs and slowly travels down to my pussy as he slowly licks his lips. Making my pussy throb. What is wrong with me, we just had amazing sex, and I could probably go again just from those looks alone.

"Fuck you drive me crazy woman." He shakes his head walking over to me. His cock already hard and ready for me. He notices me staring and shrugs his shoulders. "Sorry, this is just what you do to me, I can't control it." He places his hands under my back and thighs lifting me like I weigh nothing.

"I can walk, you know." I giggle as I wrap my arms around his neck. He leans down, gently kissing me before pulling away. Although that's a lie, I feel like if I did stand up right now, I'd probably look like a newborn animal on wobbly legs trying to stand for the first time. So, I'm thankful for his strength and him carrying me without asking for it.

"I know but that would take all the fun out of carrying you and putting you into the tub with me." He gives me his sexy grin that makes me want to jump his bones and it instantly sends chills down my body.

"You cold, Sugar?" he asks, concerned.

"Something like that." I smile looking into his brown eyes, they look a shade darker than normal, which makes his features even more attractive and dangerous. Fuck, I don't think there's anything about this man that isn't attractive.

"Well, I made sure the bath is nice and hot so that should warm your sweet body right up." He winks at me stepping into his large tub, it looks like it could be the size of a small hot tub. It's filled with bubbles and smells like vanilla. My favorite scent.

"Mmm, it smells so nice in here," I tell him as he slowly lowers us into his tub. "Fuck this feels so good, this is the perfect temperature." I relax my back against his chest and snuggle into him closely.

"I bought more of it to have here just for you, you always smell like vanilla to me, so when I went to the store yesterday, I walked by the warm vanilla sugar and bought more of it just for you," he says rubbing his hands up and down my arms from my shoulders to my elbows. Making me even more tired than I already was.

"Wow, that's so sweet babe." I turn to him slightly and kiss his cheek. "Thank you, so you knew you were going to be bathing with me again?" I giggle at him.

"Nope, I was hoping I'd be bathing with you, but either way I knew you'd need a bath to relax your sore muscles again afterwards, so I wanted you to have something here for you."

I turn around to face him and straddle his lap, feeling his rock-hard cock resting against my entrance, just waiting to be inside me. "Well Mister, what you were hoping for came true, you get to bathe with me and." I pause repositioning myself to where the tip of his cock is right at my entrance, all I'd have to do is slide down and he'd be fully inside me.

"And what? God you're driving my cock crazy, Sugar," he says in a husky tone, clearly turned on.

"And you get to fuck me in the bath too." I smile as I lower myself down onto his hard cock, letting him fill my already wet, throbbing pussy up all the way, not giving myself time to adjust to his thick, long length and Jacob's ladder. The piercings always intensifying the way it feels when he first slides into my pussy, goose-bumps spread across my entire body, a chill spreads up my spine, and I love it. We've only had sex a few times and I've never had sex feel this good or become this addicting to where I want it this much.

"Fuccck, Emerald." He lets out a groan as I slowly lift myself before pushing him back in all the way, not moving fast because I want to tease him, and torture him with how good it feels, because fuck even though we just had sex, it feels too fucking good. When he's all the way in I grind my body into him putting him as deep as he can go, and it feels fucking amazing. I rotate my body moving my hips in circles as I grind, feeling the pressure on my clit. He throws his head back, letting out a growl. Adam's apple bobbing up and down as he slowly swallows. He grips my hips hard, his fingers digging into me in the best way possible.

"Oh Goddd, fuck." Is all I can manage to say, I love the way he grips onto me, making me feel so small and fragile in his large hands as they dig into my biggest insecurities. To think that the parts of my body that I hate the most, jiggly stomach with stretch marks, and curvy hips, are his favorite.

It makes me feel sexy like he can't get enough of me as he rubs his hands up and down my body, his thumbs brushing over those stretch marks that make me feel like I've failed my body. His fingers running along my hips holding onto those parts of me like he needs them to survive. His eyes filled with lust as he eats me up with his looks. He stares into my eyes before they move down to my tits and his hands slowly travel up to them as I ride his cock like my life depends on it. "Don't you stop Sugar, you keep riding my cock, my sexy fucking slut."

"Ahh god." I love the way he talks to me; it makes me...it instantly makes my pussy fucking throb, making it wetter. Most girls would be offended by being called a slut, not me. It turns me on and makes me feel even sexier than his hands moving up and down on my body. I've never had a man make me feel so alive, so wanted and confident while being intimate like he does, and I love it.

He leans forward sucking my nipple into his mouth and I throw my head back letting out a loud moan. He's rough but gentle at the same time driving me crazy. Winding my body up even more. I feel like one wrong move, and I'll explode before I'm ready to. I'm not ready for all this pleasure to end, I'd be happy if it never stopped. I'd love to feel this way with him, forever.

I look back down, staring into his eyes while rotating my hips and grinding into him. Watching the fire grow stronger in his eyes. He reaches up and wraps his hand around my throat cutting the air off, and I instantly want to panic, but stop as the pleasure intensifies. Making my pussy throb and grip his hard cock even tighter. His piercings glide along my insides making my eyes flutter and roll into the back of my head.

"Good girl, you're riding my cock so. Fucking. Well," he growls between thrusts. "Grip my cock with that tight wet pussy of yours." He brings his other hand up and smacks my tits. I try to moan but nothing comes out from the grip on my throat. My eyes start to water, and tears start to fall down my cheeks as he stares up at me. He leans forward and licks one tear up off my right cheek before moving to the left and doing the same. And god I never thought someone licking my tears would turn me on.

"You look so beautiful with those tear-filled eyes. I love it when you cry for me, Sugar," he practically growls. "I can tell your body is getting close baby, your legs are starting to shake, now I know if I take my thumb and start massaging that clit of yours it'll take you right. Over. The. Edge," he says the words slowly while I nod my head in agreement, he knows my body so well already and I love that he pays attention to these things. "But you're not allowed to come until I say you can." And my eyes go wide because he's right. I'm about to explode and I don't think I'll be able to hold it back. "Because if you come without my permission I'll punish you even more." He winks at me before leaning in and licking another tear off my left cheek.

God he's so fucking sexy, I feel like any other woman would think he's fucked up in the head, but everything he's doing and saying is just turning me on even more than I was already turned on and now my body is wound up even tighter than it was. I feel like a wind-up toy that you keep spinning to wind up even though you know it's already ready to be played but you still keep winding it up to see how far it'll go before it can't take it and it either starts playing or it breaks. That's how I feel like I can't take it anymore and I'm about to lose it and come or my bodies going to break from holding back for so long.

"Bbb…bu…but," I barely get out in a raspy whisper from him blocking my air, which I feel like I'm going to pass out soon if he doesn't let me breathe. I feel like he's been holding my neck forever, but I don't even think it's been a minute.

"Ah ah ah, Sugar, no buts." He reaches down and starts massaging my clit with his right thumb and fuck I'm about to come I don't think I can stop it.

I start shaking my head not letting him know to stop but he smirks at me. "Don't do it, Sugar, I know it's right there baby." He licks his bottom lip. "Don't." He thrusts up into me. "Let." He thrusts harder. "It." Thrust. "Happen." He thrusts again, winding me up more.

"I'm almost there, Sugar, keep riding my cock baby, don't stop," he groans out in the sexiest voice ever. It's raspy and sounds like he's being tortured just as much as I am. He leans forward and licks my bottom lip before biting it and he continues to thrust inside me, nice and rough just the way I like it. My heart is racing, it feels like it could explode out of my chest from how fast it's racing. I don't know if it's from my orgasm, from how intense the sex is or from him holding onto my throat and blocking my air. I'm going to go with all three of those. The tension keeps building in my core and I'm about to break, I guess I'll have to take his punishment, and just when I don't think I can hold it anymore....

"Fucckk. I'm about to come," he says, thrusting in again. "Now come with me, Sugar," he growls, thrusting deep inside me as he comes inside my pussy. His cock throbbing inside me as the fiercest orgasm soars through my body. He lets go of my throat as I gasp for air, choking and coughing, as every feeling in my body is intensified. His piercings keep sending severe goosebumps through me as my pussy grips his cock, his pulsing inside me makes me never want this ride of pleasure to end. The throbbing in my clit is so extreme, I could cry from how good it feels, as his thumb keeps rubbing circles over it. This is the most intense ride of pleasure I've ever been on. The tears keep falling down my face as I try to catch my breath. He removes his thumb from my clit, as he wraps his arms around my waist to hold me up as my orgasm finally comes to an end. I'm panting, barely able to catch my breath as I move forward and lay my head against his chest, to try and calm my body down. My eyes growing heavy as it's hard to keep them open from how much energy that took from my body.

"Shit, That. Was. Amazing," I say between breaths, the tears keep falling as I cry more from how intense the overload of pleasure in my body was. I feel like an idiot. I've never cried during sex, but the pleasure was so much for my body to handle at once, especially still not recovering the last orgasms he gave me. I feel so weak and drained but in the best ways, I've never experienced anything like this ever and I'm not upset about it in the slightest. I think I found my perfect match.

"Yes, Sugar. Yes, it was fucking amazing and I'm so glad you've enjoyed everything I've done with you so far." He grabs me a little tighter. Hugging me as he kisses the top of my head.

"God yes, I've loved it all. I wouldn't complain if you did any of it again," I laugh, while still panting, slowly getting caught up on breathing.

"That's it," he chuckles, his body shaking slightly against mine from it.

"What's it?" I'm very confused, not sure where he's going with this.

"We're going to have to get married, I'm never letting you go. I don't ever want to fuck anyone else ever again." He lets out a content sigh, while snuggling his head into the side of my neck.

"Oh gee, I'm so glad your marriage proposal is going to be based on our sex and not anything else...typical man." I shake my head, laughing out a snort as I look up at him.

"Well, no, it's not just based on sex, Emerald. I fell hard and I fell quickly. I definitely believe in soulmates and love at first sight. And for me you're it." He grips my chin lightly bringing me in for a kiss. "I mean I'm not asking you to marry me right this second, but I can promise you...fuck it, I can pinky promise you." He reaches his pinky out to mine and grips it while shaking it. "That I will never let you go, I will be marrying you one day."

"God, I love you so much. I'm so glad that I'm not the only crazy one who fell hard and fast." I shake his pinky back, gripping it tightly with mine.

16

EMERALD

I'VE ALWAYS BEEN THE TYPE OF GIRL WHO BELIEVED IN LOVE at first sight and the cheesy movie romances, but never thought I'd actually get to experience something like that personally, but the first time I laid eyes on Creedence I was drawn to him, just something about him that spoke to me. And that was before I even met him in person and even talked to him. When I first met him, it was a quick hi and bye type of thing. But the second time when Carsten came to my house to talk to me about Winter, when he introduced himself again. He kissed my hand, and I blushed instantly. I truly only believed that men kissed women's hands a long, long time ago, or only in movies, so when it happened, I couldn't control the way it made me feel, like a girl with her first crush. But with the butterflies that swarmed inside me, I knew he was the one

He gets out of the bath before me letting me relax a little more while he dries off, getting dressed in a pair of black boxer-briefs and a pair of gray sweatpants, leaving nothing to the imagination when I look at his cock, that you can clearly see the outline of through the pants. He doesn't bother putting a shirt on, so when he's done getting dressed, he comes over and helps me slowly get out of the tub, setting a towel down on the stairs that surround his tub, for me to sit on. He walks to the counter and grabs two other towels, wrapping one around my shivering body, then he takes the other one and starts drying off my legs before working his way up to the rest of my body. I've never had someone take the time or care to dry me off, it's the cutest and sexiest thing ever. Watching this strong man who looks like your typical bad boy, with sexy tattoos that cover his muscular arms perfectly, taking the time to dry me off. His large hands make everything about me look tiny, the way he gently moves my body as he slides the towel up and down, making sure he doesn't miss a spot. He kneels down before he helps me stand, his face right in front of my pussy. He's not even thinking anything naughty for once and my mind instantly goes to bad things. If I could stay in a room with him for a day and not have to leave, I'm sure we'd have sex the whole time.

He reaches up, drying my stomach off before placing the towel around my back and moving the towel back and forth to get my lower back and ass.

"I never thought I'd be turned on by drying someone off, but damn, Sugar, this is doing it for me," he says in a gravelly voice.

I let out a soft moan, because the way he says it makes my pussy throb. "I was thinking the same thing, I've never had someone dry me off before and I never imagined it would be this sexy," I say in a breathless whisper, trying to calm myself down before we end up going another round. He stands up wrapping the towel around and over my shoulders before he steps out of his bathroom and walks into his bedroom. He comes back with one of his black T-shirts and a pair of basketball shorts, which I'm sure will both be extremely large on me. But I'm thankful for the warm clothes.

He gently places the T-shirt over my head and just as I guessed it's huge. The sleeves stopping halfway down my arm, past my elbows. His large shorts I have to roll up a few times because even using the drawstrings isn't enough to keep them up on my waist, even with my curvy hips and bubble ass. I look down and giggle a little at how funny I look, but I love it. I look up and see a big smile on his face. "You look so sexy right now wearing my clothes, Emerald." He starts slowly pulling me in before leaning down to place a gentle kiss to my lips. I wrap my arms around his neck as he wraps his around my waist, there's just something about his big strong hands on my body that I love. We stand there for a few minutes as he leaves gentle kisses on my lips and I feel like time stands still, every time we kiss, I feel like I'm the only thing that's ever mattered to him.

"Wanna go sit out on the back patio?" he asks slowly, pulling his lips away from my mouth, as he reaches a hand up and gently strokes my cheek with his knuckles.

"Sounds good to me." I hold out my hand for his and he takes mine, giving it two gentle squeezes before we start walking out his bedroom door.

We head out through his garage and Creedence walks right by his motorcycle without even giving it a glance. I don't want to push him, but I feel like I need to do something to motivate him to ride again, for his brother and for himself. Or to at least see if he still loves riding. I stop for a minute and look at his bike, as I slowly walk over to it and run my fingers down the black seat up to the handles. I've never been on a motorcycle before, but I've always wanted to go on one. But this has nothing to do with me wanting to go on one and everything to do with me wanting him to find his love for riding again for himself and to feel close to his brother. I've heard that sometimes doing something that you shared with a loved one who has passed helps you feel closer to them, and I know they enjoyed riding together. I stop my thoughts smiling for a second as I hear Creed's footsteps come back into the garage.

"Hey, Sugar, everything okay?" he asks slowly, walking over to me with a look on his face like he's seen a ghost.

"Yeah, just thinking about how I've never been on one before. Your bike sure is pretty and it just caught my eye, sorry for touching it and bringing you back over to it," I say, tucking my idea away in my mind, with a frown on my face. Hoping he's not mad at me for being by his bike. But I can't help it, it's so pretty, I've never seen a bike like this before, it's completely blacked out, nothing about it has color except for black. Dark black. "What kind of bike is this, a Harley?" I guess hoping it comes off sexy instead of biting me in the ass and being the wrong bike.

"It's okay, Emerald, you can be by it. Sometimes it just...makes all the memories rush back at once so it catches me off guard is all but I'm okay." He walks over to me wrapping his arms around my waist from behind as he rests his head on my shoulder. I place my head back against his chest and turn my head up to the left to look up at him.

"You don't have to hide your feelings from me, please don't let me stop you from feeling things." I give a half smile looking up at him.

"I appreciate that. I usually do try to tuck them aside when I'm around people so it's nice to know I can really be myself around you and not feel embarrassed." He lets out a sigh while staring down at his bike. "And also, yes it's a Harley Davidson Chopper." He winks at me like he knew I was just guessing but he was a little impressed by it.

"Creed, you have nothing to be embarrassed of and I'm sure your friends would understand too. You got yourself a great group of friends, I know damn well they'd never do or say anything to make you feel embarrassed or ashamed for having feelings. You can express and be yourself around them." I pause for a minute thinking before talking again. "I hope this doesn't come out wrong when I say this, but I get the feeling you haven't given yourself the time to fully grieve. If you're constantly tucking your feelings aside, which is totally okay, I'm not saying you can't ever do that. But I'm just letting you know I'm here and feel free to get it out, let yourself be free of the guilt and what if's and the it should have been me and start living your life how your brother would want you to live it for you and for him." I tighten my hold on his arms that are still wrapped around me and snuggle my face into his as we stand there. He doesn't say anything, but I can feel the sadness radiating from his body and I know he's allowing himself to feel whatever he needs too in this moment.

He lets go of me and goes around to the front of the garage pressing the button to open the big door, I stand there watching it slowly lift up. He then goes over and grabs a key off a shelf and starts walking towards his bike. He places his left hand on the left handlebar and picks up his right leg, lifting it over the side of the bike to where he's now standing and straddling his bike. Shit does he look fucking hot. He straightens it out and puts the key in the ignition, he hesitates for a second before his shaky hands slowly turn it, taking a deep breath he brings the bike to life, revving it. I jump a little not used to the loud sound and smile as he stands there with tears in his eyes and a slight smirk on his face. You can tell he's still afraid to smile and be happy, but he is happy at the same time if that makes sense. He stands there straddling his bike, tears stream down his face as he revs it. You can tell it makes him feel guilty, but it almost looks like a weight was somewhat lifted off him. Like the more he's near his bike a little more of the guilt is taken away. I hope to help him replace the guilt with good memories. I never knew his brother, but I'm sure he wouldn't want him to spend the rest of his life living in grief and guilt. He will always grieve the loss of his brother, but he doesn't need to feel guilty for being alive while doing it.

Ten minutes later he turns off the engine with an actual smile on his face, it's a sad smile but he's smiling. I stood here in silence allowing him to do what he needed, you could tell he was lost in memories, but I didn't want to bother him, so I stood here in case he needed me. He lets out a breath that sounded like he was holding the whole time and brings his hands up to his face and wipes his tear-streaked cheeks off. He takes one hand and wipes at his nose a little before getting off his bike and placing his key back on the shelf. When he's done, he walks over to me and slowly wraps his arms around me, holding me close to him while my head rests against his chest. I can hear his heart racing and feel it pulsing against my cheek. It feels like his heart might explode out of his chest so I squeeze him back tighter hoping to calm his racing heart. He pulls away slightly, looking down at me.

"Thank you." His smile is a little happier this time as he talks.

"You don't have to thank me, I'm just happy I could be here for you." I lean in and slowly kiss his shirtless chest.

"I love you, Sugar." He leans down and kisses me, swiping his tongue against my lips as I open to allow his tongue to meet mine. He sucks my bottom lip in, and I let out a slight moan without even meaning to, not even able to control the way my body reacts to him.

I pull away before I get too carried away and we end up fucking in the garage.

"I love you, Creedence, so much." I hug him again. I can still hear his heart as my ear rests against his chest. It's not racing as fast as it was but it's still a little stronger than it normally is.

"Let's head out back. I think I might need another drink." He might laugh like he's joking but I wouldn't blame him for needing a drink after that moment he just experienced.

"Hey man what's up?" Carsten says to Creed as he stands up and gives him a slight hug before doing their little handshake that they've been doing forever. If I'm not mistaken, I think Creedence said they've been doing that handshake since they made it up in middle school together. I think it's cute, but I won't tell two men that their handshake is cute, I don't want to ruin it for them. Although I don't think they'd care, they'd probably laugh and agree with me while still doing it.

"Nothing much man, just came out here to drink and get some fresh air," Creedence says with a slight chuckle.

"Ahh fresh air huh must have been "busy" in there all this time," Carsten laughs, making air quotes around the word busy as he says it.

"Something like that, what did you say that one time with Winter, you were gonna be busy talking about your feelings and stuff." He laughs at him shaking his head.

"Ohh yeah we were very busy that day, we had a lot of feelings to discuss." Carsten takes a couple sips of his beer with a big cheesy grin on his face. I'm sure he's grinning at the memories of him and my best friend fucking like crazy. Yeah, Winter and I tell each other everything including stuff about our sex lives. Except for everything Creedence and I just did. That will be my little secret. I would never tell Winter about the things I love him doing to me. That I have to keep to myself.

"Do I even want to know what this "talking about our feelings" and stuff is about?" I ask laughing, having an idea but curious as to what they'll say.

"Yeah, Carst here brought Winter over to fuck and said they were gonna go talk about their feelings like we were fucking idiots and didn't know what they were going to do." He laughs while Carsten throws a stick from the bush at Creedence.

"Hey man, that was secret information." Carsten shakes his head at Creedence. You can tell he's not really mad about it but they just like fucking around with each other.

"Well, I'll forget I even heard anything about your "talking about your feelings and stuff" conversation." I snort a little while laughing, making the guys look at me and us start to laugh some more.

Creedence walks over and sits on one of the bar stools and pats his leg for me to sit on. I love that even though there's a stool next to him he still wants me on his lap. It's like no matter how close I am to him it's not close enough and I love it.

"Thank you, Em, I appreciate that. I'm sure Winter would appreciate you not being a blabbermouth like Creedence over here too." He laughs, obviously joking but pretending to be hurt by Creedence's actions.

"Blabbermouth?" Creedence asks him as he grabs a beer from their mini fridge behind their bar.

"Are we five here bro? Who the fuck says blabbermouth these days, I felt like you were telling on me."

"Whatever man, snitches get stitches, remember that bro."

Carsten laughs as he stands up and grabs a bottle of tequila from behind the counter and three shot glasses.

"Hahah whatever the fuck you say man, whatever the fuck you say. Fuckin weirdo." Creedence is cracking up and I love this relationship they share.

"Let's do some shots guys." Carsten comes back down to sit next to him again lining up the shot glasses pouring tequila in each of them. Making my face naturally turn up in disgust because I fucking hate tequila. But I'm still gonna do it anyway.

"So, I heard uhh that you uhh..." He pauses, treading carefully not sure what to say but wanting to say something. "I heard you started her up in there." Creedence calls his motorcycle a *her,* so I think he knows what he's doing saying her instead of actually saying what he's talking about.

"Yeah man umm..." Creed stops, clearing his throat for a second before he continues. You can tell he's having a hard time talking about it, especially because we didn't know anyone else was outside when he started it up. We actually thought we were home alone. "Emerald is kinda trying to help me with all of it and stuff." He clears his throat before changing the subject.

"So, where's Winter?" And that's all we needed to see he didn't want to continue the conversation. Which is understandable, he's finally starting to open up more about the whole situation, so I think we both understand not to pry, especially Carsten who has been around it longer than I have.

"She's finishing her shift up at Lisa's Diner and then we're hanging out, not sure what we're doing yet though," Carsten says looking away, you can tell he feels bad for bringing up the motorcycle.

"We should all hang out together, I'll text Winter to see if she's up for it, if that's cool with you guys?" I ask, trying to lighten the mood before things become more awkward.

"Yeah, that's fine with me, I'm sure she'd like that a lot actually."

Carsten smiles. I love that every time he talks about Winter it brings a big smile to his face.

"I'm cool with that too." Creedence chugs down the rest of his beer before reaching for his other one he placed on the counter. Probably trying to distract his mind and calm his nerves. Sometimes dealing with grief that you've been trying to ignore can take a lot out of you and be exhausting.

I take a sip of my cherry vodka and Sprite and text Winter.

Emerald
hey bitch

Winter
sup hoe, miss your face

Emerald
Miss your face too, I'm with the guys, do you and Carsten wanna hang out when you're done working?

Winter
I'm down with that, what did the guys say?

Emerald
They're cool with it... I told them I'd ask you

Winter
yeah lets do it what do you guys want to do?

"She wants to know what we want to do?" I look back to the guys, accidentally interrupting them mid conversation.

"Well, Winter loves to dance," Carsten says sarcastically. "We can always head to Black Velvet and eat and have some drinks." His shoulders shake as he laughs at what he just said. We all know how much Winter dislikes dancing but still does it to make her friends and Carsten happy. I think she secretly likes it and just doesn't want to admit it though. I laugh to myself at that one because who am I kidding even I know that isn't true.

"That's fine with me, what about you, Creed?" I ask him, snapping him out of his thoughts. He seems spaced out since he sat on his motorcycle. I really hope me bringing it up and standing by it didn't upset him and he's just trying to act like he's not bothered to not upset me? I know he wants us to be open and honest so I think he'd tell me if he was, at least I would hope he'd tell me.

"What'd you guys say? Sorry, I was zoned out." He blinks a couple times and shakes his head quickly.

"Do you wanna go to Black Velvet to eat, drink, and dance?" I give a big smile, "Please, you know I love dancing?" I ask giving him a pouty face knowing he's not a fan of dancing, but he'll dance with me. And he has a weak spot for my pouty face.

"Anything for you, Sugar." He winks at me. "I love watching you dance; god is it sexy. So, I'm down." He rubs my shoulders a little before sliding his arms around my waist stirring the butterflies in my stomach.

"Awesome, let me see what Winter says." I open my phone back up to respond to her text.

> **Emerald**
> Black velvet?

I send it to her and see a typing response then it stops before she starts typing again.

> **Emerald**
> food, drinks and dancing please bitch you know
> you wanna shake your ass with me? Lol

> **Winter**
> was literally just typing. FINEEEE. Of course we
> can I miss shaking my ass with you lol

> **Emerald**
> fucking awesome!! I'm excited!

Winter
Me too can't wait to kiss your face. Literally I'm
going to give you a big ole kiss on the cheek, we
are living at the moment together and never see
each other I miss you skank

> **Emerald**
> good I'll kiss your cheek back hoe, I miss you too

Winter
yay! See you when I get home... we dressin like
hoes tonight betch

> **Emerald**
> HELL YEAH!! Hoes it is... the men will love it

Winter
yeah probably too much hahaha

> **Emerald**
> my thoughts exactly lol

Winter
see you lover

> **Emerald**
> see you lover face

"She said she's down. Yes!! I'm so excited, I love dancing," I say standing up looking at the guys who look not so excited about dancing. Oh well, they'll love it when we start grinding up on each other and dancing like hoes together.

"I'm not a fan of dancing but I'd let you grind up on me any day, Sugar." Creedence winks at me and I can feel my face heating up from blushing.

"Am I gonna have to walk away from the two of you so you guys can talk about important things?" Carsten laughs as Creedence throws his head back laughing. I shake my head holding back the giggle myself as a smile takes over my face. It's hard not to laugh about that even if I wasn't there.

"Yeah man, we gotta talk about our feelings and stuff. No jack-ass, you think I'm gonna fuck her outside where people can see?" He laughs again pulling me closer to him. "This right here." He rubs his hands up and down my sides like he's showing me off. "This is all mine. No one else can see any of this except for me, well Emerald of course." He kisses my neck gently. For some reason that makes my thighs tighten together turning me on just thinking about his hard cock being inside me. Fuck he's so addicting I don't think I'll ever get tired of having sex with this sexy man sitting here looking over at his friend with the sexiest smile on his face while he sips on his beer.

"Hey, sometimes you get caught up in the moment, I know there's been a few times where Winter and I have almost fucked outside." He wiggles his eyebrows with a funny look on his face and it's hard not to laugh again. I love all these people and this friend group I was sort of dragged into.

"Hey now, I'm sure Winter would want to be present for this conversation." I shove Carsten in a playful way.

"Ehh she wouldn't mind she loves you guys, plus you know Winter she'd probably be the first to go into details then pull me away for a quickie." He smirks and lets out a slight laugh. "My little Snowflake isn't shy like she used to be." He gets a look on his face like he's thinking of all the times she hasn't been innocent with him, and he smiles. "She's definitely not shy anymore. That's for sure." Then he drinks his beer.

"Gosh yes, she has no shame in sharing her business and I love that the most about her. I'm so glad you two got together, you've brought out the best version of my best friend and saved her in more ways than one." I smile over at him while bringing my straw to my lips taking a drink of my cherry vodka and Sprite.

"I can't take all the credit; she definitely saved me from continuing to live a life of doing stupid shit. I love my Snowflake more than my life, that's for sure." He stares off smiling, you can tell he's caught up in thoughts of her. Winter and Carsten have been to hell and back in their relationship. But have come out so much stronger as a couple and a family.

"What time are we going tonight?" Creed asks. "Sorry, not trying to change the subject or anything, I just figured we should get a game plan, do you guys wanna go eat first or order some pizza before we head out? Or just get food there?" He takes another chug of his beer before placing it down and lightly squeezes my love handles before pushing me down into his hard cock a little. I look over at Carsten eyes wide with somewhat embarrassment because he just did that around his friend. But Carsten is lost in his phone, probably texting Winter. Thank god. So, I get Creedence back in his own game by slowly rotating myself like I'm adjusting the way I'm sitting but grind myself down into him making him tighten his hold even more.

"I'm fine with pizza, the only good places to eat around here really is Lisa's Diner or Black Velvet. The other bars are shit and do we really want to drive a half hour or so for food?" I let out a breath. "And I know I don't want to go there on my day off and I'm sure Winter doesn't want to go back up there and deal with that bitch, Stacy." I laugh just thinking about how much we both despise her, especially Winter after she tried taking Carsten from her during their brief break up.

"Yeah, I don't feel like dealing with Stacy either, let's get some pizza then we'll head out." Carsten grabs his and Creedence's empty beer bottles, throwing them in the recycling bin.

"Winter should be home within a half hour actually then we can discuss pizza while the girls get ready...cause we both know they'll need some time to get ready." He laughs looking over at Creedence.

"Hey, nothing wrong with us taking our time to look good for you guys... Dick." I laugh shoving him as he pulls me back into his body even though I just stood up for the first time since we've been out here. Another example of what I mean by he loves me being close enough to touch me.

"I never said there was anything wrong with it, I think it's cute that you like to take your time to look good. Although you don't need to because you look sexy just wearing my clothes." Creedence wiggles his eyebrows up and down at me while slightly pushing me down into his hard cock again and it's so hard for me to not let out a moan because the angle I'm sitting his cock lines up perfectly with my pussy. Damn I swear this man is always ready to fuck and I love it. I never thought I'd find myself a man who loved to fuck as much as I do, especially with all the shit he's into. It's like he was made for me. I've been wanting to try all of that for so long and never found a man willing to. Until Creedence.

About an hour later after eating and getting ready for the night I think it's finally time to head out.

"Ready to head next door to show the boys our hoe outfits?" Winter asks as she checks her outfit in the mirror one last time. Before glancing down at her phone for the millionth time.

She always gets extra nervous with weekends away from the twins. I don't blame her, honestly, I don't know how she does it. But she's an amazing mom. Her and Carsten do everything for those little ones.

"It's okay Winter," I tell her. "The twins are going to be okay. Let's have a fun night out, you guys need it babe." I give her a quick hug. "You guys deserve it. Your littles will be okay."

"Girl, it's just so hard. I'm so thankful for a little break but damn I miss them so much." She siffles a little like she's about to start crying and my eyes widen.

"Winter you better not cry. You'll mess up your makeup." I chuckle smacking her ass as I walk over to my nightstand to grab my phone from the charger.

"Hey, that was my ass. Bitch." She tries to smack mine back and misses. "And thanks girl, I appreciate you always making me feel better about my babies." She smiles at me while waving her hands in front of her eyes like she's trying to dry the tears before they fall.

"Let's go show the boys our outfits." She checks herself out one last time before turning towards me.

"Hell yeah! I can't wait to see the look on their faces." I decided to wear a strapless tight fitted black dress, it cuts down into a V cut right between my breasts showing off how great and full they look, something I know Creedence will love. With my black low heel knee boots. My dress stops right below my ass, just enough to where I can bend down without showing it off but enough to tease him all night. God I can't wait to feel his hands on me in this dress, he makes me feel so fucking sexy, I've never had a man make me feel so wanted all the time, I love it, and I hope he can't keep his hands off me tonight.

"Well then let's go bitch," Winter says, standing there in her tight hot pink skirt with a black crop top and her black low heel knee boots that match mine, we bought them together. We buy a lot of clothes that match. Always have purposely and accidentally also another reason why I swear she's my female soul mate.

"Let's go hoe, let's go make their jaws drop." I wink at her as we start heading down the stairs and out the front door.

17
CREEDENCE

Winter texted that they were on their way, so we headed outside to wait for them. Not that they're far, I just can't fucking wait to see how beautiful she's going to look tonight. I sit on the front steps next to Carsten just bullshitting about work and the bullshit Daisy tried to pull.

"When's her next appointment?" He shakes his head, shoulders rising and falling with each laugh. "God her and Brynn are just fucked up bitches."

"Yeah dude, they're fucking crazy, should've learned my lesson from you." I laugh a little while he jokingly glares at me. "But no, she doesn't have another one, thank god, I made sure I finished her up all in one sitting. It wasn't huge anyway, so it was easy to do," I sigh, glad I'm done with her and her bullshit. I would've cut things off either way because she was too psycho for me.

"That's fucking good, at least you don't have to tattoo her anymore." And before he can finish what he's saying I cut him off.

"Well fuck dude, your woman looks hot," I say to him because he's looking over at me, all I can see is Winter right now.

"Holy fuck." He stands up quickly, adjusting his clothes before walking over to her. It's true Winter is a very attractive girl. Even when she's not dressed up, he got lucky, scoring himself a hot woman to be his future wife. Sometimes I forget they are engaged.

"Holy fucking shit," I say and it's an automatic reaction to just adjust my instantly hard cock as I see Emerald walk out next to Winter who is walking into Carsten's arms to hug him.

"Fuck, Sugar," I say pulling her into me because I can't wait to get my hands on her in that sexy fucking barely there dress of hers. I pull her closer to me, wrapping my arms around her waist as I lean down. "My cock's already hard for you baby, you look good enough to eat, like always," I whisper to her and notice the way her body shivers from my touch.

"Mmm." She lets out the quietest moan that only I can hear. "Fuck, you look so good yourself," she whispers to me as she's pulling back to check me out. I put on my black button up and rolled up the sleeves. I left the shirt unbuttoned enough to show off my chest tattoos because I know she loves seeing them. Then I'm wearing medium blue ripped jeans. Nothing special to me. But for her it's enough to want to rip my clothes off.

"Well, looks like we're gonna have to stay home," she whispers to me. "I'd tell you my panties are wet from looking at you." She gets closer to me, stirring something inside me as she does. "But I'm not wearing any," she whispers before she stands up on her tiptoes and gently bites my ear making me let out a low growl.

"Hey, we're still over here, go get a room if you're gonna rip each other's clothes off before we go out." Carsten laughs as he drags Winter up the stairs and into the house.

"Looks like you're about to go do the same," I say to him as Winter giggles as she somewhat runs in behind him.

"You read my mind, but gotta order the food first, so you gotta calm down first." He laughs at me as Emerald and I walk in holding hands behind them.

"Well, Emerald and I have some important things to discuss, so you and Winter can order that food while we uhh…go talk about our feelings and shit." I pick Emerald up, throwing her over my shoulder and she laughs letting out a high-pitched shriek.

"What is it with you guys picking us up over your shoulder, better be careful you're about to show them both my whole ass," Emerald shrieks smacking my back with her hands.

"It's ok babe, I've seen you naked and drunk before, won't be a surprise here. But I'm good on Carsten seeing you." Winter laughs, covering Carsten's eyes before he sees more of Emerald than he's ready too.

"Good lookin out, Winter," I say to her as I rush by them in the kitchen and down the hall with a giggling Emerald over my shoulder.

Once we get into the room, I lock the door and then I set her down in front of me and immediately bring my mouth down to hers kissing her passionately. Groaning into her mouth as I swallow her moans. She opens up waiting for my tongue to swirl with hers.

"Fuck, Creed, you look so sexy I just want to lick you all over." She pulls away, biting down onto my neck and sucking my sensitive skin. She slowly licks her way down to my chest where my shirt is open, biting and sucking. Hopefully leaving marks along the way. I not only like leaving marks I love when a woman marks me and makes me hers. And I definitely want to be marked by Emerald.

"Suck harder, Sugar. I want people to know I'm yours just by looking at me," I tell her as she makes her way back up to my neck making my cock painfully hard. She sucks and bites down on my neck a little longer before she comes back up to my mouth sucking on my tongue and biting my bottom lip.

God she's fucking perfect. The whole time my hands never leave her body. I can't resist touching her. I take my time memorizing the feel of her and all her curves with my hands. Before stopping my hands on her delicious fucking hips squeezing them as I imagine grabbing onto them while she rides my hard cock. Mmm, I'd let her ride me all day if it meant I got to grip onto these mouthwatering hips of hers. I step towards her, and she can instantly feel my hard cock rub against her stomach, and she lets out a soft moan.

"Please, I need your cock." She's out of breath as she pulls away from me. A look of pure hunger in her eyes.

"Beg for it, my dirty slut. Tell me how bad you wanna feel my cock in that wet pussy of yours." I smack her ass and grip it making her let out a whimper.

"Please, Creedence," she moans as I lean down and start sucking on her neck. Playing with her tits in the process. I push her dress down and groan when I feel she's not wearing a bra.

"Fuck baby, no bra and no panties. Shit you just made my night." This woman is my weakness. I can't keep my hands off her. Her perky tits feel so soft as I rub them and pinch her nipples.

"Please what, Sugar. I said beg," I growl out, so turned on I'm about to just say fuck it and bend her over and fuck that wet cunt nice and rough. Which actually gives me an idea since we don't have a lot of time.

"Please, Creedence, fuck my pussy." Shit, she is the best at begging. I love how willing she is to beg for me. I'd beg for her if she let me. Fuck, I'll beg even without her asking. "Please, I need you." She begs and it's so fucking sexy. I undo my belt with one hand and quickly whip it out of my pants, folding it in half. I quickly turn her around still holding one tit in my hand pinching her nipple. I lean down and bite her neck before I finally let go. I remove my hand from her tit and push up her dress with my free hand. My cock twitching at the sight of her bare full ass. Then whip her ass with my belt. She lets out a yelp followed by the sexiest moan, and I do it one more time, this time across both of her ass cheeks leaving welts in the process and she groans.

"Fuck, Creed." Her head falls to the side, exposing the two hickies I just left before I whipped her with my belt.

"You like that, Sugar?" I whip her again with my belt before bending her over my bed. I take the belt and wrap it around her wrists as tight as it can go, making sure it'll leave marks for later while we're out, so she can get worked up just thinking about it as she stares down at them, because that's just how my little slut is, and I love that I helped bring this side out of her.

"Yes... Mhmm...god yes," she says between moans.

I kneel down on the ground behind her and unzip her boots, taking them off one by one and then I take her left foot, pulling it as far to the left as it'll go, watching her ass push up as I do it. Then I reach under my bed and grab a strap that's connected to the cuffs I keep tucked further away and cuff it around her ankle, securing it as tight as I can, making sure It'll leave a mark. She hisses in a breath as I do it, making me smile. I smile because I know my little slut is becoming addicted to the pain, she loves it. I slowly slide my hand up her leg until I get to her pussy and swipe my finger across her slit. Yep. I knew she'd be soaked.

"Damn, Sugar, look how soaking wet you are for me baby. I bet this tight little cunt of yours will be dripping by the time I'm done with your other leg." I come up and smack her ass again leaving a handprint right across the welts. Making her head fall back as she groans.

"Fuck, Creed," she says in a moan.

I grab her right leg and do the same thing with the cuff and listen to her let out another hiss followed by a quiet moan. She's completely bent over my bed, unable to move her tied up hands from behind her back or her cuffed feet, her legs spread as far as she can go. Her ass is pushed up in the best position making my hard cock twitch just looking at this beautiful sight in front of me. Her pussy and tight little hole are on full display for me to do as I please. Too bad I don't have more time.

"I knew you'd like that. God I can't wait to fuck this tight pussy of yours baby." I come down smacking her other ass cheek before rubbing it. I lean in afterwards and slowly stick my tongue out, sliding it across the welts I left on her ass cheeks listening to her breathing quicken as I do it.

"Mmm fuccckk," she moans out another tortured moan. I slide

my tongue along her ass until I reach her pussy. I tilt my head to the side as I take my hand and slide my fingers through her slit again before swiping my tongue along her dripping wet pussy and fuck right as I taste her, I realize I've been starving and goddamn does she taste amazing.

"Mmm, Sugar your pussy, goddamn I could feast on it all fucking day, you taste so fucking good." I pull away and take my finger slowly, swiping it up and down to get it wet before I slide it inside her and curve it up towards her G-spot and I start pumping in and out before I add a second one. Listening to her sexy moans that keep making my painfully hard cock even harder than it was. Making it throb against the stupid fucking fabric of my jeans that's keeping my fucking cock trapped.

I keep my fingers pumping as I reach out with my tongue, moving right to her clit. I want her to cum all over my face and my fingers. I want my beard covered in her arousal. That way we both have something to clean up when I'm done. I'm going to make her taste herself again so she can see how good she tastes every time I lick her.

"I think I'm gonna come soon," she moans out. I figured she would with how worked up she was, tying her up, spanking her, playing with her nipples while sucking on her neck. All of that helped slowly build her arousal, getting her closer to an orgasm before I even touched her. And now that I got my tongue on her favorite spot that makes her toes curl, I swirl and suck, pumping my two fingers in faster than before and her legs start shaking. She tries to pull them closer together from how sensitive she becomes from all the pleasure. But with the way she's tied up she's not going anywhere.

"Goddamn I can't wait to fuck your pussy." I take my free hand and slap her sore ass again. Making her moan out even louder. I pull away from her pussy for a minute, making her sigh.

"Please, I'm so close, make me come, Creedence," she moans, turning her head to the side and looks back to look at me.

"Don't you worry, Sugar, I'm going to be licking up all your juices as you come all over my face baby," I growl out, so turned on myself.

I get my thumb wet and twist my fingers before sliding my thumb inside her ass. I don't even work it in, she likes the pain.

"Ahh fuck," she groans. "God don't stop."

"I'm just getting started, Sugar." And I take my tongue and place it right back on her swollen clit going right back to her favorite spot. I pump my fingers in and out of her pussy and her ass, licking at her needy bud that I crave to have my mouth on. I bring up my other hand, smack... I hit her sore ass yet again.

"Fuck yes...please babe, please." I love listening to her beg me to let her come. I take my lips and place it around her clit before sucking on it again and that's all she needed. Her legs are trembling uncontrollably, her body shakes as she screams out her release. I keep sucking her swollen clit while pumping my fingers, groaning in the process. I'm so close to getting to fuck her, I can't wait.

18
CREEDENCE

She rides out the rest of her orgasm, her body slowly going limp before I remove my fingers. I rub my hand on her red ass trying to soothe some of the pain as I stand up.

She turns her head to the side and looks up at me again, smiling as she does. She looks tired now, but I'm not done with her yet, she still has a wet pussy that's begging to be fucked.

"Here you go, Sugar, I got a present for you," I say slowly, bringing my fingers to her. "Stick your tongue out baby, I want you to taste yourself, to see how good you always taste." My voice comes out rough and hoarse.

She sticks her tongue out right as I place my pointer finger right in front of her and she doesn't waste any time, she closes her lips around it and sucks it into her mouth swirling her tongue around it and pushing it to the back of her throat. I know exactly what she's doing, teasing me because she loves sucking my cock.

"I wish I could fuck that sweet mouth of yours right now, but that'll have to wait till later, Sugar. We don't have time for that right now."

"Already making plans for tonight I see?" she giggles. "Who said we'd be fucking again?" she asks in a seductive tone.

"Oh, you'll be begging for me to fuck this wet pussy of yours, especially after I cum in it and leave it dripping out of you all night," I say, slapping her pussy with my hand, then I take my fingers and swipe it up her slit one last time before I take them to my mouth. I make sure she's looking as I slowly clean them off one by one. "Fuck, Emerald. I can't get enough of your pussy, I've never tasted something as sweet as yours before," I groan out before sticking my other finger into my mouth and doing the same. "Mmm. Mmm. Mmm baby." I smirk. Giving her my best half smile that I know she loves.

"Fuck, Creed, just you talking like that makes my pussy throb. Fuck me please." She can barely get the words out from how out of breath she is. She's doing such a good job for doing so much today. I'm surprised she still has energy left after everything we've done.

"Mmm, still begging for me to fuck you my little slut?" I ask in a husky tone as I undo my jeans and pull them down along with my boxer briefs. I don't even bother taking them off because I know neither of us will last long and I'm sure Carsten and Winter are already waiting on us as it is.

I take my rock-hard cock and place it at her entrance, slowly rubbing it up and down, making sure to tease her as I rub it on her clit. The warmth of her pussy against my cock making it throb in the process and I can't wait to feel the rest of her warmth. I slide my cock in nice and slow enjoying the feel as her pussy swallows me up. I groan at the feel of her cunt tightly wrapped around my cock feeling the walls of her pussy tightening around me, enveloping my cock in her warmth. Fuck, I could stay inside her forever. I'm only halfway in before I stop myself. I take a deep breath trying to calm my body down, so I don't come right away. Fucking her is like fucking a virgin every time, her cunt is so tight, it's like a glove made perfectly for my cock and my cock only. I refuse to let anyone else fuck this pussy now. It belongs to me.

I smack her ass lightly before sliding in more and then I start pumping quicker. The feel of my piercings rubbing against her insides is enough to drive me crazy and make me come. But again, I have to stop myself so we both enjoy this.

"Fuck, Creed, your cock is amazing," she pants out, having trouble speaking with how hard I'm pounding into her now.

"Tell me, Sugar... Tell me who this pussy belongs to," I moan out in a husky growl, smacking her ass hard in the process. I love watching my handprints form across the welts that are still there from the belt, but slowly fading.

"You," she says breathlessly.

"Ah. Ah. Ah. Tell." Thrust. "Me." Thrust. "Who." Thrust. "This pussy belongs to." And I thrust in again between each word, hitting her insides roughly hoping to make her sore in the best way.

"You, Creedence. My pussy belongs to you," she moans again. "And only you babe." She's panting her orgasm getting close. "No one." Pants. "Else's pussy but yours," she groans right as I reach around in front of her and grip her throat.

"Good girl, Sugar. That's right, that pussy belongs to me," I tell her as I fold my body over hers. Gripping her left hip with my left hand while my right hand tightens around her throat, closing off her air completely. I look down watching her hands fist in the belt. You can tell she's trying not to panic as I pump in and out of her quickly. I grip hard because I know she's close, and I want this orgasm to be intense and feel amazing for her.

"Mmm baby, I love the way your pussy grips my cock and swallows it up. Just like that pretty little mouth of yours," I groan out and I can feel the vibrations of her moan through her throat where my hand sits as I cut off her air.

"Come all over my pussy baby," I tell her as I take my free hand and start playing with her nipples pinching and rubbing them. I lean back up, remove my hand from her tits and move her hair over one shoulder and come back down to suck on the side of her neck. I love sucking on her skin. I know I'm probably leaving more marks. I can't wait to see what she looks like when I'm done with her, my beautiful, unique canvas. Her beautiful body that I get to create new marks on every time I fuck her, and I love it.

"Fuck, Sugar I'm getting close." She nods her head the best she can. "Are you ready to come for me, Sugar?" And she nods again. "Good girl, Sugar, come for me, come all over my hard cock baby."

I release her throat as she gasps for air while moaning. Her pussy throbbing and squeezing my cock hard. I can feel the intensity of her orgasm as I thrust, spilling my cum all inside her.

"Fuck. Fuck. Fuck." She pants still gasping for air trying to catch her breath.

"You like that, baby?" I ask panting in the process.

"God yes," she gasps coughing a little in the process as her body goes limp on my bed. She lays there letting her body relax as the waves from the pleasure still move through her. I look down as I pull out of her, watching my cum slowly drip from her wet pussy.

"Fuck, I love you, Emerald. I'm never letting you go, Sugar."

"It's the sex isn't it, that's why you're in love with me huh?" she asks, laughing and I reach down and tickle her.

"I will sit here all night and tickle you if I have to until you take that back, young lady."

"Okay. Okay," she's squealing trying to get away from me, but she can't since I haven't untied her yet. "I take it back, I was joking," she's giggling trying to gasp for a breath in between since she still hasn't fully caught her breath from her orgasms or me choking her yet.

"Now I said I love you, Emerald." I laugh as I stop tickling her before she really has a hard time catching her breath.

"I love you, Creedence, so much you handsome, handsome man," she says breathlessly while smiling.

"I love you beautiful." I lean down and softly kiss her cheek before I come back up and undo the belt around her wrists. She starts slowly shaking her arms, trying to get the circulation to flow through them.

"My hands are numb," she giggles again. "God I love when you tie me up." She blows her hair out of her face.

"Great now I'm gonna go out with fucked up hair that says, 'she just got fucked'. I'm gonna have to fix it now." She lets out a deep breath.

"Sorry, I'll help you fix it since it's my fault, Sugar." I lean down to untie her feet, but I stop in the process.

"Mmm, baby. The way your ass is pushed up right now from the way you're leaning is making me ready for round two. But I wish it was me fucking that tight little ass of yours this time," I practically growl out just thinking about how tight it would be if her pussy is as tight as it is.

"Down Mister. We have Carsten and Winter waiting for us babe," she snorts. "Now can you please untie me? I have to pee." She blows her hair again that keeps falling in her face from the way she's leaning.

"Keep calling me Mister and we're taking a rain check," I tell her, for some reason there's something about the way she says the word Mister that turns me on. It's never done that before, but her cracked tone and the seductive way she says it makes my dick twitch with excitement and makes me ready to fuck.

"So sorry Mister now c'mon before I pee on your floor," she pouts as she says it and I can't say no to her pout. It's too damn cute.

"Hey, I'm always down to try new things if that's what you're trying to get at," I say jokingly, at least I hope I'm joking since I'm one fucked up individual.

"No way. I refuse to pee on you." She shakes her head with her face scrunched up in disgust.

"I know, I know I'm not sure how I'd feel about that anyways." I finish uncuffing her right leg and rub her ankle gently since I see they're red and somewhat raw from all the rubbing during sex and I smile at yet another masterpiece, god her and these marks are fucking beautiful. Too bad I won't be able to see them tonight with her boots. But she'll definitely be able to feel them as she's dancing. I stand there and smile thinking about that as she runs off to my bathroom not even bothering to pull her dress down. She's fucking adorable as her ass jiggles while her tiny body sprints off on her tip toes.

"Don't clean yourself off too much, I want my cum dripping out of you while we're out tonight as you're dancing, Emerald. That way you're reminded of how good I fucked you before we went out," I say as she walks back out of the bathroom. I look down at her as she's adjusting her red lace thong that she grabbed from her little pile of clothes she has folded on my dresser for when she sleeps over. She refused to take a drawer and said it was too soon for that. But not too soon to leave clothes? I laughed at her when she said that. She pulls her skin-tight black dress down those delicious curves that I'd love to suck and bite on right now. But that'll have to wait.

"I want that pussy soaked by the time we come home tonight baby. I have a fun night planned for you so you're gonna need it to be nice and wet for me, okay, Sugar?" I ask her in a husky tone getting turned on just thinking about fucking her again.

"Yes, I'm still wet from before, and now you're cum so I don't think I'll have any issues with that." She looks up smiling at me. "Plus, I'm sore from your belt and my legs being tied so I know every time I move it's going to make my pussy throb and make me wet just thinking about your nice hard cock fucking me... Mister." She pokes me in the chest with her tiny pointer finger as she bites her bottom lip. It slowly slides out from her teeth. Mmm, those plump lips are my favorite especially wrapped around my cock.

"Now, now my little slut." I lean down and kiss her on the lips gently and quickly before pulling away again. "I know what you're doing, don't think I won't bend you over and fuck that tight little cunt of yours again before we leave, Sugar," I say whispering into her ear as she lets out a moan.

Maybe we're both sex addicts. I always thought I had a problem with wanting sex too much, but now with her I'm just a horny fucking man all the damn time who's ready to fuck every time I look at this beautiful curvy woman. Her green and black hair gets me every time I see her next to those beautiful brown eyes of hers. And her snow-white pale skin, god she's to die for. Especially with all those tattoos that curve with her body perfectly, the one between her tits is my favorite. I'd love to lick it all the way down to her pussy and then back up just to tease her.

Damn I need to snap out of my thoughts otherwise we will never leave my room.

"You okay, Creed?" Emerald gives me a knowing look. "You need to stay out of that dirty, dirty head of yours you handsome, handsome man." She stands on her tiptoes giving me a quick kiss on my cheek.

"Yes, Sugar I do, I just don't think I'll ever get enough of you baby," I say leaning down to kiss her again before slapping her tasty looking ass one more time. "Let's go, Sugar, I'm sure they are tired of waiting on us."

"I'm sure they are." She laughs. "I'm coming though," she says as she grabs my hand and walks out behind me. "Fuck I never checked my hair," she whispers as we walk out of the hall to see Winter and Carsten eating pizza at the table.

"Your hair looks good, you look beautiful," I whisper to her as we walk over to the counter with a smile on our faces.

"Man, I thought we lost you guys in there. What'd you do tie her up or something?" Carsten jokes, but man was he spot on.

"Or something." Emerald laughs and shrugs her shoulders looking up at me with a big grin on her face and the look of love in her eyes.

"Calm your ass down, it's not my fault I take my time, I ain't no minute man like you bro."

"Oh shit," Winter laughs, almost spitting her drink out. "He's definitely not a minute man but that was a good one." She takes a bite of her pizza.

"Ya. Ya. Fucker. I make her feel good too. You know what, let's not talk about this or we're both gonna end up back in our rooms and we'll never leave." He laughs because it's true, we both are that obsessed and always horny.

"Yeah, and we only have the rest of this week before Carsten's mom comes back with the twins, she and her boyfriend love having them while we finish up the work on the house," Winter says, taking a sip of her drink. "So, I want to go out, I need a night out." She laughs.

"Yeah, I'm surprised you guys have been without the twins this long, I've loved having the twins with me while you've been staying back at my house," Emerald says as she puts two slices of pizza on her plate.

"Those babies are so fucking cute," I tell them. "It's a shame you can't bring them here to stay for a couple days." I was pretty bummed but with Carsten's work schedule it was easier for them to have the twins stay at Emerald's house with her and Winter until they're done. But now Carsten's mom has them for the week while the last-minute touch ups are being done and for them to finally move every-thing back in, it'll be easier to do without the twins.

"I'm sure gonna miss having you as a roommate, I think Axton's moving out with his girlfriend soon or just on his own he mentioned," I say to them, grabbing my own pizza. I've known Carsten since we were kids and we've lived together for quite some time, so it'll be weird not having him as a roommate, he's like a brother to me and I to him even though he has Chase as a brother. All three of us have been close.

"Yeah man it'll be weird but at least we only live two houses down from Emerald, we'll still get together and shit so don't get all sappy on me," Carsten says, slapping my back as he grabs two more pieces of pizza.

"Hey fuck off, dick face. I'm not getting emotional," I say, elbowing him in the stomach.

We spend the next half hour bullshitting and eating before we're finally ready to head out to Black Velvet.

"We'll see you guys there," Carsten says, shutting Winter's door for her as I shut Emerald's door for her too. He starts walking around to the driver side the same time I do, and we both shake our heads, we do a lot of similar things sometimes without even realizing it.

"Park in the back of the bar it's going to be crowded, except for employee parking so park there with me. It'll be fine," he tells me as he opens his door, again the same time I do.

"Alright man, see you guys in about ten," I tell him, getting in the driver side of my truck and shutting the door. I put the key in the ignition and start it up.

I look over at Emerald after I do, and she looks over and smiles at me. I could get used to this, and I'm sure I've said that before. But having this beautiful woman next to me is something I'd love to have every day. Maybe I'll ask her to move in if Axton moves out or maybe I'll see if she wants me to move in with her. I shake my head, getting out of my crazy thoughts. There's no way we're moving in with each other this soon. The idea sounds crazy because our relationship is so new, but I'd love to live with her.

"Ready to go, beautiful?" I ask, placing my right hand on her thigh as she places her hand over it and lacing her fingers through mine.

"I'm ready, you handsome, handsome man you." And she winks at me before blowing me a kiss with her right hand. I take my left hand and catch it, placing it over my heart like I did the last time, and it makes her blush. I love making her blush.

19

EMERALD

Creedence opens his truck door for me and holds my hand while I climb out, I hold my side with my left hand trying to stop my dress from riding up in the process.

"Don't be shy on me now, Sugar, I love seeing that pussy of yours." He winks at me making me blush, I don't know what it is with him that constantly makes me blush all the time. But I don't think I'll ever get tired of it.

"And you and I both know what'll happen if I do let you see it." I look up at him through my lashes now that I'm on the ground giving him a seductive smile.

"Keep smiling at me like that, with that sexy fucking seductive smile of yours and things are definitely gonna happen, Sugar." He pulls me in gripping my ass, his face coming down into my green hair as he breathes me in.

"Mmm, I just love the way you smell, Sugar, so sweet, and so delicious," he growls in my ear, making me shiver, as he rubs his nose against my neck. "Makes me think of your pussy and how good it tastes when I fuck it with my tongue." His voice a rough whisper.

"Fucck." I can't help but moan out after that. "You're bad." I swat his arm with my hand, and he squeezes my ass tighter pulling me into where I'm pressed up against his firm chest, feeling his rock-hard cock against my stomach.

"You feel that, what you do to me, Sugar. God you're like a fucking drug baby and I don't want this high to end. Mmm," he growls out his voice laced with hunger, before he bites my neck.

"Down Mister. You've definitely succeeded in wanting my panties to be soaked by the time we get home. I mean back to your place, sorry." Fuck, I blush at that slip up calling his place my home. I'm there so much I feel like I should just move in with him.

"Don't apologize, Sugar. It was cute. Now let's head inside before Carsten comes looking for us." He leans down and kisses me on the lips, and I open up to feel his tongue slide against mine. There's gotta be something wrong with me to be this into someone. But I can't help it, he's addicting. Just like he said he's like a drug that I can't get enough of and every time it feels like the highs coming to an end I crave more, I feel like I won't survive without him.

I take his hand, and he leads us into the back of Black Velvet, since Carsten, his brother and mom all own the bar we get to park out back and go through the employee entrance.

We walk through the hallway and run into Carsten and Winter leaving his office. Winter's hair looks a little messy and I'm sure they just had another quickie. I smile at them and Creedence beats me to it.

"Had to just squeeze one more in there huh?" He laughs, nudging Carsten's shoulder.

"Something like that," both Carsten and Winter end up saying at the same time and laugh.

"Let's go do some shots!" Winter yells in excitement and pulls my hand to follow her down the hall and around the bar where we stop to say a quick hi to Carsten's brother Chase before grabbing some stools.

Creed and Carsten went into Carsten's office when we ran off so we're not waiting on their slow asses. I'm ready to have some fun.

"Let's not wait for the guys," Winter says, reading my mind.

"Wanna do some blow job shots?" she asks as she wiggles her eyebrows up and down at me laughing.

"Hell yeah! You know I love doing those," I say, setting my small purse on the bar top.

"That guy over there is watching you Em, seems to be a thing when you come here," Winter says, nudging me and I try to take a quick glance without making it obvious just in case he comes this way. I'll know what he looks like and fuck I made the worst mistake ever and made eye contact with him. He smirks at me, nodding a little.

"Fuck, we made eye contact. I hope he doesn't think that it's an invitation." I sigh, putting my right hand to my forehead and resting it on the counter.

"Let him, it'll make Creed jealous. Then he'll take care of it." She smiles, nudging me with her shoulder a little as she does.

"This is true I'm not used to having someone else be here to tell off the creeps for me," I say as Chase walks up to the counter.

"What can I get you ladies?" he yells to us over the music.

"We want two blowjob shots, Chasey," Winter says, slapping her card at him.

"Coming right up and get your fucking card out of here you guys aren't paying," he says as he walks away to go make them.

"I sometimes forget that my future husband is part owner." She laughs, shaking her head as she puts her card back in her small purse.

"I feel like that would be something that would slip my mind too." And before I can finish what I was saying she cuts me off.

"Fuck that guys moving closer he moved over three stools now that those other girls left. He's two away from us now," Winter says, putting cash on the counter for a tip for Chase.

"Fuck, I hope they hurry up back there they get distracted too easily." I look down the hall for any sign of either Creed or Carsten.

"Tell me about it, they take forever," she says as Chase comes back over.

"Here you ladies are two blow jobs," he says with a cheesy smile on his face, typical man.

"Woo that's fucking hot," the creep says from two stools down and I whisper yell from the side of my mouth. "Pretend you didn't hear him." Thankfully the DJ was changing songs at the moment so it was a little quieter than normal to where she could hear me whisper yell.

"Ready to do it?" Winter slaps her hands on the counter before placing them behind her back.

"Let's do this, bitch." I laugh as I put my hands behind my back just like she does. I place my mouth around the shot glass and lift my head back in one quick motion. Hearing the guy from two stools over whistle and say something about something being sexy.

"God that was delicious, we'll have to do more when the guys come back," Winter says, licking her lips.

"I'm down for more, you know I love those." I shift in my seat to turn towards her a little more to where I can still see the creep out of the corner of my eye, but my back is facing him more.

"Yeah, drinking them and giving them," Winter says, throwing her head back laughing.

"Hey bitch, there's nothing wrong with loving to give blowjobs." Just saying it makes my thighs tighten and my pussy throb as I think about Creedence's pierced cock in my throat.

"Nope nothing wrong with..." Then she's cut off.

"I wouldn't mind a blowjob from you." And I finally look over to see the creep from two stools down standing way too close to me, his body pressed against my arm.

"Excuse me?" I ask a little annoyed because one, how fucking rude and two, who the fuck stands this close to someone they don't even know and says something like that to them.

"I said I wouldn't mind a blowjob from you." He smirks at me, I mean he's attractive, but I'm not interested, and I don't think I would be even if I wasn't with Creedence, he seems like a cocky asshole and that's definitely not my type of guy. Plus, he's just straight up creepy, too creepy to show interest in.

"First off, back the fuck up," I say scooting away from him. "And I have a boyfriend, so please, leave me alone," I say, turning my back to him, hoping it's over and he gets the hint.

"Sweetie, that's not going to work on me, I saw you run over here with your friend and no man." He wraps his arm around my waist pulling me too close to him. What is with my luck with creepy men who don't like to be told to back the fuck off?

"Get off of me." I try to pry his rough fingers off me as Winter turns and looks in shock.

"What the fuck?" she shrieks. "Get off of her, she has a boyfriend." She tries to help me get his hands off me but he's strong and very drunk. What the fuck is going on right now?

"Listen baby, I'm just trying to show you a good time," he says into my ear way too close for my comfort. And I shiver in disgust.

"She said get the fuck off of her." All of a sudden, I hear the familiar voice of my boyfriend behind me and I sigh in relief at him saving me again from yet another creepy man. Must be a thing for us I think to myself.

"Listen, all I'm trying to do is talk to the lady and she was rude and turned her back to me, she could've been nicer," he slurs, his words barely making sense. Now this makes sense as to why he's not taking no for an answer, I think he's just had way too much to drink or maybe he's drunk.

"I also told you I had a boyfriend, which that's who this is, now back the fuck off of me now," I yell, irritated that even with Creedence here he's still not stopping or listening.

"Listen if you don't back the fuck off, I have no problem making you back the fuck off my girlfriend and I'd rather not," Creed says, pushing the guy away from me, which causes the guy to get pissed and swing at Creedence without him seeing, hitting him right in the lip, splitting it open a little.

"Fuck you, asshole." And Creedence swings at him knocking the guy's head back as blood pours from his nose. "She said she has a boyfriend, which that's me and I shouldn't have to tell you to leave her the fuck alone more than once. But now that you swung at me, asshole." Creedence punches him and it hits him in the cheekbone splitting it open. "I get to kick your fucking ass." And he swings again, hitting his eye this time. The asshole loses his balance and falls backwards onto the ground. I think he might be knocked out or in shock but he's not saying anything.

"Fuck guys what happened?" Chase says running over from behind the bar.

"The fucker wouldn't leave Emerald alone and I had to take care of it after the dick hit me in the mouth," he yells to Chase as he shouts over the music.

"Alright man as long as it wasn't something stupid," he says, kicking the guy's leg to see if he wakes up.

"Hey, Tony," he yells to security that his mom hired last month after someone tried to rob them while she was working by herself.

"Yeah boss?" he says, coming over crossing his arms waiting for him to respond.

"Carry him out back, his dumb ass can wake up in the parking lot for all I care. We don't tolerate fighting here," Carsten says to him.

"Well damn, I was gonna say take him to the back room but that works too," Chase says laughing.

"Hell no, I don't fuck around especially when it comes to not taking no for an answer. I don't want him in here," Carsten says, shaking his head and walking over to Winter.

"Yes sir, I'll take him out back right away," Tony says as he picks the guy up over his shoulder and carries him behind the bar, down the hallway and out the back door.

"Thanks guys," Creed says to them as he turns around and wraps his arms around me, pulling me close to him.

"No problem, man, you okay Em?" Chase asks as he walks back around the bar to grab a beer for a customer.

"Yeah, are you okay?" Carsten gives me a concerned look.

"I'm okay guys, really he didn't do much besides wrap his arm around me." I look back between Creedence and Carsten.

"I think you did more to him than he did to me," I say laughing as I look over at Creedence.

"Well, I gotta protect you, Sugar, I told you I'll always protect what's mine, that's twice here that I got to kick some guys ass for you, baby and I'd do it again if it meant I got to protect you from someone hurting you," he says as he leans down, tipping my chin up with his fingers giving me a gentle kiss. Then he pulls away.

"I'm glad you're okay Emerald." He leans down resting his forehead against mine.

"Yes, I'm good. Thanks, babe, for protecting me." I reach up to press my lips against his.

"Always, I'd do anything for you. I love you," he whispers into my ear squeezing me into a tight hug.

"I love you, Creed," I whisper back as I rest my head against his chest, squeezing him back.

"Y'all wanna do a shot?" Winter yells, breaking up the silence in our group. I'm thankful nothing more happened with that creep. I'd hate to think what would have happened if he was a little more drunk or if Creed hadn't been there to stop him from doing more.

"Hell yeah!" I shout over the music, ready to get back into a good mood, we came here to have fun not let some dick ruin it.

"Let's do some lemon drops this time." Winter smirks over at me knowing that Carsten absolutely hates these shots.

"Fuck, I hate those shots babe." Carsten shakes his head with a look of disgust on his face.

"I don't get how you ladies love those damn things, they fucking taste like shit," he laughs.

"Be a man bro pull your balls back out of your pussy and take a fucking shot for the ladies." Creedence laughs patting him on the back. The rest of us laugh along with him including Carsten who fucks with Creed just as bad. They're forever messing with each other.

"Fine, let's do a shot of fireball afterwards." He smiles at Creedence as I look back between them confused.

"Fuck." Creed's whole-body shivers. He looks grossed out just thinking about it and my face naturally turns into disgust thinking of the taste. I fucking hate fireball. "Fine, I'll be a man and do a shot of fireball, I fucking hate those shots ever since my twenty-first birthday, but whatever." Creedence crosses his arms over his chest with a smirk on his face.

"Fuck dude, I hate fireball too I thought you'd bitch out, damn." Carsten walks behind the bar to make our shots instead of bothering Chase. Since he's at the end of the bar dealing with a crowd of people.

"Nah man, I ain't no bitch I'll do it. Whisky sometimes makes me wake up naked, but it's cool as long as I wake up naked with this beauty." He grabs my ass, pulling me closer to him with his other hand.

"I'll wake up with you naked any day, you handsome, handsome man." I turn towards him and look up at him, giving him a sexy grin while biting my bottom lip hoping to keep teasing him all night. It's fun teasing him because he's not afraid to show you how he's feeling or when he's turned on. That's one of the many things I love about him.

"Fuck that was sexy." He leans down to whisper into my ear. "Keep biting that pouty lip of yours and I'm gonna take you to Carsten's office, bend you over his desk and fuck that pussy of yours," he practically growls. "Then I'll leave more cum leaking out of that pretty little cunt of yours." He reaches his hand up under my dress and grabs half my ass and pussy at once.

"What if that's what I want?" I say to him as Carsten slides the shots to us before walking back around the bar.

"Keep teasing me and that might just happen, my little slut," he whispers again in a gravelly voice clearly turned on. He reaches around and places his hand across my stomach before pulling me back into him and I can feel how hard he is on my mid back.

"Don't threaten me with a challenge that I'll happily accept babe, I'd be fine with you fucking me all night long." I wink at him before grabbing one of the two shots in front of me. Fuck this mix is going to be gross, I hate fireball and it's going to taste foul after the lemon drop, but I'll suck it up. I need to loosen up and have some fun.

"Alright bitches let's do this," Winter shouts as she holds her lemon drop up in the air. I love partying with Winter. She's so much fun. Not that I don't love her always, but when she's relaxed and loosens up, she's a blast to be around.

We all down our shots as I try not to gag. I love lemon drops, but I just hate shots, it's a weird love, hate thing I have with straight alcohol.

"Alright man, are you guys ready to do this next shot or are you gonna be a little bitch," Carsten asks Creedence who picks his fire-ball shot up and downs it before the rest of us even pick ours up.

"Fuck that shits nasty." His tone is deep and raspy as he slams his shot glass down, then sticks his tongue out clearly grossed out from it like he might gag.

"Way to wait for us dick head." Carsten laughs, looking grossed out himself from him doing the shot with ease.

"I told you I'm no bitch, I might have gagged a little but I never back down from a challenge, I may puke from that, but it is what it is." He has a sexy smile on his face, I don't think there isn't a look of his that's not sexy. Everything about Creedence Knoxx is fucking sexy. He's a fucking god and he's who I want to worship. I'll get on my knees and beg him to please me. Beg him to let me please him and worship him as my lover. I'll worship his cock like I need it to survive because I crave it like it's my favorite candy. I need him like the air I need in my lungs to breathe. I love the look in his eyes that he gets when he looks at me and the smirk that comes along with it. I love the way he looks when he smirks, his light brown beard making it look even hotter, I love a man with a beard, something about it just turns me on especially Creedence's. It makes me want to jump on him and beg him to fuck me. God I'm a psycho.

"Well, here we go ladies, I guess there's no turning back," Carsten chuckles, tipping his shot back and slamming it down in disgust.

I take a deep breath and hesitate. I hate fireball with a passion but I'm not about to bitch out, so I lift my shot, tipping it back, as a grossed-out shiver runs through my body, I shake my head back and forth sticking out my tongue as I slam down my shot glass.

"Ughh fuck that shit, fuck that's nasty." I feel the burn in my throat still as the warmth from it moves through my body, loosening me up a little more.

"Yeah, that shit is fucking gross." Winter shakes her head while a shiver runs through her body as well. Then gives Carsten a look like I can't believe you made us all do those shots.

"Guess we can all agree then, no more fireball," I shout to them over the loud music that the DJ just put on again.

"Let's go dance, Creed," I say, pulling his hand with me to the dance floor. "C'mon guys let's go," I shout behind us as I dance my way to the dance floor dragging Creedence behind me as Lil Jon 'Get Low' starts playing. I love when they do early 2000's night. They always do theme nights at Black Velvet and so far, country night and the early two thousands are my favorite nights.

20

EMERALD

Winter gets to the floor with me with a big grin on her face and starts shaking her ass grinding herself into Carsten, his smile growing as she grinds into him. His eyes fill with need as he looks down at her. They are so fucking cute together.

I turn towards Creedence and give him a seductive smile before blowing him a kiss, he catches it and places it over his heart like he always does. I love that he does that; it's the sweetest thing. I turn around and start grinding my ass into him. I slowly move my hands up over my hips before reaching my breasts, then move them up my neck till I reach his neck, holding onto him from behind while he wraps his arms around me feeling my body. I'm feeling the music and the alcohol and I'm loving it. Winter and I smile at each other with a knowing smile. Each of us turning our men on as we dance, grinding ourselves against them. Right as he says "get low", Winter and I get low with the music dropping down, grinding our asses back up against them. I take my time really feeling his body against mine, the way it forms to mine perfectly. Slowly grinding my ass right against his erection that I'm responsible for.

"Fuck, Sugar," Creedence growls into my ear. "That feels way too good, mmm baby." I can feel his hard cock growing against me as I grind into his body, doing my job right and making sure I tease him.

"The way your ass is jiggling against me as you dance is so fucking sexy." He groans as he moves my hair over onto my other shoulder. He leans down and starts kissing my shoulder as he dances with me. His hands come around as he places them on my stomach. I take my hands and place them over his and slowly move his hands with mine up to my chest making him squeeze my breasts while dancing. I don't even care if anyone is watching. To me we're the only ones here. I came here to have fun, and I'm allowed to dance like a hoe if I want to, isn't that what bars and clubs are for anyways, to let loose and dance however you want.

I turn around and place his hands onto my ass, then pull him down by the collar of his shirt and press my lips against his. I can still taste the fireball on his tongue as he swirls against mine and it's so sexy, even if I hate the shot. Something about the taste of lingering alcohol during a kiss is so sexy. It turns me on even more and I can't believe how wet I am. That's all I feel as I dance is my wet panties against my pussy from his cum and from being turned on.

"I can't wait for you to see how wet my panties are," I say into his ear, probably a little louder than needed but I wanted him to be able to hear me over the music.

"Mmm, Emerald." He pulls me closer against his body, his cock is so hard against my belly. "I can't wait to taste that wet pussy of yours." His voice husky in my ear, gripping my ass even harder.

"I can't wait to feel your tongue on me, Creed." I practically moan into his ear, and I think it's the alcohol helping me talk this way because usually I'm a little shy when it comes to talking dirty, unless I'm really in the mood. But I think this is a combination of both.

"Can't wait to feel my tongue on what, Sugar?" he asks, and I know he wants me to be more specific because he wants to hear it.

"On me. On my body," I say, suddenly becoming a little shy now for some reason.

"Ah. Ah. Ah. Feel my tongue on what? Don't be shy with me now." He grips my ass a little harder this time, probably hard enough to leave his delicious marks. I'm surprised my dress isn't lifting from it, but I know he'd pull it down if it was.

"I want your tongue on my pussy," I whisper in his ear. "I can't wait to come all over your face." I'm getting myself worked up just thinking about it.

"Mmm good girl," he groans. "You don't have to be shy with me. I want you to tell me what you want and when you want it." He smirks. "I'm serious, baby if you want me to fuck you tell me and I'm ready." He kisses my neck in the same spot he brushed the hair away from. Lightly sucking and working his magical tongue on my skin. The music changes to a slower song of Ushers 'Love In This Club'.

"Do you want to keep dancing?" I ask him, hoping he says yeah since I love dancing, and I love this song.

"I'll do anything for you, Sugar, you just tell me what you want baby." He smiles down at me with a smile that reaches his honey brown eyes. His sexy ass smile and the way his mustache and beard curve around it perfectly. I dance with him, studying his handsome face. His tattooed neck that stops right where his beard starts at his jaw line and the way they peek out from his collar. I love how he looks so dangerous and naughty. The way his strong hands feel rubbing up and down my body, and his muscular arms fit against my curves just right. Like he's the missing piece to my puzzle that makes my body complete. I'm lost in my thoughts staring up at him as he stares down at me, we're in our own world just dancing when I hear someone say something behind us.

"Oh, look who's here trying to ruin my night out." I hear a nasty voice say when Creedence turns, rolling his eyes and sighing.

"Leave us alone, Daisy, mind your own fucking business." He turns his head back towards me. I'm not even going to give her the time of day and acknowledge her, because that's all she wants is the attention. She's an ugly attention whore.

"It's kinda hard to when you're here with another one of your playthings, it's gotta be tiring never being able to keep a girl." She gives a nasty laugh as she looks at Creedence. She's talking out her ass because he doesn't have playthings, she's just trying to make me jealous, and I couldn't care less what she has to say.

"Daisy, just leave us alone." Creedence is getting pissed. I can feel his muscles tensing as he rests his arms around my waist still. Daisy stands there crossing her arms looking like a child who is about to throw themselves down on the ground and scream or cry. Hell, maybe both.

"Why? Are you afraid I'll tell your new little girlfriend here the kind of freak shit you're into." She throws her head back into a laugh and I can't help but hope she breaks her neck or something drastic in the process to shut the cunt up.

"I said leave us the fuck alone, I'm not playing your stupid games." He turns back to her, angry this time.

"Aww why, cause you're here with your new little whore and trying to impress her?" she snorts, rolling her eyes at him.

"Excuse me what the fuck did you just call me? You fucking bitch." I step forward not taking her shit. I was going to keep quiet but not anymore. I pull away from Creed to face her as he does the same thing. His arms crossed over his chest, and I swear his shirt could rip from his muscles just from bending his arms.

"You heard me." She steps closer, poking me in the chest. "I called you." Poke. "His new." Poke. "Little whore." And she pokes me two more times giving me a nasty smile as she does it.

"Don't fucking touch me," I say, pushing her away to get space since it's already crowded on the dance floor as it is.

"Aw, why's that? Only Creedence is allowed to touch his whore is that it?" She laughs again and that's it I'm not holding back anymore.

I ball my fists with anger and lift my right arm, pull it back and swing right at her, punching her in the face. Guess we all just came here to fight tonight. It hits her hard enough she loses her balance falling into Brynn behind her. Creedence stands there with his mouth open, shocked that this just happened.

"I said don't fucking call me a whore you jealous bitch." And right as I go to turn around to walk away, she grabs my hair pulling me back by my head. I let out a scream cause she's got me right at the nape of my neck. I push my elbow back hard hitting her in the jaw and she lets go of my hair. I turn around and go to swing, but she scratches me on the cheek before I can get my punch in.

"Of course, typical bitch scratching like a pussy." I smile, pushing her away from me. "Now, don't call me a fucking whore again. Just cause you're jealous he's with me and wants me instead of your nasty diseased ass doesn't mean I'm a whore," I yell back to her. Even if I am a whore for him, his little slut, or his good girl. Whatever he feels like calling me, it makes my pussy wet. Which makes my thighs tighten together just thinking about his rough voice calling me his little slut while fucking me. Mmm fuck does it get me going.

Anyways it's none of her fucking business what we do in private. She's just pissed he doesn't want her. Maybe he did some of the same things with her that he does with me. Whatever that's in the past I won't get upset about it because he's with me now and not her.

She lunges at me and punches me in the cheek, something feels like it cuts me as her hand hits my face, maybe she has rings on. I lift my arm punching her back, Creedence tries to pull me off her, but it doesn't work because I end up pushing her, she loses her balance and takes me down with her. Next thing I know I'm sitting on top of her. She's pulling my hair with one hand and slapping me with her other hand while I'm throwing punches at her, not sure where I'm hitting her because I can't exactly see what's happening.

"Oh my god stop it you guys," Brynn yells, standing back out of the way.

"You're just pissed because you know I'm right you're his next whore, his next plaything and nothing important," she hisses, losing grip on my hair.

"You stupid bitch, I might be his fucking whore but at least he loves me. He never loved you." I punch her face this time hitting her cheek.

"He. He. What?" she asks as she stops hitting me, her arms falling to her sides on the ground.

"I said he loves me. He never loved you and that's what bothers you. You jealous bitch." I smile at her as I move off her. "I'm done with your bullshit." Creedence reaches down, holding his hand out to me to help me up. Once I stand up and adjust my dress, pulling it down before my ass fully shows to everyone standing around us watching. Then I turn towards Creedence who is still in shock over the whole thing.

"God you girls are fucking crazy. That was so hot babe. I've never had a girl fight over me before." He winks at me leaning down and kissing me.

"You told her you loved her?" Daisy asks as Brynn helps pull her up, she fixes her skirt and adjusts her shirt pulling it down back over her bra that somehow was exposed during our fight.

"Yeah Daisy, I did it because I'm in love with her, I never wanted anything more from you and you know that," he tells her as we start walking away. She stands there with her mouth open in shock and a sad look on her face, that kind of makes me feel bad, but not really since she was shit talking me for no reason. Plus, I never really liked her to begin with. She's always been a nasty bitch and I'm not one to hate on girls or call them ugly and whatever else unless they deserve that shit...and Daisy, well also Brynn, they both deserve what they get because they're both nasty bitches.

"Let's go step outside and get some air babe." Creedence grabs my hand and walks me behind the bar, down the hallway and out the back door to where Carsten and Winter go out back, so we don't have to deal with a crowd.

"Dude, you guys missed it, Emerald just kicked Daisy's ass over me. They were on the floor and everything." Creedence wraps his arm around my waist pulling me in next to him as he takes a sip of his beer he grabbed on the way out the door.

"You what? You hit Daisy and I missed this shit, what the hell you should have come and got me, I would have loved to have seen that." Winter walks over to me putting her hand up to my cheek where Daisy got me. I haven't even looked at it to see how bad it is.

"Well, it looks like she barely touched you. Your face has two small scratches, that's it." Winter studies my face a little closer and it's hard for me to not laugh at how close she is. But I love how much she cares.

"Fuck, babe I'm so sorry I didn't even check you out to see if you were okay, I just wanted to get you out of there for a minute." Creedence looks down at my face in concern.

"I'm okay guys, really it doesn't even hurt." It's not a lie I honestly would've forgotten it was there if it weren't for Winter coming up and pointing it out. "The fucking bitch told me I was only his next plaything and a whore; I didn't care but she wouldn't stop calling me a whore, so I put her in her place. Then she got pissed when I told her he loved me, and the fight was over. I think that really hurt her feelings." I shake my head as the memories replay in my head. It all happened so quickly it's hard to recall how it happened.

"But babe that was so hot, Em." Creedence leans down snuggling his face into my neck as he says it. Giving slow gentle kisses.

"I would have loved to see that too; I'm sure Brynn was losing her shit over her friend getting her ass beat too." Carsten laughs.

"She was, she was screaming 'oh my god guys stop' as everyone just stood there watching," I say in my best Brynn voice, laughing. Brynn was obsessed with Carsten when he and Winter first started dating. She got pissed about it and tried to trap Carsten with a pretend pregnancy because she was pissed, he wasn't in love with her. These guys get themselves caught up with some psycho girls that's for sure.

"That's awesome, that was a great Brynn impression." Winter puts her straw between her lips taking a sip of her cherry vodka and Sprite. Her shoulders shake a little as she laughs.

"Thank you." I'm not sure if I should feel bad for the way I reacted or not. But my gut is telling me not to, that she deserved it. "That's twice tonight that someone tried to ruin our night." I push my bottom lip out in a pretend pout, actually kind of bummed at the turn our night took.

"Don't worry, Sugar, our night is just starting. I pinky promise it's not ruined." He moves his pinky and wraps it around mine. "When we go back in, we'll get some drinks and we'll go back to dancing, okay baby?" Creedence turns me around as he talks to me to where I'm facing him. He grips my ass, pulling me towards him it's hard for me to reach so I stand on my tiptoes as I wrap my arms around his neck. It's hard not to smile while looking at this sexy man in front of me. He makes me feel weak in the knees. I look up at him as he brings his lips down to mine and softly kisses me. He swipes his tongue against my lips, and I open up for him, swirling my tongue against his as he groans into my mouth.

"I need to know," he whispers in a husky tone. "How's that tight pussy of yours feel with my cum dripping out of it?" He growls into my ear.

"Fuck." Chills shoot through my body at the feel of his lips lightly brushing my ear. I practically moan from his words. "Every time I feel it come out of me, it makes my pussy throb, which makes me even more wet." I wink at him hoping that what I said turns him on. The low growl he lets out that I feel rumbling across my chest that rests against his stomach just below his ribs is enough to show me just how much he liked my words.

"Down boy." I lick up his neck slowly. "Keep making noises like that and I'm gonna wanna go home instead of going back in to dance," I whisper into his ear, it's ridiculous how much this man turns me on, I look at him and I'm instantly in the mood to fuck.

"Oh, don't you worry, Sugar, we're going back into dance. I wanna see that ass of yours shake for me some more." He pulls me closer to him again. "I want you grinding against my thigh making that pussy of yours wet, I want it dripping by the time we get home," he whispers down into my ear. "That way when my tongue swipes against you I can taste all that wetness and get it all over my tongue." He groans out into my ear pushing his hard cock against my stomach.

"You lovers done over there and ready to get back inside? I need a drink." Winter smiles, giving us a knowing look. She knows exactly how it is to be this obsessed with someone. Ever since she met Carsten, they've both been obsessed and inseparable, they actually met here for the first time, I saw the look in her eyes the minute she looked at him I could tell she was into him. Then Carsten practically stalked me waiting for me to be at home so he could come over and talk to me about Winter to see if she was single. It was the cutest thing.

I don't think I've ever been this turned on in a public place before, I wouldn't even care if he took me to the bathroom and fucked me, that's how bad my pussy is throbbing right now. He squeezes my ass one more time before smacking it.

"Yep, I definitely need a drink right about now." Creedence reaches down and adjusts his hard cock in his pants trying to hide it from everyone else. It's a good thing his black button up shirt hangs over it or it would be very noticeable.

"I could use another shot honestly." I let out a deep breath because after that fight and him turning me on like that I need something to calm me down a little.

"Hell yeah, let's do another round of shots then," Winter yells, throwing her hands up into the air in excitement as we walk back in the bar. I love how excited she gets over everything, that's one of the things I love the most about her.

As we walk back in the door you can hear 'Sexyback' by Justin Timberlake blaring through the bar and Winter starts dancing. You can tell she must have a buzz because she usually isn't a fan of dancing, or maybe she's just letting loose and having a good time.

"Having fun, Winter?" I yell to her shaking my hips a little as we come around the bar.

"Yeah, I'm a little buzzed but I'm having a great time, the music's really fun tonight too so that helps." She throws her hands up again and shakes her ass against me in the process, so I start grinding myself against her and I look over to see Creedence staring with a sexy look on his face, slightly biting his bottom lip. So, I reach out and grab Winter's ass with one hand and her hip with the other, bringing her a little closer to me to tease him some more. She brings her body closer, resting her back against my chest, moving her hands through her hair. Creedence and Carsten both look at us, mouths open. Winter looks over at me and smiles before she bends her body over and drops it down before bringing her body back up grinding into me more and as she does it both guys are in their own world as they watch us dance until the song finally comes to an end.

"Ho-ly shitttt that was hot." Carsten is the first one to speak as Creedence shakes his head to snap out of his own thoughts.

"Fuck. Yeah, I'd have to agree that was really fucking sexy." He comes over and grabs me, pulling me in to kiss him.

"What kind of shot do you guys want to do?" I slowly break the kiss to yell to them over the music.

"Let's do another blowjob shot." Winter smiles at the guys as she says it, wiggling her eyebrows as she does.

"Hell yeah, I'm down," I yell, smiling back at her, thankful the guys will be around for this one.

"I mean, I'll take the shot but I'm not doing it the way you're supposed to, I'm good without that." Creedence holds his hands out, backing away a little while shaking his head. His shoulders lightly shake as he laughs.

"Um yeah, I'm with Creed on that one, I'll take the shot but I'm not doing that looking like I'm sucking some dick, I'm good." Carsten laughs too with a somewhat grossed out look on his face.

"Whatever then you guys can enjoy the show." I turn towards Creedence and wink at him while slowly licking my lips.

"Fuck, Sugar, why you gotta keep doing that to me." He pulls me closer to him, talking closer to my ear.

"I just can't help myself; I love teasing you." It's true, just seeing the look he gives me every time he's turned on is enough to make me want to tease him all the time. It's so fucking sexy. Plus, I'm starting to feel my alcohol more and enjoying my buzz.

"Well, I love it, baby, don't stop." He leans down kissing my cheek and then moves to stand next to me.

"I don't know why I'm waiting for Chase to come over here. I'll just go behind the bar and make these shots myself." Carsten leans down giving Winter a quick kiss before walking away.

"I don't know how you guys like the taste of these shots. Honestly the more I think about it I'm just not a fan of shots I just say fuck it and do them." Creedence looks grossed out as he says it. It's funny to see this tall, tattooed, muscled man stands here and say he doesn't like shots. "The only shot I kind of enjoy is Crown Royal." He looks down at me as he talks, my mouth automatically curls up into a disgusted look.

"Eww I can't do those shots." I make a gagging noise. "Nope I'm sorry but I will never do Crown, not after my twenty-first birthday, for some reason that was the shot I kept doing and the next day was terrible. Between the headache, the hangover, and the amount of puking, I could cry just thinking about it." I shiver in disgust because the thought alone naturally sends a grossed-out shiver through my body.

"So, you won't do one with me?" he pouts a little as he asks.

"Fuck..." I let out a long sigh. "Fine, I'll do one and that's it only because you did multiple shots of the ones I like." I shiver again, the disgusted look never leaving my face.

"Hey, I need something to help you loosen up tonight." His deep voice in my ear makes my thighs squeeze together in excitement. Because that's what his voice does to me, it turns me on and gets me all worked up.

"What do you mean?" I suddenly feel nervous thinking about all the things he's said he's wanted to do to me and anal being one of them is the first thought that comes to mind. I swallow hard, my mouth feeling dry because the thought scares me, especially with his size, fuck not only is he long but he's fucking thick and it's kind of scary, especially with his piercings.

"I was thinking about fucking that tight ass of yours tonight. God just thinking about it gets me going," he groans into my ear. I love knowing that I turn him on and knowing that he's turned on turns me on.

"Shit, I don't think I'm ready for that." I'm a little worried I'm not gonna lie, I'm terrified of how bad it's going to hurt. "But I'll let you play with it more, is that okay?" I know he won't argue because even though he likes to take control he won't force me to do something I don't want to. He smirks, that sexy smirk of his it drives me so freaking crazy because of how attractive it is.

"But babe," he gives a little pout. "My cock is going to feel so good in that tight little ass of yours and you're going to love it, Emerald," he growls as his warm breath dances across my ear spreading chills through my body.

"Goddamn, Creedence, why do you have to make everything sound so sexy," I practically moan out because I'm so turned on. "I thought my panties were wet before but now my pussy is dripping for you, I think they're soaked all the way through now my thighs are starting to feel wet," I whisper into his ear, giggling a little because I know what I'm saying is getting to him.

Instead of responding he moves his hand down and grabs my thigh. "Spread your legs, Sugar." His voice is firm and deep as his hand goes on the inside of my thigh; he comes dangerously close to my pussy making it throb. I love it when he takes control. I try to tighten my thighs together, but he stops me from doing so by taking his fingers and moving my panties over a little.

"Fuck, Sugar, I can't wait to taste all this wetness, your panties are more than soaked baby." His voice comes out husky, deep. I look around to make sure no one is paying attention to what he is doing but the way he's standing he's blocking everything, and you would think he was just leaning against the bar instead of reaching up under my dress. Right as I think he's about to pull away he takes two fingers sliding them across my wet slit before pushing them inside me making me moan out, thankful the music is so loud that even Winter being next to me doesn't hear she's too busy talking to Chase behind the bar to notice anything anyways. Thank god because it feels too good for him to stop.

"Creedence, please," I whimper, so fucking turned on but trying so hard to keep it together while he's fingering me in the middle of Black Velvet. I don't know if I want him to stop or to continue. Part of me likes the idea of someone seeing what he's doing, but the other part of me is scared to be caught.

"Say the word and we'll go home, Sugar, your pussy is so. Fucking. Wet." He pulls his fingers out of me, then he moves them to his mouth sticking his pointer finger into it sucking my wetness off him.

"Mmm fuck, Sugar." He slowly brings his middle finger up to his mouth doing the same thing, it is so sexy, watching him lick my wetness off his thick, tattooed fingers. That he's the reason my pussy is this wet, that I'm the reason his eyes are practically rolling as he tastes my wetness.

"Your pussy tastes like candy, baby. Fucckkk. I can't wait to fucking taste you some more later," he growls into my ear making my body break out in goosebumps. I'm hot from how crowded it is in here, from dancing and from how fucking worked up he has me. But cold at the same time, I'm so turned on I feel like my body is ready to explode. I love the way he makes my body feel so alive.

"You are making it so hard to want to stay here, you know that right?" I bite my bottom lip trying to control my breathing in the process because my body is so worked up, I feel like I'm panting.

"Trust me, I feel the same way, I was ready to get home and fuck that sweet pussy of yours before we even left," he laughs and right before I can answer Carsten comes back around the bar with our shots.

"Sorry guys, I figured I'd help Chase out really quick with that rush while I was back there." He places our shots down in front of us. "Now who's ready for some blow jobs?" He winks at Winter, and she blushes a little. I love how he still makes her blush over certain things.

"You have no idea." Creedence's husky voice whispers into my ear and it makes my thighs tighten together with a need only he seems to know how to create.

"Shhh, Mister," I giggle elbowing him in his rock-hard abs. The ones that I can't wait to get my tongue on tonight. Or scratch all over with my nails, leave my marks of love on him like he does on me. Just thinking of the marks of pleasure he leaves on my body makes my pussy wet.

"Alright guys let's do this," Winter shouts as I wink at Creedence. I place my hands behind my back, and he gets the biggest smile on his face as I place my mouth around the shot glass and lift it back taking the shot down. I move my hands and take the shot glass from my mouth licking around it with my tongue as he stares at me with a sexy look in his eyes, clearly even more turned on.

21
CREEDENCE

THIS GORGEOUS FUCKING WOMAN IS GOING TO BE THE DEATH of me, she let me play with her pussy in the middle of a public place. Fuck she's so fucking perfect. She let me finger her and then practically melted as I licked her delicious fucking taste off my fingers. The look in her eyes as she watched me lick her wetness off my fingers was like she was going to pounce on me and fuck my brains out. Which I wouldn't mind, my cocks so fucking hard I feel like one wrong move and it's going to break. I've been ready to get out of here since we walked through the door. Forget that I was ready to leave before we left the damn house the only place I wanted to be was buried with my face between her legs, my beard covered in her sweet fucking arousal and my cock sliding in and out of her wet fucking cunt. She looks so fucking sexy tonight in her skin-tight too short of a dress that I can't wait to push up and fuck her again later in. One time wasn't enough in this dress I need to fuck her again in it. Maybe I can borrow Carsten's office and fuck her in there before we leave.

"That's it." I slam my shot glass down and look over at Emerald as she looks at me with a confused look on her face. "I'm convinced everything you do is fucking sexy as hell and made to tease me." I place my hand on my chin and cross my other arm under it.

"Ohh?" She smiles. "Why's that? I've done nothing to tease you tonight mister, I don't know what you're talking about." She giggles with an innocent look on her face, trying not to hide her smile in the process.

"Ahh, I see. Let me point out that mister definitely isn't something that teases me." I'm sure she can hear my sarcasm. "Biting your lip, licking your lips." I pause for a second tapping my chin. "You've moaned a couple times when I've said certain things, I mean we're gonna be here for quite some time, do I need to continue?" I smirk, turning myself on more in the process as I name the few things she's done that have turned me on.

"Excuse me Mister, coming from the guy who still hasn't fixed my panties yet after fingering me and I'm practically standing here with no underwear on, my pussy is soaked, my thighs are wet from it and you're going to tell me I tease you?" She bites that god damn pouty bottom lip of hers, and it's so hard to not wrap my arm around her, pull her in and kiss her.

"Okay, fair enough." I clear my throat trying not to think about how easy it would be to just lift her dress up and fuck her tight cunt right. Fucking. Here. And I know she'd be my little slut and let me do it.

"Ready to do that shot of Crown?" I give her a big smile knowing she's been dreading this shot. "You guys wanna do a shot of Crown?" I lean over and ask Carsten and Winter who are caught up in their own conversation. Probably teasing each other just like we are.

"Yes, finally something I love." Carsten slaps his hand down onto the counter before standing.

"Oh, wait." He turns around pulling Winter towards him and giving her a kiss before he walks back around the bar. I love that my best friend who is like a brother to me has found someone he's so in love with. I can't wait until they get married, he deserves the best, so does Winter especially after all the shit she's had thrown her way in the past. She deserves the world and I've seen Carsten proving to her just how well she deserves it.

"Yeah, I'm down. I'm not a fan of Crown after Emerald's twenty-first birthday and people shoving them at us." Winter looks over at Emerald and shivers at the memory, a grossed out look on her face. "But I'll do one since you guys have done all the other shots with us with no complaints." She lets out a dramatic sigh before smiling over at us.

"God I am not excited for this one Em, how'd you get us into this?" Winter sighs again resting her head on Emerald's shoulder. "I wanna vomit just thinking about doing this." She gags a little with a grossed out look on her face.

"Sorry babe." Emerald gives her an apologetic smile, trying to hide back the smirk that's threatening to creep up on her. "I didn't get us into anything. It's Creedence's fault he brought it up and said he wanted to do one, so I agreed since he did all the shots we liked and then somehow you got dragged into it." She laughs this time, throwing her head back a little.

"Ohhh, so you're saying I basically dragged myself into this because of the other shots we had them do?" Winter laughs too. "Fuck I'm stupid." She puts her hand to her head.

"You still have time to change your mind babe." Emerald throws her arm around Winter's shoulder and pats it.

"Yeah Winter, you really don't have to do it, we won't be upset," I tell her because I don't want her to think we're forcing her to do it.

"Nah, I'm just being a little bitch, I have no problem doing it, I just needed to be dramatic there for a minute." She smiles at us and Emerald lets go of her and playfully shoves her.

"Rude, you bitch." Emerald laughs at her shaking her head. "Here I was feeling bad thinking you thought I was making you take it." She crosses her arms dramatically; she's messing around too you can tell.

"Girl, you should know I would never do something I don't want to do," she says as Carsten walks back around with our shots in his hands, setting them in front of us. We're at the end of the bar now so it's easier for him to carry the shots to us.

"Alright ladies, you ready?" Carsten asks with a big grin on his face. "Damn Snowflake, you're gonna be so much fun tonight baby girl." He winks at her as she bites her bottom lip, a seductive look in her eyes. And you know that they're going to have a fun night tonight. I can't help but smile to myself because I'm excited to see where my night goes with Emerald.

"I can't wait to see how fun you'll be tonight, Sugar." I slowly lick my lips, a slight smirk forming at the corner of my mouth. I'm just hoping she's gonna be into everything I have planned, if she doesn't pass out on me from all the shots first.

"Alright fuckers let's get this shit over with," Winter shouts, she's always been fun doing shots with, especially now that we don't have to worry about what her dad will do if she goes out to have fun. It doesn't matter what shot she's doing anymore. She's excited and she's ready for it.

I wait to take my shot because I want to see Emerald's reaction and it's just as great as I thought it was going to be. She throws it back and her whole-body shakes from how grossed out she is. She gags and sticks her tongue out, which is funny seeing her gag since she doesn't when she sucks my dick unless I'm forcing my cock in her throat. I lean over to whisper to her.

"That was kind of hot watching you gag, Sugar. I'd love to feel you gagging on my cock right now," I tell her, gripping her ass and pulling her closer to me as I grab my own shot glass and down it quickly. Not taking my eyes off her the entire time I do it. I slam the shot glass down, lick the rest of the Crown from my lips and pull her in for a kiss. The taste of Crown still lingering on her tongue as mine dances across hers. She gently pushes me away with a shy look on her face.

"Down boy," she giggles.

"Sorry Em, you're just too addicting." It's the truth. Everything about this girl is like another hit of a drug, the more I get of her the more I need of her to feel okay, to feel even close to whole.

"Shit, that was better than I fucking remember," I say to Carsten as he slams his shot glass down. I look over at poor Winter who is hunched over gagging in disgust from the shot and it's hard for me to hold back my laugh.

"Shit that was a terrible idea, no more shots. I haven't even had an actual drink yet and I think I'm about ready to leave soon," Winter says in between yawns.

"Aww c'mon Snowflake, don't get sleepy on me baby girl I need you to be ready for me when we get home." Carsten nudges her a little with his elbow.

"Don't worry you handsome devil. I'm not passing out on you until after I come all over your cock." She gasps as she realizes she said it out loud. Then blushes, putting her hands over her face to hide.

"Well damn, that was unexpected. I'm proud of you for being so fucking open about that, Snowflake," he practically growls at her, clearly that did something to affect him. I don't blame him if that was Emerald, she'd already be bent over with my cock buried deep inside her.

"Damn Winter, tell us some more." Emerald laughs as she pats her on the back. Winter still has her face covered as she shakes her own head.

"Fuck dude, I can't believe I just said that out loud like that." She clearly forgot who she was around because we do not give a fuck about her being so open like that. That's how close our friend group is.

"It's all good Winter, not like we didn't know what was going down once you guys got home anyways." I give her a look raising my eyebrows at her as my body shakes from laughter.

"Shut up guys, let's go dance so we can all pretend I didn't just say that." She gets up and grabs Carsten's hand, dragging him out to the dance floor.

"Fuck I'm really feeling that shot." Emerald has a grossed out look on her face as she holds her stomach with one hand and I hope that wasn't the shot that makes her puke.

"You okay, Sugar? Do you need anything?" I wrap my arm around her waist a little, giving her a concerned look.

"No, no I think I'm good, besides needing to feel you inside me, I think this sick feeling in my stomach will pass." She giggles slurring a little and I think all the alcohol is finally starting to hit her at once. "Let's go dance handsome." She grabs my hand and pulls me to the dance floor where we spend the next half hour before we head out.

We pull into my driveway, and I walk around to open the door for Emerald. Her head is a little heavy and her body is slouched a little, so I decide I'm going to carry her inside. Not over my shoulder because I don't want to put pressure on her stomach and make her sick, so I carry her like a man would carry his wife on their wedding day. Or the way a prince would carry a princess. I could get used to holding her against me like this. She fits so perfectly in my arms.

"What are you doing handsome?" she slurs a little more than before.

"I'm gonna carry you inside, Sugar, it looks like you might need a little help." I smile as I shut my car door with my elbow and press the lock button on my keys.

"No. No. No way, please put me down, I wanna walk." She fights me a little to put her down, but that just makes me readjust the way I'm holding her. Making sure I'm gripping her a little tighter than before.

"Baby, you were kind of stumbling when we left Black Velvet, I can carry you, it's no big deal," I tell her because I don't want her to think it's a struggle to hold her when she feels like nothing in my arms.

"Please Creed, I wanna walk and sit on your front porch. I need some air." There's a nice breeze tonight and the fresh air sounds good so I start walking over in that direction.

Once we get to the stairs, I set her down and she loses her

balance a little. "Thanks babe." She sits down on the porch, stumbling a little as she does.

"Welcome Sugar." I walk in front of her. Stopping right before her knees touch me.

"God these stairs are cold on my ass." She giggles as she moves her hips back and forth, almost like she's rotating her hips while wiggling on the cement stairs completely oblivious to what she's doing.

Fuck, just watching her do that makes my cock jump in excitement as I picture her tight, wet pussy coating my hard cock in her wetness as she slides up and down on my hard length. Thinking about her pussy swallowing my cock gets my mind going in all the dirty places.

"Come sit on my lap, Sugar I'll warm your ass up for you baby." I smirk as I move to sit next to her. Our legs brushing as she stands. I pat my lap showing her where I want her and like a good fucking girl she sits right on my erection. Fuck. She giggles as she does, knowing exactly what she's doing. I place my rough calloused hands on her velvety soft skin because I can't get close enough. I can't get enough of her, or enough of touching her.

"Mmm already getting me worked up again huh, Creed?" Her tone is so fucking seductive, driving my cock fucking mad while it sits trapped under her warm center. This is why I'd rather be inside where I can take these stupid fucking jeans off and bury myself inside her where my cock belongs. Then I think about unzipping my pants and letting her ride my cock backwards out here which makes my cock twitch. Fuck it.

I lift her up for a second making her stand in front of me and her mouth drops open for a second before she pouts. Making it hard not to smile at how fucking adorable she can be.

"Hey jerk, I was just warming up," she pouts again.

"That's alright, Sugar. I'm about to warm you up again while you ride my fucking cock." I put my hands on her hips pulling her closer to me. I lean back and undo my belt removing it from my pants, then unbuckle and unzip them. I push my boxers down and my cock springs free, standing at full attention. Rock fucking hard.

"We're gonna do this right here?" she asks nervously, biting that damn lip of hers again.

"Yep, reverse cowgirl, Sugar. I wanna watch your ass bounce as you fuck me backwards." I groan at the images that flash through my mind. I can't wait to be enveloped in her wetness.

She hesitates for a minute still biting her lip, you can tell she wants to, so I give her a little encouragement. I place my hands at the bottom of her dress and push it up.

"Be my good little slut and sit on my cock, Sugar," I tell her in a husky voice so turned on just thinking about it, I've only had sex outside once and it wasn't even that exciting.

She turns around without saying anything and slowly bends down, her ass inches from my face as she pushes her fingers around the lace band of her panties. She takes them off dropping them next to me and I swear my heart stops for a second at this beautiful sight in front of me. Her pussy so fucking wet and dripping for my cock.

"Emerald," I growl. I'm so turned on. I don't think I'm going to last long. I lean forward biting her ass cheek hard, making her shriek a little before I slap it. Then to soothe the sting I stick my tongue out licking and sucking on her skin before pulling her back towards me more. I lean forward and stick my tongue out, slowly swiping it along her slit.

"Fuck gorgeous, you taste so god damn good." She lets out a soft whimper as my tongue finds her clit.

"Please, Creedence," she moans. "I'm already so close." I bet my little slut is, especially from teasing her all night and fingering her.

I pull away and she groans. "Tell me what you want, Sugar." My voice comes out raspy, hoarse.

"I want you to make me come," she pants out, it's almost hard to hear her because she's so out of breath.

"My little slut." I smile at her before slowly licking my lips, enjoying the view of her gorgeous fucking body. "Tell me you wanna come all over my face," I tell her and when she doesn't say anything I slap her pussy with my hand making her yelp a little, before letting out a moan.

"Be my good girl and tell me you wanna come all over my face, Sugar," I growl. I'm so fucking turned on my dicks so hard.

"Please, Creed." Is all she says, and I slap her pussy again. "Ahh fuckkk," she groans.

"What did I tell you, Sugar?" I lick her slowly again, circling her clit with my tongue. Making sure to put enough pressure to tease her but not enough to get her where she wants to be just yet. "What do I want you to say?" And again, she's quiet so I slap her ass first nice and hard knowing I'll be leaving a handprint and then I slap her pussy making her cry out in pleasure.

"Please, I need to," she moans even more breathlessly than before.

"Tell me that you want to come all over my face, Sugar and I'll make sure you come nice and hard all over it," I tell her practically begging her to say it because I can't wait to feel her cum while I eat her pussy.

"Please, Creedence, I wanna come all over your face," she whispers, you can tell she's embarrassed and that's the last thing I want for her is to be embarrassed.

"Goddammit, Emerald," I growl against her pussy. "I wanna punish you because you drive my mind so goddamn crazy. You drive me fucking wild. My never-ending thoughts of you and all the dirty things I want to do to you, baby. I wanna feel you come all over my face while I drown in your arousal. I wanna suffocate in your fucking pussy, baby." I am so worked up over this woman. I've never wanted someone so badly as I want her right now.

"Fuck, that was so fucking sexy," she moans, whimpering as I stop licking her pussy again.

"Don't be shy on me now, Sugar." I lick slowly again, this time stopping and sucking her sensitive clit between my lips.

"Fuck, lick my pussy, Creed, I wanna cum all over your face." It's a little louder this time, you can tell by her repeating it that it's turning her on even more from the way she practically moaned between every fucking word.

"Goddamn, such a good fucking girl, Sugar." I swirl my tongue slowly around her clit while sucking. Before adding a little more pressure with my tongue before sliding it back down her slit gathering as much of her wetness as I can with my tongue before moving back to her clit. Shit, I'll never get tired of tasting her.

"I knew you'd say it, my little slut. God, I love you." I slap her pussy one more time before I dive in and start licking her pussy like without it, I won't be able to fucking breathe.

"Fuccck, Creedence," she pants out, barely able to hold herself up in the process, so I grab her hips with my hands and get closer to her pussy sucking on her clit some more. I remove one hand from her hip and push two fingers into her, not caring if she was ready, she needs to be punished for making me wait so long to feast on my fucking pussy. Everything that was once her's is now mine. Her pussy belongs to me to take however I please, whenever she needs it and wherever she needs it.

"You're gonna have to pry me off of you, Sugar because even after you come, I'm not stopping until you beg me." I continue pumping my fingers curling them right up into her G-spot.

"Shit, Creed," she cries out. Trying to hold herself up as best she can in the awkward position I left her in.

"Fuck, you taste so good, Emerald. Always so sweet for me, my little slut," I growl into her as I lick and suck her clit, pumping my fingers in and out of her, until her body starts trembling from how bad it's shaking, her legs getting weak, so I grip her tighter with my one hand holding her up, so she doesn't fall forward as her pussy clamps down onto my fingers. She cries out into the darkness, moaning, practically screaming and she's loud. I don't even care this is mainly college street people fuck and party outside all the time, no one will even pay attention to it. I remove my fingers from her tight slit, replacing it with my tongue and start fucking her pussy with my tongue as her wetness gathers all around my mouth. Coating myself in these delicious fucking juices of hers. She tries to pull away but all that does is make my grip tighter around her waist and makes me pull her as close to my face as her pussy allows me to. I told her she was going to have to beg me to stop and I meant it, I can't get enough of her.

"Creedence, please it's too much," she says between pants, out of breath from her orgasm.

"Mmm. Mmm," I moan into her. That was my way of telling her hell no. Because I'm not done yet. Never interrupt a man during his meal, especially when he's eating his favorite thing. Emerald's fucking pussy.

"Fuck, it's too sensitive please, oh god. Shit," she cries. "Please, Creed, I'm gonna come again." Right as she says it her pussy starts tightening, gripping my tongue. This is probably the sexiest thing I've ever experienced before. I've made girls come with my mouth and tongue, but I've never felt a girl come all over my tongue while it's inside her.

"Please, Creed. I need you to stop," she moans, practically shouting while her orgasm slowly stops. Her pussy still pulsing on my tongue. Fuck, I need to be inside her. Now.

I lick up and down her slit one last time. Placing gentle kisses along the way before kissing her clit.

"Shit, your mouth is magical," she breathes out, letting out one last long breath before breathing back in. I pull away licking my lips as I do. Making sure I don't miss any of her from around my mouth. Then I slowly lick her from my pointer finger. "Fuck, I will never get tired of the way you taste." I stick my middle finger into my mouth and lick the rest of her wetness. Groaning as I do.

"Fuck that felt so good." Her breathing is still out of control as she talks.

"I need you to fuck me now," she practically begs.

"Mmm, that's my good little slut. Here you go, Emerald. Sit on my hard cock and fuck me gorgeous." My voice comes out gravelly.

Barely able to fucking speak from how worked up I am. I lean back and adjust my cock so she can sit on it.

She straddles my lap backwards and slowly slides down onto my cock. I throw my head back, a growl escaping my lips as the feel of her pussy grips my cock, squeezing my thickness tightly as she sinks down all the way. "Fuck I'll never get over how tight your cunt is, Emerald," I moan out as she slowly moves her body up and down.

"Your cock, Creed," she moans, not finishing what she was saying as she cries out grinding herself into me.

"Tell me Sugar, what about my cock?" I grab her throat with my hands.

"God, it feels so good I could cry," she pants. "It's like torture." She quivers. "And pleasure mixed into one." She's moaning in between panting. "I don't want it to end because it feels so good," she whispers from how tight I'm holding her throat. Then I get an idea. I grab my belt and wrap it around her neck, looping it through and pulling it as tight as it can go. She stops for a second grabbing it with her hands before she realizes what it is and looks back at me.

"Don't worry, Sugar. I won't hurt you, at least not in a bad way." I tighten it a little more. "Now be my good girl and fuck my cock and don't stop until I'm cuming in that tight little cunt of yours," I groan out as I hold the belt with one hand making sure it's still tight as she moans out her hands still holding onto the belt.

"Put your hands behind your back, Sugar," I tell her. She slowly moves her hands off the belt as she puts them behind her back, interlocking her fingers together, and then I hold her hands with my other hand, wrapping my large hand around her tiny wrists. I look down watching her ass jiggle as she bounces up and down, moaning my name. God this woman is perfect. The fact that she never questions anything and just allows me to do it makes me know she's the one. Fuck, I'm too obsessed with her to ever be okay with letting her go. My little slut is mine and only mine, I refuse to let another man fuck her. Besides after me, no one would ever be able to fuck her as good as I can.

I watch as she rides me making my cock rock-hard and throb in her pussy.

"Fuck I'm so close, Creed," she whispers out in a moan, so I tighten the belt a little more making her hiss in a breath from how tight it is, but I know she'll love the end result, so it'll all be worth the marks I leave and how tight it is.

"Get ready to come with me, Sugar." I let go of her hands and reach around and start massaging her clit with my thumb, her legs start to shake, and I can tell it's from her body getting close, so I massage faster, meeting her body thrust by thrust. Pushing up as she comes down on me and I don't think I can hold it any longer.

"Come for me, Sugar, come all over my cock." And she does, like a good girl she cries out as I loosen the belt. Her pussy clamps down on my cock as I empty myself inside her, filling her cunt with my cum.

"Fuck Emerald. That felt so fucking good," I say slapping her ass as she slowly stands up on shaky legs still out of breath from me choking her and how fast she was riding me.

"Let's get those panties back on baby, that way you can feel my cum leak out of you as we sit out here and cool off," I say as she grabs my shoulders and steps into her lace thong, I pull them up around her waist and then slap her ass cheeks with both hands before leaning forward and kissing her pussy over her panties. Then I pull her dress down for her. She looks down at me with a smile on her face.

"What's wrong, Em?" I ask concerned hoping I didn't hurt her. Wondering if one of my piercings irritated her.

"You just kissed my pussy over my panties, no one's ever done that before." She giggles as her cheeks turn a slight shade of red from blushing.

"Sugar, I'll kiss that pussy of yours any day. I'd take my time and kiss every inch of it, and I mean with actual kisses again." I lean in to give her a gentle, slow kiss. "I love you, Sugar," I say in a slight whisper as I pull away.

"I love you, Creedence." She rests her forehead against mine with a smile on her face.

"What are you smiling about, Sugar?" I pull her back onto my lap making sure to keep her dress down over her ass so she's not cold.

"Just you and us I should say, well all of it." She giggles probably from messing up her words. It's cute how it's like she almost forgets how to talk around me sometimes.

"What about us, baby?" I place my hand on her thigh, squeezing it a little.

"Just how quickly everything has progressed between us." She stops talking almost like she's afraid to say what's really on her mind.

"Is that a bad thing?" I'm a little worried that she's going to want to slow things down or something. And I can't do that. Not after I've had all of her, I need all of her all the time.

"No, it's not a bad thing at all, it's just crazy. I feel like you've never been a stranger to me, that you're someone I've known my whole life or something." She smiles at me before she lays her head against my shoulder, snuggling her face into my neck a little. Right where she belongs.

"That's exactly how I feel. Like I've known you my whole life. You've never been a stranger, you're my home, baby, you've always been home to me, in this lifetime and in all my other lifetimes you've been it. I never want to be anywhere you're not and I never want to be with anyone else besides you." I squeeze her wrapping my arms around her waist a little tighter. Fuck I've never been so in love with someone as I am with her. I don't ever want to fucking lose her.

"That's exactly how I feel, Creed, you are home to me, you're my safe place and I love it." She lifts her head and looks me right in the eyes. Making my fucking heart skip a couple beats.

"I love you, babe." She leans in and places a kiss on my cheek before laying her head back on my shoulder.

"I love you, Sugar, I always have in every lifetime," I tell her because it's true. I believe in soulmates. That you find your soulmate in every lifetime, that's why she's felt like home and never a stranger since meeting her, because she's been mine in every lifetime, she's what I've been missing and what I've been searching for my whole life.

"We had an eventful night, huh?" I laugh about everything that happened in the matter of a few hours at the bar.

"Right? It was definitely a crazy night that's for sure. I can't believe it happened in just one night." She lifts her head again and looks at me. "This right here has probably been the best part of the night." She gives me a sexy smile telling me she's not done with me, and I can't wait to fuck her again. I've always loved sex, but I love it more now with her than I have with anyone else I've ever fucked.

"Thank you again for getting that creepy guy away from me, that's twice now you saved me from creepy men." She smiles at me.

"Guess I'm just your knight in shining armor, huh?" I wink at her; I'll always fucking protect her.

"I guess you are my knight in shining armor. But you're a sexy ass knight in shining armor." She wiggles her eyebrows. "God, I just wanna jump your bones again, just looking at you makes me so horny." She practically moans out and I don't know if it's from the alcohol making her feel this way, because I know drinking makes me horny, well hornier than I normally am at least. Or if she always feels this way.

"Well then let's go inside now, so I can fuck that pussy again, Sugar, because you're about to have a long night ahead of you my horny little slut." I wink at her as she gets up from my lap, her legs still a little shaky from before.

"Yes Mister." She grabs my hand, her fingers lacing through mine. "I can't wait."

22

CREEDENCE

WE HEAD INSIDE AND GO STRAIGHT DOWN THE HALL towards my room. She doesn't waste any time before she takes off her boots. I didn't give her the chance to take them off when we walked in the door.

Right as she goes to take off her dress I stop her. "Ah. Ah. Ah. Sugar, not yet I want to be the one to take your clothes off you, baby." I slowly walk over to her and press my lips to hers. I swipe my tongue against her lips as she begins to open for me allowing my tongue to swipe against hers. I swirl my tongue around hers before sucking on it and biting her bottom lip making her moan into my mouth. I groan into her mouth, swallowing her moans that escape through her lips while I memorize the way her tongue feels against mine because it's something I never want to forget, especially while I'm not around her. I want to be able to think about kissing her and be able to feel her. I'm making my cock hard just thinking about it and it's pressing into my jeans making me uncomfortable. I pull away from her for a minute and I unbutton them then I unzip them, but I leave them on still. My cock pushes out of my pants where I unzipped them straining against my boxers but it's at least a little more comfortable than these stupid fucking jeans.

I cup her face with my hands, my lips meeting hers as I thrust my tongue into her mouth exploring her and showing her how much I need her, just like she needs me. I begin sucking on her bottom lip, before swirling my tongue against hers. I remove one hand and start kissing her jaw down to her neck, sucking and biting my way down. Leaving marks along the way, probably hickies too, but I don't care. My little slut loves the marks I leave on her, she tells me all the time that it turns her on when she sees them on her body. I suck on her neck more before traveling down her collarbone, biting and sucking as I go. Once I get to her dress, I quickly pull it down, exposing her bare breasts to me, her pink nipples nice and hard just waiting for me to suck on them. I cup her right breast into my hand and pinch her other nipple with my left hand, I slowly swirl my tongue around her nipple before sucking it into my mouth, nibbling on it listening to her breathy moans, making my dick even harder. I slowly slide her dress down her body until it hits the floor. Goddamn, her beautiful, curved body makes my fucking heart stop, her delicious thick thighs make me practically drool thinking about the way they jiggle with her ass as she rides me, while my fingers dig into her sexy fucking hips.

"Step out of your dress, Sugar," I tell her as she puts her hands on her black lace thong getting ready to take it off. "I said step out of your dress, Emerald. I didn't say anything about touching your panties, baby." I lean in and slowly kiss between her breasts, pinching and pulling on her nipples with my fingers. I pull hard, making her cry out and moan.

"Shit, Creed," she cries breathlessly. "Please, I need you." She looks down at me with a seductive look on her face.

"Not yet, don't worry I'm gonna get you off, Sugar, but I'm gonna take my time teasing you first."

I look back up at her. "You're gonna like that aren't you, my little slut?" I ask her as I pull on her nipples harder listening to her cry out in the process.

"Y...ye...yesss," she moans between panting. "But." She lets out a breath. "But I want to come." She pouts. I can't get over her perfectly plump lips. The way they form to mine when I kiss her. Along with the adorable fucking facial expression that goes along with it almost tempts me enough to ruin my plans for what I want to do next.

"Always so needy aren't you, my little slut?" I look up, smirking at her before I start kissing my way down her stomach.

"Yes, I love when you please me," she moans out. "I love when your hands are on me, you make me feel sexy." She looks away, like she's suddenly shy or embarrassed.

"Emerald, my god, Sugar you are so goddamn sexy, you are absolutely breathtaking, and don't you ever... ever think anything else about yourself," I tell her. "Okay?" I repeat myself because I want her to know just how fucking beautiful she truly is, I want to know she heard me.

"It's just that... I just." I don't let her continue because I'm not about to let her argue with me about this.

"I said, okay?" I ask again, this time pinching her nipples hard.

"Ahh fuck," she cries. "It's just that–I don't," she tries again, but I don't want to hear her say negative things about herself.

"What did I say, Sugar?" I asked her again. She doesn't realize that I'll just keep asking until this gorgeous, stubborn woman listens to me, and I hear the answer that I want to hear. "You are fucking sexy and so goddamn gorgeous; do you understand me?" I know she told me she struggles with being confident about her body and I want her to love her body as much as I love it. Her curves are in all my favorite places. She's thinner in the waist, nice and thick in the hips and her ass. Fuck just thinking about her delicious fucking ass she's the definition of perfection in my eyes.

"Yes," she sighs trying to stop the smirk from forming on her face as she does. She knew I was going to win. It was just a matter of her letting me instead of being so damn stubborn.

"Yes what?" I reach around her, gripping her ass with my hands before removing my left hand and slapping her left side nice and hard, watching her eyes practically roll back as I do it.

"Yes, Creedence I understand." She smiles at me this time; I think pleased with the fact that I got my way. Or maybe she loves how obsessed with her I am.

"Good fucking girl. Now I don't want you to argue with me anymore about that." I place my hands on her hips and grip onto them pulling her closer to me as I kiss my way down stopping right before the top of her lace thong. I slowly pull them down, licking and sucking her skin until I stop right before her clit.

"Don't stop," she begs in a raspy voice. "Please, Creed."

"Don't worry. I'm just getting started." I stick my tongue out, licking between her folds, swirling it around on her sensitive swollen clit. I wrap my lips around it the best I can and suck it into my mouth making her cry out in pleasure. The sexiest sounds coming from her.

"Goddamn that feels so good." Her head slowly falls back as her eyes close, her breathing picking up.

I take my hands spreading her pussy to give me better access to her clit and keep licking and sucking. I remove my hands before sliding two fingers inside her, not even bothering to get them wet first, her cunt is fucking soaked, so I don't need to worry about my fingers being wet beforehand. I pump my two fingers in and out of her hitting her G-spot each time with the way I'm curving my fingers listening to her pant and moan out each time as I suck on her clit some more.

"Fuck, Creed I'm so close," she groans, her hands reach down gripping my hair making me moan, I love when she pulls my hair it's so fucking sexy.

"Ah. Ah, Sugar you're not allowed to come until I tell you to," I tell her as I suck harder getting her closer to the release that I refuse to give her just yet.

"Wha...what?" she asks as she looks down at me with a sad look on her face. "But I'm so close." There's those damn lips of hers that she loves pushing out into a pout. I love picturing them around my cock like that, her plump lips wrapped perfectly around my cock. Shit she's gonna be an addicting problem.

"Sorry, Sugar, I told you I'm teasing you first." I lick back up her slit, gathering her wetness with my tongue as I do, goddamn I can't get enough of her taste. I stop on her clit slowly circling the bud everywhere but her favorite spot. I want her on the edge of an orgasm begging me for the release her body craves from me.

"Creedence," she pants. "But I'm about to, please," she cries. I pull away from her, standing up quickly as I walk away from a panting and pouting Emerald.

"Creed, please." I ignore her as I start unbuttoning my shirt before taking it off. Then I pull my jeans down slowly, taking them off leaving me in just my black boxer-briefs.

I lean down and grab my belt from my pants and slowly walk over to Emerald, her back faces me, her sexy ass red with welted handprints from me spanking her. Which it's about to become redder from what I'm about to do to her.

"Put your hands in front of you and don't move or I'll tie you up, do you understand, Sugar?" I get my belt ready to hit her ass and pussy with it, she nods her head slowly before trying to look back at me.

"Ah. Ah, Sugar, eyes straight ahead," I tell her. "Now spread your legs as far as you can, keep your hands in front of you, and don't close your legs no matter what." I gently slap her pussy with my belt. She lets out a soft whimper, trying to close her legs. "Ah. Ah. Sugar, what did I say?" I slap her pussy with my belt a little harder this time.

"Ddd...don...don't close my legs." Her tits jiggle from her chest rising and falling, making my cock twitch. I love watching her tits bounce while fucking her pussy and the way those perfect things fucking jiggle right now.

"Good girl." It comes out as a growl. "What else baby?" My voice is hoarse, barely able to control how turned on I am.

"Don't mov...move my hands," she stutters as her body shivers.

"Good fucking girl don't be scared. I promise it'll only hurt a little, but the pleasure is going to outweigh the pain as I whip your pussy and your ass, okay, Sugar?" I want her to be aware of what I'm going to be doing to this delicious body of hers, especially since this is the first time I'm doing it. Next time though it'll be a surprise.

"Okay," she practically whispers and it's almost hard to even hear her say it over her panting.

I don't even give her a warning before I bring my belt back and swing it forward at her ass smiling at the instant red mark, then I swing up whipping her pussy making her jolt as she cries out in a moan.

"Fuck," she hisses, and it's followed by a moan, so I repeat what I just did whipping her ass in the same spot with a smile at the welt forming.

"God, you're taking this so well." Fuck, just the thought of how well she's taking this and how much it's turning her on makes my cock painfully hard. Looking at how red her beautiful skin is because of the pain and pleasure I'm causing makes me want to stop what I'm doing and just fuck her.

"You're doing so good, my little slut," I groan, painfully turned on. She whimpers a little as I repeat the same process, letting out breathless moans with every whip.

"You like that, Sugar?" I can tell she's loving it; I can see how wet her pussy is getting from here.

"Goddd yes," she moans. "I might come just from you whipping my pussy." She puts her head down like she's ashamed.

"Emerald, baby. Please don't be embarrassed. Don't be ashamed. Fuck, you have me so goddamn turned on. I don't think my cocks ever hurt this bad from being so fucking hard. It's okay to enjoy what I'm doing to you. Alright baby?" Shit the last thing I want is for her to feel like she's doing something wrong by enjoying this.

"Okay." I barely hear it, that's how quiet she is when she talks.

"But you're still not allowed to come yet until I tell you that you can, Sugar." I smile because I know those sexy lips of hers are pouting and I wish I could see it.

"But, Creed." You can hear that she's pouting in her sad tone.

"You wanna be my good girl, don't you?" I step closer to her then lean down, placing a gentle kiss on her cheek.

"Yes, Creedence I do," she moans out. Who knew me calling her my good girl could turn her on so much.

"Good girl. Now don't come, Sugar and I promise you you'll love this." I step away, whipping her ass and pussy one last time. Satisfied with how red she is and the welts on her ass. I come up behind her and squat down to kiss the welts, trailing kisses and licking along the way until I've licked and kissed every welt and red mark. Listening to her moans of pleasure is the best part. After I'm done, I stand up and walk away, setting my belt on my bed and turning around, I see her facing me now.

"Get on your knees, Sugar." I slowly pull my cock out, it's been ready for her, rock fucking hard, every vein sticking out as I pull it out of my black boxer briefs. She does as she's told, slowly getting on her knees with shaky legs from being spread for so long.

"Now crawl to me, Sugar." And her head whips up looking at me, her eyes a little wide. I smirk, she's so fucking sweet, I knew she'd be surprised.

"Wh...what?" she asks, confused.

"Be my good little slut, baby. I want you to crawl to me and then I want you to suck my cock." I tell her as I grip my cock in my hand and slowly stroke it, lubing it with my precum.

"Umm I don't." Her tone is a little shocked. I don't even let her finish what she's saying before I cut her off.

"Ah. Ah. Ah, Sugar, you don't tell me no." I wink at her, my smile growing. I stroke my hard cock a little faster, letting out a slight groan as I stare at her tits. "You can either be a good girl and crawl over here so I can watch you choke on my cock, or you can kneel there and watch me stroke myself and get myself off. But..." I pause spreading my precum some more.

"If you watch me get myself off you don't get to come, Sugar." And her eyes go wide as they slowly fill with tears. Fuck. That's the last thing I wanted. But my smile grows a little more.

"Don't cry, Sugar, you know I love those tears of yours. Besides, I promise you'll love crawling to me." I stroke my cock faster now. Watching her eyes follow the movements of my hand as she slowly licks her lips like she's silently craving me.

I let out another groan at the thought of her on her hands and knees. Now what's it gonna be? Are you going to be a good girl and crawl or am I gonna have to punish you and not let you come. Huh, Sugar?" She bites her bottom lip while watching me jerk myself off. I know she's enjoying this, she's just unsure how to react. This is all new to her.

"Fuck, you look so hot, Creed," she moans out. "I'll be your good girl and crawl," she pants. God damn she's so fucking hot. The tears stream down her red cheeks from embarrassment, her black mascara streaking down her cheeks with her tears.

She's already on her knees as she places her hands on the ground in front of her, causing her back to arch and her ass to stick up in the sexiest way. Fuck, do I wish I was behind her to see that view. I think about coming behind her and fucking her tight pussy like that. But that'll just ruin the fun.

"God, you look so fucking sexy like that, Sugar." The way her tits slightly hang down allowing me to see how hard her pink nipples are, the way I can see her curves perfectly, with all her tattoos on display, hugging every inch of her body, she looks good enough to eat and I'd love to lick and bite every inch of her. I can see her ass jiggling and her tits bouncing as she moves towards me, one hand in front of the other, the tears streaming down her cheeks as she bites her bottom lip.

"It's okay, Emerald, you don't have to cry, Sugar," I tell her as I slowly stroke my cock, extremely turned on while watching her on her hands and knees crawling to me.

She pauses for a minute. "I just... I feel stupid is all." She looks down as her cheeks turn a brighter shade of pink from blushing.

I stop and slowly walk towards her, leaning down as I place my fingers on her chin making her look back up at me. "Please, don't feel stupid," I say in a quiet voice, just above a whisper. "You have no idea how gorgeous you look, Emerald." I swipe her tear with my thumb and bring my thumb to my mouth sucking her tear off it before placing my fingers back on her chin.

"I want you to feel sexy and confident doing this, Sugar, not embarrassed. I won't make you crawl to me anymore, you can stand up, Em." I feel like an ass for making her feel the way I did. But she surprises me.

"No, I want to crawl to you, if you think I look sexy then it makes me feel sexy and right now turning you on and pleasing you is what I crave to do, Creedence." She's a little more confident than she was just a minute ago. "I also feel stupid because I... I kinda like doing this for you." There's nothing sexier than a woman who feels confident in what she's doing. She looked so sexy before, but the confidence added to it now makes my dick even harder.

"Now let me crawl to you, Creedence, I wanna watch you stroke your cock while I do." She stops to swallow for a second, you can tell her throat is a little dry. "Please?" Goddamn my little slut makes me harder than I thought possible.

"Fuck, you're so god damn sexy." I lean down a little more and kiss her on the lips. I stand back up and walk back over to my bed, she doesn't have much further to go but I want her to feel happy with herself for feeling a little more confident this time.

She slowly licks her lips making my cock twitch again as she crawls towards me with confidence this time, staring right into my eyes. She starts biting her lip again knowing it drives me crazy, she smirks a little in the process. She stops at my feet staring up at me with an innocent look in her eyes which drives me wild.

"Stay on your knees, Sugar." I continue to stroke myself, gripping my cock tighter as I do. Fuck, it feels so good, but her mouth around my cock right now would feel even better. "Be a good girl and stick your tongue out for me." I step towards her, then rub the tip of my cock with precum along her warm tongue letting out a moan as I do it.

"Fuck, your tongue feels so good." I know she only licked the tip but damn, the warmth from her velvety soft tongue and how wet it was just from one. Fucking. Lick. Fuck, does it feel good. I place the tip of my cock on her tongue again and this time she closes her mouth around it and sucks on it like a damn sucker, moaning in the process before she moves her head making a popping sound.

"Goddd Dammmn," I groan. "That was so fucking sexy." I'm so turned on right now and looking at her from this angle on her knees, looking up at me with those beautiful brown eyes, tears streak her cheeks as the mascara shows me where they fell. God, does she look so fucking gorgeous. She's my form of heaven and I'd love to be the god she worships.

"Please." It's one word but the tone of her voice, the slight pleading that comes along with it.

"Let me suck your cock, Creedence." Her voice comes out slow and seductive. Holy shit that's probably one of the hottest things she's said to me.

"Don't you worry, Sugar, you'll get to suck it but..." I pause, pushing her hair out of her face with my hand. "I'll be in control, while you gag and choke on my cock." She pouts a little and I have no idea what's wrong.

"But I wanna be in control, please, Creedence. I just wanna please you. I wanna feel your veins sliding against my tongue as it pulses while I suck on it. I wanna feel the precum drip from your cock as my tongue swirls around your head. I wanna feel each piercing graze my teeth as I lose control in your pleasure. Please, Creed. You have no idea how much it'll turn me on if you let me do it." I've never had a girl willingly beg to suck my cock the way she is right now and it's so tempting to just let her have her way. Fuck, why did she have to sound so goddamn sexy while saying that. As tempting as it is, there's something about listening to a forced gag that's just so hot...

Maybe I'll let her have it her way first.

"You can start but I wanna finish."

She smiles before gripping my cock, her small hand just closing around my thickness. She slowly brings the tip to her mouth, licking her lips like she just can't wait to taste me. She places the tip to her tongue against the head of my throbbing cock and rubs her tongue right across the drop of precum waiting for her.

She sucks the tip into her mouth at a torturously slow pace and it feels so. Fucking. Good. I never want this form of pleasure that her mouth is giving me to end. Swirling her tongue around just the tip still, this must be her way of teasing me. It's driving me crazy that she's not giving me more, but at the same time it feels too goddamn good, and I'd love to have her mouth wrapped around me like this all the time.

She takes me as far as she can, hitting the back of her throat, wishing the rest of my length could feel her warm mouth too.Fuck, her warm mouth feels like heaven. She slides her tongue up and down my length before sucking back down to the head. Sucking on it like she would a piece of candy and I was her favorite flavor.

She opens a little, keeping her lips tight as she swirls her tongue around my shaft and I'm sure I could come just like this. But I'm not ready yet. I want to get lost in the feel of her and enjoy the softness of her tongue as it strokes me over and over. She takes it all the way to the back of her throat, angling her head to get me deeper working her mouth like she's swallowing me down, like she can't get me in there fast enough.

The way she's moaning as she does is so attractive. To see a woman getting lost in the pleasure she's giving you is so fucking sexy. She swallows me down her throat like my cock is her favorite thing to eat.

"Fuckkk your mouth feels so good, my little slut," I groan as I throw my head back from the pleasure.

She sucks on it, swirling her tongue around, teasing my piercings as she does and goddamn, I've never had someone suck my cock this good. Usually, they're afraid to hurt me because of my piercings so they barely do anything. I'm getting way too close if I don't take over now. I'll come before I get the chance to hear her gag or choke.

"My turn to fuck your face now, Sugar." I grip the back of her head, not giving her enough time to take a breath before shoving my cock all the way to the back of her throat. I tilt her head so that I can get my cock down into it. She swallows a little before gagging and making a choking sound which brings a smile to my face. I hold it there in that position as I slightly move my hips back and forth. It feels too good to move all the way and I love watching the tears fill her eyes. Her tears start streaming down her face as I slowly pull out of her throat not wanting to hurt her. I pull out enough for her to get some air before plunging back into her mouth hitting her throat again. It'll probably be sore from how rough I'm going and from my Jacob's ladder, but I told her I was going to fuck her face and I'm not going to be gentle about it, because let's be serious, am I gentle when I fuck a pussy? So why would I be gentle fucking my little sluts' mouth?

I continue to hold the back of her head while taking my cock all the way into her throat back and forth barely letting her get air. Her mascara smudges across her cheeks as her tears continue to fall and I can't help but think how beautiful she looks right now. The sound of her mouth slurping and her gagging fills the air as her drool puddles at the corners of her mouth, dripping down her cheeks and all I feel is the wetness from her chin against my balls and I love how sloppy this all is, something about the tears, the extra spit all of that messing me up and her right along with it really gets me fucking going.

My balls start to tighten, and I know I'm getting close, so I pump faster into her mouth.

"Goddamn, Sugar," I growl. "I'm about to come." I at least give her a warning before pumping two more times before slowly thrusting in the back of her throat as my cum spills into her, into her throat. I can feel her swallow it down as she moans.

"Fuck, Emerald, your mouth is so amazing," I pant, still trying to catch my breath from how good that just felt. I start to pull out of her but before moving away she grips my cock putting the tip back into her mouth sucking on it again, multiple times getting every last drop from me before making that sexy popping noise as she pulls my cock from her mouth.

"Mmm, god you taste so good." She gasps for air, trying to catch her breath from me, cutting off her breathing through half of that blowjob.

"That felt so good, I can't get over how incredible your mouth feels. I'd let you suck my cock whenever you wanted to," I tell her, wiping her tears with my thumbs.

"Next time I get to do the whole thing myself without you taking control, I promise you won't be disappointed, okay?" she pouts out that pouty bottom lip of hers, making me want to suck it into my mouth.

"Alright, Emerald, I'll let you do it next time." I fully believe she'll do great on her own, that perfect mouth of hers sure holds a lot of pleasure.

"Pinky promise?" She bites her bottom lip and holds out her pinky to me.

"Sugar, I'll pinky promise you anything if it involves that mouth of yours." I give her my pinky, interlocking them and shaking them together. I still love that she loves pinky promises just as much as I do.

"I can't wait." She starts to slowly stand up. I hold my hand out to help her up, her legs a little shaky from being on her knees for so long.

She steps towards me the same time I pull her towards me, and I cup her face with my hands, and lean down to kiss her, her mouth opening for me as I swirl my tongue with hers, kissing her tenderly. I push her back onto my bed as she shrieks a little from the sudden movement and unexpected fall. Giggling she wraps her hand around my neck pulling me towards her as she wraps her legs around me. My hard cock instantly resting against the entrance of her pussy, begging to be inside her. I'm not ready to fuck her yet, not that I don't want to be inside her, but I don't do normal sex, I still have to tie her up.

I stop kissing her and get up really quick and grab the butt plug that I bought her from my nightstand along with the lube and come back to the bed, crawling on top of her.

"Move to the middle of the bed, Emerald," I tell her as I get up onto my knees. "Lay on your stomach, knees under your chest," I tell her in a firmer tone than usual. She gets up onto her knees, turning around showing off her thick juicy ass as she gets down onto her hands and knees. Her ass pushed up into the air at the perfect angle putting her dripping wet pussy and tight hole on display, for my eyes only. No one will ever look at this delicious pussy of mine ever again, because I refuse to lose her. She crawls over to the middle of the bed at a torturously slow pace, watching her ass jiggle as she crawls. Her pussy noticeably wet just begging to be fucked. She tucks her knees under her as she bends down, placing her head against the bed as she turns to the side, placing her hands down next to her head.

"I bought something for you," I tell her as I kneel and pour the lube onto the plug. It's a smaller one, I know she's not ready for a bigger one yet and although I like causing pain, I don't want to hurt her like that. I pour the lube onto her ass and spread the lube around with my fingers making her flinch in the process.

"It's okay, Sugar, just relax baby," I tell her because if she tightens up then she'll be even more uncomfortable during the whole thing.

"Wha...what are you doing?" she asks in a nervous tone, stuttering a little as she asks.

"I bought you a butt plug, Sugar. I'm going to put it in that tight ass of yours before I fuck that tight wet pussy," I tell her as I slowly push my thumb into her ass.

"No moving sugar, or I'm going to tie you up before I'm ready." I pause, getting another Idea. "Actually, never mind, I'm ready to tie you up now." I reach for my belt and slide it under the front of her shins, closer to her knees but more towards the middle before sliding each strap over each thigh, I loop it through the buckle and push the prong through the small hole before looping the rest of the strap through the other hole. Then I tighten it around her legs as tight as it can go. Making her hiss out as I do. I take her arms and put them behind her back and grab a rope from my nightstand before tying them together making her hiss out again from how tight I tie them. Now she's stuck bent over with her knees to her chest and hands tightly tied behind her back, they're definitely going to be rubbed raw by the time we're done if she tries fighting them.

Now that I have her how I want her, on display for me to touch however I need and to tease until she begs for me. Mmm, she's fucking perfect.

I come up behind her and play with her ass again, pouring a little more lube on it before pushing my thumb into her ass again.

"Ahhh fuck, Creed," she groans. "That hurt a little." Her voice comes out pouty.

"Sorry, Sugar, the butt plug is not going to feel much better," I tell her, hoping that my little warning prepares her for what is coming next.

"I'm gonna slowly start putting this in your ass now, but don't worry, baby I put a lot of lube on the plug," I tell her, hoping it doesn't hurt her too much.

"Fuck, okay." Her voice comes out nervous.

"Take a deep breath for me and just try to relax, Sugar, if you fight it or tense up it's going to hurt more, okay?" I ask and tell her at the same time.

"Shit, yeah I'm ready." She lets out a slow breath that sounds like she was holding it in and then her body relaxes.

I take the tip of the plug and rub it against her before slowly pushing in the tip.

"Ow fuck," she hisses, tightening up a little.

"Relax your body, Sugar. That way it goes in easier." I push the tip back in and gently twist it as I do. I push in a little more, getting it about halfway in still twisting it around to help relax and loosen it to take the full plug.

"Good fucking girl we're almost there we're about halfway there, Emerald," I groan, turning myself.

"Shit, okay." She takes another deep breath in before letting it out.

I twist and push the rest of it in making her yelp as I do it. "You okay? You did a good job, it's all the way in, Sugar," I tell her as I gently slap her ass making her moan out.

"Fuck, yes I'm okay, thank god that's over with, it just feels uncomfortable, full," she tells me as I go to my phone and open the app for the vibrations. I couldn't just buy her a butt plug and not let her have fun with it. I turn it on the lowest setting, and she shrieks a little.

"Oh my god...oh goddd." Her shriek turns into little moans as the pleasure outweighs the pain.

"Do you like that, my little slut?" My lips curl up into a smile, god I love this woman, she couldn't be more perfect for me. "God look at this pussy of yours it's so wet, Sugar." I take two fingers, dragging it up and down her slit before pushing them inside her right to her G-spot and back out. Pumping in and out making her cry out in a moan.

"Fuck, Creed. That feels so good, and so strange." She giggles a little like she's embarrassed, so I remind her just in case.

"Don't be embarrassed, Sugar, it's okay for it to feel good that's why I'm doing this, I knew you'd like it," I tell her as I come down and slap her ass with my other hand.

"Ahhh goddd," she cries. "Don't stop please, I'm so, so close," she's panting as she tries to push herself into my fingers, but she struggles to do so with the way I have her tied.

"Ah. Ah. Ah, Sugar. Remember you're not allowed to come until I say you can, gorgeous." She turns her head the best she can to look back at me and pouts.

"Please, I need to so bad I'm so close," she pants out between words.

"Not yet, Em, I promise when you get to it's going to feel amazing." I remove my fingers so I can get ready to fuck her wet cunt.

"Do you trust me, baby?" I ask.

"God yes, yes I trust you, just please, Creedence." She begs and it's so fucking sexy, listening to the pleading in her voice as she does it.

"Please, what beautiful?" I know exactly what she wants but it turns me on to hear her say it. To hear her beg me to please her.

"I need to come please," she says as I place my cock at her wet entrance and slowly slide it up and down her wet slit all the way up to her clit. Rubbing it back and forth on her clit before taking it back down to her entrance and repeating the same thing again. I linger a little longer on her clit because I love how she sounds when she moans. And I want to tease her, build up the pleasure more.

"I'm about to fuck this pussy of yours, Sugar, but don't you dare come until I say you can, okay?" I push my cock halfway into her pussy listening to her cry out before pulling out again.

"But... but please, Creedence I need to come." She's practically begging me and it's the sexiest thing ever.

"Not yet, baby I promise you it'll feel good. Do you wanna be my good little slut?" I give her ass a gentle slap watching it jiggle against my hand, squeezing it tightly as I groan.

"Yes," she pants as I rub my cock against her entrance. Fucking shit, her pussy glistens as I look down. She's so goddamn wet which is good because I'm definitely in the mood to fuck. "I'll be good and wait." She's patiently waiting for me to push my cock inside her as I slowly stick just the tip in hissing out a breath because even that alone feels amazing.

"God please fuck me, Creed." She tries to push her body into me for me to slide in her pussy more.

"You want more of my cock huh?" I ask, still teasing her. Sliding the tip in and out, then I take it out and rub it against her clit again before sliding it back in about halfway this time, not ready to go fully in but torturing myself in the process.

"Shit. Your cock feels so good." Her panting voice comes out breathless.

"Your tight cunt is my favorite, Sugar," I tell her as I push my cock all the way in going as deep as I can this time, squeezing both ass cheeks in the process. I move my hands down a little and spread her pussy to get a little deeper as I pump in and out of her. Feeling my piercings rub her walls as her pussy clamps down around me.

I move my hand back and slap her ass hard, before coming around with my other hand and grab her throat. She cries out in almost a whisper from me cutting off some of her air flow as I continue gripping her throat and fucking her pussy. The sound of our sweaty bodies slapping, her whispered moans and me groaning out is all you can hear in the quiet room. I usually don't make much noise during sex, but her pussy feels so good I can't help myself. I could stay inside her forever and never get sick of it. I use my free hand and grab my phone, turning up the vibrations on the butt plug to the next level and she lets out a soft whimper, followed by a quiet

"Oh goddd." Her tortured moans from all the pleasure, those noises are my favorite. I put my phone down, taking my free hand as I reach around to rub her clit. "Ahh fucckk." Her voice raspy from me still holding her throat. I squeeze a little tighter, cutting off the air completely because I know she's getting close because her body is starting to shake, and I can feel her muscles tightening below me.

"Don't you dare come yet, Sugar," I tell her again because I want to come with her, there's something about having sex and coming with the person you're fucking that I love. I want to make sure she's enjoying it the same time I am.

"I'm getting close, Emerald, god your pussy feels so good, Sugar," I tell her as I pump faster to get myself closer to coming and I feel my balls start to tighten. "Go ahead, my good girl come for me, Sugar," I tell her as I massage her clit a little faster with my thumb.

Her pussy clamps down tightening around on my cock the same time my cock starts throbbing inside her, my cum spilling into her pussy. I let go of her throat and she starts gasping for air as she moans out, her body trembling from her orgasm soaring through her.

"Fuck that was intense." She's breathing heavily as she rests her face into the mattress. I come down one more time smacking her ass, not hard just playfully as her body slowly goes limp.

"Fuck that felt so good," I tell her because I don't think there's ever been a time where we fucked, and it didn't feel amazing.

"Mmm, god yes it did." She turns her head to the side a little, looking back at me. "My arms hurt, and my legs are sore." She lets out another deep breath. "Can you untie me please?" She wiggles her body, whimpering.

"Yes, Sugar, I'll do that right now, baby." I let her know so that way she doesn't start to panic from being in the same position for so long. "I'm going to remove the plug first." I grab my phone, shutting the vibrations setting off and slowly start removing the plug. She hisses a little as I do, probably sore from having it in for so long. After removing the plug, I go to her arms.

"Thank you." She wiggles her arms as I untie them for her.

"Fuck, my arm feels like it's going to cramp up." She pulls her arms in front of her as I undo the belt around her thighs. I help pull her up into a sitting position so she can stretch her sore legs.

"Here let me rub you, baby," I tell her as I come up behind her and softly massage her shoulders rubbing down her arms as she sits on my bed. Her slightly sweaty skin is so soft as I rub it. I get down off the bed and kneel down in front of her not even caring that I'm naked. My dick still hard just from looking at her sexy naked body. Like I said before I constantly have a hard dick around her no matter what I do to try and get rid of it.

"God that feels good." I come down in front and start rubbing her thighs and lower legs all the way down to her feet, taking my time massaging her, hopefully helping the blood flow in the process.

"Good, I'm glad it feels good, baby, but damn, Sugar, I could fuck you again right now. Just looking at your sexy body is getting me going again," I tell her as I look up at her.

"How do you think I feel sitting here with your hard cock right in front of me just begging me to suck it." She pauses, smiling. "Or sit on it and ride you again."

"Mmm, damn my little slut, just begging me to fuck you again huh?" I chuckle.

"God yes." The look of lust in her eyes. "Get up here and fuck me with that hard cock of yours please, Creed." That's all I needed before standing up and pushing her back on the bed. I crawl up over her, positioning myself between her legs.

"But wait, please this time, don't tie me up. I just want to be fucked normally."

"Don't worry, Sugar, I don't want to tie you up. This time I want to make love to you gorgeous." I position myself on top of her before slowly sliding my cock into her nice, warm pussy.

"Fuck, Emerald, your pussy was made for me, Sugar." I pump in and out of her, getting lost in the way her pussy fits around my cock, like it was made just for me. Just tight enough to hug my cock perfectly, squeezing me each time I pump in and out of her. She wraps her legs around me tightly as I interlock my fingers with hers holding her hands above her head, but not in a forceful way, in a loving way. I lean down and kiss her lips passionately before pulling away.

"I'm in love with you, Sugar," I tell her. "That's what I mean when I tell you I love you." I pant, pumping into her. "I love you and." I pump in and out, slowing down so I don't come too quickly. "And I'm in love with you, Sugar. I don't want anyone else. Ever." I fuck her a little faster than I was before now.

"God, I love you so much, Creedence." And I look up into her tear-filled eyes.

"What's wrong, baby?" I ask her with a concerned look on my face.

"Nothing. I just–I'm afraid to lose you," she says breathlessly. "I can't imagine my life without you now that I have you," she pants in between her words.

"Oh god. I'm getting so close. Please let me come this time." She wraps her legs tighter around me pushing me deeper into her with her feet.

"Don't worry, Sugar, I won't stop you from coming." I smile down at her. "I'm never going to leave you. Like I just said I can't imagine my life without you, I don't even want to think about being without you because I don't know who I am if I'm breathing without you, Emerald. I love you too much," I tell her as I come down, my lips crashing into hers.

"I love you too much too, Creedence." Then comes back in to kiss me some more.

23
EMERALD

I lay there in Creedence's bed staring at his handsome sleeping face. Biting my bottom lip thinking about all the sex and everything else we did last night. Slightly blushing in the process. I think I lost count of the amount of times we fucked last night and the number of orgasms I had. My body is so sore, I'm not complaining though because I'm sore in the best ways possible but

I'm dreading today because I'm a little hungover and I have to go to work. I'm excited to be working with Winter but hate the fact that I have to work with fucking Stacy, she's nice sometimes but it seems fake to me. She's usually one of those prissy bitches who think they're better than everyone, she whines about everything and has the worst case of resting bitch face. I'm known to have resting bitch face myself, but like I said hers is in the worst way possible making her natural beauty very fucking ugly. She's a natural blonde with beautiful blue eyes, but she tans too much and usually has an orange tint to her what could have been pretty skin. She also tries to steal boyfriends and for some reason thinks every male customer is obsessed with her. I feel bad for her, but she does it to herself honestly.

I shake my head to bring myself out of my thoughts before turning to look at the time on my phone to see that it's not even eight in the morning, what the fuck am I doing up so early? No wonder I still feel like shit. I decide to snuggle in a little closer to Creedence. He starts moving and I hope I didn't wake him up, but he shifts closer wrapping his arm around my waist and snuggling his face into the crook of my neck.

"Go back to bed, Sugar, you wake up too early," he mumbles a little, his voice scratchy and it sounds so sexy. I giggle to myself because for some reason he makes me feel giddy all the time.

"It's very early, don't worry, babe I won't wake you up yet. I'm going back to bed, I feel like shit," I groan, that gets his attention without me wanting to.

"Are you okay?" his voice a slight panic. "What's wrong, Sugar?" He leans up onto his right elbow, leaning over to look down at me.

"I'm okay, just a little nauseous from all the alcohol and hung over, that's all I think. I'll be okay if I get some more sleep," I tell him as I stretch my head up and kiss his soft lips.

"I'm sorry baby, do you need anything?" His sleepy voice comes out raspy and it's sexy and cute at the same time.

"That's sweet of you but I'm okay, babe. I just need to go back to sleep for at least another hour or so." I yawn as my eyes start to feel heavy again.

"Alright, Sugar, go back to sleep. Love you." He leans down and kisses me, then goes back to snuggling me with his face in the crook of my neck.

"I love you, you handsome, handsome man." I snuggle the rest of my body close to his, draping my legs over his before closing my eyes and drifting off.

I wake up to feeling a chill at my back where Creedence is no longer at. I turn over and see he's not in the bed anymore and roll onto my back wondering where he went and sad he didn't wake me. I look over at my phone and see I fell back asleep for an hour and twenty minutes which I hate. I feel like I wasted my morning. I'm usually up pretty early especially when I have to work at noon because I like to have some time to myself before work, but I guess I needed the sleep especially after all those nasty shots last night. I look at my phone again and see I have a text from Creedence.

Creedence
Morning, Sugar, I didn't want to wake you because you looked so peaceful and gorgeous sleeping, but I had a last minute appointment at the shop, it was a walk in and I didn't want to pass it up. Text me when you wake up, feel free to stay as long as you need to before work. Oh also yes I did kiss you goodbye before I left before you get upset. Love you.

Emerald
Morning handsome, I miss you already. Thank you for the sweet text and the goodbye kiss. Love you.

Emerald
hope your day is going well too.

I head into the kitchen to find something to eat and settle on some toast with jelly and some coffee hoping that'll at least help the nauseous feeling in my stomach. I don't feel as terrible as I did the first time I woke up but my stomach is still very upset.

After I eat, I head to the bathroom to brush my teeth and shower, that way it's one less thing I have to do when I head to my house to change. We don't have a uniform at Lisa's Diner as long as we wear work appropriate clothing that's all she cares about. I settled on a plain pink T-shirt with a pair of black leggings that I had left at Creed's house that he washed for me. I decide to wear my hair up in a messy ponytail with my pink scrunchie that Creedence got me, something to feel close to him with during my long shift and my black converse. I walk outside and sit down on the porch to put my shoes on and check my phone to see if Creedence has texted me back yet.

Creedence
God I miss you so much, Sugar. I can't wait to
wrap my arms around you. Love you baby.

Creedence
my day is good, probably got another hour here
then I'm done for the day, maybe I'll come up and
have some lunch at the Diner, does that sound
good?

> **Emerald**
> I can't wait to be in your arms babe, I feel like it's
> been days since I've seen you and it's only been a
> few hours lol.

> **Emerald**
> that would be perfect. I know seeing you would
> make my day and my shift a hell of a lot better.
> I'm working with Winter which is great ... but I'm
> also working with Stacy... uhhhhhhh :(

Creedence
That's how I feel. I'm glad I'm not alone with how
obsessed I am with you. I feel like I didn't just kiss
you goodbye this morning.

> **Emerald**
> No babe, I'm just as obsessed. I wish I was awake
> to say goodbye to you...although it was probably
> a good thing because then I'm sure you would
> have been late for work lol.

Creedence
Why is Stacy such a nasty person? I feel like the
whole Diner dislikes her except for Lisa... but
makes me wonder if Lisa truly likes her?

Creedence
I'd like to say I'm more obsessed than you are…
you have no idea, Emerald you're mine and no
one else's. No, if you would have been awake I
would've said fuck the tattoo and stayed home to
be in that tight pussy of yours.

Emerald
Thanks now I'm going to work with wet panties
and horny. Thanks babe.

Emerald
No I'm convinced Lisa just feels bad for her and
only gave her the job due to knowing her family. I
gotta leave for work now. I'll text you when I get
there.

Creedence
Damn, Sugar, why do you have to tease me like
that? Making my cock hard right before I'm about
to go back to tattooing.

Creedence
Can't wait to feel how wet that pussy is and I can't
wait to taste you ;) Drive safely. Love you,
Emerald.

Emerald
Fuck… now I'm gonna have to deal with a wet
pussy and wet panties all night. Might have to
sneak to your truck and fuck you on break. ;) Love
you babe.

I stand up to walk towards my car when I hear a noise next door, I look up to a yelling Axton on his phone and stand there with a concerned look on my face. He has been staying at his girlfriend's house so it's almost like he doesn't even live with Creedence anymore. I'm curious what's wrong though and way too nosey not to stand here and listen.

"No, if you wouldn't have cheated this wouldn't be over," he yells into his phone as he rests his elbows against his jeep, his back facing me. I feel bad listening into his conversation, but I need to see if he's okay.

"No, I don't fucking care if you're crying or heartbroken. You don't think I'm fucking heartbroken, god you fucking destroyed me. Dude, I wanted to fucking marry you and you fucking cheated." He pauses I'm assuming to listen to what she has to say. "No, I refuse to fucking take you back. Fuck off stop calling me actually delete my fucking number. Better yet, I'll just fucking block your ass." He hangs up the phone and does something on his phone, I'm assuming blocking her like he said he would. I clear my throat as he turns around.

"Fuck, I didn't see you there, I'm assuming you heard the whole conversation?" He puts his head down with a sad look on his face.

"Nah, just part of it." I look away feeling awkward and like an ass for just standing there and listening when it wasn't my business. "Sorry for listening to you. I was getting ready to get in my car cause I gotta get to work and I heard you yelling, it scared me for a second cause I didn't know what was going on. I thought something was wrong." Oh my god I'm such an idiot. I bring my hand to my face shaking my head. "I mean there was something wrong, but I thought something was wrong with you." What the fuck is my problem, could I dig myself any fucking deeper?

"Goddamn I'm an idiot, I'm sorry I'm literally just digging my hole deeper as I talk to you. I'm such an ass. He looks up and smirks at me, he's got a nice smile, not that I'm checking him out but it's hard to miss that he's attractive. He's crazy tall he's gotta be at least six foot five, maybe I'm exaggerating but I swear I heard Creedence who is fucking tall too. say that he was that height. He's covered in tattoos, which is hot. Tattoos are my weakness. It's hard to tell the color of his eyes from here but his lashes are so dark it makes his eyes pop whatever color they are. His beard really makes him look like the bad boy that he, Creedence, Carsten and Chase paint themselves to be. Bears are also my weakness. Fucking hot. Overall Axton is an attractive man. He's not my type but he's hot and I'd have no problem admitting that if Creedence asked my opinion of him, I'd have no issues telling him he has hot friends. Obviously, a relationship isn't based off of just looks but who would want to cheat on him? How could anyone cheat in general, I could never. Even if I wasn't with Creedence and I was in a committed relationship, I could never imagine doing that to someone, my heart breaks for him.

"I'm sorry I hope you get what I'm trying to say." I shake my head. Feeling like such an idiot.

"Yes, I do, it's okay. You don't have to apologize; this is an awkward situation." He's standing there putting one hand in his pocket while pushing his other hand through his already messy hair. You can tell he's heartbroken, I mean who wouldn't be, but you can tell he's trying to keep it together with the sad look on his face.

"This is going to be such a dumb question that I'm going to ask but as one of your best friends' girlfriends I need to be nosey and ask." I chuckle a little hoping that lightens the mood and he chuckles bringing his hand down over his face and then sliding it into his left pocket. He stands there with both hands in his pocket while rocking back and forth on his feet. You can tell it's a nervous habit that he can't control especially right now in the awkward situation we both caught ourselves in.

"Are you okay?" I pause. "I know that is such a dumb question to ask but I can't leave for work without asking you that." I look down at my phone. I have to leave in the next minute or I'm going to be late, although Lisa would understand she loves the boys and wouldn't hold it against me if I explained.

He lets out a long sigh bringing his right hand out of his pocket and brushing it through the other side of his hair. "It's not stupid, it's a natural reaction when someone knows someone isn't okay. That's like the first thing they want to ask no matter how stupid it might be at that moment, so I'm not upset that you're asking it. I appreciate it." He lets out another breath like he's been holding it. "Right now. FUCK." His voice grows a little louder. Not quite a yell. "I'm not okay, I feel like my whole world just came crashing down, but will I be, okay? Maybe not today or tomorrow." He looks down sounding like he's getting choked up. "Goddamn, three fucking years of my life wasted." He lets out a small, sad laugh. "I was gonna fucking marry her." He lets out an angry laugh. "I loved her more than anything, at least I thought I did. But now, not so much." He stops again, struggling with what to say next. "Fuck this sucks, never thought I'd wake up this morning to find out she was cheating. Sorry I know you gotta go. Thanks for listening to me." He sighs putting his hands back in his pocket, with a look on his face that is so fucking sad it breaks my heart. I can't just leave here without hugging him. I don't know him as well as I'd like to, he's not a stranger but with how much time he's spent at his girlfriend's house, I can't even remember the girl's name. I had only met her once, not that it's important now. But I still feel the need to comfort him. I know I'd probably want a hug in this situation. I slowly walk towards him and laugh a little.

"Sorry, this might be awkward." I hold my arms out and he comes in for a hug wrapping his arms around me. I pat him on the back. "You might not think it's going to be okay, but it will be eventually. I wish I could say more or could say something to take away what you're feeling right now, but I hope at least my hug can help ease some of your heartache." I pause. "Text Creedence, he's going to be coming up to my work for some lunch, you don't need to be alone right now I'm sure he would love the company," I tell him as I pull away from the hug.

"Thanks for that, I appreciate it. I'll think about it." He sighs a long sigh brushing his hand through his hair again. "I think right now I just need to be alone for a little bit." He gives me a sad, barely there smile.

"Well, you know what to do if you don't want to be alone. I hope your day gets better." I give him an awkward smile because that was probably the dumbest thing I could have thought of saying to him. Fuck, I don't do well with awkward situations.

"Thanks, have a good day at work." He starts walking up the driveway and hitting the lock button on his keys.

"Thanks, I'll try," I say as I walk back over to my car quietly cursing to myself because I'm officially late for work. Hopefully Lisa understands.

I pull out of my driveway quickly, driving a little faster to work than normal hoping I don't get stopped by any of the asshole cops in our town. It's like once you get pulled over one time, they're always on the lookout for you even if you're not a bad person. It's a small town so they don't have much to do besides harass everyone and I hate it.

"Of course I get stuck at EVERY. FUCKING. RED. LIGHT," I yell to myself and once the light turns green the driver in front of me sits there for a few minutes before they decide to start moving.

"C'mon asshole, DRIVE," I yell because I'm already ten minutes late and not in the mood for stupid drivers. Okay I might be a little extra bitchy from just being late but still I usually get road rage pretty easily especially when people sit there and don't pay attention to green lights, or when they drive under the speed limit. I turn the corner a little quicker than I need to and fuck. I hurry up and slow down because I see a cop clocking people in the parking lot to the left of me. I start to sweat hoping he didn't see how fast I turned that corner and of fucking course, just my luck he pulls out behind me. I put both of my sweaty palms on the wheel and pray he's not going to turn his lights on. I shut my eyes tightly at the next light and pray they just leave me alone. I have one more turn and I'm at work that's it. But no, as soon as the light turns green... Guess what? The fucker turns his lights on pulling me over. I pull over into the parking lot next to me not wanting to block traffic and put my car in park.

"Mother fucker!" I whisper yell to myself, so he doesn't hear yelling outside my car as he walks towards me. Not that my window is open yet but just in case. Don't want to give him any reasons to arrest me. He walks to my window the same time I start rolling mine down and I see in my side mirror that it's Officer Johnston, I swear he is the ONLY cop that fucking pulls me over. Wonder if he thinks I'm cute, he is pretty young, maybe I can use that to my advantage and try flirting with him. Maybe it'll help get me out of getting a ticket.

"Good afternoon." He leans down to see me. "Emerald." He smirks a little like he didn't know who I fucking was when he was pulling me over...asshole. I swear he just does it for fun.

"Good afternoon, Officer Johnston." I try not to roll my eyes in the process.

"Do you know why I pulled you over?" He rests his arms on the roof of my car looking down as he talks to me. And I swear he's looking down my shirt as he does.

"Nope, but I'm sure you're not going to waste any time telling me." I give him a fake smile back.

"Getting smart with me isn't going to help you at all, Emerald. Now look, you and I both know that you came speeding around that corner while taking that turn." His smile widens a little bit more.

"Sorry sir." I pause trying to give him a little bit of a flirty smile along with it. "I'm late for work at Lisa's Diner and now, I'm going to be even more late, but that's why I was speeding. I'm sorry. Honestly." I let out the breath I've been holding while wiping my sweaty palms on my leggings.

"Ahhh Lisa, she's great, I love the food there." I accidentally cut him off with an idea.

"I can give you a discount the next time you come in." I give another flirty smile hoping I'm helping myself out here.

"Emerald?" He chuckles.

"Yes, Officer? I bat my lashes a little hoping to help myself out here.

"Are you trying to bribe me?" He smirks again and I think this idea might be working.

"Depends on if it's working?" I bite my bottom lip, the corner of my mouth curling up a little.

"How about this one time I let it slide and then maybe I'll take you up on that offer, but–" He pauses, tapping his chin. "Please try not to speed next time, or anytime in general," he states. "Look, I get being stressed from being late, but that's not going to benefit you at all." He taps the side of my car with his hands.

"Sorry sir. I honestly didn't realize how fast I was going," I say, lying to him a little. I knew I was speeding but I don't know how fast I was really going.

"Have a good day, Emerald, try not to speed." He taps my car again and walks away.

"Thanks Officer Johnston," I yell out my window before rolling it up.

I put my car in drive and pulled out of the parking lot heading to work, my second attempt of today.

"Fuck, I hope this doesn't mean I'm going to have a shitty night." I whisper to myself as I pull into the parking lot of Lisa's Diner. See I wasn't lying when I said I was so close to work.

I pull into a parking spot and look at all the cars.

"Fuck we look busy," I say to myself again, since I love talking to myself apparently.

I put my car in park, grab my stuff and get out of the car locking it with my keys and rush in through the back door.

"Fuck, I'm so late," I whisper-growl hoping no one is back here. I need to go find Lisa before anyone spots me, especially Stacy.

I rush through the door and into the locker room to put my apron on, grab my other stuff I need and put everything in my locker texting Creed first to let him know I made it so he doesn't worry.

Emerald
Hey babe, I'm at work. I'm so fucking late. I'll explain later just didn't want you to worry since you haven't heard from me. See you when you get here. Love you.

I place my phone into my locker and turn around to go and find

Lisa right as the door opens to the back room. FUCK. Of course it's Stacy.

"Ohhh look who is super late," she practically sings out with a nasty smile on her face like she thinks I'll get fired or something for it.

"Yes, I'm fully aware I'm late. Thank you for pointing out the obvious." I give her my smart-ass answer. If she's going to be a bitch, two can play that game.

"Oohh feisty today huh? It's not my fault you can't be on time, Emerald. You have regulars that have been waiting for you. If I was them, I would have left already or went to a different section, ya know to a section of an employee that actually shows up on time." She has this disgusted look on her face as she crosses her arms while smacking her gum obnoxiously.

"Stacy. Stacy. Stacy. You obviously don't realize I'm not going to take your shit. So why don't you take your nosey ass bitchy attitude and shove it up your ass." I smile to her and right as I'm about to walk away the door opens again and Lisa comes walking in.

"Oh my god, Emerald." Her voice comes out quickly in a panic. Stacy smiles at me with an 'I told you so' look on her face which falls as quickly as it appeared, with a look on her face like what the hell? When she realizes Lisa is worried and not angry. "I'm so glad you're okay, Emerald. I thought something happened to you. Please come to my office and talk to me." She walks to me, grabs my hand and walks me out of the break room with her.

Lisa is more like a mom to everyone who works for her, it's rare that she gets mad at you for being late, or mad at you in general. What I love the most is she always gives you a chance to explain your side before she says anything about the situation.

"Come in sweet girl, come in. Tell me you're okay?" Her face scrunched up with a concerned look in her eyes.

"Hi Lisa," I start off with. "Sorry I was coming to find you then Stacy stopped me in the break room before I had the chance." I roll my eyes a little before I continue. "So, let me start from the beginning," I breathe out. "I was in my driveway walking to my car when Axton pulled in next door and was yelling on the phone. Me being my nosey self I had to stop and listen to what he was saying. I still had about five minutes before I had to leave, so I wasn't worried." I breathe out again, I'm talking so fast to get everything out quickly that I almost forget to breathe between words, or even sentences. "So, he was yelling on the phone because he had found out that his girlfriend of three years was cheating on him." She gasps, putting her hand over her mouth.

"Oh no sweetie, is he okay?" She stops, a strange look on her face before she continues to talk. "Well shit that was dumb to ask. I know he's not okay but is he okay?" She laughs at herself.

"See I did the same thing, I asked him the same question out of habit I wanted to make sure he was okay and then we talked a little and you could tell he was just so heartbroken." I sigh, thinking of the look on his face again and how sad he was. It broke my heart.

"So, when I left, I was only going to be late by a few minutes but then my terrible fucking luck." I stop putting my hand over my mouth. Shit. Oops I didn't mean to swear like that, I didn't think about who I was talking to when I said it. "Sorry Lisa." She waves it off as I squint one eye shut almost like I'm afraid for her to see me because I'm not sure if she's mad even though I think she just laughed it off.

"It's okay sweetie, I swear all the time I just try not to while I'm at work. Sometimes it's hard when you deal with asshole customers all day." She laughs to herself.

"You got that right, the rough ones really make your work shift hard, that's for sure." I start laughing with her. It's true working with people really makes you dislike people sometimes, especially the difficult ones.

"Anyway, sorry for cutting you off, continue." She smiles at me, she's on the edge of her seat waiting to see what I say next.

"I got pulled over by Officer Johnston." I stop talking, shaking my head because I'm still pissed I was pulled over. "I swear I have only ever gotten pulled over by him. I think he's into me or something." I shiver from disgust with a grossed out look on my face. He might be cute but he's an asshole. He's a cocky cop who thinks everyone owes him something or should kiss the ground he walks on. Asshole.

"Well, did you flirt with him to get out of a ticket?" She snorts, wiggling her eyebrows at me a cheesy grin on her face.

"Yes, I sure did." I put my hands on my hips proud of myself for thinking of that, especially with Officer Johnston. "Although I'm sure Creedence won't be happy to hear I was flirting with another man." I place my palm against my face not thinking about the fact that I didn't think about how it would make Creedence feel for me to be flirting with another man. But it wasn't because I was interested, it was to help me get out of trouble.

"Oh, honey he'll get over it. He'll understand it was for a good reason, now for my next question. Did you offer Officer Johnston a discount on his next meal like we talked about?" She smiles again. God I love this woman.

"Yes, ma'am I did. He was so happy, he decided to take me up on the offer and didn't give me a ticket. He didn't even ask for my license or registration. Just kind of flirted with me. I'm glad he didn't ask if I had a boyfriend or anything. He probably would have given me a ticket then." I laugh, shaking my head.

"Oh honey, the whole town knows you're with Creedence, everyone around here loves to gossip. You know this, you should hear what they're saying." She giggles in excitement. "So, he probably knew better unless he wanted to get his ass kicked."

"I didn't even think of that. You're probably right! Thank god, now I won't have to worry about whether or not he'll ever ask me out. I sure hope everyone knows we're together." I let out a sigh of relief.

"So did Axton seem as okay as he can be for just finding out that bitch cheated on him." I laugh a little, not used to her swearing like that but glad she's opening up a little more to me.

"I guess so. I told him to come up here with Creedence, because he's coming up here when he gets done at work. But he said he'd think about it," I tell her with a sad look on my face.

"Gosh, I just feel so bad for him, he broke my heart." I sigh, crossing my arms while thinking of what else I could do to cheer him up. I don't really know him, like I said before, but I'd love to find a way to cheer him up.

"Hey, text him and tell him to come up here. Tell him Lisa said to get his ass up here. The foods on the house for him today, he can order whatever he wants." She has the sweetest smile on her face.

"Aw that's so sweet of you, Lisa. I'll have to go back and get my phone though and text Creedence and wait for a response from him because I don't have Axton's number," I tell her, biting my lip a little, hoping she doesn't get mad that it'll delay me starting work a little longer.

"That's fine. I already got your tables started for you, so how about you go check on them and then swing into the break room after you give your orders to the cook." She walks towards me coming in to give me a hug. "I'm so glad nothing was wrong and that you're okay sweetie, really, I am. I was worried sick about you. Next time just shoot me a text so you don't give me a heart attack honey. Here I'll text you on my phone, type your number in for me and I'll text you so you can save my number." She is just so sweet. I swear she doesn't have a mean bone in her body.

"Awesome, thank you so much I can't believe I forgot to get your number before." I start typing my number into her phone then hand it back to her.

"It's okay sweetie, we got that taken care of now so next time just shoot me a text so I don't worry about you like you're one of my children." She places her hand on my shoulder and pats me on the back gently as I turn around to walk out the door. I walk out to the counter and grab my notepad and pen before heading to my tables to check on them.

"Hey Tom, hey Sandy," I say walking over to my first table of two of my regulars.

"Heyyy, there's my favorite waitress." Tom gives me a big smile, while he waves his hand a little.

"Hey sweetie, we're happy to see you made it, Lisa was worried sick about you. She made us worried too," she chuckles.

"I know I feel terrible, I had some personal issues going on but now everything's okay." I give them a big smile, hoping they don't ask further questions because I'm not about to add to the town gossip and give them something to talk about.

"Are you guys ready to order?" I use my sweet server voice.

"I am, but you know Tom over here he can never decide on anything, he's stuck between the steak, with baked potato or the grilled chicken with baked potato." She sighs rolling her eyes at him playfully.

"Which one do you recommend dear?" Tom asks and I was hoping he wouldn't ask me because I've never tried either of those, but I won't tell him that.

"Well, let's see last time you were here, what did you eat, it was some kind of chicken right?" I'm trying to make sure I'm remembering correctly.

"You have a great memory, yes it was chicken." He closes his menu and hands it over to me.

"Well, then if I were you, I'd do the steak this time." I smile at him while holding my pen to my pad of paper getting ready to write down their orders.

"Good idea sweetheart. Thank you for that. I'll take the steak, baked potato and a side salad with Italian if you have it." He places his hands together as he looks over at his wife.

"Perfect, now what about you Sandy?" I turn towards her holding my pad and pen ready to write hers down.

"I'm pretty easy. I'll have the grilled chicken salad with Italian dressing and extra croutons please." She smiles, closing her menu and sliding it over to the end of the table next to where I stand.

"Alright, I will go put your orders in right after I check my next two tables, and I will be right back, do you guys need anything else in the meantime?" I double check with them before putting my notepad in my apron.

"No sweetie, we're fine, you go ahead." Sandy shoo's me off politely with her hand as she says it.

"Alright you know where to find me if you need me, but I'll be back to check on you guys," I tell them as I start heading to my next table.

24

EMERALD

I TAKE CARE OF MY NEXT TWO TABLES WHICH TURNED INTO three by the time I was done with my second one and head to turn in my orders to the cook before heading to the break room to text Creed. I get my phone out of the locker and see I have a text from him already.

Creedence
I hope everything is okay, Sugar?

Emerald
As I was leaving Axton came home, he was yelling on the phone and it caught my attention his girlfriend cheated on him.

Creedence
What? Are you fucking serious, did you talk to him? Do I need to text him?

Emerald
We did talk, and yep he's heartbroken, it broke my heart.

Creedence
I bet.

Emerald
I told him to come up with you but he didn't seem like he wanted to. I was late because I was talking to him then I got pulled over. I can explain more later but I had to explain to Lisa why I was late because she was worried about me and she told me to get Axton up here so he can eat whatever he wants. She said It was on the house.

Creedence
Damn that was nice of her. Well I'll text him and then stop home before I come up and I'll drag his ass out of the house.

Emerald
Good he probably needs it because I'm sure he's going to be spending a lot of time cooped up the next few days.

Creedence
Yeah I'm sure he will. I'm about to leave here in ten. The tattoo took a little longer than I expected. Do you want anything before I come up, Sugar?

Emerald
No, I'm okay. Thanks babe. Just be careful. Love you.

Creedence
Love you baby.

Emerald
Also don't speed on your way here. You might get pulled over like I did lol.

Creedence
Thanks for the heads up, Sugar.

Emerald
No problem babe lol. See you when you get here.

Creedence
See you babe.

I get an idea as I'm about to head out to see if my orders are ready and decide to text Chastity.

Emerald
Hey Chas, do you know of any parties going on this weekend?

Chastity
Hey babe, miss your ass. How are you?

Emerald
Good just working right now, miss you too bitch, how are you?

Chastity
Actually yeah there's a party going on at one of the frat houses next Friday night, I was gonna go with Saylor, why you wanna go?

Emerald
I'm gonna get back to you on that. I think I might have a group of people who might want to go. I just gotta let them know first lol.

Chastity
You bitch, get me all excited for nothing.

Emerald
Sorry babe I'd explain more but I gotta deliver food to my tables. Call you on break?

Chastity
Of course!

I walk out the same time my food for my customers is set out, so I grab for my first table and bring it to them, then do the same for the next three tables. When I get back to the counter, I hear a familiar voice as I go to refill drinks.

"Stacy, why do you not understand that we aren't here for you?" Creedence says and I can't help but laugh at the way he's talking to her.

"I don't know why you boys don't understand that you'd have a better time with me than your girlfriends." Her attempt at a sexy smile just turns into a nasty look that doesn't make her look good at all.

"Well, I don't have a girlfriend anymore, dumped that bitch after she cheated on me and no offense, I still wouldn't want to be with you." Axton's voice is monotone. You can tell he doesn't really want to be here. I'm sure Creedence dragged him out of the house without taking no for an answer.

"Same even if I wasn't with Emerald I definitely wouldn't be going after you." Creedence clears his throat. "No offense, or something like that." He covers his mouth with his fist trying not to laugh.

I quickly take my drinks back to my first table and come over to where they stand.

"Hey guys." I walk up to them. "Glad to see you made it here, Axton." I smile at him. Trying not to frown at the sad look on his face.

"Well, dick face here didn't give me much of a choice." He scoffs, crossing his arms and kicking Creedence's shoe with his. It makes me laugh watching a grown man almost behave like a child.

"Well, I was told Lisa wanted you in here and we all know if you don't listen to Lisa, she's probably going to kick your ass." Creedence stops and laughs. "And I'm not gonna get my ass kicked by her for not bringing you in here, but I'd gladly watch her kick yours." He gives a nerdy grin as he looks at Axton.

"Fuck off, I'm here, aren't I?" He sticks his finger up at Creed and I let out a laugh as he does it. These two are quite entertaining. "Now no one's getting their ass kicked." His voice still monotone as he stares off into his own world.

"Here let me get you guys a booth, just follow me." I start walking towards the booth with them when my third table calls for me.

"Go sit at that last booth right over there and I'll be right back," I tell Creedence and Axton as I walk back to my regulars to see what they need.

"Hey guys, is everything okay?" I place my hands on my hips, smiling back and forth at the two of them. "Do you need anything?" I use my sweet server voice again that I only use for people who aren't my friends.

"Can you bring us some more ranch please, Emerald? I ended up using more than I thought I was going to." The customer smiles up at me from her seat.

"Of course. I'll be right back; I'll bring you two containers just in case." I smile, walking towards Creedence's table so I can get their drinks in as well.

"Hey guys, sorry, what can I get you to drink while I go and get my other table some more ranch?" I ask them, leaning against the bench seat, my back already starting to hurt from standing and my shift has just started.

"I'll have a Dr. Pepper." Creedence winks at me, making me blush and feel giddy like a girl in school who's crush just circled yes on the note that's asking them if they like you.

"I'll have the same, Em," Axton says looking down at his menu. I stand there giving Creedence a sad look as I look over at Axton and then I mouth "talk to him" before walking away.

Men. How do they not understand when to talk to their friends to see how they're doing or if they're okay? Why does it always have to be a woman who pushes them to do it? I smile to myself as I grab the two containers of ranch and rush it over to my table before returning and filling up their drinks

"Alright here you guys go. Are you ready to order? Or do you guys want to hang out for a bit before ordering?" I'm not sure what their plan is so I double check.

"Do you know where Lisa is?" Axton asks. "I wanted to go over and thank her without her coming to the table because I don't want customers to think I'm complaining." He smiles at me, and I think that's sweet that he even cared or thought of that.

"Yeah, if you want to go up to the counter and I'll go get her for you." I point behind me with my thumb before turning around and start walking away.

"Alright, thank you." He still sounds so sad. I mean I wasn't expecting him to be sitting there in a completely different mood just yet. But I'm hoping I can convince Creed to go to this party and then he can convince Axton to go. But I have a feeling it's not going to work because they both hate parties especially at frat houses. But maybe when I mention all the hot girls that are going to be there Axton might be interested especially after getting his heart broken, he might be ready for a rebound by next Friday.

I walk to Lisa's office and knock on her door.

"It's open," she says loudly. "Come on in."

I open the door and pop my head in not stepping all the way in.

"Hey Lisa. Axton is here, he wanted to talk to you really quickly. He's up at the counter. He said he didn't want to talk to you at the table because he didn't want it to look like he was complaining or like I was in trouble." I laugh a little at the thought and she starts laughing too.

"I never would have thought of that, how funny. I'm glad he thought of that. I would hate for anyone to think someone was complaining about you." She walks out next to me and shuts her office door behind her.

She walks out to the counter, and I walk away not needing to hear their conversation as I go over and check on my tables.

"Hey, is everything okay over here, can I get you guys anything?" I smile at Tom and Sandy as I walk over to them at my first table. They should be about done so I don't want to keep them.

"Maybe a box for me I'm getting pretty full." Tom says with a half-eaten steak and full baked potato.

"Yeah, same here I didn't put dressing on all of my salad. So, if i could get a box and a small container of dressing that would be awesome." Sandy leans back in her seat as she places her hands on her stomach like she's full from eating too much. She is a very tiny woman so I could see how half a salad makes her full.

"Yeah, I can do that, Italian right?" I like to double check to make sure I didn't forget.

"Yep, thank you sweetie I appreciate it." She smiles as she grabs her drink and puts the straw between her lips.

"Of course, I'll be right back with your stuff," I tell them as I circle around to my next four tables skipping Creedence so I can go to him after I give all my customers that had asked for boxes and anything extra their things. After giving everyone their stuff and taking the checks to the counter to check them out I place the change back on the tables of two of my four tables and walk over to Creedence.

"Hey babe, are you guys ready to order or are you gonna wait till Axton gets back?" I can't help the smile that forms on my face when I look at him. He's just so dreamy and it's so hard to believe someone that looks like him is mine. I love that I get to call this sexy man mine. It's so hard not to lean down and kiss him right now, but I have to be professional and if I start kissing him now, I won't want to stop, and I don't think I'd be able to keep my job after I do the things I'd want to do to him.

"I'm fucking hungry," he chuckles with a pout. "Sorry babe, I'm not swearing at you, I just didn't think he'd be over there that long talking to Lisa. I haven't eaten today." His pout grows bigger.

"Aww babe, I'm sorry. Order your food, I can come back for Axton. I'm sure he'll understand why you ordered it already." I reach out and place my hand on his shoulder, massaging it a little. He lets out a soft groan. "Damn that felt good, you're good at massaging and you never told me this?" He gasps almost like he's offended that I never told him. Like I had this huge secret I've been keeping from him.

"Well, I never thought about massaging you and you never asked I'm sorry babe, how about tonight I give you a massage?" I grin.

Anything that involves this man and touching his god like body I'm down for, you don't have to ask me twice. "And I mean an actual massage, before you go getting all perv like on me, Mister." I laugh when his jaw drops in shock.

"Why you gotta go and ruin all my fun like that?" his voice is dramatic and shocked. "And to tease me like that, calling me mister." He shakes his head a little. "You didn't even give me the chance to be a perv about it before you just went and took it from me. That was not nice." As if his pout couldn't get any cuter it does and it's even poutier than before, but he throws in his sad eyes with it, crushing my heart along with it.

"Sorry, babe. I wasn't trying to make you sad I just wanna make you feel good that's all and I mean in more ways than one." I wink and immediately smack my face because I just gave him the opportunity to come back with yet again, another perverted comment.

"Mmm," he growls quietly while moving his finger to show me to lean down closer to him. So, I lean down. "You always make me feel good, Sugar, don't you worry." His rough voice makes my thighs tighten together, while instantly making my panties wet.

"Fuck, Creed don't do this here please, you know I can't resist you." I pull away from him real quick before he says anything else to get me going.

"What happened to the quickie in my truck at lunch?" He raises an eyebrow at me with a sexy, seductive smirk on his face that is so fucking sexy.

"Well, unfortunately I'm only going to be able to take a long enough break to call Chastity and explain things to her and then I'm going to have to get back to work, with how late I was I can't afford to take a break and eat or anything," I tell him while glancing over at my other tables making sure they aren't looking over to me. I don't want them to think I'm favoring him over them.

"Baby, you need to eat, how about instead of calling Chastity you eat something quick." He grins before looking down at his phone that vibrates on the table flashing Carsten's name.

"I'll be fine. I ate at your house before I came to work anyways." I think back trying to remember what I ate.

"That's good, but still." He shakes his head a little. "What did you eat?" He sits back and crosses his muscular arms.

God this man is so sexy. The way the veins in his arms stick out as his muscles bulge just from bending them is so sexy, and the way his T-shirt hugs his muscles tightly like it might rip if he flexes too much makes me want to drool everywhere from how hot he is, and his muscles are.

"I umm, I had some toast with jelly," I almost whisper. I wasn't expecting him to ask me that and because I know he's going to be upset about me only eating toast with jelly for the day, but I'll be fine. I've gone the whole day without eating before, by accident of course but then I stuffed my face when I realized I didn't eat.

"Umm." He leans forward a little. "You ate what?" He puts his hand to his ear letting me know to speak up because he didn't hear me.

"I had toast with jelly and some coffee, but I promise babe I'll be fine. If I get hungry, I'll get something small and eat between customers." I look over as Winter walks out of the back room getting ready to start her shift.

"Hey girl." She starts walking over to me. "I'm so excited to be working with you." She practically throws herself at me, hugging me.

"Hey sexy." I wiggle my eyebrows. "Me too, tonight is going to be fun finally," I tell her since we are both working until ten. I was originally supposed to work until midnight, but Lisa gave two of my hours away to one of the new people which is fine with me because my back will be killing me.

"Hey, Creed, how's it going?" She looks over asking him with a big smile on her face.

"It's going pretty good, how about you?" He stands up and reaches out to hug her.

She leans in to give him a hug back. "I'm doing good, a little tired cause the twins didn't sleep well last night but I'll be alright." She yawns half the sentence. "Oh my god, excuse me." She laughs covering her mouth.

"Sounds like you'll be falling asleep." I laugh looking over at her.

"Shush, I'm gonna go get my tables started I'll see you guys around." She waves as she walks off to the tables next to my section. Thankfully Lisa lets us work next to each other and keeps Stacy on the other side of the diner.

"Bye, Winter." Creedence nods his head to her.

"Bye, Creed." She turns backwards, tying her apron as she says it.

"Anyways before you were rude and changed the subject. Tonight, let me give you a massage." I smile at him. My thighs tighten just thinking about my hands being all over his firm abs and strong muscular arms, oh yeah and his back the main thing I'll be focusing on massaging.

"Fine, but only if you let me massage you too. I can tell your back is hurting from the way you're shifting your feet, baby. I keep telling you to wear better shoes." He shakes his head at me like he's disappointed.

"I'll be fine, Creed. But I'm down, I'd love a massage." I bite my lower lip thinking about his strong hands groping me. "Hold on, let me go check my tables real quick so they don't think I'm favoring you." I tell him as I walk away to go get the checks for my last two tables and then take the drink order for my two new tables.

I walk by the counter and stop to talk to Axton really quick.

"Hey, sorry to interrupt but do you know what you want to order? Creed says he's starving and would feel bad ordering without you?" I ask with a smile on my face so that way he doesn't feel like I'm being rude.

"I'll be right there; sorry Lisa and I were just finishing up." He gives Lisa a hug.

"No, it's okay I wasn't trying to rush you, I was just asking. I figured I could put your order in while you were talking to her," I say hoping I didn't make them mad interrupting.

"It's fine, we were just about done anyway." He has somewhat of a smile on his face and it seems like he's in a little bit of a happier mood.

"Okay, cool. I'll come take your order then," I tell him as I walk behind him.

"Sorry man, I didn't mean to take that long." He sits down across from Creedence.

"It's okay, I'm just happy you're out of the house. I know what you're going through is rough and we just wanna be here for you," he tells him with a serious look on his face.

"I appreciate you guys, don't let me mope around and become depressed. That bitch isn't worth it." He laughs. "I should have listened to my parents when they told me she wasn't good enough for me." He sighs. "But you live and you learn. All I need is a couple rebounds and I should be good." He sounds confident as he smiles at us, but I can see the hurt in his eyes still because his smile doesn't quite reach his eyes.

"Oh, speaking of rebounds. Chastity said there's a big party going on at one of the frat houses next weekend. And before you guys say no, hear me out Axton, hot...single...girls." I wiggle my eyebrows at him with a smile on my face.

"Hey I'm down." He looks over at Creed for a response.

"I'm down if you are, Sugar." Credence looks over at me as he speaks. I love that no matter what we are doing his eyes always find their way to mine.

"Yes! I thought for sure you guys would say no." I have a big smile on my face as Winter walks by.

"What are you guys so happy about?" She stops walking, placing her hands on her hips.

"You and Carsten want to go to a party at one of the frat houses with Chastity next Friday?" She looks up and closes her eyes as she's thinking.

"Carsten is on his way in here right now so you can ask him but I'm down if he is." She smiles at us. "Man, it's been a while since I've been to a party, his mom has the twins again next weekend, well next

Friday night she does, so we're free. Fuck, I hope he says yes. You know what, forget him, we're going." She walks off, talking to herself in the process.

"That was interesting." Creedence raises an eyebrow at her while she walks away, laughing while she continues to ramble to herself.

"Umm yeah, I'd say." Axton laughs right along with us.

"She is weird like that sometimes, but that's why I love my best friend," I tell them. "Now what can I get you guys?" I grab my pen and pad from my apron.

"Sugar, I'm fucking starving so if you'll ignore the fact that I'm about to eat like a total fat-ass I'd appreciate that." Creed looks down at the menu, his eyes lighting up at the food.

"Creedence, when have I ever judged you for eating? I never have and never will...eat away, babe." I wink at him, hoping he understood my little hint at being dirty.

"Is that an invitation to eat whatever I want?" His voice comes out raspy, clearly getting turned on.

"Yes Mister, you can eat whatever. You. Want." I wiggle my eyebrows at him with a smile on my face.

"Umm guys I'd hate to break up this little thing you got going on but uhhh I'm right here. Thanks." Axton places his head in both of his hands, shaking it like he can't believe he's caught in the middle of this.

"Shit, sorry bro, I kinda got caught up in that conversation not thinking about my surroundings." Creedence shrugs his shoulders while giving him an apologetic oh shit look.

"Sorry Axton, I got caught up in it too, I'm sorry." I scrunch up my face a little while biting my lip in embarrassment. Sometimes when I'm with Creedence I get lost in my own world, it's like we're the only two in the room when I talk to him.

"It's all good." He gives us a smile that you can clearly tell is forced, making me feel like an even bigger ass. "I'll have the double bacon cheeseburger, with lettuce, ketchup, mustard and mayo and a side of fries with ranch please." Axton slides me his menu as he tells me his order.

"I was actually going to get the same just no lettuce and extra fries with honey mustard instead of ranch please, Sugar." Creedence slides his menu over to me with a big smile on his face.

"That's it?" I raise one eyebrow at him confused because I thought he was going to be ordering way more food than that.

"With you as the main course, that's just an appetizer, Sugar." He winks at me again; I feel my cheeks heat up. The thought making my pussy wet just thinking about all the naughty things he could be doing to me right now if we weren't here and I wasn't working.

"Guys, please I can leave if you need me to." Axton says, laughing and shaking his head again.

"Sorry man I just can't help myself when I see this gorgeous woman right here in front of me." Creedence gives me a lust filled look before looking back and forth between the both of us.

"Thanks babe, so that's all you're ordering?" I'm still so confused by his order, when he said not to judge him for how he's eating I figured he was going to order multiple things not a meal with extra fries.

"Yeah, I changed my mind and just decided on extra fries. If I'm still hungry I can order something else or eat more at home." He shrugs his shoulders like he didn't just make it seem like he was going to order a shit ton of food, or like he wasn't just acting like he was going to die if he didn't eat.

"Alright guys, well I'm going to go put your order in after I check these two tables real quick."

I tell them while walking away not waiting for an answer since I'll probably be back after checking my tables.

I check on my tables and put Creedence and Axton's orders in before heading to the back room to call Chastity while I have a minute, two of my tables are done and leaving and I have one table waiting for food and another in the process of eating, so I probably have about five minutes before I'm needed.

"Hey bitch what's up?" she answers cheerfully on the third ring.

"Hey girl, nothing just calling you while I have about five minutes to spare," I tell her peeking out the break room door to make sure no one is looking for me.

"So, you guys gonna come Friday or what?" She sounds a little excited about it.

"Yes, it's going to be me, Creed, Axton, hopefully Winter and Carsten, we still gotta convince Carsten but Winter wants to go," I tell her.

"Yay! I'm so fucking excited you guys will be there, why isn't Axton's girlfriend going, he has a girlfriend right? I only met him one time and I thought he had one," she asks me.

"Yeah, that was one reason I was looking for a party, he just found out his girlfriend of three years cheated on him. He's heartbroken. But he says he needs a rebound; I figured a party would be the perfect place." I laugh as I say it.

"What? She fucking cheated on that sexy ass man? Who the fuck is crazy enough to do that?" Her voice comes out shocked as she says it. "Girl, I'd be down to be a rebound for him any day." She giggles this time like a schoolgirl looking at her crush.

"Oh my god Chas, you would." I laugh.

"What? It's true. If I didn't have a boyfriend, I might have acted on that." She laughs again. "Let's just make sure he stays away from Brynn and Daisy because I'm pretty sure they'll be there, just a heads up." Her voice comes out like she dreads the thought of seeing them.

"Fuck. Of course they are I cannot stand Daisy, hell I can't even stand Brynn they're both crazy fucking bitches." I shake my head even though she can't see it.

"Right, not sure how they get so many guys with how psycho those crazy bitches are," she laughs a little.

"Awesome, well I'll text you some more but I gotta get off the phone because I gotta go check on my customers, but I'll text you and let you know for sure who is all going to be coming with us," I tell her as I start walking back to the door of the break room.

"Alright bitch, love you." She makes kissing noises after she says she loves me, something we always do when getting off the phone with each other.

"Love you, bitch." I make the kissing noises back.

I've known Chastity since middle school. She and I sat next to each other in Art class, and both sucked at pretty much all the assignments the teacher assigned. That's how we ended up bonding with each other was through our terrible art skills and we've been best friends since. Once I introduced her to Winter, she bonded with her right away as well and we've all been pretty much inseparable since then. We've been through pretty much everything together and I wouldn't have had it any other way, I'm thankful for my best friends.

I walk out grabbing the food for the boys as I run into Winter grabbing her food, not literally running into each other but we both went to the counter at the same time.

"Hey girl, I just talked to Chas, she said that she's excited we're going to the party but a heads up that both Brynn and Daisy will most likely be there."

"Ughh fuck, I hate those bitches." She rolls her eyes grabbing her other plate, scrunching up her face in disgust as she thinks about them.

"Girl same, but let's go with pride knowing that we got the men they both wanted, and they're stuck being miserable lonely bitches." I tell her winking at her grabbing my other plate.

"Yes! Good idea babe, so glad you have the brains of the group... well for the most part at least." She laughs, walking away from me towards one of her tables.

"I heard that meanie," I say a little loud so she can hear me from her table as I pass Stacy, who's giving me a bitchy look for absolutely no reason at all besides just to be a bitch. Typical Stacy, I would have no issues with her if she could just be a nice human, I wonder why she's so nasty all the time.

"Here you guys go." I set the food down in front of both of the boys.

"Mmm, Sugar, this looks delicious, thank you." Creedence takes my hand after I set Axton's plate down and he places a gentle kiss on my hand.

"Yeah, this looks really good, thanks," Axton says, taking a fry and biting it.

"I'll leave you boys to eat, do you guys need anything else before I go check on my other tables?" I put my hands in my apron grabbing my notepad and pen.

"Nahh I'm good thanks though, baby." Creedence picks up his burger and takes a bite of it moaning while he does. "Mmm, this shits good." I laugh a little because it's cute the way it came out all muffled from his mouth being full.

"Yeah, foods good," Axton talks through his food. "But no, I'm good, thanks." I smile at these two grown men eating like they've never seen food before.

"Alright, I'll be back to check on you guys shortly, enjoy." I blow a kiss to Creedence and walk away to check on my other tables.

I walk into the back room to check my phone real quick because I felt it vibrate in my pocket. I usually don't keep it on me, but I decided to say fuck it and keep it in my pocket of my leggings which is hidden by my apron. I look down and see that I have an email saying a package of mine was delivered and I get a huge smile on my face. I can't wait to give Creedence the gift I bought for him. I'm debating if I want to give it to him tonight or tomorrow night. I walk out of the back room and back out to the floor straight over to Creed's table to see what he wants to do.

"Hey, babe how's the food guys?" I walk towards their table, trying to keep my focus on both men, when it's so hard to not just stare at Creedence.

"Foods amazing, just what I needed to put me in a better mood." Axton has a nerdy smile on his face.

"Yep, food is awesome, tastes so good, babe thanks." Creedence smiles the same way Axton is.

"So, babe, I have a surprise for you, and I want to know if you want it tonight or tomorrow." I clap my hands together a little because I can't wait to see his reaction, hoping it's going to be a good reaction and not a bad one.

"A surprise? You didn't have to get me anything, Sugar. Whatever you would like to do I'll be happy with." He sits back a little in the booth looking at me with his sexy smirk on his face.

"Well, that's why I asked because I can't make up my mind, so I need you to tell me when you want it," I tell him, rocking back and forth on my feet as I stand there waiting patiently for him to give me some kind of answer.

"You look like a little kid waiting for an answer." He smiles, laughing at me. "Fine, how about tonight then will that make you happy, so you don't have to wait any longer or decide?" He shakes his head with a big smile.

"Yay!" I shriek because I can't contain my excitement. If I had it with me, I'd give it to him right now. "Alright after work then I'll give it to you." I have a big smile on my face as I walk away to let them finish eating.

I finish up the rest of my shift, clocking out at ten thirty. Although I was late by a half an hour late, it was still a busy shift and a long day. I'm glad it ended at ten instead of working until midnight. I'd be dead if I ended up working that late. I head home and change out of my work clothes into a pair of pajama shorts and a hoodie because I'm freezing, and I grab the package to head over to Creedence's house. I text him first to see if he's ready for me to come over.

Emerald
Hey babe you ready for me to come over? I'm home.

> **Creedence**
> Hell yeah, I missed you even though I just saw
> you at work lol.

> > **Emerald**
> > I missed you, can't wait to kiss you and feel your
> > warm arms around me.

> **Creedence**
> Same babe, when you get here I want to fuck you
> first before you give me that gift I need to be
> inside you.

> > **Emerald**
> > Damn babe, still making my panties wet.

> **Creedence**
> Well get your ass over here so I can feel how wet
> they are, the garage door will be open and come
> to my room right away.

I don't even bother responding. I grab the package, phone and house key then head out the front door locking it behind me. I walk over to Creedence's house and walk into the garage hiding the box underneath his work counter in the corner, so no one sees it. I shut the garage door and head inside, practically running to Creedence's room. But I knock before walking in just in case.

"Who is it?" I wonder if we're not home alone and take a mental note to be quiet while having sex.

"It's me silly. Can I come in?" I bite my bottom lip and the next thing I know his door is swinging open and he's pulling me into his room, slamming the door shut and locking it then pushing me against the door. It all happens so quickly I almost don't have time to process what just happened.

"Fuck, you look so good. But I'm taking these off." He practically growls while pulling my hoodie off of me, and I love the fact that he still thinks I look good in just a hoodie and pajama shorts.

"Please do," I whisper, out of breath as he cups my face. His lips come crashing down on mine, our tongues swirling together in the familiar dance of each other. He swallows down every moan my body releases. He slides his tongue against mine. He groans out as he pulls my shorts down leaving me in nothing but my lace thong. I didn't even bother putting a bra on because I knew it wouldn't stay on long and I fucking hate bras especially after wearing one all day.

He reaches down and cups my pussy over my panties making me moan again.

"Fuck, Creed, please don't tease me," I whine pulling away from his kiss.

"Don't worry, baby." He lets out a deep growl while his finger slides into my panties swiping along my folds.

"Fuck your pussy is so wet for me, my little slut, I can't wait to taste how sweet you are," he whispers into my ear. He sticks his tongue out and lightly licks my ear down to my neck, sucking and biting as he does most likely leaving his marks on me. Which makes my pussy throb just thinking of him leaving those marks on me. Some girls don't like any of that stuff, call me crazy but I love when he leaves hickies and bruises because it lets people know I belong to him.

"Mhhmm, that's from you teasing me at work and making me think about you fucking me," I practically moan into his ear because of how close he's standing to me.

"Let me get a taste you, Sugar." He removes his fingers from my pussy, bringing them to his mouth, licking my wetness off him one by one. Moaning in the process.

"Fuck always so sweet for me, I'll never get sick of tasting you." His voice raspy as he picks me up by my thighs and wraps my legs around his waist to carry me over to the bed. He lightly tosses me onto his bed before crawling over and straddling me. Then comes down again to kiss me, our lips locking together and becoming one. I moan into his mouth as he grinds his hard cock against my pussy, still teasing me. Making me even more wet than I already was making my clit throb every time his jeans rub against me in just the right way. I bring my hips up to match his movements hoping he'll rub my clit longer with each thrust, but he knows exactly what he's doing, and he's only just started teasing me.

"Please, Creedence, I wanna come," I moan as I pull away from his kiss.

"Not yet, Sugar, I'm just getting started baby, you've got a long way to go until you get to come." He reaches up and takes his shirt off exposing his tattooed muscular chest that I crave to touch and lick more than I'd like to admit. He slowly removes his belt with one hand pulling it out in one swift movement before taking it and bringing it down on my pussy, whipping it right on my sensitive spot making me scream and moan at the same time.

"Mmm, you like that, Sugar?" His seductive voice turns me on. I lift my hips trying to get close to anything that can rub against my pussy, that's how horny I am.

"Mhmm, but please, Creedence," I pout, pushing out my bottom lip hoping that'll make him give in a little.

"Ah. Ah. Ah my little slut not yet." He smirks, whipping it down on my pussy again making me whimper.

"Ohhh fuccck." I'm panting now, my breathing getting heavy, my heart racing from how intense everything feels right now. He reaches out and pushes two fingers into me, not taking his time to work them in like normal and it feels so good, too good. The pain mixed with pleasure sends an intense chill through my body making me cry out again. I don't know how much more I'll be able to take without being able to cum. My body already feels like it wants to explode. He pumps two fingers in and out of my pussy while taking his thumb and massaging my clit.

"Oh goddd," I groan out. He always finds the right spots that ignites every inch of pleasure in my body, making me feel like a bomb that can explode at any minute.

I reach down and grab my breasts massaging and playing with my nipples, moaning when I do because of how good it feels but also trying to tease him, maybe it'll work in my favor, and he'll give in and just fuck me already.

"My little slut, you look so fucking hot playing with your tits like that, Sugar." His voice comes out in a low growl, clearly turned on.

He removes his fingers making me pout again, as he brings them up to his mouth, slowly licking my juices off them. He takes his finger and licks one small line up the side, then the middle before taking the whole thing, sucking it into his mouth with a sexy smirk on his face, then repeating the same thing to the other finger.

"Mmmm, Sugar, absolutely mouth-watering. So fucking delicious, my little slut." Then he takes the belt and whips my pussy one last time before bringing it up to my hands.

"You're gonna tie me up?" I whimper, my wrists still sore from the last time.

"Actually." He gets a wicked grin on his face. "I have a better idea, Sugar." He looks down at me with fire in his eyes.

"Yeah? What's that?" I smirk, a little nervous but hoping it's going to be fun. He moves off of me and sits at the side of the bed.

"Get up off the bed and come stand in front of me baby," his deep voice, almost at a whisper.

"Oo...okkay," I stutter out, getting more nervous now about what his idea could be. I slowly sit up and scoot myself towards the end of his bed and stand up. Then I slowly walk to stand in front of him.

"Now turn around for me." His voice is scratchy. I can hear his breathing getting heavier as I turn and move closer to him. He hisses in a breath when I'm finally fully turned around.

"Mmm fuck, I love that ass of yours, Sugar." He reaches out and slaps both cheeks before grabbing them and making them jiggle in both hands. "Fuck, I can't wait to fuck this tight ass of yours, baby." He pretty much growls and it makes me smile. I love how much my body excites him and turns him on. It makes me feel sexy, wanted. Needed. Desired.

"Take your panties off for me, Sugar." I can hear the smile in his voice. I'm sure that dimple of his that I want to lick is showing too.

"Okay," I whisper breathlessly, I'm so turned on. I have no idea what this man does to my body, but it drives me wild. I slide my thumbs through the sides of my lace thong and slowly slide them down my body feeling the wetness from my pussy on them as they slide down my thighs. When they pass my knees, I drop them to the floor and step out of them. He slowly brings his hand up my thigh before pulling away and slapping my ass making me whimper. I love it when he smacks my ass, the sting is my favorite, the different sensations it sends through my body are amazing. I don't know if I want to scream from the pain or cry from the pleasure. Sometimes I end up doing both and I mean actually crying from how good it feels. Creedence loves my tears, he loves when I cry for him especially when I'm choking on his cock.

"Be my good girl and bend over for me, baby, show me how wet your pussy is now, my little slut." His voice is gravelly and it's the sexiest sound ever. I bend over a little, afraid to bend too far because I'm embarrassed about putting my ass and pussy up in the direction of his face from this angle.

"Bend over more, Emerald." He puts his hand on my lower back and pushes down a little to help guide me. "Now spread your legs, gorgeous, I can barely see your wet pussy."

"Is that enough?" I ask, because I feel like if I spread them anymore, I might lose my balance and fall face first on the bed or ground.

"Fucckk," he hisses out. "Goddamn is that sweet wet pussy, baby." He swipes his finger through my slit, making me miss his warm touch as soon as he removes his finger.

"It's fucking dripping wet." He gets down onto his knees behind me, making me nervous with his face being that close to me at this angle. He sticks his tongue right between my legs. "All." He circles my clit. "Because." He gently nibbles on it before sucking it between his lips. "Of." He slides his tongue up and down my wetness. "Me." He swipes his tongue down my folds back to my clit. "Soaking wet...just for me, Sugar." He licks it again, swirling his tongue around my clit right in the spot that makes me weak in the knees. Making me let out a soft whimper. Then he swipes it back through my folds and to my clit again just teasing me instead of getting me close to where I want to be.

"Creedence, please," I moan out.

"Ah, ah not yet, Emerald." His voice comes out rough, raspy. He leans back down and buries his face in my pussy, licking up my wetness like he can't lick it fast enough, making me squirm as he does.

"Tell me who's pussy this is, Sugar." You can tell he's smiling while saying it.

"Yours," I breathe out, panting.

"My what?" He pushes a finger inside of me, pumping it in and out of me slowly.

"Your pussy," I pant.

"Who does it belong to?" He starts pumping in and out faster and I can feel the tension starting to build. I start meeting his thrusts trying to get myself closer to getting relief.

"It's yours." I'm out of breath, my body feels so tight. "It belongs to you." I breathe out. "And only you," I moan between pants.

"Fuck, Sugar. Good girl." Shit. He makes my pussy throb when he talks like that. I try to tighten my thighs together, but he catches me off guard when his free hand comes down and smacks my ass making me scream out a moan. The ache building between my thighs, getting my body closer but not close enough.

25

CREEDENCE

I PULL MY FINGERS OUT OF HER PUSSY AND DIVE BACK IN, burying my face back where it belongs. Her pussy. And once I've tasted her again, I realize I've been starving, and I don't ever want to stop. She tastes like candy, the sweetest fucking piece I've ever tasted and I'm ready to devour her until she's screaming my name as she comes all over my face.

Her pussy is so slick from her wetness and my mouth combined. It's making my cock grow harder while I imagine my cock gliding into her tight pussy and sliding out as I look down to see how wet my cock is as it's covered in her cum.

I thrust two fingers back inside her not even making sure she's ready first, I want her sore. I want her to smile every time she feels that soreness. I suck onto her clit bringing the sensitive nub between my lips, lightly grazing it with my teeth. She cries out.

"Fucck yesss." She's breathing hard, with short breaths. "Don't stop, please. I'm begging you, don't stop," she cries out between gasps. "Please, Creed, I'm begging. It feels too good, let me come." It sounds like a tortured moan. And I love those moans coming from her. The ones that feel so good to her she wants her orgasm to come but doesn't want the pleasure to end.

What kind of man would I be if I denied her an orgasm after

begging like that? And I didn't even tell her to beg. That was so fucking sexy, giving her the release she needs is something I crave, at least when I'm allowing her to come that is.

I pull away from her pussy, just enough to tell her. "Goddamn, Sugar, that was fucking hot." Then I dive right back in to continue until she's exploding all over my face. So I can lick those sweet juices from her slit and suck the rest of them off of my fingers.

"Fuck, Creed I'm... I'm–" And she can't even finish before she's screaming my name. "Fuck, please, Creed. Fuck, right there. Don't. Stop." Her pussy clamps down tightly on my fingers, pulsing hard from the intensity of her orgasm. I have to hold onto her hip with one hand to steady her, so she doesn't fall.

"Holy shitttt," she screams, gripping her thighs with her hands as her orgasm still soars through her shaking body. I continue to pump in and out of her, slowing down as her orgasm comes to an end, her body going limp, sagging against my hand.

"Fuck, you did so good. But now it's my turn, Sugar," I tell her with a slight chuckle because I know she's tired from her orgasm.

"Yes, Creedence." I take my fingers out of her as she turns around and gets down on her knees as I take my fingers, putting them into my mouth and suck her sweetness off one by one. She crawls a little closer to me and sits her ass down on her heels. She automatically puts her hands behind her back and opens her mouth wide sticking her tongue out.

"Goddamn, Sugar, I love that you're ready for me, my little slut." I have a big grin on my face, I can't help it. She's always so eager to do anything that involves pleasing me and I love it. She always takes what I do to her so well too like the good fucking girl she is.

"Mhmm." Her mouth is still open waiting for me to slide my cock in between those juicy plump lips of hers. I love the way they feel as they slide against my cock, so soft and warm. The way they pop when she pulls my cock out and the way they suction as they pull me back in. God, I can't get enough of them. I go over to my bed and grab my belt before I come behind her and loop it around her wrists tightening it as tight as it will go. I smile as she hisses out from the pain of the leather cutting into her already sore wrists. I know they will leave marks, and possibly rub her raw if she fights it but she's usually pretty good about that. I undo my jeans, take them off and step out of them along with my boxer briefs and walk back around in front of her stroking my hard cock. I hold my hand around my thick shaft slowly pumping it up and down, my eyes closing in the process as I imagine her warm mouth yet again. She's still kneeling with her mouth open and tongue out, drool starting to fall down around her tongue, some of it running down her chin and I smile.

"You're such a good little slut. I love you, Emerald, you know that right?" I ask because I really do, even though I call her my little slut and fuck her the way I do, it doesn't change any of my feelings. She nods her head, still not closing her mouth as I slowly come up to her placing the tip of my cock on her tongue. She instantly starts swirling her tongue around the head making me let out a low growl.

"Fuck, your mouth is so warm," I tell her as she starts taking my dick into her mouth a little more, while wrapping her lips around it. Before she pulls out making my favorite wet popping sound before taking me back into her mouth. I put my hands through the back of her hair, holding a little tightly at the nape of her neck as I guide her head with my hand. She closes her mouth completely on my cock, sucking it in deep.

"Go on, suck my cock, Sugar," I tell her right as she suctions her lips around the head sucking on just the tip, driving me fucking crazy before taking me further into her mouth until I'm hitting her throat again. She moves her head at an angle to help get my cock down deeper into her throat while swallowing me down like she's starving and can't suck it fast enough. She makes a gagging noise causing her spit to pool at the sides of her mouth while her excess spit spreads all over my cock as more drool runs down her face, and it's one of the sexiest things I've ever seen. I hold her head in place as my cock sits in her throat. She still swallows my cock down like she hasn't had enough to eat like it's the best candy she's ever tasted.

Tears start to well up in her eyes, as I smile down at her. "My gorgeous girl, you know I love those sweet tears," I tell her as I start to move my hips making my cock move in and out of her warm, wet mouth. I let her get some air before I push it back into her throat, she swallows it down again as I let her choke on my cock. Pumping in and out faster as she moves her head to match my rhythm, sucking and swirling her tongue along my piercings. She moans out sending the vibrations across my cock and I throw my head back from the pleasure. I stop moving, holding her head still because I'm not ready to come just yet. I want to enjoy those beautiful tears, and that amazing mouth just a little longer. She starts making noise and I know I need to move to let her breathe but I just can't yet, my cock feels too good in the tightness of the back of her throat. I sit there for a second longer and finally start to move as she moans onto my cock again. I look down at her tear-streaked face, covered in mascara and can't get over how beautiful she looks as she cries for me, as she cries from my cock. I take my thumb of my free hand and swipe it over her tears and bring it up to my mouth, sucking it off my thumb. "Mmm." I tell her. "I swear your tears taste so sweet, Sugar." And I repeat the same to the other cheek, licking her tear from my thumb. I take both hands and grip the back of her head, taking full control of her sucking me off. It feels too good to not take control. She stretches her mouth more as I begin moving her spit covered mouth up and down my thick, long cock, fucking her face nice and rough. Like I said before there will be nothing gentle about it when I take control and fuck my little sluts' mouth. Besides I guarantee you when I'm done her pussy that I thought was soaked before will be twice as wet as it was. And I can't wait to watch what I have in store for her next.

I can feel my orgasm build up as my balls start to tighten. I move faster as she sucks harder, throwing my head back again because I just can't take it, it feels too damn good, and I wish it wasn't about to end.

"Fuck, get ready to swallow my cum, Sugar," I tell her, and she nods her head the best she can with how I'm holding my hands in it.

I pump into her as my warm cum squirts down her throat, her moaning in the process, the vibrations from it sending more intense sensations to my cock, intensifying my orgasm. "Fuck that felt amazing." I try to pull out, but she continues to suck me dry, making sure to get every last bit of cum. She finally opens her mouth and moves her head back, so my cock comes out, gasping from the lack of air. She looks up at me smiling. I take my thumb and smudge her drool and cum around her chin a little more, I can't help it it's so sexy knowing all of that was caused by me fucking her gorgeous fucking face. I lean down and place a gentle kiss on her wet lips and then I go behind her to remove the belt from her wrists. She hisses from the pain as her arms slowly fall to her sides. Then she lifts them looking at her red wrists that were rubbed raw from my belt.

"Are you okay, Sugar?" I hope she's not in any pain. It's a silly question I know, how could I ask her if she's okay when I'm the one responsible for her issues. Just because I cause her pleasurable pain doesn't mean I want to hurt her in a bad abusive way.

"I've never been better." She smiles up at me. "It only hurts in the best way, don't worry about me, babe, I'll be okay." She winks at me, and bites that pouty lower lip of hers in the process. The lip I love biting and sucking on myself because it's the perfect amount of plump. It feels perfect around my cock. It feels perfect in my mouth and against my own lips. She's the definition of perfect, that's the best way I can describe my beautiful little slut. My perfectly sweet, good girl. I'd like to think I'm obsessed with her in the best way possible, wouldn't you be if she was yours? I think to myself, lost in my thoughts about her. The only thoughts I have these days are of her, which is why I'd like to say I'm obsessed.

"Here, Emerald, give me your hands and I'll help you up, Sugar," I tell her, reaching my arms out and holding my calloused hands to her, palms facing up. She doesn't say anything as she places her soft, small hands into mine, the warmth sending chills through my body. Not that I'm cold, but just something about her touch that always sends an electric like feel of chills through my body.

I pull her up to a standing position, before taking one hand and walk her over to the bed.

"Go lie down in the middle of the bed, legs facing me." She puts one leg up, placing her knee on the bed followed by the other, then gently places her hands down on the mattress in front of her before she crawls to the middle of it and lays down on her back, keeping her legs towards me just like I had asked.

"What are you doing?" Her voice comes out nervous.

"Ah, ah, Sugar it's not what I'm going to be doing, it's what you're going to be doing." The smile on my face grows as I think about what I'm going to do next.

"What do you mean, what I'm going to be doing?" She raises an eyebrow, clearly confused by what I had just said. I climb on to the bed and lean over her, straddling her body, giving her a wicked grin. I'm excited for what is about to happen. I hope she doesn't back out. But something tells me my little slut is going to love it as much as I do.

"I'm only leaving you untied long enough for my pleasure, Sugar." She stares, still looking at me confused.

"Ww...wh...what do you mean your pleasure? Do you want me to suck your cock again?" she asks, holding her obviously sore throat, probably sore in the best way, with the best memories from my piercings and how hard I fucked her.

"No baby, I wanna watch you play with yourself." I smirk at her.

"Play with myself? Bu...but I've never done that in front of any...anyone before," she stutters out nervously.

"That's why I want to see it. I love when you touch your tits, and I know I'll love it when you touch your pussy." I lean in to whisper into her ear. "Now be my good little slut and fuck your pussy with your fingers, Sugar. I wanna watch you while you come undone from playing with yourself and massaging your own clit. What do you say?" I ask her. "Will you be a good girl and tease me while playing with yourself?" I pull away from her ear, noticing how fast her chest is rising and falling.

"Don't be nervous baby, go on play with your pussy for me like the dirty girl I know you are. I promise you'll love doing it for me, beautiful." I lick my lips trying to distract myself before I just give in and fuck her. Because that's what I want to do. I want to shove my hard cock into that tight wet pussy and fuck her till she's begging me to let her come. But I'll be patient this time because I'm excited to watch this first.

She hesitates just looking at me while slowly moving her right hand to her pussy.

"Go on, Emerald, show me how you play with yourself, Sugar. I wanna watch that pussy clamp down and cum all over your fingers, baby. Then I want to watch you lick them clean before I fuck you." I tell her smiling at the thoughts I have in my head of it playing out.

I get up off the bed and drag my desk chair to the end of my bed. Sitting down, I relax back in the chair, crossing my arms. I might as well be comfortable while I watch her play with herself and while she gets herself off.

She takes her pointer and middle finger and starts rubbing herself slowly up and down between her slit. Her breath hitches as she takes one finger and slightly pushes it inside each time she slides her fingers down, a slight moan escapes her lips as her eyes start to close.

"Eyes on me, Sugar. I want to see the look in your eyes as you come all over yourself," I tell her with a wicked grin on my face, because I can't wait to watch her, the faces she makes when she comes are unbelievably sexy.

"Okay," she moans as she comes up and starts massaging her clit with her thumb while the other two start pumping in and out of her pussy slowly at first.

"God, Sugar, you look so sexy playing with yourself like that." Fuck this chair, I need to be closer. I get in the bed and lay back in front of her, placing my left arm behind my head as I watch her fuck herself with her fingers, her breathing getting heavier with each pump. I lay there my cock painfully rock hard as I watch her. I decide to take my cock with my right hand and start stroking myself, matching her thrusts with my strokes.

"Mmm you like this that much, Creed?" Before I can answer she asks me, "Do you like watching me play with my pussy?" It comes out quiet, not quite a whisper. Her cracked tone is so fucking sexy.

"Fuck yes, Sugar, don't you dare stop. I can't wait to watch your face when you come, gorgeous."

"I can't wait to come, Creedence," she moans out, teasing the fuck out of me. "Why don't you come over here and help me play with myself." She smirks at me then bites her bottom lip.

"Is that what you want, Emerald?" I don't plan on helping her, but I know just how to get her there.

"God yes, come play with my pussy," she breathes out.

"Tell me what you want me to do, Emerald, tell me how you want me to touch you," I tell her hoping this works, not that I don't want to touch her, but I'd love to watch her get herself off.

"I want you to come next to me and take one of your fingers with one of my fingers and put it inside me, we can finger fuck my pussy together," she tells me, breathing a little heavier this time.

"Fuck, that's so hot. What else do you want me to do to that pussy of yours?" I ask her again because I know she's getting close. I can tell by the way she's breathing and the way her legs are starting to shake.

"Then I want you to massage my clit while I finger myself, and you can suck on my nipples while you do it, please, Creedence. I'm so close babe."

"Fuccck." Is all I can manage to get out. I stroke my cock a little faster, not wanting to come but I can't help myself it feels too good and she's really fucking getting me going.

"Please, Creedence come play with my pussy, come fuck me with your fingers, baby. Make me come." She's panting.

"Not yet, Sugar, I wanna watch you make yourself come, you have no idea how badly I want to see that happen," I tell her because I do. I think it's so sexy when a girl has no problem getting off in front of you, especially when she does it herself. Just watching her lose control in front of me is so goddamn sexy.

"Oh god, Creed your fingers would feel so good in my pussy, while it clamps down around them as I come," she whispers as her body trembles.

"Yes, I would love nothing more than to make you come, Sugar, I'd love to play with your clit, even suck on it with my mouth. While you finger yourself you dirty fucking girl," I growl, so turned on. I don't know how much more my body can take.

"Ohhhh god, don't stop Creed, please keep going," she barely gets out between breaths.

"Then I'll stick my fingers inside your pussy as I suck on your clit and swirl my tongue over just the right spot."

"Ahh fuccckk, I'm cumming," she breathes out, the look on her face so sexy I could come just from her looks alone.

"Shit Creed, it feels so good," she whimpers, her body shaking as her orgasm shoots through her.

I sit there smiling as her body starts to relax, just staring at this beautiful woman, who just got herself off in front of me. I've watched women get themselves off before, but it's never been this sexy, or real most of them would overdo it and turn me off in the process. But Emerald, everything she did was real, everything she felt she enjoyed. She let herself come undone in front of me and let her body lose control. I fucking loved every minute of it.

"Fuck, Emerald, that was the sexiest thing I think I've ever fucking seen," I tell her, still smiling from it.

I crawl back on top of her. My body hovering over hers. "I love you, Emerald," I tell her as I push some of the hair out of her face.

"I love you, Creedence" She's still breathing a little heavy.

"How do you feel?" I'm curious if her orgasm was any different than normal, because it seemed like it was more intense.

"God that felt so good, I don't know what it was about doing that in front of you but damn." She looks away a little like she's shy all of a sudden.

"Ah. Ah don't be shy baby, not after you just looked so goddamn gorgeous doing that. And the way you were talking to me, fuck. That was such a turn on." I grab my hard cock and rub it against her slit. "Fuck your pussy is so wet for me." I smile down at her before my lips come crashing down onto her, her lips opening for me as my tongue enters her mouth.

"I loved doing that in front of you." She pulls away for a minute. "It was so hot." And she leans back in bringing her lips to mine, kissing me. Swirling her tongue against mine. I don't even bother with tying her up this time before sliding my cock right into her wet pussy, filling her tightness up with my thickness. I thrust in and out right away, not giving her time to adjust as she scratches her nails up and down my back. I can feel her toes curling against my legs with the way her legs rest against mine.

"Fuck, Creed," she whimpers, her moans the only thing you can hear besides my grunting.

I tuck my hands under her back grabbing her with my arms as I flip us both over. To where she's straddling me.

"Ahh fuck, Creed." Her head falls back as her nails dig into my chest. "Your cock feels so good like this," she groans out, throwing her head back.

"Shit, your pussy feels so tight. Like a fucking glove, baby, I love the way you grip my cock, Emerald." I thrust my body up to match her rhythm as she rides me.

"I love it when you ride my cock, baby." Besides when I tie her up this has to be my favorite position. I love watching her tits bounce as I fuck her tight cunt, and I love being able to play with those perfectly pebbled nipples of hers.

I keep one hand on her hip and bring the other one up to grab her nipple. I start off gentle at first pulling and slightly twisting as she moans. Then I start pulling it a little harder.

"Ahh Shit," she yelps as I pull her nipple hard, pulling her down to where her chest presses against mine. I pull on her breast, as I lean up to put her nipple into my mouth. God, I love her tit's they're the perfect size and these little pebbled nipples are the perfect shade of pink. I love how soft they are when I suck them into my mouth, as I feel them get harder against my lips and tongue.

Her wet pussy slides up and down my cock as her ass bounces against me. I take my free hand smacking her ass and then squeezing it in my hand. Jiggling it as I do. I don't want it to feel left out.

I never thought I'd find someone I'd be okay having normal sex with. Usually, the thought of plain old sex sounds boring to me, but the thought of having plain old sex with Emerald sounds amazing and so far, is incredible. I wouldn't mind doing this more often.

"Fuck baby, I'm already getting close," I grumble against her nipple as I pop it out of my mouth, already missing the softness against my tongue.

She rotates her hips and grinds her pussy into me. "Mhmm, your cock always makes me want to come quickly, Creed." She's panting as she bounces up and down and grinds on my cock.

I reach down with my thumb and start massaging her clit knowing that'll help get her where she needs to be before I cum without her because that's not what I want to do. We either come together or she comes first but I will never leave a woman unsatisfied.

"Does that feel good, baby?" I ask massaging it nice and slow while she grinds and bounces on my cock some more.

"God yes, I'm so close don't stop," she cries as she reaches up and grabs her tits, I love it when she plays with her nipples while I fuck her.

"Don't you worry, I'm not gonna stop until you're done coming all over my cock, Sugar," I say, thrusting up as she comes down onto my cock.

"Shit. Shit. Shit," she breathes out. "Fuck, I'm cumming, Creed, Oh god, Creedence." My name being a moan that escapes her lips is a goddamn turn on. So fucking sexy, her whole body shakes as she cries out on top of me, losing herself in her orgasm while she curses my name through it.

Emerald's black and emerald-green hair is the only thing I see when I look down as her head rests on my chest. My cock still semi hard inside her. Not feeling the need to pull it out yet. Neither of us say anything as I lay there and rub my hand across her back as she draws across my chest with her fingers. My eyes feel heavy, and I feel like I haven't been this relaxed in a while. The comfort she brings to me is like nothing I've felt before, yet it feels like home at the same time. My heavy eyes start to close as she continues to move her finger across my bare chest, tracing over my tattoos, letting out a giggle here and there.

"I forgot I still have that gift for you." She leaves my chest cold where her head was resting as she lifts it to look up at me. I'm barely awake as I stare into her amber eyes and those beautiful light dusting of freckles that dance across her cheeks and nose.

"Oh shit, I forgot you told me about that. Not that I don't want your gift, but can we lay here like this a little longer?" I'm not ready to move yet, she's too warm and it feels too good to still be inside her.

"Is that so your semi hard dick can get fully hard and fuck me again?" She giggles because it's true, my cock is almost fully hard. It never went down after fucking before. It's not my fault I walk around with a boner pretty much all the time because of her. She excites me all the time in more ways than one, and I love that about her.

26

EMERALD

About thirty minutes later, give or take, we may or may not have fucked again before finally getting dressed. I grab my phone and keys just in case I need them and head outside to the garage so I can finally give Creedence his gift that I've been basically waiting to give him since ordering it. I'm extremely nervous because it's a touchy subject but I'm hoping that he can see where I'm coming from with the gift when he looks at it.

"So, I brought you out to your garage because I have a surprise for you." I bite my bottom lip nervously; afraid this might be his last straw with mentioning things about his brother but I'm hoping he will love it instead.

"You don't have to get me anything, Sugar. Just you is perf..." And then I cut him off handing him the black motorcycle helmet I bought him. Figuring maybe if I bought him something new to go with his Harley that's not related to something he had when he and his brother got into the accident it'd be different. It's all black with a gray and white shaded skull with bright blue roses coming out of the eyes with rose vines and leaves surrounding it. It's covering the whole top of it, if you look at it the right way it looks like the skull is popping out at you. Then going across the back bottom of the helmet it says... "In loving memory of Xander, forever watching over you big brother." But I smile because he hasn't seen that part yet, so it's still a big meaningful surprise.

"Wha...what is this?" He furrows his brows. A somewhat angry look on his face.

"I bought you a new helmet, I bought myself one too to match yours, but my skull is pink with deep purple roses, vines and leaves coming out of the eyes, I designed them myself. I thought maybe that if... if you gave it a shot, I can help you." But he cuts me off by shoving the helmet onto the desk in the garage.

"You bought me a helmet to go riding when I said I wasn't ready...when I said I was afraid too." He lets out an angry growl. "Did you ever think that maybe you should've fucking asked me. I don't know if I was fucking ready for something like this...last time we talked about this I fucking told you." He pauses, taking a deep breath. He's pissed and I feel like an ass, my cheeks turning red and getting hot from embarrassment as hot tears stream down my face.

"Creed. It was stupid I'm so sor..." I don't even get the words out fully.

"No, don't even fucking tell me you're sorry. I feel like you're only thinking about yourself in this situation and trying to... I don't know...fucking save me...or fucking fix me." He throws his hands up in the air. "Or be a hero. I don't fucking know what you thought, but you know what." He lets out another deep angry breath. "Fucking go... I'm fucking done, this was like a slap in the fucking face. Get out, go home. I'm done with this whole relationship. It's over. I'm serious. I never thought you'd be this selfish and only think about yourself in this situation." He's breathing heavily as he turns his back to me and rushes inside slamming his garage door.

I don't even try to go in there and argue. I just ran out of his garage, tears streaming down my face. Fuck I'm so stupid and hurt, I can't believe he spoke to me like that. Well, I do. I fully understand why he spoke to me like that. I'm not even hurt about it. I'm hurt over him not caring about me trying to help him trying to get him to do this for his brother, for himself. But instead, I fucked up, I'm surprised his reaction wasn't worse than that honestly. Now I have to find a way to fix all of this. Not only did I make him mad, but I also ruined our relationship and... I think he just broke up with me. I can't breathe, my chest hurts, and I can't stop crying. I feel like my whole world just came crashing down. I stop in my driveway in front of my front porch dry heaving, I feel like I'm going to be sick, but I have nothing to puke up. I walk over and I fall to the grass on my knees, leaning forward and just sit there crying for I don't even know how long but I just cry. I'm embarrassed, I'm hurt and so fucking heartbroken. And I just sit there and sob, the saddest broken sobbing you can imagine. You can hear the pain and heartache coming and probably feel the pain radiating from me. I sit there on my knees, my legs so numb I can't feel them anymore, for what feels like hours. But it's only been a half hour. I only know that from checking my phone I have a few missed calls from Winter, probably wanting to talk about the party next Friday that we were all supposed to go to. But I don't even know if I'm going now. I don't want to go unless I go with Creedence, I don't want to be anywhere without him and now that's not a possibility because there is no longer an Emerald and Creedence. My heart hurts because I thought he was the one. This can't be it, it can't be truly over, can it? Over something like this, is he being serious? I feel like I need to go over and talk to him, but I have a feeling he won't answer the door if I do. But I get up on shaking and tingling legs from the feeling coming back into them and slowly walk over to his house. Feeling like I might puke in the process as I walk up the front porch and ring the doorbell.

He comes to the door, tears streaming down his face. Trying hard to hold back his own tears now. Hurt and anger on his face, wearing them like a mask. He's no longer my happy, loving Creedence, he's replaced with the hurt I caused and the anger he's feeling.

"Leave, Emerald, I told you we're through. I don't feel like talking to you right now. Please don't make this any harder on either of us and just go." He goes to shut the door, but I put my arm in the way.

"Creedence, please," I cry out, snot flying out of my nose as I try to breathe but I'm so stuffed up from crying I feel like I'm suffocating in the process. "Please don't do this to me. I love you so much," I cry out more, my whole body shaking, wishing this was just a nightmare I could wake up from. "Please," I sob. "I need you." I fall to his porch no longer strong enough to hold myself up and I sob while looking up at him.

He looks away, before cutting me off, not even letting me continue to talk. "Emerald, just go, I have nothing left to say to you other than I was wrong about us. Now leave before I have to be even more of a dick." He shuts the door. Not even bothering to look at me one last time and I'm left there. On my knees, sobbing on his porch. My whole body is shaking, I slowly get up on wobbly legs and I run off the porch into the grass and puke. I have no food to puke up, but whatever is coming up it burns. It burns my already sore, scratched up throat from his piercings. And I want it to stop, because the memories of how good things just were minutes ago are too fresh, I'm not strong enough to handle all this alone. But it just keeps coming up until I'm dry heaving. My stomach muscles hurt from how hard I was puking, but it hasn't calmed down. I stand there dry heaving for the next few minutes on Creedence's front lawn. Alone, one of my biggest fears, being left alone.

I just want to go home now to take a warm bath. I can't believe everything was so perfect all day until about an hour ago when I went and ruined it by doing something so fucking stupid.

When the puking finally stops, I walk home on shaky legs, holding my sore stomach. Barely able to walk. I feel like I'm dragging my body in a standing up position. I grab my house key from my pocket and put it in the keyhole to unlock the door, open it and shut it behind me, locking it again in the process. I set my key in the dark blue dish that sits on the table by my front door and start walking through my house, towards my room. I need to text Winter. Right now, my heart hurts too much and I just want my best friend. But she's working so I text her.

Emerald
Creedence and I broke up. He broke up with me
and I don't know what to do. My heart is
completely broken.

Winter
What the fuck? Please tell me you're joking.

Winter
Babe, what happened?

Emerald
Long story short, I bought him a new motorcycle
helmet, and he didn't see what I had engraved on
it, but he was pissed and thought I was
pressuring him and forcing him to do something
he wasn't ready to do and he broke up with me.

Winter
Aw, fuck. I'm gonna see if I can leave early, my
shift ends in an hour.

Emerald
No it's okay, I'm about to take a bath, I'll see you
when you get here. We can drink some wine.

Winter
Okay babe, I'm so sorry, I wanna call him a jerk
but I don't know the full story.

Emerald
Well he is a jerk cause he broke my heart. But
fuck Winter, he broke my heart girl.

I walk into my room, shutting my door and take my clothes off as
I walk to my closet to grab pajama pants and another hoodie.

Winter
Babe I'm so sorry. I remember Carsten and I went
through a rough patch like this. I hope it isn't
permanent like ours wasn't.

> **Emerald**
> Girl, tell me about it. I don't know what I'm going
> to do if it is permanent. Fuck dude.

Winter
I wish I knew what else to say besides I love you
girl when I get to you we're gonna get drunk.

> **Emerald**
> Yes please. Does Carsten care if you come here?

Winter
Hell no he will understand when I tell him lol.

> **Emerald**
> If not it's okay I'll be fine.

Winter
It's fine babe I'll see you in a little over an hour.
Go take your bath.

> **Emerald**
> Ok, love you babe.

I sit on the edge of the tub, a towel wrapped around me as I wait for the water to fill up. Adding some vanilla soap to make bubbles while I wipe away the tears that just keep pouring down my face with my other hand. As soon as I think I'm done crying more tears fall without me even realizing it. I feel like there's a hole in my heart. Is this what true heartache feels like? I hate it, I feel sick to my stomach, I feel broken, and it hasn't even been a few hours. What will all the other days without him feel like? I don't know how else to explain how I feel, besides repeating my feelings. I'm devastated my whole world just came crashing down in one day and I hate it. I feel so lost and alone right now and the only person I want to turn to and cry to is the one person who doesn't want me to turn and cry to them and the only person who doesn't want me anymore. The one person I need the most and he doesn't need me.

I slowly stand up. Feeling numb all over, not from sitting but from the heartache. I walk out of my bathroom that's connected to my room and walk down the hall still in my towel. I go into my refrigerator and grab the bottle of wine I started drinking the other night and take the cork back out. I don't even bother with a glass as I take a big gulp. I have about half a bottle left after that gulp, that'll be enough to help me start numbing the pain more before Winter gets here. Right as I'm about to shut the refrigerator door I see a bottle of cherry vodka sitting in the door and decide to take a shot of that, and by shot, I mean taking off the cap and chugging some of it from the bottle.

"Ahh fuck." I shake my head in disgust as it burns going down. I feel the warmth of the alcohol move through my body and it feels good. I think I just chugged way more than I needed to but that's okay. It's just one more thing to help quiet my thoughts and numb the pain.

I head down the hall and into my room and into my bathroom over to the cabinet to grab more of my bath stuff adding warm vanilla sugar soap with bath salts making it extra bubbly. I want the smell to be extra strong on my body to erase any scents I may have left of Creedence on me. I can't handle smelling him on me and not being able to go near him. I take my pink scrunchie. Fucking stupid pink scrunchie that hurts my heart just looking at it and put my hair up into a messy bun at the top of my head. Then grab my bottle of wine and slowly step into the hot water that sends chills through my freezing cold body. Sitting down into the tub I set the bottle on my tub tray and lay back closing my eyes and let the tears that haven't stopped falling, keep falling. I didn't even realize I was still crying. That's how many tears have fallen tonight. In the short time frame of an hour, you think I would have cried out everything by now. But no, these stupid tears just keep coming.

I lay there welcoming the sad sound of silence, as I move my hands around under the hot water finally feeling a little bit of weight lifted off me. Hoping it'll also help this sick to my stomach feeling that hasn't stopped yet. I'm sure the alcohol will help get rid of it soon. I already feel a buzz from chugging that delicious, yet disgusting cherry vodka from the refrigerator and I hope this wine just keeps adding to it. I want to be drunk and have no more tears to cry for the rest of the night and hopefully I'll be able to get some sleep. Thank god I'm off tomorrow because I'll be spending tomorrow drunk too. Plus, there's no way I'd be able to go to work feeling this way, I'd probably cry all over everyone's food and that wouldn't be a good thing. Then there's the chance of seeing Creedence there because that's where everyone goes to eat all the time, especially him and his friends. Depending how I feel I may take the next day off after that too and spend the day drunk. It may not be the smartest decision I make but apparently, I'm not good at making smart decisions these days. I was just dumped so I'm allowed to spend a few days feeling bad for myself.

I finish off the rest of the wine and feel even more buzzed than I did before, but I need more alcohol. Winter isn't off work yet either, so I have some time. I stand up in my tub and step out real quick drying a little bit of the water off and wrap a towel around myself then walk out of my room out to the kitchen, grabbing a tall glass so I can drink some more cherry vodka. I don't give a fuck about mixing wine with vodka all I care about is getting drunk. I fill the glass to the top leaving a little space, so I don't spill it and carry it back to the bathroom. I hang up my towel and sit back in the tub, draining a little water and adding more hot water to it. I need it hot enough to almost burn me or else it's too cold because I'm a freeze baby. I hate that I'm cold all the time. I chug back some more cherry vodka, the warmth moving through my body again, warming me up even more. I giggle to myself because I think I might be on the verge of being drunk.

"I can't believe this is my fucking life right now. All because you had to go and be an idiot and not use your fucking brain, Emerald." Now that I say it out loud it pisses me off. I'm now pissed off at myself. Creedence was right. I shouldn't have been trying to force him to do something he wasn't ready for. Now because of that I ruined my fucking relationship and lost the love of my life.

I finally get out of the bath when my body looks like a prune and I'm drunk. I stumble drying myself off before Winter gets here. She texted me like five minutes ago that she'd be here soon, so I need to get a move on. I sloppily pull on my lace thong and put on a pair of sweatpants because now that I'm out of the bath I'm freezing and then I don't even bother with a bra I just throw on my hoodie.

"Knock, knock." I hear Winter yell from the kitchen and I'm suddenly so thankful to not be alone anymore. It's dangerous to be alone with your thoughts sometimes.

I wipe at my tears and clear my throat since I'm all stuffy and can barely talk from how much I've been drinking. "Coming," I slur a little, walking out of my room and down the hall towards the kitchen.

"Hey, bitch." Winter smiles trying to lighten the mood.

"Hey, girl." I wipe away more tears with my hands as I walk over to her to give her a hug.

"Oh babe, come here." She reaches her arms out to me and wraps them around me, squeezing me tightly in the process. "I'm so sorry."

"It's–" I take a deep breath trying to calm myself down because now that she's here I have more tears to cry all of a sudden. "It's okay," I slur and hiccup, having a hard time getting those two words out.

"Did you start drinking without me?" she pouts but giggles at the same time.

"I couldn't help it; I needed something to numb the pain." I walk over to the refrigerator and pull out two bottles of wine. I may look like an alcoholic to some but most people who know me know I like to stay stocked up on my wine. So, I keep multiple bottles in there at a time.

"What have you been drinking so far?" She gives me a concerned look as I stumble a little when I turn around.

"Some cherry vodka and about half a bottle of wine. I barely ate today." I hiccup. "I'm probably drunk, maybe," I snort. Yep, I'm drunk, and I can still feel my heartache, so I know I haven't been drinking enough. I want to drink until my lips are numb, along with my feelings. I don't want to feel anymore, at least not tonight. I'm hoping tomorrow I'll feel a little better.

"Wanna do a shot of cherry vodka?" She smiles reaching for the bottle in my refrigerator. We both love cherry vodka, so I had a feeling she would want to do one once she found out I still had that bottle from last time.

"Hell yeah, I wanna do one." I grab the bottle from Winter, very clumsily, but I don't care. I unscrew the lid, throwing it onto the counter, missing and giggling. I'll get that tomorrow. I take another chug from the bottle and pass it to her.

"I said do a shot, not chug it." She laughs as she takes the bottle from me.

"Hey, that could've been a shot worth, maybe two." I shrug my shoulders a little and laugh at her.

"Alright, fair enough." She lifts the bottle to her mouth and chugs some down before placing it back on the counter and shaking her head with disgust, for cherry vodka being our favorite it still grosses us both out when we do plain shots of it. "Fuck that was intense." She says with one eye closed still trying to get over the taste of it.

"It definitely is intense when you chug it that way, still gross too." I laugh while taking the bottle and taking another drink, not chugging it this time.

"Yep, still fucking gross, but I think that's the only vodka I'll ever truly love that won't fully gross me out like plain vodka does."

"Exactly, cherry vodka all the way." I take another sip, sliding the bottle back to her. "Let's go sit outside. I need some air." I don't even know if she could understand what I just said but she follows me as I head towards the front door.

"Cool, let's take these bottles with us. I've got some catching up to do." She grabs both bottles and the electric wine bottle opener off the counter.

"It's such a nice night out, but I'm fucking cold." I shiver a little as I take another sip, feeling my buzz intensify.

"Shit," Winter whisper-shouts as steps off the front stairs a little.

"You okay? Or did you stumble?" I giggle thinking about her stumbling since we're both clumsy, plus I didn't see what had happened since I was in front of her.

"No, Creedence is out in his driveway on his truck bed. Looks like he's drinking and playing his guitar." She tells me and it feels like I just took a knife to the chest. My fucking heart breaking at the thought of not being with him anymore. I miss listening to him sing and play his guitar so much and he just played for me yesterday while I laid in his bed, he sat next to me, his back against his headboard and just played. His voice was so sexy as he sang, I was looking forward to that memory that I got to make with him as time went on. Time that I fucking ruined.

"I should be over there with him right now, next to him," I choke out. "But I'm a fucking idiot and fucked everything up," I sob, hoping he can't hear me as Winter rushes back up the stairs.

"Oh babe, you did nothing wrong except care for him and try to do something nice. Please don't blame yourself for this." She tells me as she comes up the stairs and sits next to me. I'm thankful for the big bushes that block my front stairs because if they weren't there, I'd be able to see him perfectly and I don't think I could handle that right now, especially with how much I've had to drink so far.

"I feel like I did everything wrong, we just had such a perfect night, and I had to go and ruin it. I want to be with him so bad right now and I fucked that up." I'm crying, wiping my tears with my left hand shaking my head. "Fuck, I need to drink more where's my wine?" I sniffle, turning to Winter, wiping my tears again and taking another sip of my wine.

"Right here, babe. I just opened it for you." She hands me the bottle and I take a big sip of it before pulling it away from my mouth.

"Fuck this sucks." I let out a breath that I felt like I was holding in forever, but no matter how many deep breaths I take I still can't get this ache in my chest to ease up, or my anxiety to calm down at all.

The next morning, I wake up hung over as fuck, my head pounding, the room is spinning and I feel nauseous as hell, my mouth is so dry I feel like I just ate a bunch of sand. I can barely move my tongue as it sticks to the roof of my mouth. Gross. Drinking all that vodka and wine was the worst idea I ever had. But it did what it was supposed to do. It numbed my lips; my whole body was numb including my pain. At least until I woke up. I stretch my body and feel a leg next to mine and my stomach drops. Was all that just a dream? There's no way I had a dream that Creedence broke up with me. A rush of excitement washes over me as I slowly turn until I hear a snoring Winter next to me and my stomach drops again, my heart sinks and the tears start coming. I slowly sit up. I need something to drink and something for my head now. The room spins as I sit at the edge of my bed, breathing heavily trying to hold back the vomit that's trying to creep up my throat. I take a slow deep breath before I jump up and rush to the bathroom. Kneeling in front of the toilet I start puking, everything that comes up still burning my throat. Another terrible reminder of yesterday with Creed when everything was perfect. It already feels like it's been days without him, and it hasn't even been a full day yet. Fuck, this is the worst nightmare, and I pray I wake up from it soon.

27

CREEDENCE

I wake up the next day, feeling like shit. I got drunk for the first time in a while last night. My chest fucking hurts, my heart feels fucking heavy, and I feel empty. Is this what fucking heartache from a breakup feels like? I know I was the one who broke up with her but that doesn't mean I'm not still hurting. I've loved women before and when we broke up it didn't hurt nearly as bad as it does now. She was everything to me, my home, my world and everything came crashing down in one fucking day. Did I make the wrong choice? I have no idea but at the time I was making the right choice. I can't believe she went behind my back buying me a helmet to try and get me to ride again. I lay there in bed trying to fight the flashbacks of that day with my brother and it's so hard to do as I wipe the tears. Everything feels so fresh again, between the heartache of losing my brother, best friend. And the heartache of losing my girlfriend, the love of my life. I feel like I'm fighting a battle that has no other outcome, the flashbacks just keep getting more vivid as I lay here no matter how many times I try to shake my head to clear myself out of it.

"Sir, Sir." I keep hearing people talking but I have no idea what anyone is saying to me as I sit here and hold my baby brother's dead body in my arms, his blood all over me but I don't care. All I care about right now is my brother and how it should have been me.

"Sir please, we need you to step away from the body. Sir please. We need to look at him." Still, all I hear is their talking but I'm not hearing anything they're saying.

"Xander, please wake up man, please god dammit man please don't do this to me." I cry holding him to my chest. "Please tell me this is just another one of your stupid pranks." I shake him, freaking the fuck out I'm trying to be gentle but fuck what is going on. My baby brother lays lifeless in my arms, he no longer has a fucking pulse. This is my fault; it should've been me. I lay him down placing his head in my lap. There's blood all over my hands from his head. And I look down and feel sick again, I start dry heaving as I'm trying not to puke.

"Fuck man, please don't leave me, wake up man." I tell him as I place my hands on his chest and try to do CPR.

"Sir, please I'm sorry, sir but we need to check the body, can you tell us what happened, sir." But I can't. I don't know what happened. I didn't see the full thing; I just saw the ending and then I saw my brother lying there in a puddle of blood as I tried to rush to him.

"Xander please, I'm sorry for telling you we needed to get home, we can pull over a little longer. I'm sorry for switching lanes before you. I should've let my baby brother go first. Please don't do this to me. Tell me this is a joke. Let's wait a little longer before we head home, please, you, you have to be fucking with me. Xander don't do this." I sit there sobbing and shaking, rocking my body back and forth as I smack his chest over and over. "Please wake up." I shake him a little. You can hear people around me crying. This is not something you see every day I'm sure but that's the only thing I hear is whispers and crying. Like I said, I hear the words, but I have no idea what is being said to me.

"Xander, please I promise I won't make fun of you for being afraid to ride after it rains. I promise I'll always let you go ahead of me from now on. I won't be that asshole that goes ahead of you like we aren't

riding together, not that I always did it but you know what I mean. Please c'mon this isn't funny anymore." I slap his chest a little harder trying to get his lifeless body to wake up.

And suddenly I have two people grabbing my arms pulling me into a standing position, pulling me away from him while paramedics lay his limp body onto a stretcher. Blood. That's all I feel all over my hands and wet clothes. Xander's warm blood, the last thing from my brother that I'll always remember is his warm blood and I fucking hate that memory, that paralyzing fucking nightmare.

"Sir we need to remove the body from the scene, we're sorry. You also need to tell us what happened." One of the two officers that are holding me says to me as they help me walk away. "I'm so sorry about your loss, sir." He says again but I'm not listening. I'm too busy looking back at my brother's dead body lying on a stretcher getting covered by a body bag.

I snap out of the memory, wiping away my tears quickly as I sit up in bed gasping for air almost like I just woke up from a nightmare, but jokes on me because my life is now a living nightmare. I fucked my life up in more ways than one, when it should've been me who died that day, but I ruined my baby brother's life instead. Then I ruined Emerald's life instead of giving her the chance to explain. But I can't be with her if she's going to keep pushing me when I'm not ready, because I've told her I'm not ready. I don't even think I'm done grieving, not that I'll ever be done grieving the life my brother never got to have, but It's still so fresh. Too damn fresh no matter how long it's been.

I look at my phone and see that I have a text from Carsten. As I go to open my text messages, I realized I never closed out my last one from Emerald telling me she loved me, and it hits me like a ton of bricks straight to the heart. Fuck dude, I can't believe I lost one of the best things that's ever happened to me. But right now, it's probably for the best. My head is not right, right now and it's not fair to her, but she also shouldn't have pushed and pushed and pushed after I told her over and over that I wasn't ready. It felt like she was forcing me for her, not for me. Maybe I'm wrong.

> **Carsten**
> Hey man, Winter told me what happened. How
> you holdin up?

>> **Creedence**
>> I've been better.

> **Carsten**
> Wanna talk about it?

>> **Creedence**
>> I'll talk but not about what happened, still too
>> fresh.

> **Carsten**
> Understandable bro just know I'm here.

>> **Creedence**
>> Thanks man, appreciate you.

> **Carsten**
> Of course. You going to the shop today?

>> **Creedence**
>> Was thinking about it, but now I don't know what
>> I want to do.

> **Carsten**
> Come to the shop then we'll get lunch at the
> Diner. Both girls are off today so we'll only be
> lucky enough to deal with Stacy.

>> **Creedence**
>> Sounds good be there in about an hour.

I slowly get up, taking a couple deep breaths before heading to my kitchen for some water and something for my head, along with something to eat to help with this fucking hangover headache and this stupid fucking sick feeling from drinking on an empty stomach like a dumbass.

After eating I head outside to my front porch, avoiding the garage because Emerald left the helmet in there and right now, I'm not in the mood to look at it and bring back more memories. I barely slept last night between flashbacks of my brother's accident and then dealing with this terrible feeling of heartache. God, I feel so fucking empty, and alone and it's all my fault, yet it's her fault at the same time for bringing me back to that place when I wasn't ready. I can't deal with the demons of my past when I'm being forced to. I need to be ready in order to accept help.

I sit down on my front porch after looking over at Emeralds yard to make sure she wasn't out yet because I'm not ready to see her just yet. Or any time soon.

I take a sip of the coffee I made, and I stare out at the street not even bothering to look at my phone. I have no one to talk to now and I just talked to Carsten. I don't feel like talking to anyone anyways, I just want to be alone today. I'm sure hanging out with Carsten after work will be better for me mentally than sitting home. My feelings are all over the place right now I don't even know what I want. I take a seat on the top step when my phone vibrates in my hand.

Axton
I heard what happened man, I'm so sorry. Let me return the favor and get you out of the house tonight bro.

Creedence
It's ok man, appreciate it.

Creedence
But ehh I'm not sure if I'm down for that or not.

Axton
Oh that's cool. Glad I didn't ask.

Axton
We're going out tonight, just to Black Velvet.
Carsten is working.

> **Creedence**
> Somethin tells me ur not givin me a choice huh?

Axton
Nahh we can go up whenever.

> **Creedence**
> Well I gotta meet Carsten at the shop here soon.
> Then we are going to the diner for lunch. Wanna
> join?

Axton
Ya that's cool just text me when.

> **Creedence**
> Wait if ur not here where r u?

Axton
Friends house he had a party last night.

> **Creedence**
> Ahh ok that's cool.

Axton
Well hit me up when you go to Lisa's diner.

> **Creedence**
> Will do man.

I finish drinking the rest of my coffee and head inside to brush my teeth and take a quick shower. After my shower and getting dressed I grab everything I need for the day, putting it all in my pockets and head out the front door to my truck.

As I'm walking to my truck, I end up seeing Emerald walking to her car in the process and I look down. "Fuck." I whisper to myself. I was not ready for that; she looks so fucking beautiful. Her green and black hair braided off to the side with my pink scrunchie. She's wearing a pair of black leggings that makes her ass look amazing. With a tight purple T-shirt that hugs her tits and curves just right. Fuck, am I an idiot? But knowing her it's probably too late to even try and fix things. And I just don't know if I'm ready for that just yet.

I open my truck door trying hard not to look at what seems to be a crying Emerald, and step up inside, shutting the door behind me. I take a quick glance at her through my tinted window. She's on the phone, as she wipes her tears away with her other hand. Fuck it breaks my heart to see her like this, I just want to go over there and hug her. I snap out of my thoughts and start my truck, backing out of my driveway. Reminding myself I ended things with her for a good reason.

Ten minutes later I'm pulling into the parking lot of Crazy's Tattoos right as Carsten is getting out of his car.

"Fuck, I don't know if I'm ready for this yet," I mumble to myself, not that facing my friends is a bad thing, but I just don't know if I'm ready to explain all this shit to them yet. I turn off the engine and slowly step out of my truck suddenly feeling very anxious.

"Hey, man." Carsten comes over giving me a big man handshake, hug with a pat on the back.

"Hey, brother." I do the same thing back to him before backing away. I was fine until I got here. Now I have this strange empty, sick feeling in my stomach.

"How you holdin up?" He has a sad smile on his face. He's always been a good caring friend; we've been there for each other through everything.

"I've been better, I saw her in the driveway when I was leaving. She was crying and talking on the phone, she was shaking and every-thing. Fucking broke my heart seeing her like that." I look down, closing my eyes, trying to stop the tears from forming in my eyes. I can't let him see me cry like a little bitch.

"Why didn't you go and talk to her? I don't exactly know what happened but I'm sure she'd be willing to hear you out."

"Ehh, I'm not ready to talk about it and I'm not ready to face her yet. Still too fresh."

"I get it, trust me I went through it with Winter before." He pats me on the back as we start heading into Crazy's.

It's just the two of us working today and we're not open for long, his uncle lets us work whenever we want on the weekend and we both have appointments at the same time, two friends coming in to get matching flower tattoos on their hip.

"Hey, welcome to Crazy's, how can we help you today?" I ask standing at the counter as a female walks in smiling at me like she's never seen a man before.

"Well, hello there, how are you?" She attempts to wink but her eye just looks like it's twitching.

"I'm doing good, how about you?" I'm trying to be friendly, but not in the mood for it.

"I'm a lot better now."

"Well, that's good to hear, what can I help you with today?" I ask again, getting annoyed that she avoided the question.

"I wanted to get my tongue pierced, you guys do those right?" she asks, leaning forward on the wooden part of the front desk.

"Yes, we do, let me get my friend out here to get the papers signed and everything while I go and set everything up for you," I tell her as I walk towards the back to go get Carsten.

"Hey man, can you get paperwork set up and signed for me so I can get this set up real quick to do a tongue piercing?" I ask him in a monotone voice, just not in the mood for anything.

"Ya man, I'll go right up there."

"Thanks man, you can send her back when you're done," I tell him, walking away.

I walk into my office and start sanitizing and preparing everything for her as she walks in.

"Man, I didn't think there was going to be two hot men that

worked here." She flirts with me, staring out the door as Carsten walks by, she waves and giggles.

"Well sweetie, sorry to break your heart but he's married with children," I tell her as she looks away shocked.

"Married and has kids, damn. Well, what about you, handsome?" she asks me in a seductive voice, walking towards me slowly.

"I have a girlfriend." I lie because I'm not in the mood to be flirted with and I hope with me saying that she stops flirting.

"Well, I know how to keep a secret." She winks and I don't even react, I don't even know if I heard what she said fully.

"Here, come have a seat in my chair so we can get your piercing done." I still ignore what she says and move to grab my gloves and everything else I need.

"Alright, I'm going to place this under your tongue to absorb any spit until I'm ready, and I'm going to have you tuck this into your shirt to collect any drool that might come out of your mouth in the process."

"Yes, sir." She winks at me and It's so hard not to roll my eyes. I mean she's attractive, but not my type at all. My only type I have right now is Emerald and it still hits me like a ton of bricks every time I think about the fact that we're not together anymore.

"Alright, stick your tongue out as far as you can for me," I tell her as I grab my clamps to place on her tongue. "Now I'm going to place this on your tongue, it's honestly probably going to hurt more than the actual piercing itself," I tell her because that's what I've heard most of my customers say when I've pierced their tongues.

"Alright, I'm gonna have you take a deep breath in." I push it through her tongue, and she scrunches her eyes, slightly wincing from the pain. "Then out."

"Now take a deep breath again." I put the jewelry in her tongue and remove the piercing needle.

"Alright, we're all done," I tell her, removing the cloth from under her tongue and her shirt.

"That wasn't terrible." She smiles slowly, licking her lips, scrunching her eyes closed when the tongue ring hits her tooth, and I try not to laugh.

"Nope, I've heard it's not bad at all."

"So, do you have any piercings?" She has a smirk on her face as she looks me up and down.

"Yep, plenty," I tell her, waiting for her to ask what.

"Where are your piercings at?"

"I have a Jacob's ladder," I chuckle as I walk out of the room with a smirk, because most women don't know what that is and usually have to google it.

"Well shit." Is all I hear as I walk to the desk, yep, she must have googled it.

She comes running out of the room.

"That didn't hurt at all? I never knew that was possible." She giggles in shock.

"Nope, my girlfriend loves it." I tell her as I hand over her bag of stuff she purchased before her piercing.

"Here's your tip." She hands me twenty dollars.

"How much do you want back in change?"

"Nope, that's all for you. I don't want anything. Thank you so much." She leans on the wooden part of the desk again.

"Thank you, I appreciate the tip," I tell her, setting it down on the counter.

"If you ever become single anytime soon. Here's my number," she says, writing it down on a piece of paper. I just smile. I don't bother saying anything about it.

"Have a good day," I tell her as she starts walking towards the door.

"Thanks, you too." She waves and right as she's out of my view I take her number and throw it away. I don't need that, even if I am single right now, she was too desperate.

"Man, that was rough, huh?" Carsten's laughing as he comes out of the back hallway.

"Ya it was, she was way too desperate." I roll my eyes, shaking my head. "She practically pouted when I told her you were married with kids." I laugh.

He starts laughing and shaking his head. "That's hilarious. Thank god I'm not single." Then he pauses. "Fuck man, I wasn't thinking." He slaps his hand on his face.

"It's fine. I'm not upset. What time are those girls supposed to be here?" I change the subject. I'm not trying to talk about Emerald and not be focused on my customer.

"Should be here any minute." He looks down at his phone to look at the time, right as a car pulls up and two blonde girls get out of the car. I turn to him and roll my eyes. This should be interesting.

About an hour and a half later I'm getting back into my truck to head to Lisa's Diner, so I text Axton to let him know we're headed there.

Creedence
Hey man headed to Lisa's Diner now you still down?

Axton
Yep I'll leave here now, see you soon.

Creedence
See you man.

"Axton is joining us for lunch, is that cool?" I should probably check with Carsten thinking it's probably too late to be asking that question, but I know he won't care.

"Ya, of course I'll see you in a few." He gets into his car.

"See you," I tell him as I shut my truck door.

I pull into the parking lot of Lisa's Diner, shutting off my truck and getting out.

"Fuck dude." I say to myself as I see Emerald's car here. I thought she was off today; I wonder why she's here.

Carsten pulls up next to me and I look at him shaking my head.

"Man, I don't know if I can do this." I say as he opens his car door.

"Do what?" He raises his eyebrow, confused since he just got here.

"Emerald is here. She was supposed to be off today." I tell him, crossing my arms over my chest and leaning against my truck.

"Fuck, wanna skip the diner today then? Maybe she picked up an extra shift." He says as he shuts his car door.

"Nah, I'll be fine I just don't want to make it awkward for her, ya know?" I shrug, feeling bad that I'm about to walk through the diner door. I'm good at putting on a show, I know it'll kill her if I act okay, but I can't show her that I'm hurt.

"Ya I get it, but it's a small town, you guys can't avoid each other forever if you aren't going to be together anymore." He isn't saying it in a dick way either, he's just speaking the truth because that's just how our town works.

"Ya those were my thoughts exactly, gonna have to get used to seeing each other still even if we're not ready."

My heart sinks as I walk through the door and she's one of the first people I see, we make brief eye contact before she looks away. I can see the tears forming in her eyes and I look down trying to stop my own tears from forming, I can't believe she affects me this way. Seeing her going through a heartbreak that's caused by me breaks my heart even more. Fuck maybe this was a bad idea. She rushes off to the back room, so fast she's almost running and my heart hurts. It feels heavy and empty at the same time. I'd give anything to go and hug her. But I can't. Not anytime soon.

28

EMERALD

I RUSH OFF TO THE BACK ROOM, HE WAS THE LAST PERSON I was expecting to see for the second time today. I knew he was working today so I didn't think he'd be coming in here at all. It killed me this morning when I saw him in the driveway. I was already crying to begin with, then seeing him made it worse. It almost made me have a panic attack thinking about the fact that I'll never get to feel his hugs again or kiss his lips. I'll never get to hear his voice tell me he loves me or call me Sugar and it made my already bad anxiety worse and made it hard to breathe. My chest hurt from the pain of it all, my body was shaking I thought I was going to pass out.

Then looking up at the door and seeing how handsome he looks in his dark washed jeans, his light-blue T-shirt that formed to his sexy muscles. His tattoos showing on his arms and hands. I would've done anything to run towards him, jump into his arms and hug him. Not run away and cry because I'm fucking breaking right now.

"Sweetie, are you okay?" I hear Lisa open the door and walk into the breakroom talking to me.

"Fuck, this sucks, sorry for swearing but no, I mean I'll be ok in a minute. But fuck, Creedence and I broke up," I tell her right as Stacy walks into the back room.

"Hey Lisa, someone's–" She pauses. "Wait, you guys broke up?"

She smiles. What. A. Fucking. Cunt. I can't stand Stacy and the bitch she is.

"Tell them I'll be right there, this is none of your business, Stacy, please leave," she tells her with a mad look on her face.

"Oh sweetie." She hugs me tightly. "I'm so sorry, do you want to talk about it?" She starts rubbing my back gently.

"I appreciate it but if I start talking about it now, I won't be able to stop crying," I tell her, wiping away the rest of my tears and taking a deep breath and holding it for a second before slowly letting it out. Trying to calm my anxiety down. That seems to be my new thing, deep breathing to calm myself down and talk my body out of a panic attack.

"Okay, I'm ready to go back out now," I tell her while I'm calm before the tears start coming again.

"Are you sure? You can take a few minutes if you need to." She gives me one more hug.

"Thank you, Lisa. I appreciate it. I'll let you know if I do end up needing a minute. But right now, I think I'm good." I tell her as she starts walking towards the break room door.

"That's fine sweetie, just let me know." She walks out the break room and I'm left alone to take a couple deep breaths by myself for a minute. Hopefully by the time I come out Creedence and Carsten will be seated already, and I won't have to talk with them. Not that I want to ignore Carsten since he's my best friend's fiancé, but right now I don't really want to get into a conversation with him, especially since he's with Creed. I take a couple more deep breaths and walk out the door of the break room right as Stacy is talking with Carsten and Creedence. Fucking fuck. Right as I'm about to walk away so I don't have to talk to Carsten, Stacy starts saying my name.

"Oh, look who it is Emerald, your boyfriends here," Stacy laughs. "Oh wait, I mean your ex-boyfriend is here." Her tone is bitchy with a nasty smirk on her face. "Because I forgot he doesn't want you anymore...which I don't blame him at all. Who would want...that?" Her smile gets bigger as she points at me moving her finger up and down. Is she fucking serious right now? My face is bright red because not only did she say that to me, but she also said it in front of Creedence. And any other customer waiting in line to be seated and all the people around us could hear her clear as day. I can't believe her. I don't even say anything as tears well up in my eyes and I rush back into the break room. Fuck her and fuck this job right now.

Lisa comes rushing in behind me, the same time I hear Creedence say, "You don't have to be such a fucking bitch to her Stacy, you know damn well she's going through a hard time right now." And then the door shuts so I don't get to hear anything else before Lisa comes rushing over to me.

"Oh sweetie, are you okay? I heard what she said to you. I'm not going to let her get away with it either. I just wanted to get to you first."

I'm a sobbing mess and can't even talk, I'm on the verge of hyperventilating and my head is still all fucked up from all the alcohol I drank last night. I'm still pretty hung over and it's well into the afternoon. The crying is only intensifying my pounding headache. I knew I shouldn't have picked up any extra shifts today, but I needed to keep my mind busy, and I figured getting out of the house would be my best option instead of being drunk all day. But I'm thinking being drunk would have been the better option.

"I just don't think I can do this, I just... I just don't want to be without him," I cry out, spit flying out of my mouth from how hard I'm crying.

"Oh honey, it's gonna work itself out, I know it will. You guys are meant to be together. I have never seen Creedence so in love before, I don't know what happened, but I know it'll blow over." She puts her arm around me as she sits down next to me on the bench in the break room. I want to tell her she has no idea what she's talking about because he broke up with me and doesn't want me anymore, even fucking Stacy can see he doesn't want me anymore. But I don't want to come off as a bitch to her because I'm not trying to be bitchy.

"Do you care if I go home?" I frown. "I know when you called, I said I was fine working the extra shift today but I don't know if I'm okay anymore." I hiccup, wiping my tears with both hands.

"Of course, you don't have to explain yourself. I know what you're going through is a lot right now. I completely understand, sweetie." She pats my back again with a sweet smile on her face.

"Thank you so much, Lisa, I truly appreciate it," I tell her, pulling my apron off.

"I'll take care of the rest of your tables and whatever tips you get from them I'll put in your locker. I have a key and don't argue with me about not taking them." She laughs a little, lightening the mood.

"Lisa, I'm not going to take them when I barely did anything today. You can have them," I tell her, putting my apron in my locker.

"Whatever you say, sweetie. Whatever you say." And I know that's her way of arguing with me, telling me she's not going to listen. But I'll just give her back the money either way.

"You go home and take care of yourself, take a few days off. I'll text you to see if you're ready to come back in, in a couple days, okay?" she tells me instead of asking because she knows I'll argue with her about that too. She walks out of the break room as I finish putting my stuff away.

I grab my purse and phone, rushing out of the room.

Then I walk out of the break room and over to the computer to check out real quick. Then I head past the front counter, looking down in the process so I don't have to look at anyone as I walk out the door. I take a deep breath of fresh air when I get outside and close my eyes standing there for a minute just taking deep breath after deep breath to calm down this ache in my heart and the chest pains from my anxiety. After that I walk over to the side of the building and sit down on a bench. I need a minute before I go to my car. Then I look down at my phone, not really sure what to do with it since I don't really have anyone to talk to. I feel so alone and sad right now. I wish I had Creedence here to hug right now. But I need to start getting over it because he's not gonna be here anymore. I hear someone clear their throat and look up to see Creedence standing there. Fuck. What else could he want; he already broke my heart, did he come here to yell at me some more? I don't even bother talking. I just look back down at my phone and act like he's not there.

"Sorry I thought you left," he says, looking over in my direction. He sounds and looks sad, but I still don't say anything, I don't think I can without breaking down.

"I'm sorry for what Stacy said to you." Wow he's sorry about that but not about what he fucking said to me last night. I still don't respond. He doesn't deserve my response honestly and like I said if I open my mouth to even try to talk to him, I'm going to break down and cry and I won't give him that. He doesn't deserve to see my heartache or what he did to me, right now I'm trying to be strong and show him I'm not phased.

"None of it was true, and I felt like you needed to hear that." I don't even bother looking back up at him. I grab my stuff and stand up to go walk to my car. I need to get away from him and cry some more. But I need to cry alone, not in front of him, he doesn't deserve to see any more of my tears.

I can't believe he just went over there and started talking to me like nothing even happened between us. How was he able to talk without being affected at all? He sounded a little sad but not as sad as he should be for someone who was in love, unless he was putting on a good show to not show me how hurt he is.

I unlock my car door, getting in and starting the ignition. I drive home in silence, besides crying that's the only sound in my car. I'm too sad to listen to any kind of music and I probably wouldn't even be able to hear it over my crying anyways.

I pull into my driveway and wipe away my tears. I have a bottle of cherry vodka and some wine waiting for me inside along with a hot bath, then after I think I'm going to watch some crime shows. It's been a while since I've watched one of those and I need a good distraction, and why not watch something about crime and creepy stuff instead of something sad that'll make me cry.

I walk up to my front stairs and sit down; I need to text Chastity to kind of fill her in on everything and to see if we're still going to the party Friday. I'm still up in the air about going, especially now that I'll be going alone and single. But Winter told me I didn't have a choice.

Emerald
Hey bitch.

Chastity
Hey bitch, whats up hoe?

Emerald
Nothin really. Creedence and I broke up...

Chastity
Fuckkk babe I'm so sorry. I want to ask if you're ok
but I know you're not.

Emerald
It's ok babe. I appreciate it.

Chastity
Well then you definitely need to come out to that
party Friday.

Chastity
LETS GET FUCKED UP BITCHHHHHH!!!!!

Emerald
That's another reason why I was texting you to
see if you were still going.

Emerald
Guess if I'm going I'm going to get fucked up.
WOO HOO WE'RE GETTING FUCKED UP
BITCHHHH!!!!

Chastity
That's my girl. They always have the best drinks
there so you'll definitely get drunk.

Emerald
Good, I'm about to go in and take a bath. I'll text
you later.

Chastity
Hang in there babe. I'm here if you need me.
Love you.

Emerald
Love you babe.

I love that she didn't push me to tell her and that even though she has no idea what's going on she'll still be here if I need her. That's one thing about Chastity, she always listens no matter what the situation is, and she doesn't pry, she waits for you to be ready and if you don't ever bring it up, she still doesn't try to pry it out of you.

Right as I stand up to head inside Creedence's truck pulls up into his driveway.

"Can this fucking day get any fucking worse," I mumble to myself as I rush up my porch stairs, so he doesn't try to talk to me again. I think I'm in the angry stage of the breakup now, at least right at this moment I am, along with still being heartbroken but instead of heartbroken and sad I'm now heartbroken and fucking angry. I can't believe he just threw us away like that and I still can't believe he just tried talking to me like he didn't just break my heart into a million tiny pieces. He came over and spoke to me like things wouldn't be awkward and uncomfortable, like you would talk to someone about the fucking weather, not to someone you just broke up with that you said you were in love with.

29
CREEDENCE

I'VE BEEN SITTING ON MY TRUCK BED ALL NIGHT DRINKING and playing guitar. Each time Emerald's come outside with Winter she's had either a bottle of wine or a bottle of cherry vodka out there with her. Hopefully they've been the same bottle, and she hasn't gone through more than one of each.

I wish I was with her, part of me wishes I never reacted the way I did and that I had the balls to just go over there and apologize. But I don't have the balls yet and I know she won't accept it. Especially not after how it went earlier when I apologized for what Stacy said. I can't believe she said that to her in front of all those people. She's such a miserable bitch, but that's okay. I stuck up for Emerald and everything I had said to Stacy embarrassed the fuck out of her, like she deserved. No one fucks with my Emerald like that. Not that she's mine anymore but still… she didn't deserve that. I sit here in the bed of my truck, my back against the side and my feet over the edge listening to her mumble to herself. She sounds pretty drunk, and it almost makes me laugh.

"Yeah, fuck you, Creedence." She sorta shouts to no one since it's dark and she doesn't know I'm watching her. I'm not sure where Winter is either.

"Fucking break my heart like that, you asshole," she slurs. Taking another sip of whichever bottle she has now. She's going to feel like absolute shit tomorrow that's for sure.

"I can't believe him." Now she's crying and it breaks my heart that I broke her heart. But I'm an idiot and broke my own heart too in the process. I slowly get out of my truck, grab my guitar, my empty beer pack, and start walking towards my house when her crying becomes louder. I don't know if it's because I'm closer or if it's actually getting louder, but my fucking heart can't take it. It's taking everything in me to not go over there and hug her. But I can't do that. She'd probably kick my ass right now anyways. I head into my garage ignoring the helmet but going to my bike and sitting on it.

"Fuck Xander, I don't know what you want me to do man," I say to no one really but hoping my brother can somehow hear me.

"I don't know if I should ride again for you or stop riding permanently because of what happened to you." I sigh, tears starting to form in my eyes.

"Fuck dude, why'd you have to leave me man, I miss you so goddamn much. I wish you were here." I sit on my bike as the tears start streaming down my face faster than I can wipe them. God, I've become a bitch these last few days, an overly emotional bitch about a lot of shit. As I sit here lost in my thoughts my phone vibrates in my pocket, as I reach down to get it, I see it's Axton. Fuck I wipe my tears quickly, I forgot he wanted to go out to Black Velvet tonight.

Axton
Be home in 3 be ready cuz we're leavin then.

Creedence
Ok I'm ready.

Axton
Alright man.

Fuck I wipe away my tears some more and rush inside to wash

my face down with some cold water, then grab a towel out of my closet and dry my face off. I check my hair in the mirror real quick because I want to make sure it's not messed up from when I fell asleep earlier. Then I grab my wallet, and I head out the front door locking it behind me right as Axton is pulling into the driveway.

I open his passenger door and sit down in the seat.

"Hey, man."

"What's up?" I say, shutting the door.

"Not much, partied all night, slept most of my day away so I'm just getting up to do it all over again." He gives a slight chuckle. He's going through heartache just like I am right now except his was for three years. Not a few months. But he's handling this by partying away the pain, I don't think I could handle drinking as much as he's been every day without dying from it.

We pull into the parking lot at Black Velvet and park out back like usual and head in through the back door, almost running into Carsten as he's heading out the door with garbage in his hands.

"Fuck man." He looks at me since I'm the first one walking through the door. "You fucking scared me."

"Fuck dude, you scared me." I laugh because I wasn't expecting him to be walking out the same time I was walking in.

"Sorry for scaring you, dick face," I chuckle.

"It's cool, cock breath." He punches my shoulder.

"Glad I wasn't in the line of fire; someone could've accidentally punched me or something from both of you pussys scaring each other." Axton shakes his head, placing his keys in his pocket.

"Hey, who you callin pussy?" I ask him.

"Right, I don't know who you're callin a pussy but it ain't us," Carsten says to him with a look of disbelief on his face.

I hold the door open as Carsten walks back in. I miss hanging out with them like we used to.

"I miss the old days, man when we were younger hanging out

getting in trouble for all the dumb shit the three of us used to do." I smile back on all the memories.

"Right, all the times we got caught by the fucking cops over dumb shit that we thought was so fucking cool," Axton snorts.

"No wonder the cops hate us now, always watching out for us to make sure we're not still doing dumb shit, stealing stupid shit from the store. Blowing up shit in parking lots, shooting shit with our BB guns behind stores." Carsten laughs as we all stand there laughing with him. I stand there with a smile on my face for the first time all day before I'm hit with a lonely sick feeling in my stomach that I try to hide. I feel empty, and I know why. I hate this feeling. I've never experienced it before; sure, I've experienced heartache from breakups but never like this and it fucking sucks.

"Hey, you good man?" Carsten has a concerned look on his face as he watches me.

"Ya, ya I'm cool sorry. Was just zoning out." I lie because I don't feel like talking about it although I'm sure they already know what's wrong. They're not stupid they've all experienced heartache before, hell Axton is literally going through one right now and hasn't looked sad at all tonight. I mean he was cheated on. He should still be devastated, he wanted to marry that girl. But things don't always work out the way you want them to. I'm sure he's just trying to have a good time like the rest of us. I push my thoughts of Emerald to the side and try to get back to enjoying myself with my friends.

"You guys wanna go do a shot?" Axton yells over the music as we come down the hall. "Fireball is calling our names."

"I can do one but I'm working so I can't get sloppy, Chase will kick my ass." Carsten laughs, poor Chase had to take care of a drunk Carsten at work last year and make him go sleep it off in his office on the couch from doing too many shots. He was pissed the next day and wouldn't forgive him for a while for leaving him alone on a busy ass Friday night. Poor guy was slammed all night, and didn't get one break.

"Yeah, I'm down, I need to get drunk anyways." It's true I'm feeling too much at the moment and I just need something to numb some of it.

"Hey, guys what's up?" Chase walks up to us as he gives us a man hug, with a handshake.

"Guys wanna do a shot?" Chase yells to the three of us.

"Fuck yeah, that's what we came in here for." Axton yells as he walks around the bar and grabs two stools for us to sit on. Of course, they have to be next to some girls who are looking over at us and smiling. Fuck please don't talk to me, go straight to Axton and talk to him I think to myself because I'm not in the mood for some drunk girls.

"Here you guys go." Chase sets the Fireball shots down in front of us and waits for Carsten to come over.

"Only one shot, Carsten." Chase glares at Carsten as he says it.

"Don't worry, my man, I already told them I'm only doing one shot." He stands next to Chase grabbing the shot glass.

It was definitely a lie, four shots and one beer later I think Carsten forgot he was working when Chase comes over and punches his arm.

"Yo dick face, forget we're runnin' the bar together, you fuck." He laughs but doesn't seem too mad since they have been steady but not slammed.

"Fuck, I'm sorry dude, I got caught up in everything and forgot where I was really. Like I forgot I was working." He laughs, and Chase just shakes his head at him.

"You boys having fun?" The brunette next to me asks with a sexy side smirk on her face. Shit what am I doing I can't think her smile is sexy.

"Yeah, we're havin' a good time, what about you ladies?" I ask them, feeling the alcohol so I'm in the mood to talk a little to get Emerald off my mind.

"Yeah, we are, what about your friend, is he having a good time?" She leans forward pointing at Axton.

"Hell yeah, I'm having a good time. You ladies want a shot? It's on me?" He winks at them. And I sorta wish I could be like him and not feel my feelings right now.

"Sure, what shot do you guys wanna do?" The blonde with her asks.

"We've been doing Fireball, are you ladies fine with that?" I ask them hoping they say no because I'm now regretting the decision to talk to them. I feel like I'm cheating, and I don't like it, even if I am single now.

"Sure, I'm down," the brunette giggles, scooting closer to me. Great.

"Hell yeah, I love Fireball," the blonde yells to us as she comes and stands next to Axton.

"Hey, Carsten," Axton yells to him even though he's across the bar.

He holds his finger up and grabs a beer from the refrigerator before handing it to the guy at the other end.

"Hey guys, what's up?" Yep, he's buzzed. His body sways a little as he stands there.

"Ohh, there's three of you guys?" The brunette smiles, hand on her chin biting her finger a little.

"I'm happily engaged and have two kids at home, I'm good. No offense," he shouts out quickly before they start flirting with him too.

"Damn," she pouts and then looks back at me. "Well, you're single right?" She bites her thin bottom lip, and usually I would find that attractive even if she didn't have full, plump lips like Emerald's. I still would have found her really fucking attractive, hell I may have even tried to bring her and her friend home, I'd never turn down two kinky looking girls and a threesome. But none of those thoughts excite me, not even one of those thoughts made my cock twitch.

"It's complicated, but I'm not here to talk about relationships. Let's do this shot," I grumble trying to change the subject.

"Well alright." She gives me a pout, it's cute and all but nothing worth changing my mind over.

"Fireball?" Carsten holds up the bottle as we nod our heads, and he walks away. He comes back with six shot glasses, and I can't help but laugh knowing one of them is for him.

"Chase, get your ass over here," Carsten yells to his brother as he walks over shaking his head.

"Carsten, this is your last one, asshole. You're supposed to be working." He laughs it off like he's not pissed but no one missed the angry tone.

"So, are you single?" the blonde and brunette ask at the same time and laugh as they look at each other in shock.

"Sorry, I'm sorta taken, my uhh girl should be here shortly." He sounds really fucking confused as he says that. Maybe he's just not used to having a girlfriend or something. Him and Saylor started secretly dating before they told us. They snuck around like we wouldn't catch on. Idiots. It was very obvious that they were obsessed with each other, but they both tried to deny it.

"Damn, you guys are no fun." She gives us a dramatic pout before laughing. At least she's not truly upset.

"Right, I was thinking the same thing," the blonde pouts right along with her friend, but I think hers is actually serious.

After taking the next shot, I head outside to get some fresh air and to get the fuck away from those chatty fucking girls because they were driving me fucking crazy. The urge to text Emerald is so strong, especially with the buzz I have going on. I miss her so much and it makes me wonder if this feeling will ever go away. Then it takes me back to the thoughts I've been having. Was I too harsh or did I make the right decision? And I fucking hate second guessing myself like that. Right as I'm about to head in the guys come out to with drinks for some fresh air and we end up talking outside for the rest of it before Axton and I head on home, he probably shouldn't drive because I know If I'm drunk, he's gotta be drunk too and it's a stupid ass decision we both make. Unless he started sobering up and I'm just too fucked up to pay attention.

"I'm heading into bed, man, see you tomorrow," Axton says as he walks through the front door stumbling a little, you can tell the alcohol is kicking in more now that we're home.

"Night man," I call out after him.

I head over to my truck and lay the tailgate down hopping up on it before heading inside. I love being outside. I'd rather be outside relaxing with my guitar or someone's company than inside watching TV anyways. And even though I'm outside alone, I'd rather be alone with my thoughts outside than trapped behind my bedroom walls. Plus, I'm stupid and hoping to see Emerald on her front stairs again. This is the only spot in the driveway where you can see her stairs, because the bushes around her front porch block them unless you're standing here right where I park.

But with the way her house looks, it looks like she's probably sleeping. I look down at my phone to look at the time and see that it's one-thirty in the morning, so she's probably drunk and passed out. She's probably naked too since she prefers to sleep with no clothes on, and picturing her naked in her bed makes my cock hard.

I lie back in my truck bed, closing my eyes. I picture her on her knees, arms tied behind her back and her mouth open with her tongue out. Waiting to suck my cock just how I like it, well just like she likes it too since she's obsessed with sucking my cock.

I picture my fingers in her pussy thrusting in and out of her while she's choking on my cock and swallowing it down, her favorite thing to do. My piercings scraping her throat as she moans out from how turned on she is and I have to reach down and readjust my cock from how hard I am.

I hear a door creek and look next door to see Emerald stumbling out onto her porch, slurring whatever words she's saying.

"Fuck that hurt, stupid foot getting in my way." I laugh quietly, of course she's ruining my perverted thoughts of her. It's almost like she knew I was thinking of her and had to ruin it.

"Fuck, I'm drunk and horny. This is fucking stupid. Fuck you, Creedence for breaking up with me, we could be fucking right now," she yells a little as she starts sniffling. Shit. There goes my rock-hard cock.

I sit up trying to listen to what else she's saying but she's not being as loud now, it almost sounds like she's whispering. Fuck, I hope she's not crying.

30

EMERALD

I SIT ON MY FRONT PORCH, WITH A BOTTLE OF WINE IN MY hand and see Creedence standing by his truck, but I don't think he can see me from how dark it is, at least he doesn't acknowledge me if he does. I decide to tease him and start talking loud enough for him to hear, I don't even care right now. I'm drunk and for once my feelings are numb. Everything is numb, especially my lips. I love when I drink to the point of my lips going numb, for some reason I've always loved that feeling.

"Fuck, I'm drunk and horny. This is fucking stupid, fuck you, Creedence for breaking up with me, we could be fucking right now." My drunken teasing turned into drunken depression and now I'm crying. I wonder if he had heard me because now, he's walking away. I wonder if maybe he's sick of hearing me, so he goes inside. I talk to myself instead because I have no one to talk to right now.

"Fuck, why did I have to go and buy him a helmet thinking it would just magically fix all of his problems or bring his fucking brother back." I make sure I say that extra quietly because I don't want him to think I'm shit talking about his brother because I'm not. I just feel like such an ass for doing something with such a touchy subject like I was just going to fix his years of grief overnight. I wasn't trying to make his grieving go away, I was just trying to find a way to bring him another form of happiness.

"You're such an idiot, Emerald, how are you going to bring him happiness with such a sensitive subject," I slur to myself as I take another sip from my bottle.

I wasn't having a bad night with rotating my bottle of cherry vodka and my bottle of wine while watching crime documentaries and eating the pizza I had ordered. I made sure to get something greasy to help absorb all this alcohol I'm drinking. I stand up and start walking down my driveway to my car, I climb up and sit on the trunk to sit down with my wine. Creedence is still outside on his front porch, I saw him when I was climbing up on my trunk but I'm hoping he didn't notice me, I just needed some more air. I don't get a good breeze with the bushes blocking my front stairs and I just love being outside. I'd rather be outside enjoying the nice weather while it lasts than be inside. I take another sip of my wine when I hear someone walking in Creedence's driveway. He's back by his truck. What the fuck, now I have no way to get back to my porch without him seeing me. Right when I start to look over my shoulder to see what he's doing, he walks back up to his house. Thank god, I think he was just grabbing something from his truck.

I take another sip of my wine. Fuck I'm going to regret this in the morning. So, I take one last sip before putting the cork back in. I hop off my car and start walking towards my front door. I head inside, lock the front door and walk to my room, making a trip to the bathroom and then stripping out of my clothes before getting into my nice, warm bed. I'm drunk and I'm lonely. What a shitty way to fall asleep and a shitty way to end the night.

The next day I wake up and can barely open my eyes. The room is spinning, my tongue is sticking to the roof of my mouth from how dry my mouth is, I feel nauseous and yet again, another fucking pounding headache. I laugh to myself at that one like it isn't my own damn fault that I feel like shit. It's not like I'm sick or something, nope I'm causing my own damn problems. I slowly sit up keeping my eyes closed and place one foot on the ground to hopefully stop some of the spinning so I can use the bathroom and brush my teeth to get this nasty taste of wine and cherry vodka out of my mouth. I finally open my eyes a little only squinting, not bothering to open them all the way due to things being too fucking bright and I walk slowly in the bathroom.

After brushing my teeth and everything I head into my closet and put on some underwear and a large T-shirt before heading to my kitchen for something to eat and drink. I take something for my head and settle on some pizza from last night, not caring that it's nine-thirty in the morning. I grab my Dr. Pepper, a bottle of water, and the pizza and head to my room to check my phone and see I have a text from Winter.

Winter
Hey babes, how are you doing?

> **Emerald**
> Hungover... still drunk maybe? Not exactly sure
> yet. You?

Winter
Lol oh girl, I can't even. You are braver than I am
with all that alcohol mixing. I still feel shitty
from it.

> **Emerald**
> I did too that's why I drank some more yesterday,
> to hopefully feel better...shitty idea.

Winter
Well ya...I could've told you that one.

> **Emerald**
> Shhhh, we don't talk about that.

Winter
Hahaha I talked to Chas, you're still coming to
that party Friday just so you know.

> **Emerald**
> S, do I have to? What if he's there?

Winter
He won't be, Carsten couldn't get him to come.
He said he just wants to stay home that way you'll
go and have a good time.

> **Emerald**
> Alright. I'll go then, I already told Chas that I was
> only going if we'd get fucked up. So you have to
> get fucked up too.

Winter
Already planned on it, I haven't been to a party in
a while, so I'm getting fucked up, babe.

> **Emerald**
> Yes! I need to plan my outfit. I want to look HOT!

Winter
Good you need to look hot, maybe you'll find
someone to hook up with.

> **Emerald:**
> Seriously??

Winter
Friday will be two weeks since you guys broke up.
You need a rebound, babe. It'll help you get
over him.

> **Emerald**
> Man, I don't know if I'm ready for that yet. But I'll
> keep it in mind.

I lie, I'm only saying that to make her happy. I'm not ready to move on yet and I'm not ready for any kind of rebound even if it's only been two weeks.

Winter
I'll help you keep an eye out for sexy men ;)

Emerald
I'm sure Carsten will love that.

Winter
Well I won't be checking them out. I'll just point to guys I know you'll think are attractive.

Emerald
Mhmm keep tellin yourself that girl.

Winter
What? I'm serious. I only have eyes for my man.

Emerald
Good, that's what I like to hear.

Winter
You workin today?

Emerald
No thank god, I'd be too drunk for it.

Winter
Lol that's great. I have to work with Stacy, I was hoping you'd be there too.

Emerald
Damn, I'm sorry, babe. No, Lisa told me to take a few days off. She said she'd text me when she wants me to start working again.

Winter
Aww that was nice of her, I love Lisa.

Emerald
Same, she's the best boss ever.

Winter
She really is.

After eating my food and texting Winter I decide on a nice hot bath before I go back to drinking again for the day.

"Actually, fuck it, I'm gonna drink while I sit in the bath, it's never too early to start drinking," I say to myself, that's how lonely I am these days. I wake up, drink, get drunk, eat, and watch crime documentaries or sad movies because apparently, I think I need to cry more. I tried going back to work but Lisa knows I'm not ready for that yet, and she's right I break down a lot still.

I can't believe that in just a few days it'll be two weeks since I've had a boyfriend, since we've slept together, kissed, or done anything together. Since he's told me he's loved me even. And nothing has changed about my feelings for him. I thought I'd be over him a little but I'm not at all. I still feel the same way today that I did when it first happened and I'm sure when it hits two weeks, I'll still feel the same way.

I spend the next few days the same way. I wake up feeling depressed, alone and like shit. The room is spinning, my mouth is dry. I wake up, I brush my teeth, and barely get dressed. Only eat if I'm hungry and go right back to spending my day drinking. I've had my groceries delivered because I just didn't want to leave the house until today, Friday and now I'll *have* to leave. I don't even bother paying attention to Creedence's house next door when I go outside, I'm completely numb and broken. I wonder if I'll ever find the old Emerald again. I miss Creedence more and more each day and the pain only gets even more unbearable than it was the day before. Am I really this pathetic or is this just what it feels like to lose someone you love? I didn't respond to Winter or Chastity's texts. I just kept to myself until today. The day I promised my friends that I'd go to a party that I really don't want to go to anymore. But I'll show up drunk and leave trashed. I smile to myself at my plan, although I'll regret that being numb in the moment will be better than the aftermath.

I look down at my phone and see that I have over thirty texts from the girls in our group chat all worrying about me from the last three days. I finally feel ready to respond to them.

Winter
Are you fucking alive? Today is Friday. I'm about to break down the door if I don't hear from you today.

Chastity
Seriously dude, don't make us come over there and break that door down, I've been working out more so I've got more muscles and I'm not afraid to use them.

Chastity
Ok... obviously I'm not that strong but with the help of Winter we'll get the job done.

Winter
Exactly, I'm weak as fuck but we can get the job done together.

Emerald
I'm alive don't worry guys you don't have to break down my door.

Winter
THANK GOD! What have you been doing?

Chastity
Thank fucking god dude, where the hell have you been?

Emerald
Sleep, wake up, drink, eat, drink some more, cry, cry some more, drink till I'm completely shit faced, and repeat.

Winter
Babe, that's not healthy at all, why didn't you
text us?

Chastity
EMERALD YOU HAVE NOT?!?!? Babe, seriously we
said we were here for you.

> **Emerald**
> I wanted to be alone and drunk. I'll be drunk
> before the party so one of you will have to pick
> me up.

Chastity
Emerald, please this isn't ok babe, you need to
take care of yourself, have you been eating? I
don't remember if you said you were eating.

Winter
She said eat but like how much are we talking?

> **Emerald**
> I ate when I was hungry so at least once a day.
> I'm fine stop trying to be my mom, guys.

Chastity
C'mon babe, let's go get food before we go out
tonight.

Winter
Yes, we can go shopping and get something to
eat, maybe a new outfit? Presley has the twins so
I'm free all day.

> **Emerald**
> Not really feeling it. Already started drinking.

Chastity
Put the fucking bottle away, we will be there in an
hour.

Winter
Seriously, we are going out go shower and get
ready.

Emerald
I'm not going. Seriously guys I don't want to.

Winter
I will come over now if you don't go and get
ready.

Emerald
FINE I won't be happy about it.

Chastity
Good cause I'm fucking smiling bitch.

Winter
Same bitch same, see you in an hour and a half
be ready!

Chastity
Wait, I thought it was an hour?

Winter
She's gonna drag ass. Give her an hour and a
half. I'll meet you at her house.

Chastity
alright see you soon bitches.

Emerald
I hate you guys. See you soon.

Winter
Love you bitch.

Chastity
Love you bitches.

Emerald
Love you bitches.

31

EMERALD

I ROLL OUT OF BED, THE ROOM STILL SPINNING. I LIED ABOUT drinking already but I'm definitely going to start before they get here. I walk to my bathroom and brush my teeth real quick, trying to fight the spinning room and the nausea creeping up on me. I rinse my mouth out and throw on a T-shirt and underwear not even caring about wearing shorts since I'm alone and I walk out of my closet and head towards the kitchen, grabbing my half bottle of wine from last night out of the refrigerator and some medicine for my head. I wash the medicine down with wine and step outside wasting time because I really just don't want to go anywhere before I have to go out tonight.

Just my luck, Creedence is outside playing his guitar on his truck bed, and I look like absolute shit.

I have dark bags under my eyes, my hair is in the messiest, messy bun hanging on the side of my head with wispy pieces around my face, and loose pieces hanging from the bun. My black T-shirt is oversized hanging off my shoulder but long enough to cover my ass, but not any longer than any of my too short dresses. You know what fuck him; I don't give a fuck if he sees me either.

He's leaning against the back of his truck on the phone, his back towards me thank god. I sit down and chug some wine then close my eyes trying to feel as much of the breeze on my face as I can when I hear Creedence's voice get a little louder.

"I don't know what you want me to do Carsten," he says a little angry. "Dude no, I don't want to talk to her." Asshole, I don't want to talk to you either, fuck face.

"No, not yet at least. Why haven't I been calling you back? Cause I just wanted time to myself, time alone." He throws his hand up in the air as he says it.

"Yes, I've been drinking already, I took a couple shots." He scoffs like he's insulted.

"No, you're not coming over here." And as he says that he turns around and makes eye contact with me right as I open mine to take another sip of my wine. Fuck. He stares at me for a few minutes with anger in his eyes.

"Go to the party, seriously, I don't need a fucking babysitter. I don't want to be around her either, not after what we went through." Then he turns around like he wasn't just saying that to me pretending like he was saying it to Carsten.

"No. I said no, I don't need you here, I want to be alone."

"Fine you can come over when Winter is at Emerald's but you're going to the party and I'm staying alone. I will kick your ass out, you know that." He glances over his shoulder in my direction. I can't keep the tears away any longer. I can't believe he just looked me right in the eyes and said that. Either he's still hurt, or he just truly didn't love me. "Okay, I'll see you later then just text me when you're on your way."

"No, I won't be passed out, I've been pacing myself, don't worry." His voice is angry and loud.

"Okay then text me or have her whatever's easier." His tone is annoyed. I'm sure the look on his face matches the sound of his voice too.

"Alright. Okay. Bye man." Then he hangs up and keeps his back towards me while he sips from whatever glass bottle is in his hands, looks like it could be Fireball. Gross.

Glad we're on the same page of our breakup. Just kidding, if he wasn't a dick head, we wouldn't fucking be here we could be in his room, in my room. Fucking on the fucking roof for all I care, we'd be together that's all I want, at least I think that's what I wanted. But now I'm so heartbroken I'm not even sure what I want anymore.

An hour and a half later, Winter and Chastity come barging in my house. I forget that Winter has a key. At least she didn't have to break down my door.

"Knock, knock bitch," she shouts from the kitchen.

"Hey." I stumble out of my room a little, holding onto the wall so they don't realize how drunk I am. I didn't mean to drink this much before going out. But I can eat something and sober up a little.

"Dude, you're already drunk?" Chastity crosses her arms. She looks disappointed in me. Which I don't care she's in a happy relationship with her douche fuck boyfriend that everyone hates now, but she's not going through a heartache like I am. I don't even respond, I just stand there and lick my lips, holding the almost empty bottle of wine I opened after drinking that half bottle earlier.

"Babe, have you eaten yet?" Winter looks really concerned. Not sure why she knows what this feels like.

"No, I'm not hungry." Is all I say as I lean against the wall holding myself up. My arms are too tired to hold myself up.

I chug down the rest of the bottle before they can take it from me and head inside. They can't say shit. I showered, washed my hair, shaved, and made myself feel good and clean. Even though I was buzzed. I still did it. Then I got out and actually styled my hair. I curled it in big loose curls, leaving it down. So that way it was ready for tonight. I put some makeup under my eyes, so I didn't look like I was dead. And I did a smokey eye with thick cat eyeliner, and mascara. My usual look. Then I put on some black fishnets with black high waisted shorts that show the bottom of my ass cheeks, and a hot pink crop top T-shirt, the fishnets covering the part of my stomach that shows, and my hot pink converse. I'm going to find a new outfit to wear to the party tonight, this is just to go shopping and grab food. I may be drunk, but I at least did a good job getting myself put together. They may be disappointed in me for being like this, but they should be proud that I put myself together even though I didn't even want to leave the damn house.

"Let's go eat first, you need to sober up, babe." Winter tries to say in her polite voice, but I can still hear the sadness in her tone. Plus, her face gives it all away that she's sad to see me like this but disappointed in how I'm behaving. I just can't help it, I'm completely heartbroken.

"I'm down, you guys want to eat at Lisa's since it's on the way?" Chastity speaks up, I'm sure to change the subject and clear the air of this awkward, uncomfortable energy. I'm hoping that Creedence won't be there if we do go.

"I'm fine with that, let me go grab my things real quick." I go into my room and grab my purse, and a bottle of cherry vodka I found sitting on my nightstand, might as well drink up now if they're going to try and sober me up and make me feel things again.

"Emerald!" Chastity practically shouts in my ear, "c'mon I think you need to chill for a minute." She takes the bottle from me, and I roll my eyes giving her a dirty look.

"It was just the rest of it anyway. I didn't want it to go to waste, besides I can drink if I want, I'm an adult." I give a polite yet bitchy smile before walking towards my front door and grabbing my house key.

"Still, you don't need to be drunk when it's only one in the afternoon." Winter starts getting loud.

"We're just worried about you, that's all." Her tone is a little angrier. It makes me feel bad that I'm hurting her. Her father was an abusive alcoholic so I'm sure this triggers things for her. But I'm going to be a little selfish right now because this isn't about her. It's about my life, my happiness. And right now, I'm fucking dead inside. Creedence killed whatever was alive inside me, he took my heart with him, crushing it with each word he spoke. Slowly dragging a knife through it as he continued to kill me. So, I think it's okay that I'm being selfish and only caring about myself at this moment.

"I know and I'm fine." I try to say clearly but the slur my voice decided to add to it isn't allowing me to as I realize maybe I shouldn't have chugged that cherry vodka down as the nausea starts stirring in my stomach. I shake off the feeling. I refuse to puke; I just need some food.

Or maybe a lot of food. I've lost some weight so I could eat and not worry about gaining for once. I turn the handle and open the door, motioning for them to go first so that way I can lock the door behind me.

And of course, guess who is outside sitting on his truck bed playing his guitar? And he just so happens to have his back against the side of the truck to where he's facing my driveway.

"Hey Winter, where's Carsten?" He's swaying a little and she looks over at me before looking at him. "Christ," she mumbles to herself, but I hear it, I don't know if they did but I know I did.

"He'll be coming over later, we're about to head to eat and go to the mall for some clothes for tonight," she tells him, not sure why she gave him all the details.

"Okay, I wasn't sure if he came with you now or not, I haven't heard from him since this morning," he tells her as he looks over at me and I look away. He looks sad, his eyes are bloodshot and a little puffy, either from crying or lack of sleep, but I'm gonna go with lack of sleep and drinking. I doubt he's been crying over me.

"I'll tell him to head here a little earlier for you." She gives him a quick smile; you can tell she feels awkward talking to him in front of me.

"Alright, thanks, you ladies have fun. Oh, and since I won't see you, please be careful at that party later. I've heard some shady shit goes down at those parties," he slurs a little before he turns, walking towards his house. Not even waiting for an answer.

"Fuck, dude, why does he do that to my heart." I refuse to

fucking cry. I put this makeup on because I didn't want to cry anymore. I wanted to feel beautiful for the day instead of a lazy mess so I'm putting my foot down. I refuse to fucking cry. "The fact that he just talked to you like I didn't even exist fucking sucks." I sniffle. Fucking shit.

"Aw babe, I'm so sorry he put me in a tough spot there and I didn't know what to do." Winter bites her bottom lip, you can tell she feels terrible by the look in her eyes along with the sympathetic look on her face. I hate when people feel bad for me.

"It's not your fault, I just miss him. What I would have given to just run over to him and jump into his arms. To even feel his arms around me again. Fuck." I quickly blink back tears because I still refuse to let him win. I will not cry.

"Babe, I'm so sorry I wish I could do something for you." Chastity grabs my hand and gently squeezes it as I lean against the back of my car. I so badly want to just go back inside and drink the day away until I pass out drunk and do it all over again the next day until I no longer have to numb this pain.

"It's fine. I'm ready to go." I turn towards Chastity, squeezing her hand back.

"I'll sit in the back seat of Winter's car, you two can sit in the front." Chastity walks to the back of the car and opens the back door behind the driver's seat. I don't even bother responding. I'm just ready to get this day over with and get to the party where I can drink away my heartache again.

After lunch we head out to the mall to go shopping. I end up buying a black, skin-tight, mini Bodycon dress that I'm lucky even covers my ass. It hugs all my curves and my tits perfectly, fitting my body like it was painted on and showing off my tattoo sleeves, and the tattoos on my thighs since it's far too short to be wearing. If Creedence saw me, he'd freak out or bend me over and fuck me.

God what I would give for him to push me up against his bed, push my dress up and shove his hard pierced cock into my wet pussy right now. I haven't had sex or even had the desire to touch myself since he broke up with me. I walk out of my room right as the girls come back to my house, they left after shopping to go get ready at their places because I practically kicked them out so I could nap before getting ready again. I didn't have to shower or anything. I'd just have to fix my hair and touch up my makeup after changing into my cock teasing dress.

"Holy shit girl, I knew you would look fucking hot in that dress. I'm so glad you just went with it and didn't bother trying anything else on when we were shopping because you look fucking hot!" Chastity whistles and claps her hands in excitement.

"Holy fuck, if I weren't straight, I'd totally fuck you girl, you look so hot." I smile at my best friends who actually brought me out of my mopey mood I've been in this afternoon. I actually enjoyed myself and had a great time with them once I sobered up.

"You girls look fucking hot yourselves; damn Carsten is lucky to have that piece of ass to go home to every day." I wink at Winter.

"And girl, you're going to be pushing guys off of you tonight since your man ain't comin' out." I say to Chastity, who's been with the same douche for about a year now. We all loved him at first until he cheated on her and she took him back. But that's her business I just stay out of it and I'm a good friend when she needs someone to vent to.

"Where's Carsten?" I'm confused because he was supposed to be coming with us.

"He went to get Axton and talk to...ummm..." Winter pauses for a second.

"It's okay, Winter, you can say Creedence," I tell her with a small smile. It still makes my heart sink through my stomach when I hear his name. But I can't stop my best friend from talking about him when her soon to be husband, also father of her children, is best friends with him. I'll just have to learn to suck it up eventually.

"He went to talk to Creedence before he left with us to make sure he's okay. He's been drinking a lot too just like you have. I guess he's been pretty bummed out since you guys broke up," she says, looking down knowing she feels awkward saying it.

"He should feel bummed out." I can't help but roll my eyes. "He's the asshole that broke up with me, he could be going out with *this* tonight," I practically shout, waving my hands up and down my body. Like I'm showing myself off. I'm not conceited one bit. I'm just feeling a little confident tonight especially after being a bum for almost two weeks. I'm thinking maybe I will try to find someone to hook up with tonight if I can get drunk enough to forget they're not Creedence.

"Well let's go get the boys then. Well, you guys can, I'll go by the car."

"Hell yeah ladies, let's get fucked up tonight!" Chastity yells, throwing her hands up and doing a little dance.

"Wooo! Let's get fucked up," Winter yells along with her.

"Hell yeah bitches!" I shout, laughing along with them, actually excited about this party.

About a half hour later we walk into the party, the house is filled with so many people they're practically dancing on top of each other, and I fucking love it. The music is so loud the base practically shakes the walls and you can feel the vibrations from it through the floors. The lights are off and there's blue strobe lights that light up the party along with what look like blue Christmas lights lit up around the ceilings and around the baseboards of the floor on every wall. There are two tables with alcohol along with kegs that line the walls with guys standing at the table mixing drinks and passing them out to everyone that walks by. There's also what looks to be punch bowls I'm assuming filled with whatever alcohol they threw in there too. I can't wait to get over there and sample all the drinks. Except for the beer, I fucking hate beer.

I haven't been to a party in so long. Usually this would stress me out with how many people there are but everyone's giving off such fun vibes, I love it. Either that or it's the fact that I'll be getting drunk right along with them.

"I'm going to get a drink," I shout to the girls, walking away from them. I'm at this party to have some fucking fun and I'm not giving a single fuck what they say to me, I'm doing me and I'm having fun. So, I walk away not waiting for an answer from them because I'm sure their first reaction was an eye roll.

I walk over to the table taking the first drink I see and down it right away. That was probably a reckless move right there. Just grabbing a glass off the drink table and trusting that it's not roofied.

"Hell yeah, baby, did you like that?" the guy passing out drink's yells to me over the music.

"Yeah, it was strong, what was that?" I ask him, hoping he'll tell me so I can make these tomorrow at home after I stop at a liquor store of course.

"It's our house secret, we can't tell you guys what's in it. Do you want more?" he shouts, and I hold up two fingers. He gives me two cups and I walk away with them, downing the one and throwing it in the first trash can in the middle of the room I see. I walk to the other side of the room where everyone is dancing. Feeling the music and the alcohol I start moving my hips to the music. Holding both hands up dancing when some guy comes up behind me.

"Looks like you could use a drink." His deep husky voice sends chills through me as he talks into my ear. That's how close he is to me as I dance, downing my second drink.

I turn to look at a cute blond guy with messy hair, he's not Creedence but he will do to dance with, for now. He's tall, not as tall as Creed, about six-foot-two, blue eyes, and built like he works out every day.

"Yeah, I can go for another one." I stand on my tiptoes and shout loudly by his ear so he can hear me.

He takes my hand and walks me over to the table and he hands me a drink from the guy behind it.

"Here you go, gorgeous." He lightly hits his glass to mine without saying cheers.

"Thank you." I smile at him and down half the drink. I don't care if I look like an alcoholic to him. I just chugged my full drink in front of him before he got me this one and then I chugged this one about three quarters of the way down. He can judge all he wants. My lips start to tingle, and I feel a heavy buzz already, I giggle to myself as more of the warmth spreads through my body. I don't care though. I'm ready to get drunk.

"I'm Matt," he yells, holding his hand out to shake mine.

"I'm Emerald," I yell back, shaking his strong hand. His skin doesn't feel anything like Creedence's hard working calloused hands. His are soft, too soft and doesn't feel manly at all for someone as big as he is. Maybe I'm just being a bitch because he's not Creed.

"Let's go dance again," he yells to me and I'm thankful for the distraction from my annoying thoughts. He takes my hand and leads me back to the middle of the crowd. I hold my drink and close my eyes, feeling the music as he comes up behind me and places his free hand on my hip. Bringing me closer to his body as he grinds his clearly hard length into my lower back and top of my ass. Because that's where he comes up to when he stands behind me. I grind my ass into him, hearing him groan into my ear. That's how close he is to me, and I smile, it's nice knowing I can turn another guy on. That I didn't lose myself when Creedence broke my heart. That I can still excite a man. But I'm not getting turned on myself which sucks because I'd probably fuck this guy if he wanted to fuck me that's how horny I am. But he doesn't try making any moves besides grinding his erection into me and I feel like he could probably get off this way and its actually kind of turning me off.

"I'm gonna go find my friend, I need to go smoke." I lie to him, although I'm drunk to the point where I wouldn't mind bumming a couple cigarettes. I enjoy drinking and smoking sometimes.

"Want me to go with you?" he asks, and I shake my head. Kinda disappointed that my fake smoking didn't turn him off. Apparently smoking doesn't bother him.

"You don't have to, I'll come find you when I'm done, I might be a while." I smile at him, so he doesn't think I'm fucking around and not coming back. Even though I haven't decided if I've wanted to come back yet.

"Alright I'll see you in a bit." He winks at me, and I actually feel bad because I might forget to come find him. But that's alright, I'm not here to meet a guy I'm here to get fucked up. I need to stay focused on numbing this fucking heartache.

I walk around the party giving zero fucks. Like I said before, I'm doing me and giving zero fucks as I do it. I'm downing drinks and shots with people I haven't seen in a while or people I've just met and I'm having so much fun. I'm pretty drunk so I start looking for the girls, so they don't get mad. Although they should be happy that I even came out. Even though I came here with one goal in mind. To get fucked up. To drown my sorrows in alcohol and numb my pain with shots. I think I've become an alcoholic these past two weeks because all I do is drink since I'm not working, and it takes way more alcohol to get me drunk now. My heart hurts and the pain hasn't gotten any easier, if anything each day it's gotten worse. I just wish things would go back to normal. Every morning, I wake up wishing it was a terrible nightmare that I'm waking up from only to be hit by this extreme anxiety as I realize it's not.

I walk back over to the first table I got drinks from and hold up two fingers to the guy again and he just winks at me as I make my way out back and sit on the edge of the porch swinging my legs over the side. As I down my first drink and stack my full drink into the cup. I light the cigarette I bummed from one of my friends I ran into and take a hit, feeling the buzz from it tingle through my body and I smile. I love the way it makes me feel when I'm drunk. Yep, I'm officially drunk now, but I'm not shitfaced yet. I sit there and smoke my cigarette enjoying the continuous tingle it brings to my body, or maybe that's the alcohol, or both? I snap out of my thoughts when I hear footsteps behind me.

"Hey, Emerald." I jump at the sound of my name. Although I heard footsteps, I wasn't expecting anyone to come up behind me and talk.

"I'm sorry to hear about you and Creedence, I heard about it from Stacy at the Diner." I hear Daisy say while she stands next to Brynn.

"Thanks," I mumble as I take another hit of my cigarette before taking a sip of my drink. I end up drinking half of it down. I look down at my almost empty cup. Fuck, I need to get up and get more. But I'm really enjoying this cigarette.

"Do you need another drink?" she asks me, and I look down at mine remembering that I just downed almost half of it. And I giggle at the fact that I forgot about it that quickly. Shit, I'm fucked up.

"Yeah, I'm about to go get one though so I'm okay." I take another hit of my cigarette while she smokes hers, wanting to just be left alone. I figured if I came to a spot on the porch that was empty people would get the hint and leave me alone. Guess not.

"Here girl, you can have mine. I just grabbed it from that guy at the first table over there, the one who won't tell you what's in this delicious drink. I didn't even drink out of it yet." She places it down next to me and instead of telling her no I think to myself, zero fucks tonight, I'm here to have a good time. Plus, she just grabbed it before coming out here. I need to be a little more trusting and stop thinking everyone is out to drug me. Especially a girl.

"Thanks, I appreciate it." I down the rest of my other drink and stack hers into the other two solo cups I have.

"No problem." She smiles as her and Brynn put out their cigarettes and walk back inside giggling like something had happened that I apparently missed.

Weird, maybe they went to get more alcohol, or they were just done smoking and went inside. Emerald, stop being so paranoid I think to myself.

I pick up the cups and take a sip out of the drink she just gave me, actually more like I chug half of it down and feel the burn in my throat finally going away. My throat is starting to go numb, and I no longer feel the strong burn from the alcohol. I take another hit of my cigarette before putting it out and lighting up another one that I borrowed from someone else. Zero fucks tonight. I'm not ready to go inside yet either. The weather is perfect and I'm enjoying the slightly cool breeze as I sit here and swing my legs still looking down at the ground. I'm also super warm from the alcohol so it's nice to feel the cool breeze blow across my hot skin. I sit here in silence, staring up at the sky as I take a hit of my cigarette, kind of getting grossed out by it. This is why I don't smoke regularly, just for fun when I'm shit faced.

My mind automatically wants to go to Creedence, and I know I need to take another sip of my alcohol because I haven't erased my feelings just yet. I chug down the rest of it and put my cigarette out not wanting to finish the rest just now, I'll hide it out here and save it for later. Or go find what's her face, I forgot her name. And bum another one I'm sure she won't care if I promise to buy her another pack tomorrow. Or give her money for them. I need to go get another drink first. I'll come back out later.

I slowly stand up, feeling a little dizzy for a second before it finally passes, and I walk inside through the back door. My stomach turning a little as I walk. Almost like a motion sickness feeling. I still haven't seen the girls or even Carsten and Axton since we got here. Maybe I shouldn't have left them, but I'm sure I'll find them eventually. They've gotta be around here somewhere. I'm surprised they haven't tried to come looking for me either honestly. It can work both ways, if they wanted to find me, they would have.

I start walking towards the table stumbling because I'm starting to feel weak, almost like my body is feeling heavy and I'm feeling a little dizzy again. I haven't been taking much care of myself over the last two weeks. I've consumed more alcohol than I have actual foods or other liquids, and I think it's finally starting to catch up to me. It's probably from how much I had to drink so far though. I haven't exactly gone easy on the drinks or the shots for that matter. I finally get over to the table after feeling like I dragged my body there and attempt a smile at the guy, hoping my cuteness will hide how fucked up I actually am.

"Are you sure you want more, sweetie? You're looking like you're past your limit," he yells to me, his brows scrunched up with a concerned look on his face.

"Just two more please, one is for my friend. I told her I'd grab our drinks for us." I think that sentence made sense as I slurred the words together. I give him a flirty smile hoping it'll convince him. But he's not going to tell me how much I can and can't drink.

"Okay, but if you come back, I'm going to have to tell you no," he yells to me again, over the music and I nod my head as he hands me two more drinks. He's not being a dick either, you can tell he's just truly worried. I've come to the table and grabbed two drinks for myself of this crazy concoction they've made up all night. And I haven't shared any of them with anyone. They've all been for me and I'm sure if the guy knew that in the beginning, he might have slowed down on how much he was giving me. Thank god he didn't see how many shots I did. I'm surprised I'm not passed out or black out drunk from how much I've been drinking. I guess my body really is building up a tolerance.

My head starts to feel foggy as I make my way back towards the back door. I want to sit back on the porch again but I'm starting to feel a little funny. I start feeling shaky, like I'm cold. But I'm not, in fact I feel like I'm burning up, so I know that's not it. Maybe this morning when I woke up feeling sore it was due to me getting sick and not just from the drinking.

I take another sip of my drink and set them down on the nearest table. I need a bathroom; I feel like I'm going to be sick. I saw a lot of people going up and down the stairs all night so I'm going to assume the bathroom and the bedrooms are up there. I stumble my way upstairs, catching myself with my hands as I do. I probably look like a pathetic idiot who doesn't know how to handle their alcohol to all these people that I'm apologizing to as I run into them from my body feeling so heavy. I feel like someone is pulling me down as I try to walk. I stumble up the stairs, dizzier than before and start to panic. What the fuck is wrong with me? I've never felt this bad from drinking before. Maybe it's from mixing all the alcohol. Or all those shots and those drinks I had tonight and they're just all hitting me all at once. I start to sweat so I reach down and grab my pink scrunchie from Creedence and put my hair up into a high ponytail as I search for the bathroom, I finally find it, the third door on the left and there's someone in there. Fuck I feel like I'm about to pass out. The person finally opens the bathroom door and as soon as I get in there, I fall to the ground on my knees feeling nauseous and dizzy again, like I'm about to pass out. My vision is blurry as I start attempting to crawl towards the toilet. My shaking body barely allows me to move as I attempt this crawl. I start dry heaving my hands give out under me and I smack down onto the ground. My head hit the floor pretty hard because I didn't have enough time to catch myself. My eyes are barely able to make out what's in front of me as black dots dance in front of my eyes.

32
CREEDENCE

It's been two weeks since I've talked to Emerald. I feel like such an asshole I can't believe I spoke to her how I did. I never talk to women like that.

I've seen her in passing in the driveway and she's just quickly gotten into her car. She's only tried talking to me once, that was the night we broke up and after that she didn't try again. Not even when I tried talking to her the next day at the diner. I don't blame her, I treated her like shit. I've been miserable, my heart hurts. I've never felt this way about anyone before. This really must be like what it's like to lose the woman you love, I can't eat, can't sleep, I'm barely functioning. I've been staying home instead of working, I've been drinking almost every day, all day. But I just can't man up and face her. I wouldn't even know what to say or where to start.

I'm sitting at my table attempting to eat when Carsten comes walking through the garage door. I left it open for him after I talked to Winter, and he came over about two hours later.

"Hey, man." He's quiet. I'm sure he's not sure how to talk to me, especially after how I talked to him on the phone earlier. I was kind of a drunken dick.

"What's up, brother." I look over at him before taking a small bite of my sandwich I was eating so I don't have to talk.

"I like your helmet out there, when did you get it?" He smiles. Kind of excited. As he's trying to start a conversation but I'm just not in the mood. I never went into details about why I broke it off with Emerald, so unless Winter told him because I know Emerald told her. Then he doesn't know about the helmet. But I don't respond, I just take another small bite of my sandwich pretending to be hungry.

"Okay, fine," he sighs. "Where'd you get the engraving done? It's awesome, I'd like to get some engraving done on mine." He looks back to the garage before he looks over at me. And that gets my attention. I look up at him a little quicker than normal and raise one eyebrow.

"What engraving?" I'm getting angry, and I'm really confused. I feel like he's fucking with me right now or something.

"Bro, are you losing it? You get yourself a new helmet and forget you had something engraved on it?" He's laughing a little, shaking his head. "Maybe you've been drinking too much."

"What the fuck are you talking about?" I snap getting up. I'm not in the mood for games. I rush out of the house into the garage and pick up the helmet. I don't see anything on it until I turn it around and on the back of the helmet along the bottom, below the gray and white shaded skull says *In loving memory of Xander, forever watching over you big brother.* And I lose it. Tears start falling down my face and I hear the door open behind me, fuck I'm such an idiot. I slam the helmet down on the desk in my garage, hard, but not hard enough to cause any damage.

"FUCKKKK," I shout.

I see Carsten standing there, arms crossed in the doorway one shoulder against the door frame.

"Emerald had this made for me, she said she got a matching one too. She's been trying to get me into riding again. She's been wanting me to go for a ride for my brother she said she knows he'd love it and fuck man I'm afraid to but fuck I'm an asshole." I let out the breath I was holding.

"She asked me if you and Xander had any nicknames for each other, and I didn't know why so I just told her. I didn't realize this is what she was doing," he states before asking, "but why are you an asshole?"

"Because I didn't really pay attention to the helmet I just kind of went off on her because I felt like she was forcing me to ride again when I wasn't ready. I felt like she was forcing me to be ready for her, not for myself. But really she wasn't, she was just trying to help me find happiness in it again and I'm an asshole. I broke up with her and everything over it," I sigh. "I was caught off guard and wasn't expecting this as the surprise that she had for me, so when I saw it, I reacted before thinking and I reacted like a fucking asshole. I was pissed, I felt like she wasn't listening to me and just thinking about herself but really, she wasn't thinking about herself she was thinking about me."

"This is why you broke up with her dude?" He looks shocked and a little disappointed maybe.

"Man, I mean I love you like a brother, but I'm gonna be honest, you fucked up big time." He shakes his head at me with a disappointed look on his face.

"You don't have to tell me because I just realized I fucked up big time. Fuck dude." I push my hands through my hair, pulling at it. Fuck, fuck, fuck. I cannot believe I was such an idiot. I've had this fucking helmet sitting here on this desk for two weeks that I've avoided it each time I've been out here and all I had to do was stop and actually pay attention to it. But instead, I was a dumbass and avoided it like it had a disease.

"What are you going to do now?" he asks me with a concerned look on his face.

"Fuck, dude. I have no idea, but I know I need to think fast and find a way to fix this mess." I let out the breath I was just holding, suddenly feeling stressed as fuck.

"Well, I can help you think of something, I can come over tomorrow after work with the twins and we can come up with some kind of plan if that works for you?" He crosses his arms again and leans against the opposite side of the doorway.

"That sounds good, anything will help, I appreciate it," I tell him because as of right now I have absolutely no idea as to how I could even begin to get her back.

Right as I'm about to say something the doorbell rings and I know it's Winter coming to get the guys, that could be me going with them too but I fucked up big time and now I'll be spending my night sobering up so I can come up with a way to get my girl back before it's too late.

DURING THE PARTY

I sit on the couch at home feeling miserable. This seriously must be what it's like to miss someone and feel heartbroken. Because it feels like fucking shit. I feel like I need to go find her and apologize tonight, but I know she'll be drunk and will probably not care or like I said before, try to kick my ass. Plus, I need to come up with a good way to get her back, not even just get her back but to find a way for her to forgive me for being such a piece of shit with how I spoke to her and then for pushing aside her gift like it didn't mean anything to me, when now that I look at it and actually pay attention to all the details, means more than the world to me. Just like her.

I feel my phone vibrate in my pocket and look down to see Axton's name and decide to ignore it. I know everyone is at that party, including him so I'm not sure why he's even calling and I'm not really wanting to talk to anyone. Not right now, I'm busy trying to think of ways to save my ass and win Emerald's heart back. I look down after I ignore his call and see I have a bunch of texts from Carsten and Axton right as I'm about to open them Carsten starts calling and instead of ignoring them again, I decide to answer it.

"Listen man." I'm angry answering the phone. "I already told you guys I didn't w..." And then he cuts me off rushing out his words that I almost don't hear what he said.

"Emerald, dude, somethings wrong." I barely hear him say because it's so loud and my stomach drops, my heart starts racing and I break out in a sweat.

"Dude, what the fuck I can't hear you. I told you I'm not ready to apolo..." I start saying.

"Dude, you need to get here NOW, something is wrong with Emerald, we keep trying to wake her up, but she's passed the fuck out. I don't know if she drank too much or if someone drugged her. Get here now!" he shouts. "Fuck, I think we need to take her to the hospital dude, her pulse is barely fucking there. What the fuck," he shouts, and I sit up all the way feeling instantly sick to my stomach at what he just said. Her pulse is barely there.

"What the fuck, dude, what do you mean, what do you mean," I shout not giving him a chance to respond but rushing to get an answer from him because I'm pissed he didn't start with that shit.

I jump up off my couch rushing to my keys and shoes. I don't even care that I'm only in a wife beater and basketball shorts. I put my slides on and rush out the door running to my truck.

"I don't know, she said she was gonna get drunk tonight, she's really heartbroken man. I don't even know what she fucking drank. She left us when we got here, and we've been searching for her for a half an hour now. I don't even know how long she's been like this." My turn to cut him off.

"Fuck, she was left alone, Carsten, what the fuck man, you guys know these parties aren't exactly safe."

"Someone said they saw her, one of the guys at the drink table. He said she was being reckless and doing shot after shot and taking drinks left and right, she even took one from Brynn and Daisy," he shouts.

"Are you fucking kidding me? I swear to God if those two have anything to do with this I'm gonna let the girls beat their asses. Actually no, I'm gonna get the police involved fuck those psycho bitches."

"Then someone found her passed out on the bathroom floor and started panicking. Then that's how I found the guy who told me about her, he was the guy serving drinks. He recognized her and remembered her coming in with us and got us," he rushes out in a panic trying to tell me all the details.

"We just got her in the car, meet us at Fernfield Hospital."

"Fuck man, I swear I hope she's okay. I'll be there in ten," I say speeding out of my driveway. "Actually, fuck it, make it five. I don't care about the speed limit tonight, the cops can suck my dick," I say, hanging up the phone and pushing down on the gas pedal. Feeling extremely sick to my stomach trying to ignore these terrible thoughts that keep trying to surface.

I pull into the parking lot parking my truck in the first spot I see; I don't even know if it was an actual parking spot, and I really don't even care. Fuck it if it gets towed. Right now, Emerald is where I need to be, she's who is important. I run in through the emergency room doors, practically knocking someone over.

"Fuck, fuck. Are you okay?" I grab the older gentleman's shoulder, stopping him from losing his balance even more.

"Shit son, you almost knocked me out there," he chuckles. C'mon speed it the fuck along.

"Sorry, I can't wait." And he gives me a confused look as I run off further into the emergency room waiting area. Running straight for the desk I don't want them to stop me and delay this any longer.

"Emerald... Emerald Hart," I accidentally shout. "My girlfriend, she was just brought in, please she... she was unconscious, and her pulse was barely there. Please, I need to see her," I rush out hoping they'll allow me to go back there and at least wait for her.

"Sir please, please, I'm going to need you to calm down for a second, please you can't go back there this worked up," the lady behind the counter says in a sweet calm voice, not even affected by how loud, or angry I sound or the fact that I'm breathing like I just ran a marathon and can't catch my breath.

"Sorry please I just…" I pause feeling defeated for a minute. I can't let anything happen to her without her knowing how I feel about her and that I'm sorry. "Please, she's all I have left. I just need to know she's going to be okay."

The lady looks around to see if anyone is looking and leans forward. "If you could please lower your voice I could help you, sir." She smiles.

"Sorry, miss." I'm fucking furious, does she not realize how fucking important this situation is. Right as I'm about to go off on the lady I hear someone from down the hall yelling my name.

"Creed, Creed." I look over and see Winter running down the hall towards me. "She's down here, follow me."

The lady gives me a look and I smile at her as I turn towards Winter and run down the hall towards her. "Thank fuck, I don't think that lady was going to let me go back she was being a bitch."

"She was a bitch when I came in yelling that we needed help. She was going to make us wait out here and not let us go back with her," she says out of breath as I catch up to her. Damn that was a long fucking hallway.

"How is she?" That's all I care about. I'll ask what exactly happened after finding out if Emerald's okay.

"Here umm, let's talk to Carsten." She gives a quick smile before turning into the room I'm assuming is Emerald's. I walk into the room and there's a curtain drawn around her bed to where you can't see anything in the room.

"What's going on guys, where's Emerald?" I'm pissed. "Tell me what the fuck is going on."

"Man please, Creed. I need you to promise me you won't do anything–" I cut him off. I'm not promising shit.

"I'm not making any promises man, tell me what the fuck–" It's his turn to cut me off.

"She fucking overdosed man," he shouts at me. "She fucking overdosed," he chokes out and I look over to a sobbing Winter.

"What the fuck...what the fuck do you fucking mean. Please tell me. Is she okay?" I'm losing my mind I feel like I'm about to have a mental fucking break down. I just need to hold her; I need to kiss her. Please let her be okay.

"She's unconscious. But she's okay," he chokes out. "I'm sorry I couldn't get the words out sooner. It was the scariest thing I've ever experienced. Man, we didn't know what she drank or took, so they had to pump her stomach." He's wiping his tears that are falling as quickly as he's talking. "She was so lifeless. I was so fucking scared for her, for you. Fuck, her whole family. Goddammit, I need to know what the fuck happened," Carsten shouts. He's protective of Emerald like he would be of a sister.

"Wait, you said she took a drink from Brynn and Daisy?" The thought pisses me off. The fact that anyone could purposely hurt someone is so fucked up.

"Yeah, that's what I was told, I don't know how true it is," Winter says to me as she opens the curtain to an unconscious Emerald lying in the hospital bed. IVs in her hand and arm. A couple hospital bracelets on both arms. She's so fucking pale, I question if she's even breathing. Shit I feel sick. But I try to hold it in. I can't throw up not here.

"We're lucky we got here when we did, Creed. If we would've been a few minutes later, they may not have been able to save her." Winter starts rubbing Emerald's cheek as she talks to me. I slowly walk over to her. Thoughts of my brother lying lifeless on the cement try to flash through my thoughts, but I push them aside. I need to focus on my sweet Sugar. I get next to her and Winter moves away. Standing at the end of the bed. Wiping her tears away as she looks down at Emerald. I sit next to her and grab her cold hand.

"Fuck, Em," I choke. "Why isn't she awake?" I turn to Winter and ask her or Carsten whoever wants to answer.

"They don't know what she took yet. They said whatever it was could be the reason she hasn't woken up fully yet. They're waiting for the results of her blood work and as soon as they know they'll tell us." She gives me a sad smile.

"Sugar, I'm so fucking sorry, baby." I lean down kissing her hand. "Please, please come back to me." I have no idea what I'll do if something happens to her. I can't lose her too.

"Fuck, Creed." Carsten places his hand on my shoulder crying next to me. Then my idea that I thought of before returns and I look over at Emerald I lean down and kiss her. "I love you, Sugar," I whisper to her. "I'll be right back." I stand up and look over at Carsten and Winter. "I'll be right back guys, trust me." And I don't wait for an answer, I run out the door. Running through people that are walking through the halls, doctors that are staring at me like I lost my mind, with a look of confusion on their faces as I run from yelling nurses and other people who work here, I finally make it to the doors when I see security coming. What the fuck? Security because of me running in a hospital? Fuck this. I pick up speed. I used to play football, so I'm used to running. Our coach was a psycho about our speed. I make it to my car before the two overweight security guards get to me and speed out of the parking lot. Fuck the speed limit tonight I need to get to this party.

I get to the party and rush in through the door, I'm immediately greeted by Brynn and Daisy, who hold cigarettes in their hands like they were about to come out and smoke.

"Damn, you look fucking hot," Daisy slurs a little trying to rub her finger against my chest but misses. I'm out of fucking breath from all that running and anger. I don't have the energy to react to more than what I need to.

"What the fuck did you do to my girlfriend. Daisy?" I'm fucking fuming and it's taking everything in me not to fucking choke her.

"Word around town is she's not your girlfriend so why does it matter what I did?" She has the ugliest smile on her bitchy face.

Fuck her. I push her up against the wall pushing my hand against her throat, fuck being nice. Fuck her and Brynn.

"Tell me what the fuck you did to her, what the fuck did you put in her drink? My friends are calling me freaking the fuck out cause she's not waking up then next thing I know they're rushing her to the hospital. I can't get into detail I'm too fucking pissed. I'll do something I regret if I do. So save yourself and tell me before I fucking hurt you." I'm seething with anger. She suddenly has a panicked look as all the color drains from her face.

"I roofied her drink, okay. That's all I did. I wanted her to pass out and for someone to see her and sleep with her so that way she'd be cheating on you and you guys would be done for good. That way maybe you'd want to get with me." She smirks a little, looking away from me, tears in her eyes.

"What the fuck is your problem? You wanted someone to fucking rape her?" I'm fucking furious now. She's lucky she's a girl and I can't kick her fucking ass.

"Well, no, I didn't think about it that way, please don't be mad at me, Creed," she whispers then sticks her bottom lip out in an ugly pout. She never was cute when she pouted. I don't know what I ever saw in this nasty fucking girl or why I ever gave her the time of day. I should have ran when she showed interest in me, especially after what her friend Brynn did to Carsten last year when she tried to pretend she was pregnant to get him to leave Winter for her.

"Don't be fucking mad at you? You roofied my girlfriend and wanted someone to fucking rape her. I'm not mad..." She smiles like she's relieved. "I'm fucking livid." I slam her body into the wall a little while walking away. I don't care if I fucking hurt her, she's lucky I didn't do more.

"What the fuck did you give her Daisy?" I yell in her face not caring how shitty I'm being to a woman right now.

"The guy called it liquid ecstasy," she shouts in a nervous voice squinting her eyes closed like I'm about to hit her or something.

"You fucking gave her GHB! What the fuck is your fucking problem. Dammit," I shout and shove her against the wall one last time before running out of the house back to my truck.

Once I arrive back at the hospital, I park in the same made-up spot I parked in before and I run back inside, bypass the desk with the bitch behind it and run down the hall dodging everyone until I get back to Emerald's room. "GHB," I pant, out of breath from how fast and how far I just ran. "They gave her liquid ecstasy," I breathe out.

"Knock. Knock." In comes a man with what looks to be a tablet in his hand. "Good evening, I'm Dr. Franks, we're still waiting on the results from her bloodwork."

"GHB," I blurt out. "The girl at the party who did it told me. I went to the party and got it out of her."

"Thank you for that information. Well that definitely explains why she overdosed. I was told she was drunk all day and then overdid it on the alcohol at the party. That mixed with gamma hydroxybutyrate, also known as GHB, mixed with that amount of alcohol mixed with however much GHB can cause someone to overdose. She should be awake sometime tonight, if not depending on how much was left in her system she could be out until morning. But she'll have to stay for a day or two to be monitored."

"When she comes home will she be back to normal? Will she be okay or?" I'm worried about her; I can't help all the questions that come to mind.

Dr. Franks gives me a kind smile. "She may have suffered some memory loss. She may not remember the night of the party or why she's in the hospital. Little things, nothing major like she will remember who you are and everyone else in her life. She'll be okay, she'll just be groggy for a few days." He turns away towards the door before turning back. "I'll have her moved up to the third floor, that's where she'll be for the rest of her stay. I'll be back to check on her before she's moved though. I'll let you guys visit." He walks out the door not waiting for us to respond to what he had just said. I wish

Emerald was awake so I could talk to her about how fucking scared I am right now that even though Dr. Franks said she'll be okay it's still hard to fully trust it. I can't lose her. Ever. I need to tell her how much I love her, and how sorry I am.

"We're gonna head out." Carsten comes over to me. "That way you can spend time with her plus we gotta go get the twins from my mom's."

"We love you guys so much," Winter says, as she comes in and gives me a big hug from her little body.

"Love you too, Winter. Em loves you too." I squeeze her back.

Carsten comes in and gives me a hug and pats me on the back. "Love you, Creed." Carsten squeezes me tight, a hug I didn't know I needed from him.

"Love you too, Carst." I smile to myself while hugging my best friend, my brother. Thankful for them and their support.

After they leave, I gently slide into bed next to Emerald. Being careful not to move her too much as I adjust myself next to her. I miss her so much; I just need to be close to her. I need to feel my body next to hers. I need to warm her up, so she won't be so cold when she wakes up. I lay there in the bed next to her, brushing the hair away from her beautiful face and just stare at her. God I've missed having her next to me, the warmth of her body and to just be able to reach over and feel her soft skin under my rough skin, just knowing she's there, even if I'm not touching her. I've missed it. Now I just hope in the morning I can convince her to forgive me, after she wakes up and realizes where she is of course. I end up closing my eyes, getting some rest while I'm next to her. It's been so long since I've slept well, being without her has sucked. I fall asleep to the sound of the machines around Emerald beeping and the slow beat of her pulse, I feel as my fingers grip her wrist gently. I find comfort in her pulse knowing her heart still beats for me, even if she doesn't realize it yet I know she fought for us.

33
EMERALD

I wake up the next morning with a splitting headache. I don't even want to open my eyes fully yet, so I close them as quickly as I opened them. What the fuck are those beeping noises? The room is spinning which I'm surprised I'm not used to by now and my mouth is so fucking dry. I hate waking up like this. What the fuck happened last night. I barely remember anything. I remember getting to the party and drinking those mixed drinks that the one guy at the table wouldn't tell anyone what they were made of because it was a house secret, and I remember doing a bunch of shots with random people. But that's it, I don't remember leaving or how I got home... Wait a minute... Panic sets in. Where the fuck am I?

I slowly open my eyes again, as I think about how I got home, and I realize I'm not in my room. I open my eyes and see bright white walls with weird signs hanging on the walls. White curtains cover the windows, but the room is still so fucking bright. I look down and see white thin bedsheets, no wonder I'm so fucking cold. Where the fuck am I? What the fuck? Then I think back to the party and remember dancing with that blond guy, what was his name? Mike? Matt? I don't remember it was something with an M, fuck what am I going to do if I wake up and I'm with him, how am I going to remember his name.

I try to stay still as I look around some more, my head is still foggy and my headache making it hard for me to focus and then it hits me... No, how the? What the fuck? How did I end up in the hospital? Where the fuck, what the fuck?

"Hey, Sugar." Creedence walks in with two cups of coffee and what looks to be like a bag of donuts. He rushes over to me quickly. "Fuck, baby, I'm so happy you're awake. I have so much to say to you, but I don't want to overwhelm you but I'm so, so fucking sorry, babe." He sets the coffee and donuts down on the table next to me. Shit, did I text him? I sit here in a panic; I look down and see I'm not in my dress anymore but in a huge hospital gown that's practically falling off of me.

"What...what are you doing here, Creedence? Why am I...am I in the hospital?"

"Baby, relax, you're okay, you're safe now, Sugar. Fuck babe," he sighs. Then looks at me, tears forming in his eyes. "I thought I fucking lost you, Emerald. You almost didn't make it. Daisy and Brynn gave you liquid ecstasy, which is GHB, a form of date rape drug. With the amount of alcohol you had in your system you overdosed, babe," he chokes. "If they would have gotten you here a few minutes later you wouldn't have made it." He wipes at his tears as he pulls me closer to him, gently pulling me onto his lap. "Babe, I can't lose you too, please."

"Creedence." I barely get the words out with how dry my mouth is. Tears start to form in my eyes as I think about the past two weeks, and I lose it. I start crying, making my headache feel even worse. My body starts shaking as I try to calm myself down when his arm squeezes me tighter around the waist.

"It's okay, Sugar, don't cry, baby. I'm right here," he says in a calm voice. Sugar? Baby? What the hell is going on, I'm so fucking confused right now.

"Creedence, wh...what...what happened last night with, with us?" I ask, struggling to get my words out from how dry my mouth is.

"Nothing yet and I'd like to fix that." He stops for a second placing his hand on his face. "I don't mean sex. Not that I wouldn't enjoy that, but you get what I mean. Right now isn't the time for sexual comments. What I mean is let me explain." He gives me a tired, sad smile that breaks my heart.

"Creedence, please let's just forget it even happened. I don't want to be apart anymore. I've missed you so much," I breathe out.

"Fuck, Sugar, I've missed you so fucking much babe." He leans in and gently presses his lips to mine and shit I've missed the warmth of his lips against mine. "Fuck, Emerald, these fucking pouty lips of yours, gorgeous," he growls into my mouth. Before swiping his tongue across my lips, I open my mouth meeting his tongue with mine before swirling my tongue with his. Moaning into his mouth. It's hard not to be turned on so quickly when you have a man like Creedence Knoxx sitting underneath you, his hard length digging into your ass. "Mmm, I've missed this," I moan. "Can we?" I giggle. Because why not if he does all the work?

"Emerald, fuck babe. It is so goddamn tempting to say yes to you, fuck I'd love nothing more than to bury myself deep inside you," he grumbles against my lips. "But you need the rest, Sugar."

"But," I pout, it's been way too long since I've had sex, and way too long since I've felt Creedence's hard, pierced cock inside of me.

"Baby, please don't do this to me," he growls. "Fuck." He lifts me and readjusts his length underneath me.

"Sorry, I don't know what's gotten into me. I've just missed you so much." I kiss him quickly at first then slow it down deepening the kiss. I don't want to go fast right now, I've missed this. I want to kiss him and memorize the way his lips feel against mine.

"How are you feeling, Sugar? Are you hungry or thirsty? I brought your favorite donuts and coffee." He smiles at me.

"God yes I'm so thirsty, and I'm starving," I pout though.

"Emerald, what's wrong, did I hurt you?" Creedence looks so worried as he looks me up and down to make sure I'm not hurt.

"No, you did nothing wrong, don't worry. I feel so sick to my stomach, and dizzy. My head's pounding." Tears start to form in my eyes. The pressure from the tears only intensifies my headache.

"You know what, hold on, babe. I'm gonna go get your nurse real quick, see if she'll bring your medicine." He walks out the door real quick and comes back a minute later.

"She'll be in soon." He smiles at me as he walks in. Before the look on his face turns serious.

"Emerald, please don't cry, baby." He gently rubs my cheek as he stares down into my eyes. His kind smile bringing butterflies to my stomach, and it makes me feel safe. Which is a nice way to feel after what I just went through last night.

"I'm sorry I'm just feeling emotional right now for some reason," I whisper, wiping away my tears as I do.

"Probably a combination of everything going on, babe, you've been through a lot. Fuck, you need to lay back down." He slowly picks me up and gently places me down on one side of the bed and he sits down next to me. Lying back tucking one arm behind his head like a pillow and the other behind my head, his big, strong arm wraps around my shoulder and down my arm hugging me close to his warm body. God, I missed this.

"Be mine, Emerald, please?" He squeezes me tighter, not hurting me, making me feel loved.

"I'm always yours, Creedence. But what do you mean?" I chuckle against his firm chest as my head rests against it, feeling his heart drum underneath me and hearing it in my right ear.

"Be my girlfriend again, be my girl. Please. I need you to be mine." He looks down at me, placing his hand under my chin lifting my head to look up at him. I stare into his honey brown eyes, brown messy hair, probably from sleep and stress. His beard is a little longer than the last time I saw him, but it's a good look on him. In fact, I think it's my favorite look on Creedence.

I feel something vibrate against my leg and realize Creedence's phone is going off the same time he sits up to reach into his pocket and grab it.

"Hey, man, what's up?" he answers his phone.

"Ohh yeah, that'll be perfect." He smiles.

"Fuck yeah. Thanks man, tell her thanks too and everyone else. We appreciate you." His smile grows.

"Yeah, see you soon, brother man." He hangs up.

"Carsten and Winter are coming up; they're bringing breakfast from Lisa's Diner. So now you'll have your favorite donuts and your favorite breakfast." He smiles down at me and it's so hard for me to not melt every time his eyes land on any part of my body.

"Em, we gotta talk about last night." My stomach drops a little, I don't really want to talk about last night, but I know I'll have too eventually.

"What about it?" I'm truly curious about what he wants to talk about.

"Babe, you drank a lot last night. Eddie, my friend at the table serving drinks, he told me how reckless you were. I was texting him last night after I left the party and came here. He told me how crazy you were with drinking and how careless you were with accepting drinks from people." He sighs, taking a deep breath.

"Fuck, Creed. I'm not usually so careless." It's true. "Usually, I'm very careful when I go to parties and about who I accept drinks from. I've just, you know... I was crazier tonight because of how bad the last couple of weeks were." I let out a breath. "It doesn't make it okay, I could've prevented the whole thing if I weren't so reckless, I know," I tell him. And then I realize something.

"How come the police didn't get involved?" I thought they would've wanted to talk to me about what happened at the party and whatever else.

"I took care of them. I told them you'd talk to them when you came home, that right now you weren't able to talk and might not be mentally ready yet after everything that happened that you might need a few days. So, they talked to Dr. Franks who agreed, and they said they'd call you to set up a time and I gave them your cell number."

"Thank you, Creedence." I smile at him. "I truly appreciate you; we weren't even together, and you were still finding ways to take care of me."

"Babe, I'll take care of you for as long as you allow me to take care of you." He leans down and kisses me gently before pulling away.

"Fuck, I'm so sorry I wasn't there last night, Emerald. I'm so fucking sorry I wasn't there to stop you from taking that drink, from preventing the whole thing. For breaking your heart and even causing this whole issue." He gives me a sad smile. "If I were there that wouldn't have happened to you." There it is, I knew he was going to feel that way and say that. But he has no reason to even feel this way, we weren't together when it happened and it's not like he knew it was going to happen.

"Creedence, you still came to my rescue, even if it wasn't during, you still saved me afterward. By being here for me and not leaving me alone." I smile up at him. "And you're here for me now, Creedence and that's enough for me." He's always been enough for me.

"I love you, Sugar." He leans down cupping my chin again with one hand and kisses me softly.

"I love you so much you handsome, handsome man." I kiss him and he pulls away quickly like something is wrong.

"Emerald, I'm so sorry for how I reacted when you gave me the helmet, I didn't even see the engraving on it, I just saw the helmet and I panicked," he tells me, closing his eyes in sadness.

"Carsten pointed it out, and I lost it. It means so fucking much to me that you did that." He opens his eyes as tears start to fill them.

"It's okay, I'm hurt, I'm not gonna lie but I can forgive you and move past it. I understand why you reacted the way you did but I'm more hurt by the fact that I felt like you threw me away, like you threw us away." I sigh as tears start to fill my eyes again from feeling the heartache of our breakup all over again.

"You broke me, I've never felt so empty or alone in my life." I start crying a little harder as he pulls me onto his lap again. I rest my head against his chest and cry.

"I felt the same way and I'm the asshole who fucking did this to us, I'm so sorry, Sugar." He puts his fingers on my chin, lifting my face to look up at him, and his lips crash down on mine as I open my mouth inviting him in, he starts to explore my mouth, making long strokes with his tongue, devouring it like it's been ages since he's tasted me. I pull away from the kiss.

"It's okay, Credence," I say before bringing my lips back to his. Forgetting that we're in my hospital room. It's okay, the nurses just checked on me. They think I'm resting and said they'd be back in two hours. So, no one should be coming in before Carsten and Winter get here.

I slowly turn my body, throwing my left leg over his, straddling his body, feeling his hard length under my already wet pussy, I don't know how my body is turned on in a moment like this, but I can't help it, it's been so long since feeling him this close to me, my body craves to be touched by him, it craves to feel him inside me.

"I need you," I tell him breathlessly. "Please."

"Show me what you need, Sugar," he groans, and I slide the hospital gown down, leaving myself completely naked, exposing my naked breasts, and hard nipples to the hungry look in his eyes.

"Fuck you're gorgeous." The hungry look in his eyes grows stronger as he looks me up and down, slowly devouring me with every movement.

"Thank you," I whisper against his lips as he brings his mouth back to mine for another hungry kiss, his lips taking their time, slowly grazing against mine. Like he's memorizing the feel of them to remember when he's not with me. He groans into my mouth as I start grinding against his shorts. He leans forward, sliding his wife beater up over his head, before lifting his hips, I lift myself up a little as he removes his shorts and slides down his boxer briefs. His hard, warm length resting against my entrance, one movement and he could be inside me. But I'm not ready yet. I place his cock between my folds, not at my entrance and I slide my wetness against him.

He throws his head back growling out quietly, "Fuck. Your pussy is so wet for me, Sugar." He moans before pulling me forward, my head falling back as he begins kissing my neck. I'm desperate for him. It's been so long, too long I'm desperate for his kisses, his hands all over my body, and to feel him make me feel full inside. I slide myself forward, reaching down and wrapping my fingers around his hard cock and hold it still while I slide down onto it, stretching me, making me whole again as he fills me with his fullness. I've missed this. He has no idea how much this kind of intimacy means to me.

"Fuckkk." I moan as one of his hands finds my tits, gently tugging on my hard nipple between his thumb and pointer finger. "Goddamn, I missed the feel of your pussy," he growls against my neck before coming in and biting down, sucking on my now sweaty skin.

I lift my body up and down, his cock thrusting in and out as I grind my hips into his hard length. I've missed the way his piercings feel, the way they touch my walls in all the best places and send a chill straight through my body.

He grabs onto my hips squeezing them as he thrusts up into me a little quicker, taking what he needs from me, while I take what I need from him, each other. Our bodies together becoming one. He wraps his arms around me and slowly moves me onto my back, I've missed the feel of his body on top of mine. The warmth, the safeness and the way he makes me feel like I'm the only thing he'll ever need always as he looks into my eyes. His lips gently brush mine, as I moan into his mouth. The fullness of his cock being everything I'll ever need when it comes to making love, because he is all I'll ever want. And this closeness being everything I've missed in our time apart. He thrusts deeper, taking his time with my body as I wrap my legs around his waist to hold him close. There is something different about the way he's making love to me, we've made love a couple times before, but this is something different. Something special about this moment we're sharing. Like each of us is afraid this whole moment isn't real, like if we blink or let go one of us will disappear.

"I love you, Emerald, you have no idea how much I love you, Sugar," he whispers against my mouth as he pulls away from my kiss.

"I love you so much, Creedence," I whisper back against his lips as I grip the back of his head and pull him close for another kiss. The way his tongue moves along mine, dancing with it like we've been dancing this way together our whole lives. Like we've always been two halves of the same whole. Searching and finding our way back to each other this whole time. Our breakup was just another obstacle in our way, challenging our love for each other to see if we're both strong enough and worth the fight.

He grabs my hands, placing them on each side of my head, inter-twining our fingers together. My fingers fitting between his like they were always meant to be there. He pumps harder, taking himself deeper with each thrust, getting me closer to my release with each thrust and I cry out from the pleasure, as he hits just the right spot each time.

"Get ready to come with me, Sugar," Creedence grunts between thrusts.

"Ohhh goddd," I moan as I nod my head because I can't find the words to use, just moans.

"Be my good girl, come with me, Sugar," he moans out as he fills me with his cum, pumping into me faster and as deep as he can go.

My eyes roll back and my toes curl as my orgasm soars through me. It's so intense I don't want it to end. I could cry from how good it feels and I'm pretty sure he feels the same way as he growls out into the crook of my neck.

"Fuck, Emerald," he pants, slowing down his thrusts.

"Uh huh." I can barely find my voice to get words out as my heart races so fast it feels as if it'll rip out of my chest. I try to catch my breath as my body becomes tired, I relax my legs that I had around him so tight they're now sore.

He lets go of my hands as he lays his head next to me. He slowly slides out of me as I feel his cum drip out with him. He stops staring down at my pussy.

"Mmm, if we weren't about to eat food, I'd take my time eating you, Sugar. You look fucking sexy with my cum dripping out of you," he growls.

"I have two weeks to catch up on." He smirks. "I'm gonna take my time with making it all up to you, nothing rough until you're feeling better."

And I pout, "But I like when you're rough." I bite my bottom lip hoping to get him going again because I suddenly don't care about my headache or the food anymore, I just care about him bending me over this bed and fucking me again.

"Creedence," I whisper. "You are such a dirty man," I giggle as my hands instantly go to my pounding head that has now intensified. He looks over at me, concern written all over his face.

"Are you okay, Sugar, what's wrong?" He moves one of my hands to get a better look at me.

"My head is fucking pounding. I woke up with a bad headache from whatever she put in my drink and it's worse now, hopefully that medicine starts working soon," I sigh as I slide my hospital gown back on my cold, naked body. Creedence stands and quickly gets his clothes on.

"I figured you were probably nauseous from both the alcohol and whatever she gave you. Here let's eat those donuts I brought for us and see if eating something helps your head." Creedence grabs the still hot coffee and the bag of donuts and sits down on the bed next to me, handing over the food.

"Knock, Knock." Carsten and Winter come walking through the door with two bags filled with food containers.

"We didn't know what to get so we got all of Emerald's favorites, along with yours. We already ate so all of this is for you guys." Winter smiles setting the bags down on the little table that sits next to my bedside.

"How you feelin, Em?" Carsten sets his bag of containers down, and walks towards me.

"Like death, my head's pounding, dizzy, nauseous, I could go on but I'd rather not." I let out a breath. "Thank you, guys, for everything last night. For saving my life. Fuck, I can't believe how bad last night could've been." Tears start forming in my eyes as my voice starts to feel shaky.

"I could've died." I cry.

"Baby, it's okay, everything's okay now. Please don't cry." Creedence wraps me in his arms, pulling me up off the bed to stand on shaky legs. But I know he'll support my weak body; he'd never let me fall.

"I'm sorry you're feeling that way, if you need anything please don't hesitate to ask for it honey." Winter adds in.

"I'll be alright, things are just kinda coming back to me as I process last night. I was stupid and I'm sorry." I sniffle. "I should have been more careful, less reckless."

"You don't have to apologize, Emerald, we understand." Winter is the first one to say something before Carsten and Creedence both agree with her.

"Seriously, we all do stupid shit, Sugar, please don't be sorry baby." Creedence grabs my hand, squeezing it.

"You guys, I was reckless, careless, irresponsible, the list goes on. I almost fucking died." I don't understand why they're not upset with me. Not that I want them to be upset with me, but shouldn't they be?

"Emerald, Sugar. I'm relieved that I didn't fucking lose you too, babe. We're all fucking relieved we didn't lose you. No one's upset with you. We're just thankful you're okay." He gently kisses my forehead.

"Bitch, I'd be pissed if I lost my best friend, but I'm not mad at you. Fuck, I'm just so happy you're okay that's all we care about." Winter sniffles a little and my heart breaks knowing I've caused the people I love a pain like this.

"Seriously, Em, we're just glad you're okay, no one's mad." Carsten rubs my shoulder, sounding choked up himself.

"Here, you sit down, I'll get you some food. You need to eat, Sugar." Creedence walks me back over to the bed where I sit down at the edge and I slowly sit down, my body sore for some reason.

"They boxed everything up in different containers, so you guys had a decent amount of food. It was Winter's idea. Don't worry Stacy didn't help." Carsten laughs as he walks over pulling the containers out of the bag.

"Thank god." I roll my eyes. "I haven't missed her at all." Not since the bullshit she pulled when she said everything to upset me in front of everyone, I still can't believe she went that low to make herself feel better.

"You haven't missed anything, between me being there and everything Winter has told me these past few weeks, she's just the same old bitchy, jealous Stacy."

"I figured nothing has changed with that bitch." I laugh as I grab plates from the cabinet, my head starting to feel a little better from the medicine Creed gave me.

Creed gathers a lot of food on a plate for me and my mouth practically waters. It feels like it's been days since I've eaten. Well, it might actually be, I paid more attention to drinking than I did eating. Then he grabs himself a plate and sits next to me on the bed.

While we eat, we talk about what happened with Daisy, the cops came by earlier and I told them I wasn't interested in pressing charges. When I see her, I'll have a mouthful to say. I'm sure she deserves more but I'm not an asshole like her. Plus, I just want to move on with my life and forget this shit ever happened.

34

CREEDENCE

It's been two weeks since Emerald and I have gotten back together, and we've made up for the time apart in more ways than one. It's also been two weeks since Emerald's been out of the hospital and she's doing better than ever. We're doing better than ever.

I lay here in my bed, excited for today as I have a surprise for Emerald that she has no idea is even coming.

She lays next to me, her back towards me, part of her body still covered up except for one of my favorite parts, her ass and her legs stick out. I place my hand on her bare, smooth skin, rubbing it up and down slowly, taking in the feel of her and how happy she makes me.

I don't ever want to forget the feel of her body next to mine, in fact I'm going to ask her to move in with me soon, whether it's her house or mine. I don't care where I'm at as long as I'm with her day and night. I want to wake up with her and fall asleep next to her every day for the rest of my life. Emerald is home to me, wherever she is that's where I belong.

"That tickles." She gives out a sleepy giggle.

"Sorry, Sugar, I can't get enough of you. I was just feeling how soft your skin is and got lost in my thoughts, I wasn't trying to tickle you." I reach my arm around her and pull her in closer to me, her back now to my chest and my hard cock now resting against her ass.

"Mmm, someone's excited," she giggles, wiggling her ass against me. You can hear the smile in her voice.

"I'm always excited when I'm around you." I take my rock-hard cock in my hand, rubbing myself against her ass. "I just can't help myself. You're just so fucking sexy." I let out a low grumble that vibrates through my chest against her back, as I groan into the crook of her neck. I start kissing and sucking on the sensitive skin, listening to her sleepy moans.

"I need you, Creed," she whispers as she turns over to face me, her lips instantly finding mine. I swipe my tongue against her lips asking for her to let me in and she opens immediately, her tongue finding mine, sliding and swirling against it. I moan out, god this woman drives me absolutely crazy.

"I'll always need you, Sugar," I tell her as I pull her on top of me, she giggles again as I grip onto her hips. "Mmm, already wet for me, my little slut?" I ask her with a smirk on my face. I can feel the wetness from her pussy pressed against my hard length and it's taking everything in me not to just thrust up inside her.

"I don't know, why don't you check and see." She slowly winks at me, biting her bottom lip.

"Ohh, do you want me to go down and see if you're wet?" And she nods her head. "Tell me what you want, Sugar." I hope she says what I want to hear, because I love when she tells me what she wants and isn't shy.

"I want you to lick my pussy, Creedence." She practically moans out the words.

"Mmm, I thought you'd never ask, I bet you still taste just as sweet as you did last night, my naughty little slut." I smack her ass hard, she throws her head back, letting out a moan as I rub the spot I just smacked before slapping it again. "I love how much you love when I take control." I growl at her because I do, it is so fucking sexy how much it turns her on when I take control. I love that she gets turned on by all the dirty things she lets me do to her, that we both equally enjoy.

"Please, Creed, I wanna come all over your face," she pouts and how can I resist, even if she didn't do that I'd still go down on her, I'm starving to taste her, and I haven't eaten anything yet after all.

"I want you to sit on my face, gorgeous. Smother me with your pussy." I barely get the words out. They turn me on as I think about it, making my cock twitch with excitement.

"You...you want me to do what?" She blushes a little, I love making her blush.

"My little slut, you're so fucking sweet, you're such a dirty girl yet so. Fucking. Innocent."

"Creedence, I've... I've never done that before." Her face is so red it's so sweet.

"Now is not the time to be embarrassed, Emerald. None of the guys you were ever with in your past have ever had you do this?" I'm actually curious. I thought she was into freaky shit just as much as I was.

"No, they were all boring and..." She pauses. "I've never done that with anyone because I was always afraid I'd hurt them." She looks away from me and I place my hand on her chin and turn her to look back at me.

"Well, I'm about to change that." I grin at her. "Straddle my fucking face, Sugar, I want your eyes on me while I eat my fucking breakfast. I want to watch you come alive while you come. I want to see what you look like when you come undone because of me." Every time I've gone down on her I've never had a good angle of her face and this time. I'm not fucking missing any of it.

"Shit, Creedence," she moans as I slowly pull her forward, trying to get her to move her body over my face.

She slowly crawls up my body, one knee on each side of me before finally placing her right knee by my head.

"Right here?" She sounds so nervous as she asks.

"Perfect." I slide her other leg on the other side of my head. "Goddamn baby, your pussy looks fucking delicious."

I stick my tongue out swiping it along her slit, groaning with how good she fucking tastes.

"Fuck, Creed," she whimpers as she holds herself up with the headboard.

I grab her thighs and pull her down a little more, making her squeal.

"Creedence, I can't hold myself up being that low," she whispers breathlessly.

"Emerald, I said smother me with your fucking pussy. Sit on my face baby, I don't care as long as you're enjoying it. Let me please you." I stick my tongue out again, licking up her slit until I hit her clit, circling the sensitive numb with my tongue before grazing it with my teeth. I gently pull it between my teeth listening to her cries of pleasure as I wrap my lips around her sucking and swirling as I do. She starts grinding into my face, slowly at first, back and forth she loves it against my tongue before gyrating her hips in a circular motion.

"That's it, baby, let go, ride my face." I grumble into her pussy. "Drown me in your wetness, fucking smother me please, Sugar." She finally lets go, relaxing fully onto my face. Riding me, grinding into my tongue.

"Fuck, Creed, you feel too damn good," she moans, reaching down and grabbing both breasts in her hand as she throws her head back in pleasure.

"Eyes on me, baby," I growl and suck her clit back into my mouth.

"Fuck, sorry," she breathes out. Looking back into my eyes.

"Good girl." I slap her ass back and forth on both cheeks hard, five times on each side, making her cry out tortured moans. "Don't." Slap. "You Dare." Slap. "Disobey me." Slap. "Again, Sugar."

Two more slaps on each cheek as she whimpers, grinding into my face, my beards covered in her arousal and I fucking love it, she's so wet for me my little slut and I love how much she's letting go and enjoying herself. Her heavy eyes rolling with each stroke of my tongue as I lick her clit like I'd die if she removed her pussy from my mouth. I slide my tongue slowly down her slit until my tongue starts to swirl inside her as I eat up her pussy, starving for more with each swirl of my tongue, trying to taste as much of her as I can because I can't get enough of her.

Her body starts shaking, her legs trembling on each side of my head so I grab her thighs, holding the weight of them for her so she can ride out the intense orgasm she's about to experience.

"Creedence, please. Oh god yes," she cries, her eyes rolling and head falling back.

"Eyes on me," I grumble into her.

"Fuck." She looks down. "Please. Yes. God, I need more, Creed please, I... I need something." Fuck that is the sexiest thing she could have done right now, beg me for more.

"My little slut is getting greedy, huh?" I can't help the smile that forms on the face of the monster I created.

"Mhmm, yes, Creed. Please. I wanna come on your face," she pants. "I wanna see the look on your face as you watch me come, please, Creedence." She slows her pace, slowly rotating her hips as I circle my tongue on her swollen clit. She's so close it's like her body is slowly dragging out the build up getting her there just enough but still not enough to give her what she needs. I circle my tongue on her favorite spot giving her everything she needs to get her closer. Not too hard but enough pressure to feel good as I slowly stick two fingers inside her pussy and one in her ass.

"Ahh, fuck, Creed." She hisses because I didn't prepare her ass for it. I just kind of went with it in the moment.

"Shit, sorry." I continue to pump in and out of her while swirling and sucking her sensitive clit. Her grinding is getting faster and more intense as I help her ride my face.

"Come for me, Sugar." And as if my words were magic her body explodes, her pussy clamping down on my fingers, pulsing around them as her orgasm soars through her. Until her body stops shaking, her head falling down as she giggles, staring into my eyes with a big smile on her face.

"Fuck, that. Was. Perfect," she whispers out of breath from her intense orgasm and how fast she was just riding my face. I wish she wasn't so sensitive right after I'd have her keep going until she came again. But I'm too horny to play that game right now. My dicks rock hard and I need to be inside her.

She lifts her left leg, removing herself from around my head and falls onto the bed next to me, her breast jiggling as she breathes heavily, her hard nipples looking lonely, making me want to suck them into my mouth. I quickly sit up, and push myself between her legs, resting my cock at her entrance enough to touch lightly and feel that she's so fucking wet and so warm, my cocks begging to be inside her. But I'm not ready yet. I lift her chin with my thumb and press my lips to hers, swiping my tongue against her soft plump lips, thinking about how they'd feel if they were around me right now. Our tongues slide together, dancing together so perfectly. I lean down onto my left arm placing it next to her and cup her right breast, playing with her nipple as I continue to kiss her. Swallowing her moans as she moans into my mouth. I twist and pull her hard nipple with my pointer finger and thumb. Before pulling away from her kiss, she pouts.

"Now, now Sugar, how will I give you what you want if you pout?" I ask her with a smile on my face as I trail kisses down her jaw working my way to her neck as I kiss and suck, her sweet skin, making sure to leave my marks along the way. I said it before and I'll say it now, I want people to know my little slut belongs to me, even if that means leaving marks on this beautiful piece of art, that I happily call mine. I kiss my way down her neck making my way down to her perky tits, sucking her pink nipple back into my mouth as she cries out.

"Fuck that feels so good. Please, Creed, don't stop," she moans.

"Don't worry baby I'm just getting started," I tell her smiling as I suck her nipple into my mouth again. I kiss and suck, working my way over to her other breast before sucking it into my mouth and gently biting on it. I love hearing her moan and cry out my name. I'll never get tired of listening to it. I take my hand and thrust two fingers inside her, not even working them inside her as she's already soaked.

"Fuck look how fucking wet you are for me," I growl as I pull them out and show them to her, before I lick the wetness off one by one and then stick them back inside her, thrusting them in and out. I remove my fingers from her pussy adjusting my cock at her entrance, but she stops me. Placing her hand on my chest.

"What's wrong, Emerald, are you okay?" I scrunch my brows while raising one.

"My turn," she says, licking her lips.

"Your turn?" I have no idea what she's talking about, so I wait patiently for her to explain.

"My turn to suck your cock, Creedence. Please?" She has a sweet, innocent smile on her face as she asks. Fuck I was so close to being inside her.

I get up, slowly getting to my knees, curious as to what she wants to do with that pretty little mouth of hers with those juicy plump lips. She sits up scooting herself closer to me, inches from my cock as it stands at full attention right in her gorgeous fucking face.

She slowly licks her lips before wrapping her small hand around my long, thick shaft. Stroking it, pumping her fist up and down as she takes her tongue and swirls it around the head of my cock.

"Fuckkk." I groan and she sucks the tip into her mouth swirling her tongue as she does it, slowly taking me in deeper, bobbing her head back and forth. She scoots her body closer to me before she places her hands on my ass. Holding me in place as she sucks my cock. Her head moves back and forth as she looks up at me with fire in her eyes, she's loving this. She loves sucking my cock. I reach my hands down and slide my fingers through her hair and just hold onto her head, I don't move her. I let her have this and take control of the situation. I've come to learn that I love her being in control just as much as she loves me being in control. She sucks me into her mouth, tightening her lips around me as tight as they'll go as she sucks me to the back of her throat, swirling my piercings with her tongue along the way. She moans as she does it and that's another thing I love about my girl, she gets worked up sucking my cock. It makes her extremely wet and horny. She tilts her head, taking me into her throat as she does it, swallowing and moving her head back and forth, relaxing her jaw and taking me down further as she does. I swear I'm halfway in her throat, I have no idea how she does this. But it's super fucking sexy. She starts moving her head back and forth again, swirling her tongue faster around my cock, sucking as she goes, taking her hand she wraps it around the rest of my cock that her mouth doesn't cover and grips my shaft with her small hand that barely closes around it and starts pumping her hand up and down with her spit covered mouth. Spit pools at the corners of her mouth as she takes me back into her throat again, her tongue sliding along my piercings as she does it and I can't help myself. I take control, taking my hands and holding her head in place as I thrust my hips back and forth, going in and out of her mouth. She moans as the tears start to form in her eyes and I smile down at her, she looks so beautiful when she cries, and she does. She cries for me as I fuck her face. I thrust faster getting closer to my orgasm as I do.

"Get ready to swallow my cum, Sugar," I groan out as she moans around my cock the vibrations from her mouth getting me closer as she sucks me in tightening her lips around me as I lose control. I feel my balls start to tighten as she relaxes her jaw and throat for me. I thrust further in pumping faster and harder as I fuck her face and my orgasm comes to life. I spill my warm cum down her throat, she moans and swirls her tongue as I slowly pull out of her throat.

"Fuckk, your mouth, Sugar, feels so good when it's wrapped around me," I moan out breathing heavily. I pull out of her throat fully and move my hands from her head as she gasps for air. I let my head fall back for a second before lifting it back up. I look down at her as she sucks the rest of my cum from my cock, licking me clean like it's the last thing she'll eat for days. I wipe her tears with my thumbs and lick them off one finger at a time. I'll always love licking her tears. I can at least wipe her tears for her and licking her is my favorite thing to do and if I can't lick her tears from her face then I clean them off with my fingers and lick them that way.

When she finally catches her breath, I flip her over onto her stomach and pull her ass towards me. "Spread your legs. Sugar, I'm not done with you yet, my little slut," I demand as I smack her ass hard leaving a handprint, she lets out a soft moan and looks back at me and smiles.

"I love it when you spank me." Goddamn does that make my cock twitch with excitement. I grab a handful of her ass and squeeze it, then jiggle it with my hand before letting go and slapping it again, a little harder this time, smiling as it jiggles because there's something about a nice, thick and juicy ass that gets me fucking going and her. Mmm, does her ass make my cock hard.

"Ohhhh goddd," she cries as I bend down slowly licking her ass where I slapped it before I open my mouth and bite it, letting out a low growl as I do. Fuck her ass is so delicious I love that she lets me bite and lick it.

"God, Creed, I love feeling your mouth on my body." She moans out into the mattress before turning her face to the side. "Please, I need to feel your cock inside me." She's panting while rocking her hips back and forth teasing me with her ass.

"Mmm, I wish you'd let me fuck that tight ass of yours baby girl," I say in a husky voice from being so turned on.

"Please, Creed, please just fuck me. Fuck my ass," she cries, making my cock twitch.

"Emerald, it's going to fucking hurt, baby you're not ready." And it's true. I'm definitely bigger than average and with my piercings. She cuts off my thoughts.

"Please, Creedence, I know what I want, I'm ready. Please," she cries, and I reach over to my nightstand, grabbing the lube and the vibrator I bought for her. I hand her the vibrator.

"Turn that on a low setting, place it on your clit. It'll help distract you from the pain, baby," I tell her, pouring a generous amount of lube on my palm. I want enough to cover every inch of my cock I growl as I stroke my cock, getting myself worked up. When I'm done making sure my cock is fully covered, I squirt some lube on her ass, spreading it with my thumb as I push my thumb in and out of her preparing her for my thickness.

"I'll go slow," I tell her as I place my cock against the entrance of her tight hole. Rubbing it back and forth pushing against her entrance with each swipe slowly getting her used to the tip before pushing myself in as gently as I can. She whimpers a little, her body begins to shake as I try to push myself deeper but she's so tight it's pushing me out.

"Relax, Sugar." I rub circles on her lower back with my free hand helping her body relax a little as I do before pushing myself in further.

"Fuck, Creed," she hisses. "I don't think I can do this."

"Do you want me to stop?" I freeze, stopping mid thrust afraid that I'm hurting her too much.

"No, please. Don't stop," she pants as she turns up the speed on the vibrator.

"Circle your clit for me, baby," I growl. "Nice and slow, but don't come baby girl. Not until I tell you that you can."

"O...okay." I push myself in deeper, the head finally all the way in and I grit my teeth so tight I'm afraid I might break them; I need to stop myself from busting inside her too soon. That's how tight she is. I'm afraid to even move just the tip because I might come.

"Tell me what you want, Sugar." My voice comes out deep, husky, breathless.

"Please, Creed. Give me your cock. I need to feel you inside my ass," she begs, and you can tell she's being serious and not just saying it to sound sexy. She truly wants to feel my cock in her ass, and I can't wait to be buried in her tightness.

"Mmm, I love it when you beg me. Tell me who this ass belongs to, baby." I slowly start sliding the tip in and out, little by little. Sliding a little more of me in with each thrust.

"Shittt," she cries out. "You, Creed, my ass is yours and only yours," she moans as she pants waiting for me to fully enter her. "Same with my pussy, no one else's ever, Creed. Only you."

"Mmm, fuck. Good girl," I moan as I thrust into her halfway. Not able to resist anymore but I can't just shove myself all the way in. I don't want to cause any damage. I pump in and out of her slowly, pushing deeper each time pulling it almost fully out, teasing her, as her breathing picks up some more. I thrust back in, loving the feel of her tight ass as it tightens around my cock with each thrust, pumping in and out slowly still giving her time to adjust.

"Shit Creed," she whimpers a tortured moan. I love those moans from her, the moans where you can tell it feels so good to her it's like torture, almost like she could cry from the intensity of the pleasure. She makes my cock throb in her ass as I listen to her.

"You feel so fucking good." Fuck. "Your ass is practically swallowing me up, Emerald, you're so fucking tight." I push in a little more. "You're doing so fucking good, I'm almost fully in."

"Fuck, please hurry. It hurts. When is it going to feel better," she whimpers.

"Shit." I stop. "Emerald, please tell me to stop. I can't unless you tell me to. You feel so fucking good, I'm not strong enough to stop this on my own."

"Come in my ass, Creed, please," she moans out and fuck is it hot when she talks like that, making my cock pulse inside her as she says those nasty fucking words to me. My sweet naughty girl loves being dirty for me.

"Is that what you want, my little slut, for me to come in that tight little hole?" I groan.

"God yes, fuck me, Creed." I slow my pace, making her growl a little as she attempts to wiggle her ass closer to me, but I hold her still so she can't move.

"So greedy, Sugar. I fucking love it so much," I groan. "But babe, I'm not in all the way." I chuckle a little, waiting for her reaction.

"What? You... You're not in all the way?" She pauses. "Fuck, Creed. Just...please. I need all of you to make me come." She's out of breath and pants between each word. Fuck she's perfect.

"I'll try to go slow." I don't want to hurt her, and she's already done such a good job taking me so goddamn well. I grip my cock and slowly guide the rest of myself inside her. Trying so hard not to cum, I didn't think it was possible for something to be this tight.

"Your ass is so. Fucking. Perfect. So. Fucking. Tight," I grumble between thrusts.

"Oh god, Creed, don't stop please I'm so close."

"Don't worry, baby, I'm not stopping. This is going to hurt but I promise it'll feel good just as quickly." I thrust into her hard. "Fuck, Emerald. So. Fucking. Tight. I can't get over it, so fucking perfect."

She hisses, letting out little whimpers in between tortured moans, with each thrust I give her. She's taking me so fucking well. "You're doing so well, Emerald."

She giggles a little. "It feels so fucking good, I can't believe I waited so long to try this," she says between pants, as her body shakes, her orgasm close as my cock slides in and out of her tight ass, I can't help the noises I make, I sound like an animal growling between each thrust and moan. It feels too fucking good to control the way I'm feeling.

"I'm getting close, baby."

"Fuck, Creed, me too please," she cries, and I reach down, removing the vibrator between from her hand, tossing it on the bed without even shutting it off. I pinch her clit gently, before rubbing it with my thumb.

"Fuckkk, come with me, Sugar," I tell her and that's all she needed to hear, as she comes all over my cock, milking me with each fucking thrust, tightening and grabbing everything that's left inside me.

"Shit, Creed, don't stop," she screams out as I keep pumping into her until her body goes limp, she falls down onto the bed, I gently pull myself out of her, making her whimper as I do. Then I slowly fall down next to her, holding her in my arms trying to catch my breath and cool off my sweaty body.

Later that day after we finally got out of bed, showered and got ready for the day I take her into the garage, it's a nice day out so I have a few ideas in mind.

"I wanted to try the helmet on for you while we're out here." I hesitate a little as I say it because it still triggers bad memories. But I've been working on them more. "And I wanted you to try your helmet on so I could see you with it on."

"Is that why you had me go get it?" She nervously stares down at hers on the desk next to mine.

"Yep, I've decided today is the day, Sugar." I pause to see if she can guess what I'm talking about.

"Today is the day for what?" She raises an eyebrow confused.

"I'm taking you for a ride, baby." I pause. "And I don't mean on my cock." I laugh, smiling at her feeling like a weight is being lifted off of my shoulders just saying it out loud. Like I'm setting some of the bad memories free and making room for new happy memories with Emerald.

"Creedence, are you sure?" She has a worried look on her face as she stares up at me then back at her helmet. Then back to me, biting her lip.

"I've never been more sure of anything in my life, for once I'm ready, and I'm ready to take you with me, I'll do anything to protect you and I won't let anything happen to you."

"I trust you, there's never been a time where I haven't trusted you. You know what you're doing babe." She smiles up at me, like she's trying to hide how big her smile truly is.

I walk over to my bike and straddle it, starting it up, revving the engine as I look at Emerald with a big smile on her face. It's been a couple weeks since I started it so I wanted to let it run for a minute. I rev the engine again, smiling at the vibrations below me. I've missed this and I've never felt as close to my brother as I do now, thanks to Emerald.

"You've been on a motorcycle, right?" I ask her because I can't remember if she said she has or not.

"Kinda, well I rode on one once and went around in a parking lot with a guy I dated but that was about it, so I guess yes I have, just not on the streets." She's biting her lip; you can tell she's nervous.

"You have nothing to be nervous about, babe. I know it's been a minute since I rode on my bike, but I'd never forget how to ride, it just comes natural to me."

"I trust you, Creedence, I pinky promise." She winks as she holds out her pinky to me and I take her pinky in mine and shake it, smiling down at her. I can't believe how incredible this woman is right in front of me. How did I get so fucking lucky?

"I want to take you to a place I used to go to with my brother. It's about a half hour from here, do you think you're okay with that?" I don't want her to be uncomfortable, so I double check before just to be safe.

"More than okay, Creed, I'd love to see it." She smiles at me. Getting a look of excitement in her eyes.

"Great, let's get ready to get out of here then." I walk over to her wrapping my arms around her waist, bringing her in for a hug. "Thank you, Em, for always believing in me, and for bringing me back to something I hadn't realized I missed until now." I pause, getting emotional. "You have no idea how much this means to me, and I have you to thank."

"Anything for you, Creedence. I'm so glad you're doing this too." She lays her head on my chest for a second before looking back up.

"Wait, is this why you said I needed pants, boots, and my hair braided?" She's giggling a little, and it's cute how excited she is to do this.

"Yep, I needed you to be ready without knowing what we would be doing." I tell her. "Because I wanted you to be surprised."

"Well, I definitely am surprised." She smiles. "I'm proud of you, babe." She comes over wrapping her arms around me, hugging me tightly.

"Thank you, Emerald, that means a lot to me," I tell her as I kiss her forehead.

We both get our helmets on and goddamn does she look fucking sexy. I mean everything about her is sexy but seeing her with her helmet on, mmm I could bend her over right here and fuck her, mmm or I can have her ride me on my bike. So many ideas. But I'll save that for later. Right now, I have more important things that I need to do.

She hops on the bike behind me, wrapping her arms tightly around my waist, and I slowly pull out of my driveway, turning left as her body leans with mine.

We pull onto the highway and my body tenses up a little as I fight the urge to pull over and freak out, Emerald must sense it because she lightly squeezes my waist twice like she's telling me it's okay and that's all I needed to calm back down again and focus on the road and get us to where we need to be safely.

As we pull into a parking spot, she slides off the bike and I get off behind her.

"For someone who has only been on a bike once, you did awesome," I tell her, and she smiles.

"That's because you make me feel safe, if it was with anyone else, I probably would've had to have them pull over. But I wasn't scared with you, I told you I trusted you." I walk up to her and wrap my arms around her waist again, leaning down to kiss her as my lips slowly graze hers. She opens her mouth for me, and I deepen the kiss. She leans into me, standing on her tiptoes as she slightly moans into my mouth. If she moans again, I'll be tempted to take her right here in the middle of this parking lot. I pull away and move my arm, readjusting my hard cock in my pants.

"Sorry." She giggles a little as she looks down at my cock through my dark washed jeans.

"But are you sorry?" I laugh as she playfully smacks my arm, giving me a slight smirk that tells me she's not sorry at all.

"Okay, okay, I am sorry I didn't mean to... I can't help it." She laughs. "I could blink and make you hard, I literally do nothing and your cock's hard, why is that my fault?" She giggles as I start tickling her, grabbing her wrists together with one hand and tickle her love handles making her laugh hysterically.

"Stop okay okay I'm sorry," she laughs hard.

"Are you though?" I ask again, smiling trying to hold back my laughter as I try to keep a somewhat serious look on my face, even with a smile.

"I know, it's okay I'll just punish you later for it." I wink at her.

"What? All that tickling and I don't get anything as an apology," she pouts, crossing her tiny child-like arms. Everything about her is tiny, even though she's thick and curvy, I'm not sure how to explain it. Or maybe she's just tiny to me because I'm like a big fucking dude. Either way I love how small and fragile she is. I love being the one to protect her from everything.

"Sorry, Sugar." I laugh. "You secretly loved it."

I take her hand and walk her into a path through the woods, after walking for what felt like forever, making me think I took the wrong turn since it's been so long since I've been here. Memories flash through my mind of the days my brother and I used to come here and just walk around through the woods, eat some food that we'd buy and take back here. This whole place is one big heart aching memory. But I suck it up and do this for Emerald, and for myself because whether I want to admit it or not, I needed to do this a long time ago, I'm just thankful I'm doing it with Emerald by my side.

"This is all so beautiful." She smiles as she looks around with every step she takes, and then she looks forward and finally sees it.

"Holy shit, is...is that a waterfall?" She has this big, beautiful smile on her face. "Wow, it's so...beautiful." She takes my hand again, walking forward.

"My brother and I found it one day when we took a break after riding. It was a hot-ass, humid fucking day and we were sweating our asses off. We decided to walk through the woods to find some shade, somewhere to cool off and as we walked through we found this."

"Did you guys swim in it?" She has this huge smile on her face like she's remembering the memory with me.

"Hell yeah we did, we started making it a tradition every month when the weather was nice we'd ride out and swim out here, just the two of us. I've never taken anyone here before because we promised each other we'd keep it to ourselves, but now I'm sharing this with you, in hopes that you'll keep this between us and make it our place. He would love that, just like he'd love you," I tell her, trying not to get choked up. But when I look at her, I see tears forming in her beautiful, brown eyes.

"I wish I could have met him; I'd love to be a part of this memory and new tradition between the two of us." She grabs my hand again, leaning up on her tiptoes to give me a quick kiss. "I love you, Creedence." She wipes at the few tears that fall freely on her cheeks as she attempts to blink away the new ones.

"I love you, baby. Thank you for wanting to be a part of this." I wipe her tears away then turn to look at her taking both of her hands in mine, she smiles up at me as she glances back over at the waterfall. The peaceful sound of the water falling into the lake, is such an amazing sound. Yet it's so quiet like all the noise in the world is gone except for the water around us. I could listen to it all day.

"I've been doing a lot of thinking and have come to the realization that life is too short. I've been living the last few years feeling guilty, guilty that my brother died and that It wasn't me and guilty for still being alive. I don't want to live feeling that way anymore because if I wasn't the one who survived that day then I would have never had the chance to have met you and to have fallen in love with you. I realize I can't keep living my life in guilt, it's killing me living this way. Emerald, you saved me, baby. You've given me back my life, before you I was a depressed, grieving mess and now I actually want to go out and live again, and I actually want to start riding again, with you, if you'll ride with me more." She stands there smiling and listening to me talk not wanting to interrupt at all.

"I said this all to you before and I'm going to say it again because I want you to hear me say it to you, you deserve to hear it today and every day. You've never felt like a stranger to me, you've been my life in this lifetime and all my lifetimes before this one. You've been my rock and my better half. You're my drug and I'll never stop or want to stop being addicted to you. When I met you, I knew you were the one, there was just something about you that told me to never let you go and then when I did, I thought I had lost you forever, I thought I'd never get you back. I don't ever want to be without you because I don't know who I am if I'm breathing without you. I belong wherever you are, you are my home, you are my world. All I've ever needed is you and all I will ever need will always be you, today, tomorrow and every day, only you. So, remember the time when we both said we were crazy for loving each other so quickly?" I look at her beautiful face smiling at me, with fresh tears in her eyes. I smile back at her feeling really fucking nervous. I get down on one knee and grab her shaking left hand with my shaking hands.

"Emerald, I'm already the happiest man ever when I'm with you, but I'd be even happier if you were my wife. Emerald, will you marry me?" She puts her right hand over her mouth and continues to cry, a little more intense now than she was a minute ago.

"God yes, I'll marry you," she says between sobs. "I don't care how crazy we are, you're my crazy and I'll happily be your crazy any day." I placed the ring on her finger. When I went to pick it out, it was ironically the first ring I saw, and I knew it was meant to be. It's a heart shaped emerald, with black smaller diamonds surrounding it and going down the sides of the white gold band. I've never seen anything like it, but like I said it was the first ring I saw when I walked into that jewelry store, and I knew It was the one.

"Oh my god it's an emerald," she squeals in excitement. "I've always wanted an emerald wedding ring; how did you know?" she asks, holding her left hand that's still shaking with her right hand while moving it back and forth watching it sparkle under the sun. "It's so fucking beautiful."

"I didn't know, I just saw it and knew it was perfect. It was the first ring I saw and just knew it was meant to be yours." I smile at her as I pick her up by her thighs wrapping her legs around my waist. Her lips crash against mine, she opens her mouth, her tongue swiping against mine as I kiss her passionately. I want to cherish this moment forever, not a day will go by where I won't think of this sad memory of a place that my brother and I went to that is now turned into a happy memory. Where I can come here with my future wife and remember the good times my brother and I had while I create good memories with her. She pulls away from the kiss and smiles at me.

"I love you so much, Creedence."

"I love you, Emerald," I tell her, and she lowers herself down out of my arms.

"I have an idea." She has a big smile on her face as she slowly starts taking her clothes off. I look at her with an equally excited smile as I follow her lead and do the same. She strips down leaving her lace bra and thong on and I strip down to my boxer briefs as she giggles in excitement.

"If you can catch me, I'll let you fuck me on the dock." She giggles as she runs away from me, I start after her, chasing her slowly. I don't want to catch her yet. I'll definitely be fucking her on that dock, but I want to enjoy this happy moment with her. I stop running as she jumps off the dock and splashing into the water. She comes above the surface as I stand there watching her, my future wife with the biggest smile on her face as I smile at her. I never thought I'd see the day where I found pure joy and happiness again and I don't ever want to do anything to fuck it up again.

EPILOGUE

CREEDENCE

I STAND THERE AT THE ENTRANCE OF THE DOCK, WITH THE waterfall behind me. Carsten's Uncle Kane, who happens to be our officiant to my right and my best friends Carsten, Axton and Chase to my left.

While we watch Winter, Chastity, and Saylor walk down the aisle that we made, our guests line up across from us. We wanted to keep this place a secret but when we decided we wanted to get married we couldn't think of a better place to have it than here. On top of that it made me feel like my brother is here with us since this was our place to hang out. It made it more special for the both of us.

The music changes and the song "A Thousand Years" by Christina Perri starts playing and I close my eyes, taking a deep breath for what's to come. I know when I open them, I'm probably going to cry and I have no shame in crying because of the beautiful woman that I will get to call my wife here shortly. Everyone stands and I close my eyes again, partly from nerves, wanting to be surprised and trying to calm myself down as tears already start to fall down my cheeks, who knew I'd be this emotional on my wedding day.

I take another deep breath in as I feel a hand on my shoulder.

"Holy shit," Carsten whispers behind me, he's the one putting his hand on my shoulder. "She looks fucking gorgeous man open your eyes, brother."

I open my eyes as Emerald walks towards me and the breath is literally taken from my lungs. She takes my breath away in her beautiful white halter top dress, the whole upper part of her dress that covers her breasts and stomach are all laced flowers that almost looks see through, but it's the tan fabric underneath giving it the illusion of nothing being underneath. It's tight all the way down to her hips before the lace fabric starts flowing out into a long train, covered in lace flowers that match the rest of the dress. She looks absolutely gorgeous. Her green and black hair is braided off to the side with loose strands curled around her face. I look at her smiling as the tears fall down her cheeks, she takes her hand away from her bouquet to wipe them before placing her hand back on it and letting out a small giggle that I feel like only I could hear. I smile with her as she gets closer to me, and the tears just keep coming down both of our faces. I feel like a pussy until I look over and see all three of my best friends crying as well as the three girls. At least I'm not the only one, but even if I was, I wouldn't give a fuck, how I could I not cry while looking at someone as gorgeous as Emerald, she looks absolutely breathtaking in that dress, and I want to remember this moment forever. I stand there completely lost in my thoughts not listening to anything Kane is saying as I stare at Emerald's beautiful face, as she listens to Kane talk to us and to our guests. I can't focus, how can I focus when I can't wait to permanently make this woman mine.

After asking for the rings, he looks at me, hands me Emerald's wedding band, that's white gold and filled with black diamonds to match the black diamonds around the emerald heart on her engagement ring.

I take her left hand in mine and look over to Kane finally paying attention.

"Repeat after me."

"Emerald, I choose you. To be no other than yourself. Loving what I know of you and trusting who you will become. I will respect and honor you, always and in all ways. I will take you to be my wife. To have and to hold, in tears and in laughter, in sickness and in health, to love and to cherish, from this day forward, in this lifetime and every lifetime after that."

I repeat everything he says fighting back tears as Emerald's hand shakes in mine.

"Emerald, I want you to repeat after me." He looks to her as she grabs my left hand holding the ring at the tip of my finger.

"Creedence, I choose you. To be no other than yourself. Loving what I know of you and trusting who you will become. I will respect and honor you always and in all ways. I will take you to be my husband. To have and to hold, in tears and in laughter, in sickness and in health, to love and to cherish, from this day forward, in this lifetime and every lifetime after that." Repeating the words through sobs. She still looks so beautiful.

"Do you Creedence take Emerald to be your wife, from this day forward always and forever?" He looks between the both of us, smiling.

"I do." I smile, sliding her ring onto her finger.

"Do you, Emerald, take Creedence to be your husband from this day forward, always and forever?" he asks Emerald, smiling while looking at her and then back to me.

"I do," she says, smiling while sliding my wedding band onto my finger.

"I love you forever, Creedence," she whispers to me as she stares into my eyes.

"I love you, Sugar forever and always, gorgeous," I whisper winking back at her.

Kane continues talking as we stare into each other's eyes, smiling. I can't wait to kiss her and fully make her mine.

"Did you guys hear me?" He laughs, we're both in our own world, just lost in each other. We both look over in confusion.

"Umm, no sorry," Emerald laughs.

"No, sorry I was lost in my thoughts of Emerald." I laugh looking over at Kane.

"I said you are now Husband and Wife." Then he looks over at me and smiles.

"You may now kiss your bride." I wrap my arms around her waist as she wraps hers around my neck and I slowly lean down pressing my lips against hers, as she opens her mouth a little, her tongue dancing with mine, as I kiss her deeply, passionately. Knowing she'll be mine forever makes me the happiest man I've ever been, and the happiest man I'll ever be. Today, tomorrow and forever, in this lifetime, the next lifetime and in every lifetime after that. She'll always be mine.

ACKNOWLEDGMENT

To think I'm an indie author of not only one but TWO published books is so crazy to me. It doesn't seem real that I'd be sitting here one day writing books for people and making my dreams a reality.

I couldn't have done it without the support of my husband, Michael or my children. I love you guys so much, thank you for always being there for me through all of it. Even when I feel like giving up on myself, I'm thankful you guys kept pushing me to keep going. Thank you, Michael, for always telling me how proud you are of me and just being my shoulder when I needed it.

To my sister for always being there for me, when I needed to make sure something sounded okay, for always telling me I can do it and for pushing me to keep on keepin' on that people out there loved my book, and will love my future books.

The rest of my family, my parents, my brother and his wifey, thank you so much for always supporting me and congratulating me on all of my little milestones I've made along the way and just being there for me. I appreciate you all.

To Erica, with Logophile Editing. THANK YOU for always being there, answering my endless questions as best as you could. For working with me and taking care of my book, for guiding me when I needed extra help. For all your hard work you put into editing, proofing and everything else you did for me that involved both of my books. You helped make my dreams into a reality and I couldn't thank you enough. I appreciate you more than you know!

To Kate, with Kate Decided To Design. THANK YOU for everything you did. All your extra help and guidance when I needed it. For always answering my never-ending questions. For working with me for both of my books and putting all your love into my book inside and out, my graphics and BOTH OF MY BEAUTIFUL COVERS. I can't get over how amazing your work is. Thank you so much for everything. I appreciate you more than you'll ever know.

To my READERS, Alpha readers, Beta readers, ARC readers, and just everyday readers who have read and continue to read my book. I FUCKING LOVE YOU GUYS!!! THANK YOU! Thank you for giving my books a chance and loving my book. It means so much to me. All my readers that became friends over this past year you guys mean more to me than you know. I love the personal relationships I've built with some of my readers and gotten to know on a more personal level and created friendships with, thank you so much for being there for me and continuing to support me. I LOVE ALL OF YOU SO MUCH!!! THANK YOU!

CONNECT WITH ME

Come find me on social media!! I'd love to know when my books find a home!

Facebook: Author Christina Maria
Instagram: Author.Christina.Maria
TikTok: Author.Christina.Maria

Don't be shy, send me a message to say hello, I love making new friends :)

ABOUT THE AUTHOR

Christina Maria lives in Cleveland, Ohio with her husband Michael, their five kids and two black cats. Before becoming a stay-at-home mom, she worked at a salon as a licensed hair stylist for almost eleven years. Christina has always loved reading and getting lost in a good book. Along with writing, for as long as she can remember she has always loved anything that told a story or using her imagination to write her own story. She remembers writing stories on her computer or in notebooks as a little girl. It has always been a dream of hers to write a book of her own. One day, after taking a four year break on a book she started writing she finally picked it back up and decided to turn it into her dream of being a first time Indie Author on her very first Dark Romance book, Breathing You In.

CONTENT WARNING

Death of family member
Tying her up
Choking/breath play
Excessive alcohol use at times
MFC drugged not by MMC